More praise for

The Collective

"Hilarious and winning . . . smoothly told. . . . Threads a perfect line between the theoretical dogfights of the classroom and the actual dogfight of experience." —John Freeman, *Boston Globe*

"Lee comes with an agenda—an important one—about ethnicity and art, but he also delivers a heartbreaking, sexy, and frequently funny story about fractured friendships." —Stephan Lee, *Entertainment Weekly*

"Smart, subdued. . . . Lee, a third-generation Korean-American, is obviously familiar with the complexity of identity fixation, and his characters ultimately discover the danger of becoming martyrs to a cause." —*The New Yorker*

"Sometimes heartbreaking, sometimes hilarious. . . . Lee explores themes of identity he's contemplated in the past—the allure of the cultural bond, the bristle of the stereotype—but this time through the lens of the college novel." —Susan Stamberg, NPR

"Brilliantly sorts through issues of friendship, intimacy, idealism, art, sacrifice, racism, and publicity." —Rachel Meier, *Christian Science Monitor*

"Offering strong characterizations and thought-provoking prose, Lee addresses the Asian American experience from various vantage points, realistically examining themes ranging from personal relationships to racism and artistic censorship. His novel has enough depth to spark uninhibited discussion in any book group and, given its time frame, will have special meaning for Gen X readers."
—Shirley N. Quan, *Library Journal*

"Lee smashes Asian stereotypes to pieces to present a provocative look at what it truly means to have one's identity tied to not just oneself but also an entire race." —Carolyn Kubisz, *Booklist*

"We're huge fans of the campus novel, and this morning we're adding another great one to our collection: Don Lee's *The Collective*."
—Emily Temple, *Flavorwire*

"Engrossing. . . . A compelling work of literature." —Noah Cho, *Hyphen* magazine

"Lively and suspenseful, this novel masterfully probes the high-stakes contest between integrity and belonging. Lee's sympathy for his deeply human characters will captivate any reader."
—Sun Yung Shin, *Minneapolis Star Tribune*

"Lee is a fine prose stylist who shares something of Philip Roth's talent for digressing into tangential episodes without ever halting the momentum of his narrative. Here, he credibly addresses the political and social concerns of a specific demographic, while also rendering a work that will feel relatable to nearly everyone who reads it." —Timothy Bracy, *Time Out*

"*The Collective* is an enjoyable feast of artistic abandon, one that sweeps up readers in a colossal tidal wave of bewilderment, as these protagonists go on to have their shares of success and failures."

—Zachary Houle, *PopMatters*

"Lee manages to pull the dialogue away from the traditional parent-child storyline that often overwhelms the themes of many Asian stories. . . . If life imitates art, then perhaps this novel could serve as a different life beyond the normal art we see. Lee ought to be commended for pushing the envelope." —bigWOWO blog

"*The Collective* is, undoubtedly, [Lee's] most personal novel, although don't let the overlaps with his real life fool you—Lee's an incorrigible storyteller." —Terry Hong, *Bookslut*

"A must-read for everyone interested in the discussion of racial identity and its place in our supposedly post-racial world."

—Poornima Apte, BookBrowse

THE
COLLECTIVE

a novel

DON LEE

 W. W. NORTON & COMPANY | NEW YORK LONDON

for

Jane Pappalardo

Copyright © 2012 by Don Lee

An excerpt from this book originally appeared in *Narrative* magazine.

For information about permission to reproduce selections from this book,
write to Permissions, W. W. Norton & Company, Inc.,
500 Fifth Avenue, New York, NY 10110

For information about special discounts for bulk purchases, please contact
W. W. Norton Special Sales at specialsales@wwnorton.com or 800-233-4830

Manufacturing by Courier Westford
Book design by Chris Welch
Production manager: Devon Zahn

Library of Congress Cataloging-in-Publication Data

Lee, Don, 1959–
The collective : a novel / Don Lee. — 1st ed.
p. cm.
ISBN 978-0-393-08321-7 (hardcover)
1. Creation (Literary, artistic, etc.)—Fiction. I. Title.
PS3562.E339C65 2012
813'.54—dc23
2012008851

ISBN 978-0-393-34542-1 pbk.

W. W. Norton & Company, Inc.
500 Fifth Avenue, New York, N.Y. 10110
www.wwnorton.com

W. W. Norton & Company Ltd.
Castle House, 75/76 Wells Street, London W1T 3QT

1 2 3 4 5 6 7 8 9 0

THE
COLLECTIVE

1

There's a road in Sudbury, on the outskirts of Boston, called Waterborne. Famous for the great blue herons that nest there, the road cuts through the immediate floodplain of the Sudbury River. It's lined with red maple, white oak, and dead ash yellows, long ago decimated by a virus. It curves and dips, wending through hills and an alluvial marsh, rising once again past meadows and farmland, then descending in a series of hairpin turns. It's a beautiful road—smooth, continuous, unsullied by houses or businesses—and therefore popular with bikers, runners, and drivers in a hurry. To no one's surprise, hardly a month goes by without some sort of accident on Waterborne.

It was around three o'clock on a Saturday afternoon in late September 2008, partly cloudy and unseasonably warm at seventy-six degrees, the tincture of fall edging the flora. Joshua Yoon, thirty-eight, was on his afternoon run on Waterborne, hugging the road's left edge so he could watch for approaching cars. He had intended nothing for that day. The week before, in fact, he had arrived upon the method he'd use, suggested by a group on the Internet: he was going to put a clear plastic bag over his head, fasten the bottom of it around his neck with Velcro, open two canisters that would pump helium through tubes into the bag, and within minutes he would be unconscious and dead. Painless, quick, and efficient.

Once you decide to kill yourself, studies have said, there is clarity. You become focused. Your mood brightens. You're blessed with a profound state of well-being. These sorts of decisions, momentous as they are, come willy-nilly. They begin as passing whims, an indulgence of reverie, and then, unbidden, they sharpen and coalesce within you, and you begin to fixate, and plan. You pay your bills, you write letters of instruction, you update your will, make funeral arrangements, buy an urn, label all your keys. There are only two things left to be determined—how and when. You have choices. You feel relief and joy.

This is not to say that Joshua was entirely lucid then. He was taking pills, so many pills. He was on antidepressants, anti-anxiety meds, mood stabilizers, sleeping pills, and painkillers, their effects aggravated by a recent experiment with robostripping, something he'd learned teenagers were doing, spinning a bottle of Robitussin centrifugally on a string to distill pure DXM to the top. He was high, perhaps even hallucinating—not that it mitigates anything.

He was running on a stretch of Waterborne where drivers are slingshot out of a curve and accelerate. He heard a car coming, and, rather than keeping to the edge of the road, he drifted a few feet onto it.

Did he really mean to do it, to be hit by someone and killed? Could he have been so callous, willing to burden an anonymous driver, through no fault of his own, with a lifetime of trauma?

To this day, I am not sure. I go over and over it, and still I don't know. Maybe Joshua, my old friend, had only wanted to feel the whoosh and rev of the car as it went by, the inches between death and continuance, how arbitrary the sway can be between the two. Maybe he had yawed drunkenly into the car's path without volition or meditation. Yet the impulse had probably come across Joshua before, more than once, running on that road, to step in front of a speeding car, ending everything right then and there. Whatever the case, there was a witness, a driver approaching from the other direction, who claimed she saw Joshua veer abruptly and unmistakably into the path of the car.

The timing of it, the multiple, trivial interruptions that could have prevented any of it from happening: a stoplight, a phone call, a detour for ice cream, a playmate needing a ride home. A few seconds would have made all the difference.

A few seconds before the car came out of the turn, the little girl in the backseat, three months shy of her fourth birthday, had unbuckled herself and climbed out of her safety chair to pick up a book she had dropped. Her father was driving too fast, a bit impaired himself, having had a few drinks earlier at lunch. He disliked seat belts and would have eschewed them altogether if not for the insistent warning beeps. That day, he had compromised by clicking in the lap belt and flipping the shoulder strap behind his back. He turned around to yell at the girl to get back in her chair right this minute. Then he glanced around and saw Joshua, ten feet in front of him on the road, too late to do anything, but swerving on instinct to avoid hitting him head-on. The car swiped out Joshua's legs at an angle, crushing one of them and snagging the other on something, maybe the bumper, so his foot disarticulated at the ankle, much like twisting a chicken bone off at the joint. The impact vaulted his body into the air in deranged cartwheels, and the car itself flipped and rolled in the other direction, tumbling repeatedly and brutally, until it squashed to a rest against a stand of white oak. By then, the man and the little girl were slowly dying inside the car. Joshua was luckier, if one could call it that. He landed on his head on the asphalt, and the blunt-force trauma to his brain killed him instantly.

2

Joshua did not have any identification on him that Saturday on Waterborne Road, and originally he was listed as a John Doe, the police unable to figure out who he was, no one recognizing or missing him, until his original preparations became apparent.

The week before, he had scheduled a housecleaner to come to his rented cottage on Monday morning. It was a first appointment, the arrangements made by email, and Joshua had told the woman that if he wasn't home, she should just walk in—the door would be unlocked for her. By habit, he never bothered to lock his front door, but it was uncharacteristic of him to hire a housecleaner. In general, he shunned visitors, and he had never been known for his cleanliness.

She arrived at the appointed time, and when she came inside, she saw a letter addressed to her on the kitchen table, a letter with the numbers for the Sudbury police and an attorney in Cambridge, with instructions that the woman should first call the police, who should then contact the attorney, giving him possession of the labeled keys on the table, along with the urn in the box that was in the hallway closet. The letter explicitly instructed the woman not to enter his bedroom. She should depart immediately, Joshua wrote, not touching or cleaning anything. He left her payment in cash on the table, and apologized for the trouble.

In the bedroom, the police found the helium canisters and plastic hood. They deduced that Joshua had been planning to kill himself by this method (the Internet history on his laptop revealed the particulars) sometime between Thursday, when he'd bought the materials (date-stamp on a receipt), and Monday, when the housecleaner was due to arrive. He had been very meticulous, working out a way for his body to be discovered before it bloated and decomposed, yet for some reason, after devising such careful plans, he had suddenly annulled them, running out in front of the car instead of gassing himself.

There was a criminal investigation, replete with autopsies, toxicology reports, an accident reconstruction, interviews, and search warrants. If Joshua had survived, he would have been charged with two counts of manslaughter.

I am certain that Joshua never imagined anyone in the car would be injured, much less killed. But the little girl's death, much more so than if just her father had died, overshadowed the entire episode, redefining it from a tragedy to an atrocity. Consequently, what I initially felt for my friend of twenty years—besides a numbing shock—was shame, not grief.

Why couldn't Joshua have waited and killed himself in the privacy of his cottage, instead of imperiling innocent bystanders? Although I learned later that the driver had not been so innocent. His blood alcohol level had been .092, above the legal limit. Skid marks showed he was weaving on Waterborne on the preceding straightaway, and he was driving an estimated fifty-one miles per hour in a thirty-five zone. Just hours before, he had ordered three glasses of Malbec with his pork Milanese at a Concord restaurant, and perhaps had drunk more after he'd left with his lover—a sales associate—and gone to a motel with her.

No matter. Instead of flattering obituaries and tributes for Joshua, there were articles tinged with rebuke. Instead of being celebrated as an Asian American novelist of minor yet significant renown, Joshua Yoon was being remembered as a murderer.

There's an established protocol to this, writers committing suicide. It has to be done with some dignity, honor, perhaps even panache, in order to establish the proper legacy. Gas would have been acceptable. Plath used gas, as did John Kennedy Toole. Hemingway and Brautigan shot themselves. Hart Crane jumped off a ship, Primo Levi down a stairwell. Woolf drowned. Mishima chose the most gruesome method, seppuku, Malcolm Lowry the most commonplace, pills, which—combined with his chronic alcohol abuse—had led, the coroner concluded, to his "death by misadventure."

Yet suicide is an act of solipsism, or narcissism—I've never seen much of a distinction. The suicidal are incapable of thinking about whom they might affect, whom they might harm. They have vacated all rational considerations. They're only thinking of themselves, and the exigency of the situation, which is to make it all stop.

Why had Joshua wanted to die? In the days afterward, everyone (except my wife, who knew better) kept asking me that question. My answer, only half in jest, was usually: He was a writer.

Yes, he was depressed—obviously. But this was not something new or atypical for him. Aristotle called it melancholia, the predisposition artists have for depression, prone as they are to being morose and antisocial and self-flagellating and megalomaniacal. Indeed, without that inclination, no one would probably become an artist in the first place.

Still, everyone wanted a *reason*, something concrete and understandable, like a degenerative disease or excruciating heartbreak, and I suppose I hoped for one, too. But no, Joshua wasn't sick, and he wasn't in love. He didn't have a psychotic breakdown, he wasn't bipolar and hearing birds speaking in Greek, nor was he facing sudden destitution. He had had money at one time, but frittered away almost all of it. Nonetheless, he was getting by. Although he rarely received any royalties for the three books he'd published, he had a part-time position as a writer-in-residence at Wheaton College that provided him with a modest income and health benefits. He wasn't a gambler or a sex addict or a (nonprescription) drug user, he wasn't a pervert, he wasn't having an affair with a student, he wasn't being extorted by pimps or dealers or loan sharks (unless you want to count credit card companies). No one was threatening or blackmailing him, there were no scandals in the offing, he wasn't about to be disgraced or lose his job or reputation.

So he had no reason to do it, and yet he had every reason. He had never married, never had children, never even lived with anyone. He had chosen to steer clear of any distractions or obligations that might interfere with his writing. He was willing, nay, *eager*, he said, to make whatever forfeitures were necessary in the pursuit of his art. This was what you had to do if you wanted to be a real writer, he said, if you wanted to strive for greatness, for perfection. You had to be dedicated. You had to sacrifice.

That was why he had moved out to Sudbury nine months before, to that dank, isolated little cottage in which he had lived as an ascetic. The place came with a few basic furnishings, and Joshua kept it spartan, bringing only his files, laptop and printer, clothes, flat-screen TV, and extensive book collection. I visited him there once. Wood paneling and appliances circa 1950s roadside motel, thumbtacked sheets in lieu of curtains. Instead of getting shelves, Joshua had stacked his books against the walls, and then screwed hooks into the floors and wood panels and connected them with a series of bungee cords to keep the stacks from toppling. In the kitchen, he had boxes and boxes of Sapporo Ichiban ramen, purchased from the Japanese market in the Porter Square Exchange. It was, essentially, what he had been eating every meal for weeks. He was like that, obsessive with his habits, eating the same thing or listening to the same album over and over, until he finally got sick of it and switched to something else. He made the ramen with—I'm sorry to report—packaged bologna that he sliced into thin strips, cabbage, and the yolk of an egg.

He would get up early, make coffee, write, eat ramen, write, go for a run, shower, write, drink a beer, eat ramen, write, watch TV (the Red Sox) or a DVD (mindless action thrillers, his taste in movies surprisingly lowbrow), then get into bed with a book. He did this pretty much every day, save for occasional treks out for fast food or take-out meals, and visits to his psychiatrist. His schedule had varied only twice a week during the spring semester when he had had to drive to Wheaton to teach a fiction-writing workshop. He didn't go into town, didn't go away for vacations or holidays— only trips to New York for research. His parents were dead, and he had no relatives to speak of. He didn't have a girlfriend, and he no longer saw any of us, his old friends, albeit our little group had by then fragmented and dispersed of its own accord. That was the extent of it, his life. To me, it was a rather lonely and—I don't want to say this, but I will—pathetic existence.

In point of fact, Joshua didn't seem particularly happy about it, either. After he'd gotten a fair amount of attention for his first novel, each successive book had met a poorer reception, and he felt he had become irrelevant as an author. It bothered him that he wasn't famous, that his books weren't selling more, that he wasn't winning the big prizes and grants, that he wasn't better reviewed, that he wasn't more influential, that he wasn't among the *anointed*.

He was, in other words, a typical writer. However, he had talked excitedly about his current project, saying the new novel might be his magnum opus, his breakout book. Supposedly it was about residents of Koreatown and Chinatown in Manhattan after 9/11, and supposedly he was almost finished with it. I don't know if this was true or not. No one had ever seen a single word of it.

How well do we really know anyone? We only know what people are willing to reveal. It's not that people change. People don't change. They merely hide things from you, and lie. Was Joshua lying about his new novel? Had he been working diligently on it in that cottage in Sudbury, amassing pages, as he claimed, or had he been blocked, unable to produce anything, and prevaricating? It could be that he was writing some, but fitfully, and he knew it wasn't working, the language flat and uninspiring, the story line increasingly ludicrous. Perhaps he sat at his desk all day, unable to squeak out more than a few sentences after hours of effort, and could no longer envision what should come next. Perhaps what he feared most was happening—his imagination had abandoned him, the well had gone dry.

We will never know. This is what shocked me the most. It might have been foolish of me, but I had expected Joshua to appoint me as his literary executor. I thought he might have left instructions asking me to edit or finish his last novel, or, at the very least, cull through his papers and archives to donate to a library, so they might later be examined by biographers and academics. I knew he had kept everything—his journals, each manuscript draft and outline, the index cards and notebooks in which he sketched out ideas, research materials and maps, calendars, annotations in the books he read, his correspondence with editors and his agent and other writers, grant applications, sample book covers, even all the rejection slips he had received from magazines for story submissions.

But the attorney in Cambridge told me that there were no pro-visions for a literary executor. Joshua's will mandated that all of his personal possessions should be donated to Goodwill, his book collection to the Cambridge Public Library. His car, a two-year-old Subaru, was to be auctioned, and the payout from his term life insurance and the proceeds from what was left in his portfolio (which wasn't much, after debts and taxes, and after the driver's widow filed a wrongful-death suit, which was eventually dismissed due to "contributory negligence" yet racked up court and attorney fees) were to be given to the Asian American Adoptees Fund. He was to be cremated, and the urn buried next to his parents' plots in Mount Auburn Cemetery. He wanted a plain bronze gravestone, with just his name and the years of his birth and death on it. He forbade any type of funeral or memorial service.

But what about his journals and papers? I wanted to know. What about his last novel? His files and notebooks? His photo albums? Nothing was located inside his cottage, nothing in his office at Wheaton, nothing in his storage space in Somerville. Adding to the mystery was that no note was found. Even though it might have been disappointingly prosaic, as most suicide notes are, a variant of "I'm sorry," I couldn't believe that Joshua would not have taken the opportunity to memorialize his last thoughts for posterity. This was a man, after all, who had aspired to join the canon, the pantheon, of American writers, who believed that his every doo-dle should be preserved for the historical record. Perhaps he had intended to write a note before using the helium, which made what happened on Waterborne Road even more puzzling.

For a brief time, I held on to the insane notion that Joshua had been driven to suicide because someone had been keeping the mate-rials hostage from him, or that everything, including a note, had been stolen from his cottage immediately after the accident, which might not have been an accident at all, but staged to look like one, in a cover-up. Joshua had always been a scrupulous researcher. He once did not eat for four days while writing about a character on a hunger strike. In researching his latest novel, had he uncovered something he shouldn't have, something dangerous? Perhaps in the netherworld of organized crime in Koreatown or Chinatown? The smuggling of illegal immigrants, sweatshops, money laundering, drugs, the trafficking of sex slaves. Had someone wanted to shut him up, get rid of whatever evidence he had gathered?

I called the detective in charge of the investigation. I was going to suggest looking into Joshua's cell phone records, his text messages, his bank and credit card statements, his emails and documents on his laptop, his datebook, to find out what he had been doing in the last year, whom he had been talking to and meeting, where he'd traveled. The detective told me there was no need, there was no mystery. Joshua himself had destroyed everything. He had burned all his manuscripts and journals and files in two fifty-five-gallon drums behind his cottage. A neighbor, worried about the smoke, had watched him doing it over the course of several days, using barbecue lighter fluid, a wheelbarrow, and a shovel to turn over the layers and remove ashes. Joshua had also wiped everything off his laptop, all the email messages in his account, all the bookmarks and Internet history prior to the previous week, all the documents, folders, and programs on the computer except for a utility that he had purchased and downloaded to ensure the foolproof, irrevocable deletion of his hard drive.

I was staggered. I refused to believe it. I clung to conspiratorial scenarios. It seemed impossible that Joshua would have voluntarily elected the complete erasure of his life. What must he have been going through? He had made vague references to suicide over the years, comments like, "I don't know why I keep doing this, I might as well just check out," but we never took him seriously. He had a histrionic bent. He exaggerated and embellished, he would often call in the middle of the night with a crisis that would turn out to be wholly trivial. He could be a total pain in the ass.

His psychiatrist would not offer any clues when I contacted him, saying doctor-patient privilege extended into death. Exasperated, I told him that he, if anyone, should have been able to see through Joshua's bluster and melodrama, he should have sensed Joshua was suicidal and pink-papered him into a psych ward. In response, the psychiatrist somberly explicated Kübler-Ross's five stages of grief to me: denial, anger, bargaining, depression, acceptance. These stages are not necessarily progressive or discrete, he intoned. They'll occur out of sequence and merge and mingle. He encouraged me to seek out therapy for myself while going through this difficult process.

So I am only left to wonder, and imagine. I imagine Joshua was drinking too much, not eating properly, not sleeping well. I imagine he was waylaid further by a cold and started taking cough medicine and doubling up on his pills. I imagine his work had stalled into impasse, and he anguished in self-doubt and loathing, so he began sleeping in later and later, past noon, time no longer being precious nor perishable, not wanting to face the bright insolvency of his talent, the paltry rations of what had become his life and career, the terrible miscalculations he had made about what would fulfill him, since everything he had done, everything he had worked toward, seemed pointless to him now, utterly meaningless. I imagine he mourned, and he raged, and he despaired that it would never stop, it would never get better, he would never be content, he would always be alone.

What I can't imagine are his last few seconds. As the car was about to hit him, did he welcome it? Was he relieved, happy, even, or was he terrified, recognizing too late that he had made a horrible mistake? Did he realize at that moment that he did not want to die? Perversely, a part of me wants to believe that. The alternative is too sorrowful to consider.

The fact is, he did not think to call upon us, his friends, least of all me, for help, no doubt convinced we had forsaken him. Maybe his suicide note, had he completed one, would have been in some measure a reprimand, decrying our neglect and implying it had been contributory. But I wonder, if he had reached out to us, if our little group had remained intact, would we have been able to save him, do anything to allay his unceasing, unalterable disconsolation? I don't know.

We had loved Joshua, but we'd gradually grown tired of him, and of one another. The fact is, if pressed, we would each have to confess that we all saw it coming, and we did nothing to prevent it.

3

There were occasional emails or, more rarely, phone calls, but we had been drifting apart for quite a while, and actually I hadn't seen them—any of them, including Joshua—for almost a year. There wasn't a particular reason for the lapse, a blowout or feud or any intentionality of severance. It was, I reasoned, just the natural way that groups evolve and dissipate.

An intimacy develops among a circle of people, you do everything together, you can't imagine this tight cadre ever breaking apart, and then, quite mundanely, one friend slips away, and then another. It might be because they're moving across town or to another part of the country. It might be because they've started a new relationship, or are getting married or having a kid or changing jobs. It might be because everyone's getting older and more preoccupied, *busy*. And, of course, it might simply be that everyone's become a little bored with one another, doing the same things over and over, hearing and telling the same stories.

Despite your best efforts and intentions, there's a limited reservoir to fellowship before you begin to rely solely on the vapors of nostalgia. Eventually, you move on, latch on to another group of friends. Once in a while, though, you remember something, a remark or a gesture, and it takes you back. You think how close all of you were, the laughs and commiserations, the fondness and affection and support. You recall the parties, the trips, the dinners and late, late nights. Even the arguments and small betrayals have a revisionist charm in retrospect. You're astonished and enlivened by the memories. You wonder why and how it ever stopped. You have the urge to pick up the phone, fire off an email, suggesting reunion, resumption, and you start to act, but then don't, because it would be awkward talking after such a long lag, and, really, what would be the point? Your lives are different now. Whatever was there before is gone. And it saddens you, it makes you feel old and vanquished—not only over this group that disbanded, but also over all the others before and after it, the friends you had in grade and high school, in college, in your twenties and thirties, your kinship to them (never mind to all your old lovers) ephemeral and, quite possibly, illusory to begin with.

So it was with us, although we had a longer and better run than most. It began with Joshua, Jessica Tsai, and me as freshmen at Macalester College in St. Paul, Minnesota, in 1988.

Joshua was from Cambridge, a 1.5—born in South Korea but raised in Massachusetts, not first generation or second, but somewhere in between—and his last name at the time had been Meer, not Yoon. His parents were Jewish professors of history and sociology at Harvard, and they had adopted Joshua late in life, when they were both well into their fifties.

Jessica was second-generation Taiwanese American, her father an optometrist in Saratoga Springs, New York.

I was third-generation Korean American from Mission Viejo, California, the son of an engineer for an aeronautics firm that built navigational equipment for Lockheed, and although I hadn't gotten accepted into Princeton, as I'd dreamed, I was ecstatic merely to have escaped the banality of Orange County, where I had lived all my life.

Freshmen at Macalester were required to take a first-year course, which often had a residential component, all the students in the class living on the same dorm floor. Even though it wasn't our first choice, the three of us were thrown together into a course called "The Vietnam War: Apocalyptic Visions and Imperialist Hegemony," team-taught by professors from the English and humanities departments.

At the initial meeting during orientation, Joshua sidled into the room late and took a seat next to me near the back. It was hot outside, but he was wearing a raggedy gray car coat and Doc Martens. He had a stringy goatee and lank hair that flopped over his eyes, and he reeked of cigarettes. He badly needed a shower. He was of average height and rather thin, but, incongruously, he had a noticeable paunch. Coming from Southern California, land of ab-defined, yogafied, body-obsessed boobletons, where even I—never much of an athlete—had felt compelled to work out and keep trim, this impressed me.

He glanced at the name tag stuck to my shirt. "Eric Cho," he read. "What do you know, another Korean." He wasn't wearing a name tag himself. An act of defiance, apparently. He took a look around at the other kids in the Vietnam War class—overwhelmingly midwestern, upper-middle-class, white-bread—and said to me, "What do you think, bro? We were put in here to provide the Oriental perspective, weren't we?"

Jessica, who was sitting in the row in front of us, peered around and gave us a brief head-to-toe.

Joshua raised his eyebrows. "You like that?" he nudged me.

I had been staring at her from the start of the session, wondering how I might broach a conversation. She was petite, tiny, really, with long fine hair that curled at the ends. She had a small flat nose without much of a bridge, making her eyes appear slightly crossed and farther apart than they were, and her eyebrows were set unusually high, so her neutral expression seemed to be one of haughty annoyance. Attracted as I was to her, she frightened me a little. She had on a sleeveless Neil Young T-shirt, no bra, nipples poking in the air-conditioning, bell-bottom jeans streaked with paint and smudges, and leather sandals. There was a suede sling purse with fringes on the floor beside her chair. Yet she also had on black toenail polish, and black fingernail polish, a studded wristband, earrings that seemed to be snips of real barbed wire, and a silver chain with a circle-A pendant—the anarchy symbol—her fashion sensibilities crossed between retro-hippie and post-punk. Mainly what I kept staring at was the small of her back, exposed as she leaned forward on her desk, her T-shirt lifting, the waist of her jeans gapping, to reveal a curve of skin that went all the way down to the cleft of her buttocks. She wasn't wearing underwear.

"*Or,*" Joshua said more loudly, "you strictly *vanilla*? As in boarding-school shiksas, frosty Mayflower mungie cakes, pinkaloid pooty, Ritz cracker chirp-chirp Marshas. Or maybe you prefer the local corn-fed variety, the gopher winkle Triscuits and chalky Betty Crockers and Miracle Whip doozers and tapioca hayseed cream pies."

By now, everyone in the room had swiveled around and was looking at us.

"I'm sorry," Joshua said, quite pleased with himself, "was I speaking out of turn?" Then, as a postscript, he told me, "Not that I have anything against white girls, understand. After all, as Kierkegaard once said, pussy is pussy."

Jessica raised her hand. "Is it too late to transfer to another class?" she asked the professors.

"Ditto for me," I said.

"Damn," Joshua said. "Once again, betrayed by Asian nation."

■   ■   ■

We were assigned single rooms on the fourth floor of Dupre Hall. Macalester—or Mac, as everyone abbreviated it—was considered a premier liberal arts college, small and selective, with fewer than two thousand students. The campus was pretty and well maintained, and the school itself was rich, its coffers bursting with donations from the founders of *Reader's Digest*. Yet Dupre Hall, designated for freshmen and sophomores, was an ugly brick bunker with vertical slit windows, and it was generally acknowledged as the worst dormitory on campus. Dupre—alternately referred to as Duprojects, Duprived, and Duprison—was the only hurricane-proof building on campus, in an area that was not known to have hurricanes. Supposedly the building plans, intended for a coastal location, had been available at a discount. The single rooms in Dupre indeed felt like a prison, so narrow that the beds had to be lofted on stilts, with the desks and dressers directly underneath. There was a rumor that Macalester had to pay a fine to the state every year because the rooms violated a human-rights code, not meeting the minimum legal size for juvenile detention cells.

Joshua was on one end of the fourth floor, the smokers' end, and Jessica and I were on the other. I was curious why we'd been given singles, unusual for freshmen, and not doubles or even triples.

"You're complaining? You *wanted* a roommate?" Jessica asked.

"I wouldn't have minded." I had a sister, Rebecca, who was four years older, and no other siblings. She had left for college when I was entering the ninth grade, and consequently I'd gone through high school feeling like an only child. I would have welcomed the company of a roommate.

"It's going to be claustrophobic enough around here," Jessica told me.

She was right. The orientation schedule was chock-full of activities that weekend, everything emphasizing *community*: lots of meetings and group sessions and pep talks, tours, picnics, resource fairs, advising appointments, dances, and talent shows. Parents had been invited to participate in the festivities. Naturally, all three of us had asked our parents not to come, but Joshua's were the only ones who complied. While Jessica and I grudgingly escorted our parents around the campus, Joshua sat in the quad, leaning against a tree and listening to his Walkman CD while he smoked and read a novel or scribbled in a notebook.

We were encouraged to sign up for as many student organizations as possible, and there was a dizzying number to choose from. We could join the newspaper, the student government, clubs for minorities, civic engagement, and international relations. We could join clubs with political or religious affiliations, clubs for artists and musicians, for feminists and queers, for bicycling and other athletic pursuits.

There were sports teams at Mac, even a football team, but they weren't entities of much importance. There were no athletic scholarships, so not surprisingly the teams were perennial losers. No one ever wanted to be identified as a jock, a pejorative term on campus. Pointedly, there was no Greek system, no fraternities or sororities, the school much too progressive for any of that nonsense.

The only things I was truly interested in were the literary magazine and Ultimate Frisbee, the latter because all summer, knowing Frisbee was popular at Mac, I had been practicing, able now to throw sidearm with two fingers and overhand with a wrist flip. I had wanted to be good, competent, at *something* upon arrival. I ended up, however, joining two other organizations—Amnesty International and Habitat for Humanity—because I saw Jessica Tsai going to their tables and signing up. Joshua, of course, abstained entirely.

"I'm not a joiner, man," he told me in the dining hall. "This group-participation shit is driving me crazy. I mean, what happened to developing the individual, to encouraging subversion and independence? I thought that's what this place was all about. Instead, it's, you know, just the old bourgeois concept of togetherness—i.e., conformity—under the guise of PC liberalism. It's fucking oppressive, man. It's downright totalitarian."

"It's not that bad," I said. Truthfully, I appreciated the intimacy of Macalester. In high school, and in Southern California in general, I had felt lost, merely another Asian American kid among the multitudes.

"Let me ask you something," Joshua said. "Who do you read? Who are your favorite writers?"

At one of the orientation meetings, we had been forced to reveal our career aspirations, and it turned out that all three of us wanted to be artists—Jessica a painter, Joshua and I novelists, the latter a coincidence that immediately distressed me.

I set down my fork. "I don't know," I said. "Cheever? Updike, maybe. Chekhov. Fitzgerald."

"Jesus, how'd you get to be such a fucking Twinkie? Chekhov's okay, but the rest of those guys are just WASP apologists."

"What about you? Who do you read?"

"Pynchon, Nabokov, Kundera, Joyce. DeLillo, Rushdie, Hawkes. Calvino, Dostoyevsky, Barth. Coetzee. Bernhard."

"I like all of those," I said, although I hadn't read many of them, much less heard of some.

"Wait a minute," Joshua said. "Did you come here because Fitzgerald was born in St. Paul? Is that it? It is, isn't it?"

I felt myself warming. I had already visited the house on Laurel

Avenue where F. Scott Fitzgerald had been born and the ones on Summit Avenue where he had lived.

"I knew it," Joshua said. "You're a romantic. God, I'm going to have to look after you, Eric, make a special project of you the next four years, because if you take that shit out into the world, that kind of fucking idealism, you'll get slaughtered. You'll get creamed. It'll be the death of you."

4

kept hearing a church bell ring. I'd be in my dorm room or the library and hear the bell, and I'd look at my watch, thinking it must be the top of the hour or a quarterly increment thereof. But the clanging appeared random, occurring anytime, most often at night or in the wee hours of the weekend.

"What the hell *is* that?" I asked Joshua one evening. We were sitting in the fourth-floor study lounge of Old Main, both reading Michael Herr's *Dispatches* for the Vietnam War class.

"Oh, you don't know?" he said with a smirk.

"Know what?"

He dog-eared the page he was on and led me to the window. "Look across to Weyerhaeuser."

It was dark, but I could see a few lights outside Weyerhaeuser Hall, across the quad, where a couple was gamboling on the sidewalk, skipping and giggling and kissing.

"Ever notice the bell there?" Joshua asked.

I had, now that he mentioned it. Next to Weyerhaeuser Hall, there was a small gazebo with an old church bell hanging inside of it.

"It's a tradition here," Joshua said. "You lose your virginity on campus, you ring the bell."

"All these people were virgins?" I asked. This did not seem like a school of erstwhile prudes. Then again, there were a lot of dorky students at Mac, teenagers who in high school had likely been unpopular and excluded from the active coital roster.

"No, no. It's when you lose your *on-campus* virginity," Joshua said, "your first sexual liaison here, not necessarily the first time you've ever glazed the donut."

"Oh."

"You're not a virgin, are you?"

"What?"

"Have you buttered the muffin? Dipped the corn dog? Ridden the wiki wiki all the way to tuna town?"

"Of course I have."

"Yeah? When?"

"Eleventh grade."

"What was her name?" he asked, testing me.

"Leigh Anne Wiatt."

"Ah, you see? I was right about you. A *baekin*. Addicted to mayonnaise."

"What's a *baekin*?"

"You're such a banana," he said—a.k.a. Twinkie, yellow on the outside, white on the inside. "It's just disgraceful you don't know Korean."

We had had this argument already. Like many third-generation Asian Americans, I had resisted learning Korean as a kid, not exactly ashamed of my ethnicity (though there was some of that), but wary of being defined solely by it. Unlike my sister, I didn't take Korean lessons on Saturday mornings at the Garden Grove church my parents attended, and eventually I stopped going to services on Sundays as well. Most of my friends in Mission Viejo had been white or Chicano, and I was probably more familiar with Mexico's culture and history than Korea's.

Joshua's Korean, on the other hand, was quite passable. He had left Pusan at five, but in high school, when his memory of the language was beginning to dim, he retaught himself Korean with books and tapes. He also enrolled himself in Hebrew classes, much to the befuddlement of his atheist, anti-Zionist parents. He knew a lot about his homelands, was proud of his split (tripartite?) heritage. The Seoul Olympics were taking place during the start of our first semester, and, watching broadcasts, he rooted for the Koreans first and the Israelis second over the Americans. He called himself a "Kew," and joked that Koreans and Jews had more in common than any other ethnic groups: they both begot a disproportionate number of classical musicians, both feared and were reviled by black people, and both tried to inundate Harvard with their progeny. He was always complaining he couldn't find kimchi or a decent bagel in St. Paul.

In many ways, our quick friendship was a surprise. In coming to Mac, I had thought my ethnicity might work in my favor, sort of as a reverse exoticism, a radical chicness, that would redound well, especially with the girls. I worried that hanging out with other Asian Americans would lessen my distinctiveness and I might be stereotyped. And the last thing I needed was someone constantly harping on me that I wasn't Korean or Asian enough. But Joshua, for all his insistent Asianness, was, well, cool. He was putatively brilliant, always with a bon mot or clever rejoinder at the ready, he wanted to be a writer, and he seemed well versed in all manner of things to which I was not yet completely privy, like sex.

"So," he said in the study lounge, "was it serial mambo with this chick Leigh Anne, or was it a one-off?"

"A one-off."

"She's the only one you've ever schtupped?"

"Yeah," I said forlornly, and it almost had not counted. I'd barely had time to put on the condom and jab myself inside her (where the hell was the *entrance*?) before I had ejaculated. Little wonder Leigh Anne hadn't seemed very interested in going out with me again.

"You need to get cracking, old sport."

"I suppose you've had a lot of experience."

"You suppose right," Joshua said, although I would learn later that he was lying, that at that moment he was still a virgin, on campus and otherwise.

During the next few days, I became increasingly disconcerted every time I heard the Weyerhaeuser bell. The whole idea of it bothered me, that all these kids had already paired off and were rutting in their dorm rooms, and then broadcasting their new sexual status to the campus. Instead of a celebration, it seemed more like a taunt. To my ears, the bell began to acquire a competitive tenor, a challenge to join the initiated. It seemed, all of a sudden, imperative that I get laid and be able to ring that fucking bell myself.

The first partner *in flagrante delicto* I considered was Jessica Tsai. My visceral attraction to her was somewhat mysterious to me, since, as Joshua had guessed, up to that point I had been almost exclusively partial to white girls, in particular blondes. Leigh Anne Wiatt, for example, had not been exceptionally pretty. It would have been fair to have described her as plain, verging on homely. Yet she had been blond.

Jessica gave no indication she might be amenable to participating in my campaign. In fact, she was proving to be very elusive. I'd figured out her schedule—when she'd wake up, walk across Grand Avenue to her classes, when she'd be getting out and perhaps going to the library or the student center—and I tried to bump into her as often as possible.

One Wednesday morning, I stepped out into the hallway of Dupre, holding my dopp kit, just as she was heading to the shower in her white silk bathrobe.

"We've got to stop meeting like this," I said.

Jessica regarded me without expression. "How long you been working on that?" she said, then flipped her towel over her shoulder and brushed past me.

Days—I'd been working on that line for days.

I finally had a chance to corner her the next week, when I sat beside her on the bus to Dayton's Bluff, where we were going to renovate a house for Habitat for Humanity. We'd just finished midterms, and we compared grades. She had received all A's, and I'd gotten—typical for me, despite my prodigious efforts—mostly B-pluses.

"How'd Joshua do?" she asked.

"B-ish," I said, which had shocked me until I found out that he sometimes did not hand in all of his assignments. He was bright, but lazy.

I told Jessica I'd once asked Joshua why he hadn't gone to Harvard. He didn't even apply. With his off-the-chart SAT scores and as a legacy applicant, with his parents (one of whom was an alum) both professors there, he would have surely gotten in. "I thought I should learn some humility," he'd told me, "mingle with the little people."

"Like us?" Jessica asked.

"No doubt."

"He's always had it so easy," she said. "He's been coddled. An only child, an adopted child. You know what my father did the day

I was born? He sent out for applications to Harvard and Yale. He was crushed I didn't get into an Ivy."

Her parents had immigrated to Flushing, New York, from Taiwan, and it took many years before her father's English was proficient enough to pass the intensive three-part exam for his optometry license. In the meantime, he had slogged away as a lab technician at LensCrafters, and Jessica's mother had worked in a Korean nail salon. Every day, they had reminded Jessica and her two younger sisters that they were in America for one purpose and one purpose only: so their children could attend the best universities in the world.

Jessica had always loved drawing as a child, but until a junior high field trip to the Museum of Modern Art, she had never seen—*experienced*—real art in person. Thereafter, she kept returning to MoMA and venturing to other museums and galleries, not telling her parents that she was riding the No. 7 train by herself to look at paintings. By ninth grade, she knew, with a certainty and urgency she had never felt about anything before, that she wanted to be a painter, but she told no one. The following summer, her father relocated the family to Saratoga Springs, where he had bought an eyeglass shop. The move made Jessica heartsick, yet she told herself to be patient. She would be escaping to college in just a few years.

She daydreamed about going to RISD or Pratt or the Art Institute of Chicago, but her parents, who had long-standing ambitions for her to become a doctor, would never have allowed it. She figured she could surreptitiously study art at one of the Ivies. That was her plan, but it was thwarted by an unexpected disaster: she bombed the SATs. Three times. All her prep work and practice tests aside, she had panic attacks each time she sat in the exam hall with the Scantrons and No. 2 pencils, and she could not, for the life of her, think. Although she graduated as her school's valedictorian, she was rejected by all eight Ivy League colleges. Yet her parents still held out hope for an Ivy *medical* school, and they still believed Jessica would be a premed major at Mac, which explained why she was taking organic chemistry and cell biology her first semester.

"My parents," I told her, "still think I'm going to apply to law school. Why else would anyone be an English major? They've never really pushed me, though. Princeton was my idea."

"What's your excuse for not getting in?"

"Look at my midterm grades. I'm just not that smart." All my life I had tried my best, but I had never been academically gifted, which contributed to my parents' lowered expectations for me.

"At least you know that," Jessica said.

"Do you think it was psychosomatic?"

"What?"

"The panic attacks. Maybe it was your mind trying to find a way out. Maybe you subconsciously wanted to fail."

"And join the ranks of Asian American underachievers, rare as they may be?"

"It's not such a bad thing. It's kind of freeing."

"Maybe you're right. I never wanted to be one of *those* kids, know what I mean?"

I knew. The model minority. The Asian American nerds, goobers, spazzes, and lame-o's, as Joshua would say. The nine-irons, bug eaters, and grinders, the panface Post-its and dim-sum tapeheads. One of the UFOs, the Ugly Fucking Orientals with their high-pitched hee-haw laughs and bowl haircuts and dweeby clothes, the obsessive-compulsive doofuses who poked at the bridge of their eyeglasses and twitch-blinked and read the fine print for everything and always followed the directions, the ping-pang ninnies who were so stultifyingly sincere, diffident, and straight, who wouldn't recognize irony if it bit them on their no-asses, the wei-wei Hop Sings who perpetuated all the stereotypes and gave us, the Asian kids with some style and cool and fucking *balls*, a bad name. I never wanted to be one of those kids, either.

The conversation on the bus changed things for us. Afterward, Jessica softened toward me, and we began to hang out more often. We had an understanding, it seemed, and I started to think there could be something between us.

Joshua quickly quashed the thought. "You're barking up the wrong twat," he told me.

"Why do you say that?" I asked.

"She's a yellow cab."

"A what?"

"California slang for Asian chicks who'll only date white guys."

"That's bullshit."

"She's got a haole boyfriend back home."

I had, stupidly, not considered this possibility. "How do you know?"

"I asked her."

"The topic just came up?"

"It's some dude she went out with in high school named—I kid you not—Loki Somerset. He ended up staying in Saratoga and going to Skidmore."

"How come she's never mentioned him?"

"I don't know. Maybe she's embarrassed. He's fucking studying Chinese, man. He's a rice chaser."

"A what?"

"California slang for white dudes with a fetish for Asian chicks."

I was suspicious. I thought perhaps Joshua was interested in Jessica himself and had lobbed a verbal probe to see if there was any reciprocity. Jessica, trying to be kind, might have lied to Joshua, exaggerating the importance and currency of this high school romance. After all, how many of these adolescent relationships survived the separation of college? And perhaps Joshua, after being rebuffed, was now trying to derail my prospects with her.

As we sat at a table for Amnesty International in front of the campus center, attempting to recruit new members, I asked Jessica, "Do you have a boyfriend back home?"

"Joshua told you."

"Is it still going hot and heavy?"

"'Hot and heavy.' That's a quaint phrase," she said. "Your language can be so old-fashioned sometimes. I hope that's not indicative of your writing style—or, worse, your morality."

"You're avoiding the question."

"I don't know. I've had two boyfriends my entire life, neither of which my parents were ever aware of. What do I know about hot and heavy?"

"You guys still writing to each other, talking on the phone?"

"Some."

"I want to know something: Do you only like white guys?"

"Joshua told you that? He is full of it. You know that thing he said in class? 'What they lacked was testicularity'? You know where he got that? He stole it straight out of *Franny and Zooey*."

I thought it had sounded familiar, and later that afternoon I would go to the library and confirm that Joshua indeed had lifted the expression—uttered by Franny's boyfriend, Lane, no less, that pompous little shithead—from page eleven of Salinger's book.

"Okay, so he's not original all of the time," I said. "But you have to give him credit. He says what's on his mind. He doesn't give a shit what people think of him."

"Are you kidding?" Jessica said. "That's *all* he thinks about. He's exactly like you."

"What's that mean?"

"You're always trying to please everyone. You're quick to adopt other people's opinions, because you haven't formed any of your own yet. You're kind of like this empty vessel right now, a cipher, waiting to be filled up."

"Thanks a lot," I said, stunned and insulted, while at the same time sensing she might be right about me.

"It's not irredeemable. You'll grow out of it eventually."

"Like you'll stand up to your parents someday?" I asked.

"I never claimed I had any testicularity," she told me.

■   ■   ■

So I turned my attentions to Didi O'Brien, a freshman I'd met playing Ultimate Frisbee. I ran into her in the student union during Seventies Disco Night. There were themed dances nearly every month on campus, none of which Jessica or certainly Joshua would ever deign to attend. That night, as soon as I entered the lounge, Didi pulled me onto the floor for "That's the Way (I Like It)."

"You look fantastic!" I said. She was wearing a tangerine-orange minidress and white go-go boots.

"You, too!" she shouted, admiring the powder-blue leisure suit I'd picked up at Goodwill.

If possible, Didi was a worse dancer than I was, gawky and arrhythmic, yet wholly unselfconscious, which endeared her to me. We stayed on the floor for two more songs—"Dancing Queen" and "Cold as Ice"—and then coupled for a slow one, "Killing Me Softly."

"You're kind of cute," she murmured. She was drunk. We all were. The drinking age was twenty-one in Minnesota, but booze flowed freely in the dorms, and we always tanked up before going to the dances.

"You're not so bad yourself," I said, nuzzling her. She was tall and gangly, with long legs and arms, big hands and feet, but she had a classical air about her, her face strongly angular yet alluring. She was blond, of course.

A few days later, I asked her out to a movie that was playing at the Grandview, the theater half a mile from campus. They were showing *Running on Empty*, a new film starring River Phoenix as the son of two former Weather Underground–type radicals on the run from the FBI. I figured afterward I could ply Didi with what I had learned about the antiwar movement in my Vietnam class.

But we didn't end up staying until the end of the movie. Halfway through, I turned to her, and she to me. She was chomping on a piece of gum. I was about to ask if she wanted the rest of the popcorn, and as I opened my mouth she spontaneously spat her wad of gum right into it. Startled, I took a sharp intake of breath, which lodged the gum in my throat, and I started choking. Alarmed, Didi punched me in the solar plexus, which made me hawk the gum out, directly into the hair—a nesty brown bouffant—of the woman in front of us. Didi and I gasped, but when we realized the woman somehow had not noticed the new appendage that had been projectiled into her hairdo, we began giggling, which escalated into a paroxysm of near-pee-in-the-pants guffaws. We were kicked out of the theater.

We went to Dunn Bros Coffee for cappuccinos and carrot cake, and talked. Didi was from Massachusetts, Irish Catholic, and intended to major in math and computer science. Her father, like mine, was an engineer. He had grown up poor in Dorchester and gone to UMass Amherst and then had started a hugely successful company that specialized in hospital software systems. He expected Didi to work for him after she graduated.

"Did you want to follow in his footsteps, or were you feeling forced?" I asked, thinking the story didn't change much across ethnicities.

"Oh, I don't know. I'm the only one of his kids with any facility in math. I actually *like* math."

"You don't look like a math geek."

"What's a math geek supposed to look like?" she asked.

"Well," I said, "probably like me."

I walked her back to her dorm, Turck, and outside the front door we smooched a little, but it was all rather chaste, without presage of ardor. This might be a dead end, I thought.

Nonetheless, the next Friday we joined a gang of students to go to the Sonic Youth concert at First Avenue, the club Prince had made famous. Macalester was in a quiet residential St. Paul neighborhood, miles from downtown Minneapolis, which usually required two buses and forty-five minutes to get to, but the school had decided to make a semi-sanctioned event of it, offering a couple of vans to transport us to the club, and we all eagerly piled into them, Joshua included.

"This is Didi," I told him.

"Hey," he said, barely registering her. "Fucking-A, how cool is this, huh? We're finally getting off the goddamn reservation. First Ave! Sonic Youth!"

I wasn't all that familiar with Sonic Youth, or that entire classification of punk rock. Truth be told, before I came to Mac, my favorite musician—I'm ashamed to say—had been Billy Joel.

Sonic Youth was touring for a new album, *Daydream Nation*, and Joshua ran through the song list, citing the allusions to Denis Johnson, Saul Bellow, Andy Warhol, and William Gibson. "It's, like, a lit major's wet dream," Joshua said, laughing. "I mean, yeah, it's the most mainstream, commercial thing they've ever done, and they're going to get some flak for it for sure, but it's still got its subcultural, seditious connotations, you know?"

When we got out of the van near the club, Joshua pulled me (and I pulled Didi) into an alleyway. "We've got to get in the proper mood for this," he said, and produced a pipe and a lighter from his jacket pocket. Mac was known as a haven for potheads, so I wasn't surprised that Joshua had gotten hold of some weed. "This is primo Buddha," he said. "Thai stick. Phoebe, ladies get the honors."

"It's Didi," I said.

Didi seemed somewhat hesitant, but gamely fired up the lighter and took a toke, then promptly gagged and hacked.

"Yeah, it's righteous strong shit," Joshua said. "It might have some opium laced in it."

Between the three of us, we smoked two bowls, and then went in for the show. An all-girl punk band did an opening set that was shrieky and uninteresting, but I was enthralled just being inside the club. Until then, my only concert experiences had been at the Hollywood Bowl and the Forum in L.A.

Sonic Youth took the stage with "Teen Age Riot," which commenced slowly, quietly, but once the band started lashing into the main part of the song, the crowd came alive, everyone raising their arms and headbanging and pogoing, and it didn't stop for an hour and a half, the energy overwhelming and exhilarating.

"I'm going in!" Joshua said after a few songs, and he waded toward the mosh pit that had formed in front of the stage.

He disappeared for the rest of the show. Only occasionally would we glimpse him bouncing in the mob. Near the end, I had to pee. I didn't want to miss anything, but I had to go. "Stay here," I yelled to Didi.

When I returned from the bathroom—a forever ordeal—I

couldn't find Didi at first, but then caught sight of her on the far side of the floor.

"You missed Joni Mitchell!" she told me.

"What?"

"Joni Mitchell came out and played a song with them!"

This sounded odd. Joshua had said one of the songs, "Hey Joni," was partially a tribute to Joni Mitchell, but it seemed improbable she would appear with Sonic Youth. "Are you sure?" I asked.

"Yes!" she said. She blinked. "I think." Confused now, she rolled her tongue around her lips. "Wait, maybe it wasn't Joni Mitchell?" The Buddha had gotten to her.

I turned toward the mosh pit. People were flailing and slam-dancing and stage-diving, and in the midst of it all was Joshua, who had been lifted into the air and was being passed overhead from hand to hand while lying stiffly supine, arms akimbo in crucifixion, a smug grin on his face. Then he vanished. Someone had dropped him. A ruckus broke out. Bouncers converged.

In the van to campus, Joshua told us what had transpired. "Racist skinhead dickwad," he said, elated. His eye was welting, his cheek and neck were scratched, his knuckles were cratered and bleeding. "Cracker called me a chink and told me to get back on the boat. I clocked the motherfucker. I put him *down*."

When we returned to Mac, we made our way to Wallace, the party dorm, where there were several rooms hosting festivities, everyone sweating in the close quarters. We flitted from room to room, toking and drinking, until Didi passed out. I half carried her to Turck. "Not the bed, not the bed," she kept saying when we got to her floor, so I took her into the women's bathroom, where there was a tub. I set her down inside of it. She was already snoring away, drooling. I could have sold tickets: Yeah, five dollars, grow your vegetables here.

The following afternoon, I sat with Joshua in the library, trying to finish the rest of *The Quiet American*. His eye was puffed and bruised black, the lid half closed.

"That guy really called you a chink?" I asked.

"You think I'd lie about something like that?"

In my entire life, I had never been on the receiving end of such a slur. I could not deny that there were ethnic tensions in Southern California, but I'd never been affected by anything directly. In this respect, there was comfort in numbers: there were so many Asian Americans in the L.A. area, I could throw a stick in any direction and hit six of them. "I'm just surprised, that's all," I said to Joshua. "Everyone's been so friendly here. I thought maybe people might look at me funny once in a while, but it's never happened. Not that I've noticed, anyway."

"Don't buy the whole 'Minnesota nice' thing," he said. "This place is as racist as anywhere else. It's because of all the Hmong refugees. They think we're boat people, man. It's as bad as Boston. Over there, you've got the ofays in Southie, the yokels in Dorchester—you know exactly what to expect from them—but the more sinister, corrosive, subtle shit comes from people like your chickadee, what's her name, Didi."

"What about her?"

"Were you purposely *looking* for WASP City?"

"She's Catholic."

"You know what I mean. She's so white-bread. She's, like, the apotheosis of white-bread. She's sour*dough*, man. She has no soul. She's never suffered or wanted for anything a day in her life."

"I like her."

"Do you, or you just on bush patrol? The story about the bell get to you?"

"Of course not."

"Yeah, right. Listen, she's a lemon sucker."

"What?"

"A yellow dipper, a paddy melt, a Chiquita muncher. California slang for white chicks who want a taste of Asian."

"How come I'm from California and I've never heard of *any* of these terms?"

"I can't account for your ignorance," Joshua said. "I hate to be the one to tell you this, but Sourdough is just slumming, man. It's a phase, like every chick in college needing to go girl-on-girl at some point. Chicks like Sourdough like to think they're pluralistic, but when it gets down to it, they'll stick to their own kind."

"Meaning what?"

"Meaning Sourdough would never get serious about you."

"Jesus," I said, "we're just hanging out. Who said anything about getting serious?"

"Just so you understand. Have fun, wet your wick, but don't expect it could ever go beyond that."

I didn't believe Joshua, not really, but I kept thinking about what he had told me, and, against my better judgment, I started scrutinizing everything Didi said and did, as if searching for incriminating evidence. Was it significant, for example, that she bought a silk happi coat (Exhibit A) and began wearing it around campus? Was there something to her having a late-night craving for moo shu pork (Exhibit B) and making us take the bus up Snelling to the House of Dynasty on University Avenue? Should I have been perturbed that she once sang the chorus to the song "Turning Japanese" (Exhibit C) apropos of nothing? What about the fact that she wanted to learn tai chi (Exhibit D), or the time she uncupped her hands to give me an origami (Exhibit E) of a tiny blue bird?

Then there was the night she wanted to cook me dinner, an odd whim, because she couldn't cook—at all. Turck had a lounge on every floor with a stove, sink, and microwave, and there she whipped up an unholy concoction of frozen vegetables, shredded day-old chicken-salad sandwiches from the snack bar *with* the bread (which was sourdough!), a sprinkling of cashew nuts, and an entire jar of plum sauce (Exhibit F), all mashed together and sautéed in a wok (Exhibit G) and served in rice bowls (Exhibit H) with chopsticks (Exhibit I).

"It's good!" I told her, naturally.

And then there was this conversation:

"Your hair is so straight," she said. "Is it this straight all over?" (Exhibit J.)

"All over? Well, not completely straight. A little wavier, maybe."

"Let me see." She lifted my left arm and peered through the sleeve at my armpit. Then she said, "What about down there?"

"Where? You mean . . . my pubes?"

"Uh-huh."

"The same, I guess."

"I suppose I'll have to check it out sometime for myself."

Things like that last statement made me ignore the strong circumstantial case that was building up against Sourdough, the sobriquet becoming more apt by the minute. I told myself I was being paranoid. So what if she was going a little Asian on me, so what if she'd contracted a bit of yellow fever? Maybe all the evidentiary pieces were merely coincidental, or just gestures of attraction, misguided as they were. She was simply trying to tell me she liked me. Anyway, I was being unduly influenced by our increasingly avid make-out sessions, by all the smooching, sucking, and licking, the groping, stroking, and grinding—they were turning me Japanese, making my testicularity bluer than origami.

Finally, one night in my dorm room, after hours of spit-swapping on the floor, Didi whispered, "Do you have a condom?"

Did I have a condom? Was she kidding? Did I have a condom? I had at least eight *dozen* condoms. I had condoms of every shape, color, size, material, texture, thickness, and flavor. I had condoms that were ribbed and studded, that tickled and tingled, that were lubed and edible, that heated up and glowed in the dark. For a month, I had been hoarding condoms—buying variety packs at the drugstore, palming them from the bowl in the health clinic, grabbing multiple free handouts during Safe Sex Week.

"I think I might have one," I said.

"Okay," she said, "let's do it."

"Are you sure?" I asked, then regretted asking. I'd had a feeling that tonight might be the night, and had even leaked the premonition to Joshua, yet everything felt as if it were tottering in suspension. I didn't dare do anything that might make Didi change her mind.

"Turn off the lights," she said.

I did.

"Take off your clothes and get into bed."

I did.

"Put on the condom."

I did.

I waited. I lay on my tiny bed on its stilts, sheathed by the condom, and I waited. "Didi?"

She was still standing below me. "Wait, what time is it?" she asked.

"The time?"

"It's eleven-seventeen! I totally forgot. I have another date!" she said, and chortled weirdly. "I'm late!" Then she ran out the door.

What the hell?

I glanced down at my sensi-dotted, ultra-invigro, xtra-stimulation condom (orange, mint). Didi was not a virgin, but she was as inexperienced as I was and somewhat priggish—the residual Catholic schoolgirl. Or so I had assumed. I had never imagined she might be dating someone else simultaneously. If anything, I had worried she might be attaching too much significance to our dalliances. But now I had to recalibrate. Had I been completely mistaken about her? Was Didi, in fact, a closet hussy?

I snapped off the condom. I was miffed and angry, but eventually I fell asleep, only to be awoken at around one in the morning by a knock on the door.

In the hallway was Didi, holding a pint of Ben & Jerry's White Russian ice cream and a bottle of vodka. "I'm sorry," she said. "I lied. I didn't have another date. I don't know why I said that. I freaked out a little. Okay, a lot. Do you like White Russians? Do you have a couple of glasses and a spoon and maybe another condom?"

All was forgiven.

An hour later, I dragged Didi out of my room, both of us buzzed on vodka and post-copulatory euphoria. It was relatively warm outside still. Thick clouds stretched out across the sky, peeks of a few stars in between. I'd often wondered why the sky seemed so low in the Midwest, as if the firmament were balefully compressing against the plains, and then had learned it wasn't the sky that was lower, it was the earth that was higher—the elevation was almost a thousand feet here, flat as everything was—and for once, instead of feeling landlocked and claustrophobic, I perceived myself as being closer to the heavens. I was young. I knew nothing about the world. Already I was half in love with Didi.

"I'm so sleepy," she said. "Do we really have to do this now? Can't it wait until tomorrow?"

"Tonight!" I said.

We were crossing Grand Avenue when, by happenstance, we heard the Weyerhaeuser bell tolling, and as we rounded the chapel, we saw, in the shadows, a couple walking away from the gazebo toward us. Compadres! I wanted to shout out. Brother and

sister! Another pair of lovers following their biological imperative! O life, love, joy! I had to embrace this couple, I thought,
have them witness our own induction into the hallowed circle of
campus fornicators.

The guy was wearing a brown three-piece suit, the girl a blue
halter dress with a shawl covering her shoulders, her arm hooked
into his. As they came closer, I realized it was Joshua, and with
him was not a girl but a woman, late twenties or early thirties,
Asian, with long hair, made up rather heavily but quite beautiful,
and something in the way she walked or carried herself made it
obvious to me that she was, without question, a high-class hooker.

"Hello, kiddies," Joshua said, and he and the woman kept going,
strolling past us into the darkness, leaving our faces slack with
astonishment.

He had called an escort service, insisting that the woman be
Asian. He had met her at the Saint Paul Hotel downtown, knowing
she probably wouldn't show up if he had specified Mac as a rendez-
vous, and then, after offering her an extra fifty bucks, got her to
take a cab with him back to Dupre. She rather enjoyed herself, he
would tell me. She thought it was cute, fucking in the dorm.

I'd wonder about it later. It was too much of a coincidence. Yes,
I had told Joshua this likely would be the night, but how had he
timed it so he'd be at the gazebo just before we came along? Was
he clairvoyant? Had he been monitoring us from down the hall?
Planted some sort of listening device in my room? It would remain
a mystery.

Whatever the case, Joshua had demonstrated, for the first of
what would be many times during our lives and careers, that no
matter how desperately I tried, he could, and would, beat me to
every momentous bell.

5

One day I walked outside, and it was twelve degrees. The weather had turned. Up to that point, I had been thinking it wasn't too bad in Minnesota, not as dire as everyone had warned. In late August, when I'd arrived in the Twin Cities, it had been hot and humid—disagreeable but not extreme. The only unsettling thing had been the thunderstorms that would trundle through the area in the middle of the night. It had seemed so strange, to be awoken by riotous rumble at two, three a.m., the thunder clapping for hours, instead of during the dewy peak of late afternoon. Once, alarms had blared a tornado warning. (Perhaps constructing a hurricane-proof dormitory had not been a bad idea, after all.)

Yet when the humidity waned, the fall became sunny and pleasant, and although the nights dipped into the low thirties, it was entirely tolerable. I had felt confident the winter wouldn't bother me. Contrary to people's assumptions, it got cold in California. I wasn't a pussy to cold, I'd told myself.

This kind of cold, though, was different. It was bone-penetrating, teeth-shuddering cold. Blood-constricting, testicle-shrinking cold. We began layering. We doubled up on T-shirts and then sweaters. We bought long underwear. The first snow—the only time

I'd seen snow beyond a family ski trip to Big Bear Mountain—we joyously ran outside and, per Mac tradition, had a snowball fight across Grand Avenue, played pushball, and feasted on a lamb roast. What we didn't know then was that it would not rise above thirty-two degrees for the duration of the winter, and that this snow would never melt, it'd remain on the ground, getting packed down and frozen and dirtied as it accumulated, until April. Everywhere there was ice, and everywhere white smoke billowed, from vents and chimneys and manholes and tailpipes. We breathed out plumes as we shivered across the quad, bundled in parkas, scarves, hats, gloves, and boots, and then peeled off the clothes—mounds heaped upon the backs of chairs and on the floors—once ensconced in the blister of heated rooms. With the first subzero day, we stopped venturing outside if it could be helped. We retreated into hibernation.

Mainly I stayed in bed—with Didi. She had a roommate and I didn't, so we spent most of the time in my room in Dupre. To reduce the number of trips back and forth, Didi brought over some of her clothes and toiletries, then her books, boom box, and CDs, and in short order my closet and bureau were subsumed by her things. She essentially moved in with me. The RA's attitude toward this was surprisingly lax. Students were written up for lighting candles or incense, and if you were caught with alcohol you had to pour it out, but no one seemed to care about new arrangements of cohabitation. You could sleep with anyone you wanted, it seemed, as long as you didn't burn the place down.

Didi and I were constrained only by my tiny bed. I began to suspect that, for the original designers, putting the twin mattresses on stilts had not been so much a space-saving measure as an underhanded way of discouraging conjugal overnights. It was a wonder neither one of us ever rolled over and plummeted to the floor as we slept. Not that we slept that much, although Didi did everything possible to make the bunk bed comfortable. She replaced my bedding with hers—four-hundred-thread-count Egyptian cotton sheets, feather-down pillows and a mattress pad, a comforter and a duvet. It was the softest, plushiest material I had ever lain on. I had never thought about thread counts before; it was possible I had never heard of the term. My mother had always bought generic sheets on sale for us at Sears.

Nonetheless, Didi and I did not take advantage of the luxurious linen, at least for slumber. We were constantly mucking it up, fucking. If we weren't in the midst of carnality, we were in the faux-tristesse of post-carnality, moonily staring at each other, limbs and fingers entwined. Occasionally we'd catnap, then one would rouse the other and we'd begin anew. We spent more hours naked than clothed. When we were forced to get out of bed and stand, we'd nearly keel, verticality having become so unfamiliar to us. We lost weight, unable to make it to the dining hall for meals, and we were forever woozy from hunger and dehydration. We clung to each other as if our lives depended on it.

What dawned on me was that no one had ever described sex properly in literature, the sheer sloppiness of it, the excretions and stickiness and sweat, the pungent smells and tastes, the slurps and smacks and pickled inelegance of daily congress. We soon used up my stockpile of condoms, and decided to go without. We wanted to *feel* each other, and there was something much more arousing about the perils of relying on me to pull out in time. Didi sometimes would not let me withdraw when I felt I would rupture. "Not yet, not yet," she'd whisper.

Her poor lovely sheets. We ruined them. We slept on the wet spots, because the bed was too small not to. We couldn't wash the sheets and duvet often enough, and they were indelibly stained with crusty yellow patches. I would use a towel to wipe the semen off myself, off Didi's stomach and breasts and back and face, and each day the towels would become stiffer—scruffed and mangy. After a while, I didn't bother trying to wash them anymore. I threw them away and asked my mother to mail me another set. "Why do you need so many towels?" she asked on the phone. "Is someone stealing them from the bathroom? You need to mark your name on them."

We tried different positions, making things up as we went along. We became expert at fellatio and cunnilingus (the intricacies of which had previously been an utter mystery to me), gymnastically hanging halfway off the lofted bed.

"Your skin is so smooth," Didi told me. "You're practically hairless." She plucked at my arm with her fingers, unable to gain purchase on a single strand. "I love your body."

Both of us, quite unintentionally, through our starvation and acrobatics, had acquired washboard abs. I hadn't appreciated how much of a workout sex could be.

"You don't realize how beautiful you are yet, do you?" she said.

This was true. No one had ever described me as beautiful, or even good-looking, and I knew that objectively I had not changed in the course of a few months, metamorphosing from middling to handsome. But something in me *had* changed. I carried myself differently now. I had crossed a line of maturation, stepping from callow to experienced.

Once, as I was entering her from behind, I touched upon the wrong opening. I started to retreat, but Didi said, "Wait. Stay there."

"Really?" I asked.

She lowered her ass and pressed back into me.

When we were done, I went to the bathroom and washed myself off in the shower. "Was it disgusting?" she asked.

"No." I didn't know what I had imagined. Probably the same

thing Didi had: my penis excrementally and perhaps permanently browned, flecked with bits of feces. Yet, as much as I'd looked, I hadn't noticed anything really unusual.

Didi scooted against the wall and lifted the covers as I climbed back into bed. "How did it feel? When you were inside."

"It was . . . weird."

"Didn't it feel good?"

"It was okay, I guess." I had been too self-conscious amid the act to derive any enjoyment from it. I had kept thinking to myself, with wonder, We–are–having–anal–sex. "How'd it feel to you?" I asked Didi.

"I don't know," she said. "But I'm glad we did it."

A taboo had been broken, and we were a little awed with ourselves, though we never tried it again. From then on, we stopped at nothing, even making love when she had her period, adding blood to the blotter of her sheets. Our intimacy was freeing and intoxicating. I had never been physically and emotionally so close to anyone. We were at ease, unabashed. We could do or say anything without fear of ridicule or retribution. It didn't matter what we looked like, if our breath smelled or we farted or had a zit. This was acceptance, I thought. This was love.

We kept going, experimenting, exploring every inch of each other's body, learning each other's likes and dislikes. (She liked when I raised her knees to her chest, feeling me deepest that way; I liked when she straddled me and rubbed the folds of her vulva along the underside of my erection before reaching down and sinking onto me; she liked when, as I tongued her clitoris, I inserted a finger and hooked the tip and pressed against the roof of her vaginal canal; she disliked, though, her earlobes being sucked, and I didn't much care for the insertion of her pinkie into my anus one time.)

Nothing had prepared me for this education—not any of my sister's women's magazines that I used to sneak away to read, not the two copies of *Playboy* and one issue of *Penthouse* that I had found in my father's closet. I realized that, before Didi, I had been a complete neophyte. I had known as much about sex, real sex, as I had about thread counts. And yet I wanted to know more. I could not get enough. I wanted to become a great lover.

I didn't see much of Joshua and Jessica during this period. I let my studies go. I didn't attend meetings for the school literary magazine or for Amnesty International or Habitat for Humanity. Reluctantly I went to my classes—sleepy, unshowered, bowlegged—but all I could think about was getting back into bed, naked again, with Didi.

The four days we spent apart for Thanksgiving, flying to opposite coasts to our respective homes, were interminable. I met her at the airport with flowers, took her back to Dupre, and stripped her down as soon as the door was shut.

"I love you," I said.

She laughed as I backed her into the room toward a clear space on the floor, waddling with my jeans around my ankles, cock standing acutely upright.

Only three weeks were left in the semester, and there was a rush of activity as we geared toward finals. The first Saturday in December, the school held the annual Winter Ball, a semiformal dance for which you were supposed to show up in your nicest outfit, replicating—sardonically—what you had worn to your prom or homecoming. In high school, I had gone through a preppy phase, and I pulled out my blue blazer, pink button-down oxford shirt, argyle sweater vest, and penny loafers. Didi teased her hair into a poodle perm, adorned with a lacy bow, and donned a taffeta dress with spaghetti straps, white tights, and granny boots. She was, all irony aside, gorgeous. As we made our entrance at the gallery of

Olin-Rice, the science building, I was proud of her, of us, of our identity as a couple.

Joshua was sporting a beat-down leather motorcycle jacket, holey jeans, and a Red Sox cap—his usual garb. "I didn't go to my prom," he said. "Where the hell have you been? I haven't seen you in a dog's age, and we live down the fucking hall."

I nodded toward Didi, who was loading hors d'oeuvres onto two plates for us. "Doesn't she look beautiful?"

"Jesus," Joshua said. "You're a goner. You're totally pussy-whipped."

For the rest of the term, Didi and I had to buckle down, catch up on everything we had neglected. We studied in my room—with our clothes on, for a change. I sped through *Dog Soldiers* and *Going After Cacciato* (the author, Tim O'Brien, was a Mac alum), and I wrote a paper on the role of drugs and surrealism as a counter-exposition to colonialism. Didi integrated partial fractions and differentiated logarithms and calculated polynomials. I marveled at our industry, our focus. We were actually studying, getting things done, while sitting in the same room, although all it took was a single glance from either of us to abandon everything for a quickie. But then, miraculously, as if nothing had occurred, we would slip our underwear back up and return to our books.

During exam week, we stayed up all night, cramming for tests. The school held a midnight breakfast for us, with professors and administrators—including the president—in aprons, serving us pancakes, the repast occasionally interrupted by primal screams and the time-honored appearance of students, Joshua among them, streaking nude through the hall.

And then, before I knew it, it was over. I was back home in Mission Viejo, Didi was in Massachusetts, and we would not see each other again for a month.

I moped. It was seventy-two degrees and sunny out, but I stayed in my bedroom, trying to puzzle my way through *Gravity's Rainbow*—the first title on the recommended reading list that Joshua had given to me for my vacation. I slept late, watched TV, and hoggishly ate the meals my mother prepared for me ("You're so skinny!" she had said, horrified, when she met me at John Wayne Airport).

I saw a few friends—high school buddies who had remained in Southern California, attending one of the UC or Cal State schools—but I felt little connection with them anymore and preferred staying home, renting videos of foreign films from Blockbuster and listening to Lou Reed (first on the recommended albums list that Joshua had given to me) on my headphones, occasionally interrupted by my mother as she brought in my folded laundry and asked if I wanted a snack.

I let her pamper me—something I had resisted mightily in high school, something that had, in fact, led to awful rows and appalling cruelty on my part.

My mother, Junie, had been born in 1940 in Korea and had come to the States soon after World War II, when her father, a prominent chiropractor in Seoul, was hired to teach at Palmer College of Chiropractic in Davenport, Iowa. He eventually moved the family to L.A., where he set up his first clinic in Koreatown (he would build a chain of them dotting the Los Angeles Basin, yet was lousy as a businessman and was perpetually in debt). My mother grew up in Boyle Heights and attended community college, LACC, then worked as a postal clerk, a job she held until my sister was born.

From then on, her focus was solely on the maintenance of her home and her children, making our lunches and getting us to school every weekday, fastidiously cleaning the house, gardening, grocery shopping and prepping our dinners, picking us up and ferrying us to various places and activities. My mother's typical sack lunch for me included two homemade chicken salad sandwiches, sticks of carrots and celery, cookies, potato chips, and an orange. It wasn't a fancy lunch, not like the elaborate bentos some of my Japanese American classmates clicked open, but it was meticulously prepared, exemplified by the orange. My mother would slice the outer skin so it would open up like the petals of a flower, still connected at the base. She would peel off the inner white membrane of the orange, then put it back—now pristine and tender—into its protective skin. An ordinary piece of fruit turned into an art form.

She tried to spoil us rotten, my father, sister, and me. And how did I repay my mother for her devotion in my teenage years? I snapped at her. I belittled her. I was sarcastic and rude. Unconscionably mean. I yelled at her to stop trying to *do* everything for me, stop *doting* on me, stop being so *nice* to me ("You're not my maid! Don't you have any self-respect?!"). I raged when she cleaned my room ("Don't ever come in here again without my permission!"). I fulminated when she ironed my clothes ("I'll look like a nerd!"). I was apoplectic when she uniformly bleached my acid-washed jeans ("You're an idiot!"). Her mere presence, taking a seat beside me on the couch, inquiring how I was doing, was enough to provoke my fury ("Why can't you leave me alone?! You're suffocating me!").

It shames me still, the insufferable way I treated her. She had no career, no intellectual pursuits, few hobbies or interests other than horticulture, her world almost entirely confined to the domestic, to caring for us, and I thought less of my mother for it. I took her completely for granted.

She would die prematurely, when she was just fifty-nine, a month before I turned thirty. In the latter part of her life, she was diagnosed with high blood pressure, but wasn't good about taking full doses of her medication, disliking the side effects. While she was

swimming laps at the local pool, she had a stroke, a massive cere-
bral hemorrhage. The lifeguards were late pulling her out of the
water and couldn't revive her. Technically she drowned. My father
called me with the news from California, incoherent as he wept.

For several years afterward, I could not get one question out of
my head. Its arrival—usually when I was in the middle of the most
humdrum things, riding the subway, washing the dishes, peeling
an orange—would undo me. I was always afraid of breaking down
in public. The question was this: What was going through her
mind those last few seconds, after the sunburst in her brain, as she
was choking facedown in the water, knowing she would likely not
survive? Unlike with Joshua's suicide later, I knew exactly what her
last thoughts must have been. I knew she was thinking she would
never see her children again, me and Rebecca, she would never see
us marry or have children of our own, would never spend another
Thanksgiving or Christmas with us, would never be able to hold us
and say she loved us, and I knew this must have been unbearably,
heartbreakingly sad for her.

I am forty-one years old now. Indeed I did not fully appreciate
her until—relatively recently—I got married and had children. In
retrospect, it dismays me how little curiosity and empathy I had
toward my mother when I was young, how rarely I tried to imagine
her inner life, or even acknowledged that she had one, with hopes
and disappointments of her own. That image did not come complete for me until the last Christmas our family spent together, in
1999, before she died. I found a bunch of old slides in a closet, and
I set up a projector in the den for my parents, Rebecca, and me to
view after dinner. They were slides of my mother and father's wedding and honeymoon. We howled and cried, we were laughing so
hard, looking at the antiquated fashions and hairdos, but privately
Rebecca and I were impressed by our parents' youth, how hand-

some and vibrant they were. Our mother recounted their courtship, and she made fun of my father's strenuous pursuit of her, but
she was plainly delighted by the memory.

My father, Andrew, came, strictly speaking, from peasant stock,
and it had apparently taken a herculean effort to convince my
mother and her family that he was worthy of her. My grandfather
had been among the first wave of Korean immigrants, recruited as
laborers for sugar plantations in Hawaii. Later, he became the manager of a small Brussels sprouts farm in Rosarita Bay, California. My
father was the last of three children to be born, but the first to go to
college, at UCLA. He met my mother at a social in Koreatown, and
thereafter, almost daily, drove the twenty-five miles between campus and Monterey Park on the pretext of mailing a letter or needing
stamps, claiming he was, just by chance, in the neighborhood, in
order to see my mother at the post office where she worked.

"You sure mail a lot of letters," she once said. She invariably
weighed each envelope and checked the zip code (which, perplex-
ingly, always needed to be corrected) before stamping the postmark, stalling their time together.

"I like writing letters."

"Pen pals?"

"They're friends. People I met in my travels."

"You've been to Kalamazoo, Michigan? Weeki Wachee, Florida? Eros, Louisiana?"

He blushed red. He hadn't intended the double entendre of the
last address. He had never been to any of these places, had never
journeyed outside of California. He picked the cities randomly
from a road atlas and fabricated the names of the recipients and the
street addresses. All the envelopes contained blank sheets of paper
and were, in due course, returned to sender. "Sure," he said. "It's a
beautiful country, if you have the time to explore it properly."

"Lucky man," she told him.

I'm thankful that, during that first Christmas home from Macalester, I began to thaw toward my mother and initiate a long-overdue détente, although my behavior could hardly have been called angelic. I could still be unforgivably judgmental, condescending, and pissy, and for that, I blamed Didi.

Joshua, in addition to his lists, had given me a calling card number and code, ostensibly to report my impressions of the recommended books and records to him. The number, he told me, was a covert account that was charged to the FBI, which I never verified yet which terrified me for years, thinking I might be arrested retroactively for interstate fraud. However, that December and January I used it with impunity to phone Didi every day, and what distressed me, each time I called, was that she was not as miserable as I was.

"Doesn't everyone seem like a stranger to you?" I asked.

"What do you mean?"

"I mean, nothing's really changed, but *we've* changed. Don't you see the hypocrisy and futility of everything all of a sudden? Like, it was there all along, but now that we've been away, now that our eyes have been *opened* vis-à-vis what we've been studying and discussing, it's blatantly obvious just how sad and empty everything is, the bourgeois vapidity of everything that surrounds us." I was cribbing a few of Joshua's expressions. "Like, the people who used to be our friends—I mean, I get so *bored* talking to them. They're going to end up just like their parents—*our* parents. Do they ever think about anything other than money? There's this inertial deadness that's pulling everyone down. I mean, they should all just shoot themselves right now and get it over with. Why even bother? Doesn't it seem like that to you?"

"Not really."

"It's like Pynchon says: entropy reigns supreme."

"What?"

"It's the heat-death of culture."

"Eric," Didi said, "have you been smoking dope?"

I wished I did have some dope. Didi seemed so *happy*. Each phone call, there was a bustle of jocularity, gaiety, in the background, people talking and cackling—a party every minute, it seemed. Didi was always distracted, continually interrupted. "What's going on there?" I'd ask.

"Oh, it's just my family," she'd say. She had three sisters and a brother, a plethora of aunts, uncles, and cousins.

In contrast, my house in Mission Viejo was marked by an unearthly silence. My father would come home from work in his short-sleeved white dress shirt and clip-on tie, fix himself a bourbon and Sprite, and read the newspaper before the three of us sat down to dinner, during which no one would utter a word. I'd look at my father as he cut into my mother's chicken cacciatore (her stab at Western food, made with Campbell's tomato soup, yet admittedly tasty), and I'd try to recall any advice he had ever imparted to me, father-to-son, any statement of profundity or wisdom, even a bad joke, and I'd come up with zilch. After we finished eating, I'd help my mother with the dishes, and then they'd go to the den to watch TV while I went to my bedroom, from which I could hear purls of canned laugh tracks, but never my parents' own laughter. Not a titter.

Even when my sister visited, the decibel level barely wavered. Rebecca had graduated from Whittier College—Richard Nixon's alma mater—with a business degree and gotten a job at First Federal Savings & Loan in Hacienda Heights, processing mortgage applications. She was renting a one-bedroom apartment in West Covina and had a Chinese American boyfriend who was in dental school. It was about as dull a life as I could imagine. My father and mother approved of it wholeheartedly.

Parents believe they have such an impact on their children's lives, yet I knew, from the moment I had set foot on Mac's campus, that I'd become a different person, unfettered from whatever gravitational influence they had tried to extend. I'd moved beyond them. They only served now as proscriptive examples.

One afternoon, while my mother slipped freshly laundered, neatly folded briefs into my chest of drawers, I asked her, "Why don't we have any books in the house?"

"What?"

"Why didn't you read to me as a kid?"

"That's what school is for. Do you want something to eat?"

"How come you never sang any lullabies to me?"

"What?"

"It's like I was in a coffin of sterility and cultural deprivation, growing up."

She stared at me, baffled. "Maybe you should get out of the house. Do something."

I drove to Laguna Beach and walked up the pathway bordering the ocean to Heisler Park. It was a weekday, but there were plenty of people about, playing volleyball, basketball, jogging, rollerblading. I passed by a group of twenty or so adults of various ages, sitting in a circle on the grass, and I caught a snippet of what was being said. Only in California would they hold, outside like this beside a beach, in full view and earshot of the public, an AA meeting.

What I mainly noticed, though, and what made me ache, were all the couples. They seemed to be everywhere, cuddling on benches, spooning on towels, strolling with arms encircling each other, all smiling goofily, brazenly in love. They repulsed me. I despised them, because I knew now the full range of things that couples did behind closed doors, and I was beginning to suspect that Didi might be doing those things with someone else. I wondered if she had lied to me that first night in my dorm room: perhaps she had had another date after all.

She did not love me—not like I loved her. How else to explain the fact that she did not seem to miss me one iota, that more and more she wasn't home in Chestnut Hill when she said she would be, and then did not return my messages right away?

"Where were you tonight?" I asked.

"Oh, we went to see a movie in Cleveland Circle."

"Where?" I wasn't familiar with the geography of Massachusetts. As far as I knew, she could have flown to Ohio for the day.

"Nearby. On the edge of BC," she said, not clarifying anything for me.

"How far away is Chestnut Hill from Cambridge?"

"Twenty minutes driving, forever on the T. Why?"

It was much closer than I had thought, not a distant suburb. "You could go visit Joshua. His parents' house is near Harvard Square."

"Why would I want to visit Joshua? He hates me."

"He doesn't hate you," I said, although Joshua had never expressed anything but indifference or disdain for her.

"What would be the point?" Didi asked. "It's not like we're friends or anything."

I didn't know what the point would be, exactly. I supposed I was desperate for something to ground her, connect her, to me again. She seemed so removed from me.

"I called twice tonight," I said. "Didn't your mother give you the messages?"

"I was going to call you back tomorrow," she said. "I'm beat."

"Did you go somewhere after the movie?"

"Hey," Didi said abruptly, "I was wondering, where were you born? I've never asked you. Were you born in Korea?"

"What?" The question befuddled me. "No. I was born here, in Mission Viejo. At Sisters of St. Joseph."

"Do you speak Korean or English at home?" she asked.

"English," I said, even more flummoxed. "I don't know Korean. I thought I told you." I had explained to her that I was a *sansei*, third generation. I had assumed she understood. All this time, had she been thinking of me as a fobby, an immigrant fresh off the boat? Was that how she saw me?

"What about your parents and sister?" Didi continued. "Do they speak to each other in Korean?"

"Why are you asking me these things all of a sudden?"

"No reason. I was just wondering."

"Did someone in your family ask?"

"No, not really. Well, maybe the subject came up."

"When you told them I'm your boyfriend?"

"I don't know if I used the word boyfriend," she said.

"Why not?"

"They'd pester me endlessly!"

"So what? They've got to know what's going on—I call you every day."

"You don't know my family. They're always in my business. They never leave me alone. Nothing's ever private. I can't ever get a moment's peace around here. You have no idea what it's like."

"It doesn't seem to bother you that much. From what I can tell, you've been having fun, a lot of fun, being back home."

"I don't know. I guess so." She yawned. "What time is it? It's late. That movie sucked. We should have walked out halfway."

"Who'd you go with?"

"Abby and Michael." Her younger sister and brother.

"Just you guys?"

"We met some people there."

"Yeah? Who?" I asked, noting the original omission.

"Nina and Sean. Friends from Milton."

"Is Sean an old boyfriend?"

"Sean? Sean Maguire?" She laughed. "No."

"He's not the guy you lost your virginity to?"

She laughed again. "That's so screwy to even suggest. So to speak. Naw, Sean's like a cousin to me. That was Kurt, at music camp in Lake Winnipesaukee. He was from Montpelier. I don't know where the hell he is now. Oh, my God, for a moment I forgot his last name."

"Sean never had a thing for you?"

"Pamplin."

"What?"

"That was his last name. Kurt Pamplin. I wonder what ever became of him. He was a really hot guitarist. I bet he's up in Burlington, in a band or something, playing at Nectar's. That's where Phish got their start, you know. They went to UVM. God, I could go for an order of their gravy fries right now. If you ever go to Burlington, you have to go to Nectar's and get their gravy fries. But you have to get them from the little window outside and eat them standing on the sidewalk. And you have to be drunk, and it has to be, like, two a.m. and wicked cold out. If you eat them inside, it's not the same thing."

I did not want to hear about Kurt the hot guitarist, or the band Fish, or the club Nectar's and the culinary delights of eating their fries al fresco. "Tell me about Sean," I said.

"What about him?"

"Where's he go to school?"

"Princeton."

The fucker. "Have you been hanging out with him a lot?"

"My mom's best friends with his mom. He's like my brother."

First a cousin, now a brother. "I bet he's always had a thing for you."

"What? What are you talking about?"

"Did you tell him you have a boyfriend?"

"I told him I've been seeing someone, yeah."

"'Someone.' Not anything more definitive than that, huh? Why won't you tell people about me?"

"I just explained."

"Are you ashamed of me?" I asked.

"Don't be silly. Of course not."

"Why do you want to keep me secret, then?" For the first time, I thought there might be something to Joshua's lemon-sucker theory.

"I'm really tired," Didi said. "I'm going to sleep. Let's talk about this tomorrow, okay?"

We didn't talk about it, though. She kept skirting the topic, and our conversations devolved into prickles of irritation the rest of the vacation.

Nevertheless, when I got back to St. Paul at the end of January, I had hopes we could somehow go back to where we'd left off at the end of the fall semester.

I met Didi at the airport, flowers in hand, reenacting our reunion after Thanksgiving. She looked wonderful. Gone were the pallor and dark circles and emaciation from finals week. She radiated health—well rested and well fed. I had a surprise planned for her: I had bought new sheets for us, exquisitely soft, with a thread count of four hundred and fifty. But Didi demurred when I tried to take her to my dorm room.

"I have a yeast infection," she told me.

"A what?"

"The doctor said maybe it has something to do with my sugar

levels. I'm not feeling that great. You mind if I sleep in my own room tonight?"

I was certain now that she had been cheating on me. Yeast infections were from sex. Too much sex. Not for nothing was it called the honeymoon syndrome.

The next morning, as I knew she would, Didi broke up with me.

"It's Sean, isn't it? You've been fucking him."

"Sean has nothing to do with this," she said, packing the belongings she had stored in my room.

"That's not a denial."

"I haven't been fucking him, all right? I haven't been fucking anyone. This is what I mean. I can't breathe around you. I feel suffocated by you. You're always all over me. All we ever do is have sex. Have you noticed we never talk about anything? I can't remember a single conversation we've ever had. We don't have anything in common."

"You never loved me, did you?" I said.

"This is what I mean. All this talk about love! For God's sake, we're *eighteen*! Why couldn't we have just enjoyed ourselves and, you know, been casual about it? Why'd you have to get so serious and obsessive? You want too much. You wrecked it."

"You were just slumming."

"What?"

In the liberal protectorate of Mac, she had felt uninhibited, free, but once she went home, she had woken up to our outward differences, and had lost her nerve. She had begun to envision my life on the opposite coast, and had been terrorized by the specter of a bunch of strange Orientals sitting on the floor in *hanbok*, eating live octopus and hot chili peppers, speaking in unintelligible barks and yips. "People like you," I said, "when it gets down to it, you'll always stick to your own kind."

"What are you talking about? What's that even mean?"

"It was all a lark to you. A little walk on the yellow side. You used me."

"If anything, Eric," she said, "we used each other."

I brooded and cursed and cried in my room in Dupre, alone, the entire weekend, and then went down the hallway to Joshua's room.

I walked in without knocking and sat down on his battered bean-bag chair. There was detritus all over the floor: books, clothes, CDs, magazines, squashed cigarette boxes, food wrappers, an old guitar missing several strings. A red bandanna was draped over a lamp, batiks and posters of Sartre and Iggy Pop were tacked to the walls, and a black surfboard, inlaid with the prism design from Pink Floyd's *The Dark Side of the Moon*, hung down from the ceiling, held aloft by a fishnet. "Blister in the Sun" by the Violent Femmes was playing on his stereo.

For reasons unknown, Joshua was wearing a green Bavarian alpine hat with a tassel and feather and puffing on a big, curved cal-abash tobacco pipe. He was hunched over his desk, gluing together an arched, three-foot-long bridge, made wholly of toothpicks.

"What are you doing?" I asked.

"These are catenary trusses," he said. "Check this out." He propped up the bridge so it spanned his file cabinet and desk, then, to a middle strut, he hooked a rope that was tied to a cinder block. Suspending the heavy, slowly rotating block, the bridge did not give. It did not bend. "You believe that?" Joshua asked, admiring his handiwork. "Fucking toothpicks."

"You were right about Sourdough," I told him. "I should have listened to you."

He nodded. "I've missed you, bro."

6

I t was a school for the bookish and nerdy, for geeks and losers, for kids who liked to study, who actually *wanted* to learn. During our four years at Mac, we would read Foucault, Hegel, Derrida, Saussure, Gadamer, Lacan, Barthes, Deleuze and Guattari—never the full texts, mind you, just xeroxed scraps and smidgens that still we would not understand, but from which we could lap up the lingua franca of pseudo-intellectualism. We'd sling around words like synecdoche and hyperbole, ontology and eschatology, *faute de mieux* and *fin de siècle*. We'd describe things as heuristic, protean, numinous, and ineffable. We'd discuss Maslow's hierarchy of needs and Plato's cave and Gödel's incompleteness theorem, Heisenberg's uncertainty principle and Laffer's curve and Schrödinger's cat. We'd embrace poststructuralism and existentialism and epistemology, semiotics and hermeneutics. We'd see everything as an allegory or a metaphor for something else, and ultimately we'd deconstruct everything as divisive or patriarchal or sexist or homophobic or racist or neofascist—a product of heteronormative exclusivity, a metanarrative propagated by the oligarchy. We'd answer almost every question by decrying it as a syllogism, or a trope, or tautological, or phallocentric, or reductive, or hege-monic (undoubtedly our favorite buzzword). We'd come to believe that any text—be it Shakespeare or a comic book or a supermarket circular—had the same intrinsic value, and we'd insist that all truth was relative, that there was no reality without signifiers, that there was no there there, that nothing, in fact, really existed. We'd argue and rant, we'd foment for empowerment and paradigm shifts and interstitial hybridity, we'd make grand, sweeping pronouncements about subjects of which we knew nothing. We would become artic-ulate, well read, sensitive, open-minded, totally insufferable twits. We would graduate as nihilistic, atheistic, anarchistic, moralistic, tree-hugging, bohemian, Marxist snobs. We would love every min-ute of it.

All of this we did without a trace of irony. Only Joshua, ever the devil's advocate, would call us out at times (although, on the whole, he tended to be the most pretentious and reactionary of any of us: "Hemingway was a racist." "Flannery O'Connor was a racist").

"Look, this is all just intellectual masturbation," he said once in class. "The fact is, no one here will ever be poor. In ten years, what do you think you'll be doing? *Maybe* the best-intentioned of you will be working for a nonprofit, but you'll be living off your trust funds. More likely everyone will have caved in and become corporate attorneys."

That spring semester of my freshman year, I took Problems of Philosophy, Metaphysical Diasporas, Faith and Doubt in Nineteenth-century Literature, and Introduction to Creative Writ-ing. Jessica was in the first class, Joshua in all four. Our education began in earnest, and so, too, did our friendship, Joshua and Jessica working assiduously to lift me out of my funk over Didi. (I'd see her now and again on campus, and each encounter would fill me with heartache. I could not imagine then that, after a year, we'd reach a rapprochement of sorts, born mainly out of disinterest, since we'd both be involved with other people, and that eventually, when I left Mac, I'd forget about her almost entirely.)

Jessica got me to start running with her on the treadmills in the Field House. To counteract such a frightening aspiration for health, Joshua got me to start smoking cigarettes. We watched reruns of *Magnum, P.I.*, of which Joshua, peculiarly, was an aficionado, and for each viewing in the lounge, he'd make us wear Hawaiian shirts and drink mai tais. We visited the Walker Art Center. We spent hours browsing in Cheapo Records and Hungry Mind Books, inhaling the musty acid odor. We ate greasy fish fries (made with the ever-present walleye) at the St. Clair Broiler. We listened to live jazz at the AQ. We rolled frames at BLB, the Bryant-Lake Bowl, a combo restaurant-coffeehouse-performance space-bowling alley. We rented snowshoes and clumped up Summit Avenue, past the Victorian mansions, and trekked along the Mississippi. We had long bull sessions about the meaning of life ("Do you see the world as mean or sublime?" Joshua would ask, and he'd shake his head pityingly when we answered sublime).

We spent so much time together, people began referring to us as the three musketeers, the three amigos. "No," Joshua said, "you know what we should call ourselves? The 3AC. The Asian American Artists Collective." And thereafter, especially when we were drunk, we'd use the acronym as a rallying cry, a toast to our solidarity: "To the 3AC!"

Mostly what we did, though, was study and read (I entered college with 20/20 vision and left needing contacts). My grades had suffered the first term, and I was determined to do better overall in the spring. Nonetheless, the only course that I truly cared about was Intro to Creative Writing.

In the class, we started by reading selections from a poetry anthology and then taking a stab at writing our own poems. This was, without exception, a ludicrous exercise. None of us were poets. We didn't understand poetry. We didn't know what to write about. There were sixteen students in the class, and the majority were not English majors. Intro to Creative Writing was considered a Mickey Mouse course at Mac, and it fulfilled a fine arts requirement.

So we presented weepy elegies for our grandmothers and family dogs, self-pitying monologues about teenage angst, hackneyed pastorals about meadows and fluorescent moons, angry apostrophes to divorced parents, soaring heroic couplets about unrequited love, mawkish paeans to pain and sorrow, and fiery sonnets about loneliness. It was the most wretched stuff. Everything alliterated and rhymed. Most of it was incoherent drivel. There were repeated appearances of tears and rain, usually in combination. But, true to the ethos of Mac, no one in the class laughed or disparaged any of these sorry efforts. We were supportive and kind. We made gentle suggestions. We lauded the intentions.

The poetry part of the class didn't matter to me. What I was nervous about was the second part of the course, when we would write fiction. For all my ambitions to be a writer, and for all the encouragement I had received in high school, told by more than one teacher that I possessed a creative flair, I had never written an actual short story, just unfinished vignettes or scenes.

We did a few fiction writing exercises, and then we scheduled ourselves for the real thing: a workshop rotation wherein we would make photocopies of our stories and pass them out in advance, then have them critiqued in class after reading a handful of pages aloud.

Joshua, of course, volunteered to go first. After he finished his brief recitation, we sat in silence in the classroom. The story portrayed a ten-year-old boy in Seoul after the Korean War who accompanied his father every day as they pushed a cart to deliver and sell charcoal. It was a quiet story, with not much happening and hardly any dialogue, the only fracas of significance an argument with a racist GI. Yet the language was lyrical and precise, with none of the bombastic flourishes and hyperkinetic rhythms I had expected from Joshua. At one point, the boy recalled a long-ago trip to visit relatives in Inchon: "He remembered looking out over the Yellow Sea, where the water lay undulant in the sun, the waves glinting as they moved toward shore, folding over one another like the ruffling of curtains." The story had grace and gravitas. There wasn't, as far as I could discern, a single misstep in it.

The professor, Peter Anderegg, cleared his throat. He wasn't a real professor, just a visiting instructor, an adjunct. He was fairly young, perhaps twenty-seven, and was in his first year out of graduate school. He had published a few stories in some obscure journals, but not a book. Bashful, diffident, at any other college he would have been run over by the students.

"This is really . . . extraordinary," he said. "It's really quite beautiful. "

Our initial reaction confirmed, the class began chiming in, ladling out our own effusive praise. Peter had a workshop rule, which was that the author could not speak during the roundtable critique, but I kept sneaking peeks at Joshua, and he was beaming with obvious pride. With his literary references and quips, he had already established himself as the class leader, but now he had elevated himself so he wasn't just another blowhard. He had authentic talent, and from then on, his authority in the workshop was unassailable.

We walked to the Tap, a neighborhood dive, for burgers and beers, and sat across from each other in one of the big wooden booths. I asked Joshua, "How about giving me that story for *Chanter*?"—the literary magazine at Mac.

"That little rag?" he said. He swigged his Summit IPA. He had made Jessica and me get passport photos, without revealing why, and then had procured fake IDs for us. Mine was laminated with the name Nick Carraway. His said Seymour Glass, Jessica's Frida Kahlo. "It'd be kind of a waste, don't you think? Those guys are idiots."

I was low man on the totem pole on the journal's staff, but I was certain I could convince *Chanter*'s editors—who were known to be snitty, once turning down a story they had solicited from a prominent author who'd read on campus—to take Joshua's piece. "Don't worry," I said. "I'll guide it through."

"No, that's not what I mean," Joshua said. "I was thinking I'd submit the story to a real magazine."

"Yeah? Like where?"

"Maybe *The Atlantic Monthly*."

"No shit?"

"Or maybe *Esquire* or *Harper's*," he said. "Fuck it, I might as well go for *The New Yorker*."

Such an idea would never have occurred to me. His story was good, but it seemed arrogant—outrageous, really—of Joshua, an unpublished eighteen-year-old, to presume he had a chance at any of those prestigious venues.

As my turn in the workshop approached, my anxiety ratcheted. I kept eking out opening paragraphs of short stories and then tossing them. Finally, I finished a hasty draft, typed it out on a computer in the library, and ran off copies. It was about a couple standing in an alleyway next to the man's motorcycle, a Suzuki Katana, having an argument. There were vague allusions to illegality: a rigged poker game, a pimp. The woman wore a sequined dress slit on the sides, and there was a recurring image of her blond hair falling aside, exposing the curved nape of her neck, as she reached down to adjust the clasp on her stiletto shoe. It was called "Nighthawks Rendezvous."

I had rushed the story, I knew. Twelve pages long, it was filled with mangled phrasings and inexplicable tangents and more than a few typos. Writing it, I had had severe doubts that it displayed any merits whatsoever, yet, irrationally, as I read the first four pages out loud in class, I began to think that it wasn't that bad. As a matter of fact, I thought it might be pretty inventive and original—kind of edgy.

"Comments?" Peter said to the class. "What did you think?"

No one said a word, just like when Joshua had presented his story, and I wondered if the class was similarly awed.

Ben, a political science major, raised his hand. "I'm not sure I understand what's going on in the story."

"Yeah, is this real, or, like, the guy's dream?" Stephanie said.

"I was kind of confused, too," Tyson said.

"I'm wondering what the author intended," Elizabeth said. "Was the author intentionally trying to be abstruse?"

This was another one of Peter's commandments. In order to protect students from feeling they were being attacked, we never addressed the author by name or by saying "you." We were told to use "the author" exclusively. We weren't supposed to look at the author, either. We were to pretend that the author was not in the room.

Rules for decorum aside, the discussion began to take a bad turn—the first time in any of our sessions, in fact, that the critiques were unequivocally negative.

"It's like a really slick music video," said Geoff, "but I don't know if it has any more depth to it than that."

"I don't think there's enough of a character arc," said Cory. "No one changes during the course of the story."

"We don't know enough about them," said Jeremy. "They aren't developed very much."

"There's no conflict that I can define. What's at stake? Is anything resolved?" asked Drew.

"The prose gets a little grandiose," said Lara. "It's reaching for highfalutin but it comes off as ostentatious."

"The hair and neck thing got to be really tedious," said Carey.

I waited for Joshua's verdict. The hair and neck thing—at that moment I realized, with panic, that I had completely ripped the image off, almost word for word, from Alain Robbe-Grillet's *La Maison de Rendez-vous*, a novel that had been on Joshua's recommended books list.

At last, Joshua said, "You're all missing the point. The story's working on an atmospheric or impressionistic level, on mood rather than plot. Character development and conflict are irrelevant in a modality like this. There's an inherent tension beneath the recurrences, the circularity, of the sado-erotic imagery, and the entire story relies on the flux of linguistic excess. Stylistically it has a kinship to the *nouveau roman*. It's phenomenological, in the Heideggerian sense. Structurally and conceptually this story is really sophisticated—I'd say it's even brilliant. I loved it."

God bless Joshua's soul.

After a pause, Megan said, "You're right. It's surreal, that's what it is. The unpredictable way it flows is disturbing and kind of magical."

"I'm going to retract what I said before," Geoff said. "I didn't get it. Now I see how intense the story is."

"The story's actually very sexy," Carey said.

More revisionist compliments accrued, and Peter concluded, "I think there's a great lesson here, which is that we need to be more flexible in our approach. Not everything's going to be in the conventional realist tradition, so we have to be prepared and more open to ambitious work like this, not be knee-jerky judgmental when anything smacks of the experimental. Otherwise we'll be blind to this kind of stylistic innovation."

Joshua and I went to the dining hall. It was Tortellini Thursday. The kitchen staff had celebratory themes for nearly every day of the week: Sundae Sunday, Chili Monday, Taco Tuesday. I said, "You didn't really love it, did you?" I knew the story hadn't been great—in no shape or form had I meant it to be experimental—but, illogically, I was angry that it hadn't been universally extolled by my classmates. During the workshop, I had felt myself on the verge of crying, and I still trembled with wounded indignation.

"I loved parts of it," Joshua said.

"Not the part I stole from Robbe-Grillet."

"Sometimes the distinction between theft and homage is murky." One half of his plate was piled with tortellini with tomato sauce, the other half with tortellini with alfredo sauce. He sampled each mound, then mixed them together.

"They hated it," I said. "If you hadn't stepped in, it would've gotten truly ugly. I would've been hosed. Deservedly so. That story's a piece of shit. I don't know what the hell I was thinking, ever believing I could be a writer. I should just give up right now."

Joshua tasted his tomato-alfredo tortellini, and then shook a sizable amount of salt and parmesan on it. "Let me ask you something. How long did it take you to write that story?"

"Forever!" I told him. "Like, seven hours. I pulled an all-nighter."

"So you got the idea for it at midnight or something and

wrote the whole thing in a Kerouacian binge, all bagged out and wired?"

"Yeah."

"Pretty impressive, then. Shows a lot of promise. But look, you can't claim ownership over something you spent so little time on. You know how long it took me to write my story? I'd say *seventy* hours on the first part alone. Just think what you might be able to do if you were more disciplined. That's what it takes to be a writer, Eric. Grinding it out, showing up at your desk every day and clocking in and clocking out. It doesn't happen overnight, you know. It's *work*, man."

"I suppose you're right," I said despondently.

"Listen, don't worry about it. You'll write other stories. You'll get better. I'd say you were trying too hard to impress, that was the main problem, but there was something genuinely interesting happening there, a *vision*, you know, a leitmotif of people searching for transcendence amid the muddle. It's indisputable, man. You're a writer."

"You really think so?" I said, more than willing to be persuaded.

"Absolutely." He showered red pepper flakes onto his tortellini. "Let me ask you something else, though."

"What?"

"Why did you make all the characters white?"

I was nonplussed by the question. I hadn't consciously made my characters anything. "They're not white."

"No? The girl has blond hair. The guy's last name is Lambert."

"Oh," I said, embarrassed. "I didn't realize."

"The only thing that's Asian in your entire story is the motorcycle."

"I don't know why I did that."

"It's all the writers you used to idolize. They fucking brainwashed you into whitewashing *yourself*, man."

"All the authors you like, the ones you've been recommending, they're all white, too."

"Yeah, but the difference is they're subversive."

A feeble justification, I thought. "For the sake of argument, what's wrong with having white characters?"

"What's wrong with it?" Joshua said. "Isn't it obvious? It's tantamount to race betrayal."

"Come on. Seriously?"

"Are you ashamed of being Korean?"

I thought of what I had asked Didi: *Are you ashamed of me?* "No," I told Joshua, "I'm not."

I'd gone to Korea only once, when I was eleven, with my family. In Seoul, I had been shocked by how chaotic and dirty everything was, the traffic and noise and pollution, the old men pulling carts on the street with flattened cardboard boxes stacked fifteen feet high, the women who'd lower into a kimchi squat without thought, the drunk businessmen pissing against buildings, everyone cutting in line and pushing you aside, the phlegm-gathering and spitting, the profuse smoking and drinking, the slurping and masticating with open mouths, the toilet paper rolls on the dining table in lieu of napkins, the gaudy materialism and unabashed sexism. It had all seemed so vulgar, crude, Third World. In truth, I never wanted to go back.

"So why make your characters white," Joshua said, "when you could just as easily make them Korean? What do you gain by doing that? A bigger audience? You haven't even started your career yet, and you're already selling out."

That wasn't the issue for me. The problem was, I didn't feel

Korean. I didn't know what it meant to be Korean, or Asian, or Asian American. I only felt American.

"Are you saying I'm obligated to always have Asian characters?" I asked.

"Yeah, that's exactly what I'm saying," Joshua told me.

"And write about race?"

"I don't know, something like that. I mean, don't you think your stories would have more power and emotion if you tap into your personal experience? You can't deny that's a part of who you are."

"But I haven't experienced racism."

"That's a joke, right? Of course you have," Joshua said. "You've never had someone ask, 'What are you?' or 'Where you from?' or 'What's your nationality?' because there's no fucking way you can be a real American? You've never had a kid pull his eyes slanty at you or some asshole tell you it's National Hate Chinese Week? You've never had anyone tell you your English is pretty good or ask you to 'chop chop,' hurry it up? You've never walked by a bunch of punks singsonging, 'Ching chong, Chinaman'? What about all the jokes implying you've got a small penis or that you can't possibly parallel park?"

Our experiences, East and West Coasts, couldn't have been any more different. Yes, I had always been acutely aware of my ethnicity, but that awareness had been almost wholly self-inflicted, not because I had been the victim of taunts. "No, not really. Maybe the what-are-you stuff, but that's mostly been from other Asians."

"What about what went down with Sourdough?"

"Okay, maybe," I said. "All that shit's happened to you?"

"And worse."

He told me about coming to the U.S. as a five-year-old, speaking only Korean. He had been in the orphanage in Pusan since he was a few days old, literally left on the doorstep. Nothing was ever uncovered about his parents or background, and the director of the orphanage had arbitrarily named him Yoon Dong-min. But now he was Joshua Meer, living on Walker Street, a stone's throw from Harvard Square, with two extraordinarily tall, white professors as parents. They could have afforded sending Joshua to Shady Hill or Fayerweather, then to Concord Academy or BB&N, but the Meers believed in public schooling, and he attended Baldwin and Cambridge Rindge & Latin.

He received the predictable abuse: ridiculed for not knowing English and being placed in special needs; having it regularly pointed out to him that the Meers were not his real parents; asked if he ate dog; called pancake face and yangmo; told his skin looked like mustard—did he have a liver problem, was he full of bile?; asking a girl to dance and having her turn away from him, saying, "I don't understand you. I only speak English"; entering a junior high writing contest and being given third place instead of first because the judges—once they learned he was Korean American—suspected he had plagiarized the essay.

The nadir was in eleventh grade. A classmate named Stevie was going fishing off Pleasure Bay in South Boston, and Joshua tagged along. On the pier, four thugs started taunting him. "Hey, Mr. Miyagi, do you know karate? *Haiya!*" All afternoon, they badgered Joshua, who refused to respond to them. At last the men disappeared, and Joshua thought it was over, but then they returned with a rope. "Hey, slope, where're your glasses? How do you see out of those slits? Can you see at all?" Joshua's friend dropped his fishing rod and ran away. "Stevie!" Joshua yelled after him. "Don't leave me!" The men tied Joshua to a railing and left him there after duct-taping his eyelids open. Two cops found him hours later (dozens of people had

walked by and done nothing, just laughed at him), and when Joshua
began describing the four men to the cops, they told him to forget
about it. "It was just a stupid prank, kid. No harm done, right? They
didn't hit you or nothing. Boys will be boys, right?"

"Jesus," I said to Joshua. "That's unbelievable."

"It's not just Boston," he said. "It's everywhere. You need to wake
up to it."

7

Spring break came. Like most freshmen, I didn't travel anywhere, and it was quiet on campus. We slept in and goofed around, not getting much done, in spite of our vows to catch up on our studies. The following week, we returned to classes and the dead doldrums of midsemester. It seemed that winter would never end, until, in mid-April, the snow slowly began to thaw, and then all of a sudden it was gone, and we celebrated at the annual Springfest, an all-day outdoor concert on Shaw Field. Impossible to believe, but we were nearing the end of our first year.

One of the last students to workshop a story in Intro to Creative Writing was a girl named Kathryn Newcy. I didn't know much about her—just that she was from outside Duluth, where her family, implausibly, owned a Christmas tree farm. She struck me as timid and odd. The entire semester, she had never joined in any of our discussions, even though class participation was twenty-five percent of the grade. The one time she had to speak, reciting her poem (a forgettable ballad about lake-effect snow), her voice was barely audible and warbled nervously, and she began hyperventilating. I worried she might faint. There was a rumor she had some sort of a heart problem, a pacemaker implanted in her chest.

Her short story was called "Water of Heaven." It took place in a rural Chinese village in the eastern province of Shandong during the Cultural Revolution. The central character was a fifteen-year-old girl named Meihui who lived on a farm collective and worked in a boot factory, where, one day, she was raped by a party official's son. Against her family's wishes, she reported the rape, and instead of persecuting the rapist, the Revolutionary Committee censured Meihui, forcing her to say she had lied and shaving off her hair at a public denunciation in the village square.

I thought it extremely peculiar that this dowdy girl from Duluth would choose China as a setting, but I couldn't help admiring the story. All the historical and panoramic details seemed authentic: the grim descriptions of the living and working conditions, the corruption and cruelty of the officials, the strictures of Chinese family and village life, the allusions to mysticism and folklore. There were even Chinese words and proverbs sprinkled throughout the piece. Kathryn Newey somehow seemed to know this world, inhabit it. Moreover, the story, despite its overwrought elements, was gripping and emotional.

"I thought this was stunning," Tyson said.

"Gorgeous," Cory said. "I loved how carried away I was into life in this village."

"It was really touching," Megan said. "I cried when I got to the end."

"I have to agree," I said, then quickly added, "although I didn't cry"—which got a laugh—"but I was surprised by how moved I was."

The plaudits kept coming—unanimous and lavish—until Joshua said, "I guess I'll have to be the lone dissenter here."

"Yes?" Peter said.

I hadn't had a chance to talk to Joshua about the story before class. We'd gotten copies two days before, but, as usual, didn't peruse them until the last minute. I knew he would have qualms with certain sections of the story, which was hammy and purplish in spots, but naively I assumed he would give Kathryn Newey credit for exploring an Asian society so convincingly, and that he might even consider it a tribute.

"I thought this was fatuous and interminable," he said. "It's contrived and melodramatic and bogus in every respect. I found it completely offensive."

We were used to Joshua's provocations, but this sort of wholesale condemnation was unlike him. A zinger or two notwithstanding, he generally played along with Peter's entreaties to be diplomatic and constructive.

Peter, who was leaning against the lip of his desk, shifted uncomfortably. "Well, I wouldn't—"

"Offensive to my aesthetic sensibilities, and, above all, offensive to me, personally, as an Asian. This *author*," Joshua said, "had no right writing a story about China."

"Why not?" someone blurted.

I turned around, and was startled to see that Kathryn Newey had asked the question, and she was not quaking or palpitating, about to swoon. She was livid.

Peter cautioned, "Let's remember our rule about the author not being allowed to—"

"Why can't I write about China?" she asked.

"Have you looked in a mirror lately?" Joshua said.

"I'm Caucasian, so I can't write about Chinese people?"

"Ah, clarity begins to beckon."

"What about Pearl S. Buck? She won the Pulitzer for *The Good Earth*. She got the Nobel Prize."

"Yeah, interesting, isn't it? They'll give the Pulitzer to a white woman for a novel about Asians, but no Asian American novelist has ever won a Pulitzer."

"Isn't writing supposed to be about imagining other people's lives?" Kathryn Newey said. "Isn't that the whole point?"

"Not when you do it by exploiting another race. Not when you romanticize or commodify the Other. I mean, come on, the humble village peasants, the despicable commie officials—could you be more patronizing? You're stealing what you want from another people's culture and not respecting their right to tell their own stories."

"This could be a fascinating topic for discussion," Peter said, trying to regain control of the class, "but why don't we table it for—"

"Do you honestly think you have one clue what it's like to be Chinese?" Joshua asked.

"I've been to China!" Kathryn Newey said. "I spent two summers there. I know Mandarin."

"And that gives you license? So you spent a couple of summers there. So what? You were a tourist. You only saw the culture from a position of white privilege."

"My grandfather was born in Shanghai. His parents were Presbyterian missionaries there."

"Missionaries are just religious colonialists."

"They are not! We've always loved the Chinese. We respect everything about the Chinese."

"You're just reinforcing stereotypes," Joshua told her. "What you say you're honoring, you are in fact mocking."

"They *aren't* stereotypes," she said.

Pleadingly, she looked to Peter, but he was entirely unprepared for this kind of debate. Then she swiveled toward me. She knew that Joshua and I were friends, that I alone in the class, as the other Asian American, could intervene on her behalf, steer the tone of the discussion astern, just as Joshua had done for me. I glimpsed her thin, pale, beseeching face, and turned away.

"No?" Joshua said. "Look at this. 'Her long, lustrous blue-black hair,' 'her deep, fathomless almond-shaped eyes,' 'her neck, delicate as a swan's.' Those aren't stereotypes? What's sacrificed in their stead? Oh, I don't know—originality, wit, genuine emotion, one or two other things. It wouldn't be as egregious if, at the very least, your prose weren't so atrocious. It's almost laughable, how bad it is. I've never read so many insipid clichés. This has all the craft and profundity of a romance novel. Maybe that's being too generous, an insult to romance novels."

"That's so unfair!"

"Your story is a maudlin, lugubrious, exploitative piece of tripe."

"You're a racist," Kathryn Newey said.

"*I'm* a racist? That's quite a spin."

"An asshole," she said, eyes watery with rage.

Joshua smiled. "Now you're talking, sister."

■   ■   ■

After class, Joshua said to me, "You agree with me, don't you?"

I shrugged. I didn't know if I did or not.

I discussed it with Jessica in the Field House. Recently we'd taken to jogging outside, but it was raining that afternoon, and I preferred the treadmills, anyway. It felt more intimate, being side by side with Jessica like this, being able to chat.

"Joshua *is* an asshole," she said. "And a racist. One of these days, someone's going to pop him one. Tyson Wallafer's in that class, isn't he?"

"Yeah. Why?" I had never given much thought to Tyson—a

nice enough kid, not handsome, not ugly, not smart, not dumb, just average in every respect.

"He's Kathryn's boyfriend. Didn't you know? He lives in Dupre, the floor below us. She's always hanging around there. It's not a secret or anything."

It had never occurred to me that Tyson and Kathryn Newey might be a couple. They sat next to each other in class, but I had never noticed any signs of affection. "I had her pegged as a spinster till the day she died."

"Was her story that bad?" Jessica asked.

"I thought it was good, actually, but now I'm not so sure. I'm starting to doubt my ability to judge. The things Joshua pointed out, I have to admit, they were pretty hokey, but I don't know—I think she deserved better."

"It's a stupid argument, Joshua's."

"Do you think, as an Asian American artist, you should have Asian themes in all of your work? That it'd be a betrayal not to?"

"Is that something else Joshua told you? He's fucking whacked. You need to stop listening to him."

She had complained to me recently that I had started talking (and growing a goatee, in addition to smoking occasionally) exactly like Joshua, but she, too, had picked up on some of his mannerisms, particularly his use of profanity. "You're doing exactly that in your drawings," I told her.

"No, I'm not."

"Yes, you are."

"Coincidence," she said. "Art should not be a polemic."

I was confounded. The political context of her drawings was obviously more than coincidental, and I couldn't understand how she could deny it so baldly. "That's a total contradiction."

"No, it's not."

She had been working with ink on paper this semester, and her newest project was a series on Mao. The largest piece measured four-by-three feet and was an adaptation of Zhang Zhenshi's famous portrait of the Communist leader. Seen from afar, the contours of his face appeared to be composed like a topological map, with ragged, pixilated lines and blobs. But the drawing drew you in, and, looking closely, you could see that the lines and blobs were actually made up of infinitesimally tiny, intricately etched tanks and ships and cannons and soldiers, thousands of them. It was fiendishly elaborate, painstakingly detailed. You could make out the facial features on the soldiers, the threaded hilts of their bayonets. The hours, the dedication, the obsessiveness that must have been required to do this was breathtaking. Staggering. But you walked away not so much with admiration for the artist as concern for her mental health.

"I don't know," I said. "I'm starting to think all art is political, whether you intend it to be or not."

"I still say Joshua's full of shit," she told me. "His story, yeah, everything was well done"—I had lent her my copy to read—"but a poor Korean merchant and his kid in postwar Seoul—has Joshua even been to Seoul? He's from Pusan, right? What the hell does he know? He's so assimilated, he's no more Korean than I am now."

"It could be that he's just fucking with us. Maybe he's not serious about any of this. Sometimes I get the feeling he does things just to get a rise out of us."

"It's easy being outrageous. Much harder to offer real meaning." She wiped the sweat from her forehead and glanced at herself in the mirrors that lined the wall. "Do you think I got fat? Loki told me I got fat."

Like the rest of us, she had not been immune to the freshman fifteen, but the extra weight, just five or seven pounds, became her.

More filled out, curvier. She was wearing green sweatpants, rolled at the waist, and a T-shirt with the midriff cut off, exposing that lovely swale on the small of her back. "You look good," I said.

I still carried a little torch for Jessica, although her relationship with Loki Somerset seemed more secure than ever. During spring break, she had finally introduced him to her parents, and she had been both pleased and stumped by how welcoming they were to him, particularly after he began speaking to them in Mandarin.

"You know, maybe Loki and Kathryn ought to get together," I said. "They could geek out in Chinese."

"That rice-chaser comment still burns me," Jessica said. "Fucking Joshua."

I had let that comment slip. I considered myself a discreet person, yet it was sometimes difficult for me not to let a few things leak. I was in an awkward position, being between Joshua and Jessica. From time to time, each would criticize the other, and they would make me promise to keep it private, but did they really expect such things to remain submerged? Frequently I felt that these confidences were a sneaky stratagem, ensuring that their scorn would be conveyed, but allowing them to avoid confrontation. We were friends, we were the three amigos, the 3AC, yet occasionally I wondered if we even liked each other.

■   ■   ■

On each dorm-room door was a small chalkboard for messages. The Saturday morning before finals week, we arose to find communiqués scrawled on all three of our boards. Joshua's read GOOK PIG. Mine read DINK WEENIE. Jessica's read CHINK COIN SLOT.

First the RA came. Then the Dupre Hall director. Then the residential life director. Then the dean of students, Bob Nordquist. They each looked at the chalkboards, pursed their lips, and shook their heads mournfully. At another college, this might have been dismissed as a regrettable yet relatively minor act of vandalism. But not here. At Mac, this was sacrilege. This was the worst kind of profanation, an affront to every belief held dear. Nordquist asked the residential life director to have a custodian wash the boards clean, making sure no remnants were visible.

"Wait a minute," Joshua said. "What about fingerprints?"

"Pardon?" Nordquist said.

"You're not going to call the St. Paul police?"

"Why don't we talk about this."

We sequestered ourselves in Jessica's room, just the four of us. "I'm so sorry this has happened to you," Nordquist said. "I can't begin to tell you how sorry. We're a college that respects each other's differences, that's committed to tolerance and understanding. When something like this happens, it's an attack on our entire community."

We were all standing, huddled in a cramped circle. For a moment, Nordquist was distracted, looking over our heads at Jessica's sketches, drawings, watercolors, and oils pinned to the walls. He had wavy reddish blond hair and rimless eyeglasses, and he was dressed neatly in a mango-orange Mac polo shirt and pressed khakis. "These are very good," he said to Jessica.

"Thank you," she said tentatively.

"My immediate concern is the three of you. I want you to know, we'll do everything within our power to meet your every need." He told us that if we felt threatened and wanted safety escorts, even round-the-clock security, they would accommodate us. The head of Campus Security, the nurse and counselor from Health Services, the minority program director, the provost, the president—they would all come to visit us soon. "So will the chaplain, if you so wish. I don't know your spiritual affiliations." He would talk to our teachers. If we wanted to leave campus right now and postpone our final assignments and exams, we'd be free to do so without academic penalty. They'd make special arrangements, and we could worry about the makeups later. "I'll talk to your families as well, if you so wish. Our biggest concern is that you don't suffer the aftereffects of this trauma any more than you have to. So my question to you at this point is, how do you want to proceed? You said you want to call the St. Paul police?"

"Damn straight," Joshua said. "I want to find the son of a bitch who did this."

"Let me assure you, we all do," Nordquist said. "But in incidents like these in the past—"

"What incidents?" I asked. "Things like this have happened a lot?"

"I wouldn't say 'a lot,' but unfortunately, yes, there have been a few in the twelve years I've been here." He mentioned a noose found in the library, a swastika drawn on the wall outside Doty Hall, KKK painted on the dorm doors of several Japanese students, a hate-mail letter sent to a Native American student. "We all like to think of Mac as a perfect place, but the sad reality is, it's not perfect. The measure of a community, however, is in how we respond to these situations. In some instances in the past, students wanted the incidents to go unreported."

"You mean you covered it up," Joshua said.

"It was entirely the students' choice."

Needless to say, Joshua's inclination was to distrust all authority figures. I wasn't of the same mind back then, at least when it came to the administrators at Mac. Nordquist might have had a tendency to pontificate, but he was an honorable man, I thought.

"We'll do whatever you want us to do," Nordquist said. "It's completely up to you. But let me give you a couple of scenarios and gradations therein. The reason why some of those students

chose not to go public was because they wanted their privacy pro-
tected. The last thing we want is for victims to feel they're being
revictimized. Conversely, going public could be an opportunity, a
teachable moment, for the entire college. It could be a platform for
us to recommit ourselves to our principles and values of tolerance
and"—he searched for a word he hadn't already used—"inclusion.
We could open a campus dialogue on diversity."

"What do you mean by 'campus dialogue'?" Jessica asked.

"I'm not sure what could be done so close to the end of the term,
but meetings, forums, perhaps a convocation in Weyerhaeuser
Chapel."

If we decided to go public, he said, they would post flyers on
every bulletin board on campus, describing the incident and asking
anyone with information to come forward. They would not reveal
our names, and they could—"if you so wish"—describe the epithets in nonspecific language to keep our ethnicity hidden.

"We're different ethnicities," Joshua said. "Korean and Taiwanese. You mean race."

"Yes. I'm sorry," Nordquist said.

After the flyers, articles would appear in the *Mac Weekly*, the
student paper, and perhaps, especially if we involved the police, in
the *Pioneer Press* and the *Star Tribune*, the St. Paul and Minneapolis
dailies.

"So I need for you to decide," Nordquist said. "How do you feel
about all of this? What do you want to do? It's a big decision. These
sorts of things tend to have larger ramifications than you can imagine. They can gain a certain traction or momentum."

He left us alone to ruminate, telling us to call him at his office
once we'd reached a decision.

"We're all in agreement here, right?" Joshua said. "We go public."

"I don't know," Jessica said.

"I don't, either."

"Why the fuck not? We can't let this racist bullshit stand, man."

"It's not such a big deal," Jessica said. "I've been called worse. I don't want this thing to become a carnival act."

I felt the same way. I could imagine the hysteria that would surely erupt, the overkill of political correctness. I could imagine the pitying looks, everyone expressing their sympathy and outrage, the teach-ins and speak-outs, the candlelight vigils and songs of unity, worst of all the convocation in Weyerhaeuser Chapel, having to speak in front of four, five hundred people.

I did not want to be an activist. A martyr. A victim. I wanted all of this to disappear. I was hurt and in shock, but I told myself I would get over it.

"Look," I said, "finals start Monday. Nothing's going to get accomplished. Let's forget about it."

"We are not going to forget about it," Joshua said. "You think everyone doesn't know already? The chalkboards have been up all morning. Everyone on the floor's seen them, and I'm sure they've tittle-tattled the news to the entire campus. What would it look like if we did nothing? It'd look like we're cowards, like we're fucking coolies, willing to accept whatever abuse is doled out our way."

"He has a point," Jessica said to me.

"I've dealt with this shit all my life," Joshua said. "No one has to tell me racism exists, even in a liberal enclave like this. But the kids here, these chummy Crisco Gomers, they have no fucking idea. They'd say there's no way there's any racism at Mac. They don't understand it's in the media and in every aspect of society. They don't understand they have racist attitudes hidden within themselves. It'd be a wake-up call to them. Yeah, it might seem inconsequential, just some dumb fucking slurs, but you let this go, and then what happens when someone wants to pass out white supremacist literature on campus? Or print a Holocaust denial ad in the school paper? You do nothing, it becomes approval."

He kept sermonizing for several more minutes, using the same rhetoric. Finally, Jessica and I looked at each other, and nodded.

"We're all in?" Joshua asked.

"I don't want to have to go to any forums or meetings," I said.

"Not a problem."

"I don't want to give any speeches."

"You won't have to worry about that."

"Okay," I said. "Full disclosure."

■ ▩ ▧

The question—so obvious, it was overlooked by everyone until the flyers were already posted on the bulletin boards—was not asked until the next afternoon, in Nordquist's office: "Do you know of anyone who might've wanted to target the three of you?"

"Kathryn Newey," Joshua said without hesitation.

As he recounted to Nordquist what had happened in the workshop, I wondered why I had not thought of her immediately. Subconsciously, I must have suspected her all along. Yet it had been more than a week since that class, and in the life of a college student, a week was an eternity, other matters promptly taking precedence: needing to finish *Middlemarch* and *Howards End*; writing two term papers, the theses for which were eluding me; trying to arrange a summer job at Dutton's Books in Brentwood, even though it would mean driving through two hours of traffic each way on the 405; and flirting with a sophomore named Amber, who said she might be in SoCal in July. There was also another factor. If it had indeed been Kathryn Newey, her sole object of ire should

have been Joshua. Maybe me in addition, as a casualty of association, and because I had not defended her in class, but why include
Jessica? It didn't make sense.

"There had to have been more than one person," Jessica said.
"The handwriting on the boards doesn't match. And there were
two different types of chalk."

None of us—not being artists like Jessica—had noticed the
disparity in the white chalk or in the hastily scribbled, childlike
block letters. We examined the three chalkboards, which had been
unscrewed from the doors and ferried to Nordquist's office, and
saw that Jessica was right.

The likelihood of an accomplice abruptly changed things. This
was racially motivated after all, not merely a personal vendetta
between Joshua and Kathryn Newey. Jessica and I were impli-
cated in this as much as he was. We had been targeted because we
were Asian.

"Tyson Wallafer," I said to Nordquist. "Her boyfriend. He must
have been in on it, too."

■   ■   ■

Everything proved anticlimactic. All the fuss I had dreaded, the
protests and rallies, never materialized, because Kathryn Newey,
once confronted, confessed. She had followed a progressive—
a series of parties that moved from one off-campus house to
another—and had gotten wasted on beer pong. It was the first time
she had imbibed so much alcohol, she said. In the middle of the
night, getting up to use the toilet on the third floor of Dupre, she
had gone up the stairs and written GOOK PIG on Joshua's door in a
foolish, drunken moment of spontaneity.

"Didn't I tell you?" Joshua said. Yes, he had, but then I wondered why he hadn't accused her from the start. Why had he waited until the incident was made public?

Kathryn Newey would not, however, own up to writing the slurs on the other two chalkboards, and neither would Tyson Wallafer. He vehemently denied any complicity. He said he had passed out once he and Kathryn returned to Dupre from the progressive, and didn't realize anything was amiss until the flyers were put up. His own brother back home in St. Cloud was a KAD, a Korean adoptee (before then, I had not heard of the acronym, nor did I know that Minnesota had one of the largest populations of KADs of any state). He would never, ever consider doing such a horrible thing to another Asian American, he told Nordquist, and then he had cried.

Nordquist negotiated a settlement. Kathryn Newey agreed to apologize to Joshua in person, write a statement admitting she had been drinking and had put the slur on his board, and submit a signed apology to him and to the entire community for publication in the *Mac Weekly*. She would be suspended for one semester and, to be considered for readmission, would have to enroll in a racial sensitivity course, attend AA meetings, and receive treatment from a therapist.

In the agreement were also stipulations that the school would amend its student handbook, adding penalties and procedures for hate incidents, and create a racial harassment committee. There were also pledges that, sometime in the future, Mac would institute diversity awareness workshops for all incoming freshmen, establish a multiculturalism center, and make an ethnic studies course a core requirement.

In exchange, we all consented, with our signatures, that we wished to resolve the matter without litigation or any further proceedings.

It was important, what we did, I feel now. We made the right decision, and a lot of good came out of it—a perforation in the parchment. The following year, despite my apprehensions, I joined Joshua and Jessica on the twenty-seven-member racial harassment committee, and I participated in a few forums.

Kathryn Newey never returned to Mac. She transferred to Winona State University, I heard. I don't know what became of her, how much the incident altered the course of her life, although it must have. Winona State was not Macalester. The notation of a suspension on her academic record must have made it difficult for her to get into a better school, or to go on for a graduate degree, if that had been her plan. She was, I'm sure, bitter and depressed. She might have spent the rest of her days working on her family's Christmas tree farm in Duluth, ruing the unfairness of her fate. Or maybe she wasn't much affected at all, and, wherever she is, she's fulfilled, Mac a distant and negligible memory.

In retrospect, I think we killed a promising literary career in the making—maybe not as a serious fiction writer, but possibly as a commercial novelist. She had had incipient talent as a story-teller, certainly more than I did at that juncture. I could have stood up for her during workshop and precluded all the ensuing events, but I did not. Sometimes I feel guilty about it. Just as often, I acquit myself. She was not, after all, altogether innocent. Maybe she was a racist. Maybe her story was, at its roots, patron-izing and exploitative.

No evidence was ever found to connect her, Tyson Wallafer, or anyone else to the other slurs. Of course, then, after a while I began to speculate that Joshua had fabricated them. Perhaps he had heard Kathryn Newey bumping against his door that night and, after dis-covering what she had written, had shuffled down the hall, found a piece of chalk, and inscribed the epithets on our chalkboards. It was, given the lack of alternatives, the likeliest explanation. Maybe his intentions were even noble, albeit manipulative and perverse: to incite our ethnic pride and stir our ideological passions. Joshua would refute any suggestion of chicanery to his grave. But I always thought, and still do, that it would have been very much like him, doing something like that, in order to bind us together.

8

The 3AC did not become a formal organization until 1998. After Macalester, we scattered to different parts of the country, all for our graduate degrees. Joshua received a scholarship to the Iowa Writers' Workshop, where he became Frank Conroy's darling. Afterward, he landed another coveted sinecure, the Stegner Fellowship at Stanford, then was given a Jones Lectureship, a cushy teaching gig that allowed him to stay in Palo Alto.

He didn't get published in *The New Yorker* or *The Atlantic*, but his stories started to appear with regularity in literary journals. He was twice nominated for a Pushcart Prize, and one of his pieces was reprinted in an anthology of Asian American writers. Things were going well for Joshua, it seemed, but then he went off the rails.

Both his parents, in their late seventies, died in quick succession in 1997. During the funerals, Joshua wept inconsolably—genuine anguish that was heartrending for me to witness. "I didn't deserve them," he sobbed to me. "I took them for granted because they weren't my real parents, because they weren't Asian."

On several occasions, I had seen him together with the Meers, both of them bespectacled and spindly. They had been extraordinarily kind people, but Joshua's relationship to them—and, I have to say, theirs to him—had seemed to be one of gentle indifference.

Be that as it may, their deaths precipitated several perplexing, contradictory episodes in Joshua's life.

First, he took a temporary leave from his Jones Lectureship and went to Korea, spending weeks in search of his birth parents. At the orphanage in Pusan, he learned of a rumor that he had actually been born on Cheju-do, and he took a ferry to the island, hoping he might be able to uncover more, but the trip was to no avail. With no further leads, he migrated north, up the peninsula. He had an amorphous idea that he might repatriate and stay in Seoul, yet he felt uncomfortable in the city, and in the country as a whole. By bureaucrats and policemen, by clerks in hotels and stores, by waitresses in restaurants, by bus and taxi drivers, he was chastised for not being able to speak Korean well enough, for not being a real Korean, for being too American—all of the things he used to berate me for. He felt denigrated for having Meer as his last name, for being an adoptee, someone who was unwanted, illegitimate, abandoned, who had no lineage or family history he could claim as his own. He felt *baekjeong* to them, an outcaste, the lowest class, contemptible and polluted, untouchable, unspeakable. He didn't belong in Korea.

Returning to Palo Alto, he legally changed his name from Meer to Yoon. He started a KAD support group in the Bay Area, helped organize a Korean heritage festival, became a Big Brother to a Korean teenager, joined a Korean dragon boat team, taught ESL to Korean immigrants, and, briefly, unbelievably, became born-again and attended a Korean Baptist church.

Then, abruptly, he withdrew from all these activities, denouncing them as preposterous and futile. He began siding with the burgeoning anti-TRA (transracial adoption) movement, arguing that white families who adopted Asian children were selfish and ultimately cruel, that snatching Asian babies from their homelands was a vestigial, devious form of imperialism, colonization by kidnapping, nullifying the adoptees' ability to ever identify with any ethnicity, an effacement equivalent to genocide.

"Asian babies should grow up in Asian households," he told me. "Otherwise, they don't stand a chance."

Then, just as swiftly, he rescinded this stance, deciding that the Meers had been decent and compassionate and should be honored for their altruism. He gave up his Jones Lectureship and, bankrolled by his inheritance, moved to Paris for five months.

Jessica had a tough time of it as well. Her parents might have found it acceptable for her to date Loki, but not what she chose to do next. She applied to all seven Ivy League medical schools and, unexpectedly, got into two: Harvard and Penn. She had only cursorily prepared for the MCATs, intending to do poorly on them and rid her family of this Ivy League fixation once and for all, and perhaps as a consequence—no pressure, no panic attacks—she aced the test. But she decided to turn down Harvard and Penn and attend the one other school to which she had secretly applied, the Rhode Island School of Design, to get her MFA in studio art.

Her parents disowned her. She took out loans to pay for her tuition to RISD. When she graduated, she moved to the Lower East Side in Manhattan, but floundered trying to make a name for herself as an artist while working two different jobs as a waitress and a third as an after-hours proofreader at a law firm. Enervated and losing hope, she at last found rescue through a one-year fellowship to the Provincetown Fine Arts Work Center. It meant living in a tiny, makeshift, barely insulated studio from October through April, seasons that were gloomy and desolate on the tip of Cape

Cod, and the stipend was paltry, but Jessica leapt at the opportunity for a respite.

I went to Boston, of all places, for my MFA. Unlike Joshua, I was rejected by Iowa, and UVA, and Michigan, and every other top creative writing program in the country. Walden College, a former secretarial school in the Back Bay, was small and third-rate. It didn't have a single famous author on the faculty, and it didn't offer me a scholarship, but I went, anyway, because they were the only ones willing to take me. "Why an MFA instead of an MBA?" my mother asked me, as if it were only a matter of changing a consonant. But I had prepared her and my father over the years, tamping down expectations of my going to law school or having any comparable professional ambitions. I was going to be a writer. Nothing they said or did could stop me. I think back now, and wonder what might have happened if I had not met Joshua. As a freshman, I had not even known a master's of fine arts in creative writing existed.

As mediocre as Walden was, it had one redeeming attribute, an affiliation with a literary journal called *Palaver*, where I signed on as an intern my first semester. It was edited by my principal workshop teacher, Evan Paviromo, a British-Italian scholar, bon vivant, and wastrel. He was a charismatic, towering presence at six-foot-five, beefy verging on portly, with thick brown hair he kept long and swept back, always elegant in his blue Savile Row suits, bow tie, and matching hankie. He had no money of his own and relied on his wife's income to fund his indulgences, including the magazine (he told me he'd come to the U.S. from London "looking for a rich widow with a bad cough"). A raconteur extraordinaire, he unfurled story after story to anyone who would listen. Stories about producing art-house films, hanging out with movie stars and politicians, spending weekends at the Kennedy compound in Hyannis Port, and running guns and drugs for Central American dictators under the aegis of the CIA. I had a hard time believing any of it, and came to suspect that Paviromo was a con artist, questioning the authenticity of his credentials and even his Oxbridge accent.

There was no question, however, about *Palaver*'s reputation, which was outsized compared to its meager resources, its office a rented shithole in Watertown. *Palaver* had a history of discovering young writers, their stories and poems regularly plucked for prize annuals. Agents and book editors kept close tabs on the journal, scouting for new talent. A publication in *Palaver* had the potential to launch a career, and Evan Paviromo kept promising to launch mine.

As Joshua had predicted, with discipline I had gotten better as a writer, and in such a lackluster MFA program, I was treated with almost Joshuaesque regard. In general, Paviromo was admiring of my fiction, although I can't say he was of much value to me as a mentor—lackadaisical and distracted and not terribly interested in his students' work. Joshua still served that role for me, reading all my short stories and critiquing them exhaustively during late-night phone calls from Iowa City. "Paviromo said what?" he'd ask. "That asshole doesn't know shit. Where the fuck does he come off? He's not even a writer." Then Joshua would break down my stories, pointing out each blunder in the structure and prose, nitpicking about words like "desultory," "recalcitrant," and "askance." The ritual was withering, excruciating, but it helped, and by the time I finished my master's thesis, a mélange of various projects that included a screenplay and a long story called "The Unrequited," Joshua said about the latter, "Now you're fucking cooking. This is the best thing you've ever done, by far. Honestly, unequivocally, all bullshit aside, you know I wouldn't say this unless I meant it, it's brilliant. You've made a huge fucking leap." Paviromo agreed, telling me, "You know, I believe this is eminently publishable. In fact,

I might want to publish it myself in *Palaver*," and for years he kept stringing me along with that pledge.

Joshua tried to circumvent matters, submitting "The Unrequited" for me to journals in which he'd previously appeared, telling the editors they'd be blind to pass up such a gem, yet they always did, saying the story had come close but wasn't quite right for them. Every week I'd send out photocopies of "The Unrequited," wait eight months to a year for a response, and each time, I'd get the copies back in their self-addressed, stamped envelopes with the same apologetic rejections. I could not, for the life of me, get anything into print.

After I graduated, I was hired as an adjunct instructor at Walden, mostly assigned freshman comp and the occasional Intro to Creative Writing class. Paviromo also took me on as the office manager of *Palaver*, a quarter-time, minimum-wage job. I had loan payments, no health insurance, and a mounting balance on my credit card. I was making $17,000 a year.

I lived in a basement studio apartment on Marlborough Street, and the bay windows—covered with iron bars—faced the rat-infested back alleyway and were right next to the rear door, which tenants kicked open at all hours to lob their garbage into the trash cans. I was miserable there. I was miserable in Boston.

It was an old, crumbling, restive city. People were brusque and rude. No one ever said "Excuse me" or "Thank you" or held a door for you. And, yes, as Joshua had warned, it was a racist town. I didn't have my eyelids duct-taped open, but a lot of the sinister, corrosive, subtle shit that had happened to him, I experienced, too. Everywhere I went, I found myself to be the only nonwhite person in the room. I got so tired of the where-are-you-from, what-are-you inquiries, I began to answer, "I'm a third-generation Korean American, born and raised in Mission Viejo, California," hoping specificity would curtail stupidity, and still I got: "Hey, you speak pretty good English." The assumption was always that I was an MIT student. That I studied engineering. That I was a foreigner fresh off the boat. That I was an overachiever, a model minority, a wimp.

Paradoxically, I kept dating white girls, mostly other aspiring writers, but there was a difference now. I no longer predicted a future with any of them, and it could have been, in fact, that I subconsciously chose women who were so fucked up, disaster was virtually assured, providing fodder for the stories I was now writing about Asian guys who dated fucked-up white girls.

The most recent one, Odette, had been from Atlanta, an assistant editor at the literary journal *Agni*. Things had been going swimmingly, if a little quickly. Almost right away, she began discussing marriage, kids. "What do you think of the name Genevieve if it's a girl?" she asked. "I want to have three children, the first when I'm twenty-nine, okay? Do you think your mother will like me?"

Odette spoke on the phone to her own mother in Atlanta, who asked what my name was. "Is he Asian? What? Korean?" Then her mother shouted to her father, "Did you hear that, Sam? You're going to have slanty-eyed grandchildren."

But we didn't have children. The relationship didn't last more than a few months. Out of the blue, Odette's ex-boyfriend sent me a letter, claiming that every day for the last two weeks he had been fucking her in the afternoon, just hours before Odette came to my basement apartment to fuck me. He added that, according to her, I was lousy in bed and had the penis of a pygmy.

"That is fucked, man," Joshua told me. "*You* are fucked. Why do you keep going out with these rimjobs?"

By then, the spring of 1998, Joshua had returned from Paris and had moved into his parents' old house on Walker Street, in Cambridge for good now—or at least as permanently as he could fore-see. A few probate issues notwithstanding, he had money from his parents' estate—their retirement and investment accounts, their life insurance. If he was frugal and sold the house, a three-story Victorian worth well over a million dollars, he could write full-time almost indefinitely and live anywhere. He was in a quandary, unable to decide what to do or where to go, not prepared to put the house on the market just yet. "It's the only home I've ever known," he said. So for the moment he was living in the house alone, four bedrooms and three and a half bathrooms to himself. Again and again, he asked me to move in with him. "Come on, man, I won't even charge you rent." It was a tempting offer. Certainly it would have been a welcome financial reprieve for me, but I kept hesitating.

It wasn't that the house was inhospitable. Far from it. It was over a hundred years old, gray, weathered clapboards outside, but the interior had been continually renovated, decorated in a mini-malist, modern aesthetic that was inviting: Swiss Bauhaus furni-ture with clean, straight lines and warm blond woods, Max Bill stools, Alvar Aalto bentwood tables. There was an Eames chair and ottoman. There were comfy upholstered sofas, faded red Persian rugs, bright still lifes and black-and-white landscapes on the walls, lots of light and quiet, stainless steel appliances, central heat and air-conditioning.

And it wasn't just that Joshua was a slob. It was a given that he wouldn't pick up after himself, do the dishes, pitch in with chores. I'd have to take care of all of those things if I moved in, I knew. That didn't bother me so much—an acceptable trade-off if I were living there gratis.

Rather than domestic, it was more the prospect of emotional servitude that made me waver. I remembered our sophomore year at Mac, when Joshua had gotten a tattoo on his upper left arm that

read, in inch-high, mineral-black Futura Bold letters, 3AC. Jessica
and I had first thought it was fake—stenciled with a marker. Temporary tattoos were all the rage then, and there had been a fuss
when some high school kids in Maple Grove had supposedly been
given lick-and-stick blue star tattoos that were soaked in LSD,
prompting Mac officials to put out an advisory.

But Joshua had told us no, it was real. "So when are you guys
going to get yours?" he'd asked.

"No fucking way," I'd said.

"Why not? It's a badge of solidarity."

"We'll probably have a falling-out next week and never speak to
each other again," Jessica said.

"No, no, you don't understand," Joshua said. "This—this thing
with us—it can never die."

We did not get matching tattoos. A part of me had agreed with Jessica. The three of us had become close at Mac, especially in the wake
of the brouhaha with Kathryn Newey, but I hadn't felt our friendship warranted an indelible symbol of commitment and fidelity.

Now that Joshua and I had known each other for ten years, however, I had the opposite concern. Although I relished his counsel
and company, I was wary of him at times, wary of how critical,
noisome, and dogmatic he could be, of his predilection for creating drama and havoc, of the inequity in our roles, and wary, too,
of his dependence on me, his neediness. Already there were the
phone calls, the panicked intuitions that he might have leukemia
and maybe should get a lumbar puncture, or that he might have a
brain tumor and maybe should get a CT scan. More systemically,
there were the calls, both during the day and late at night, when
he thought it imperative to convey an idea he'd had, an epiphany,
or to read me a particularly piquant passage he'd just written or

read, or calls about nothing, really, just wanting to check in, shoot the breeze.

There were the spontaneous hankerings for pizza or Bass ale or a movie or a hike, for just hanging out, because he was bored and lonely. There were the favors to help him trim a tree or fix the gutters, to go with him to Tags Hardware or Home Depot, to pick up a prescription at CVS or do some research in the microfiche archives of the BPL for him. He didn't understand that I had work to do, grading papers and prepping for classes and stuffing envelopes in *Palaver*'s shithole. He didn't understand that not everything revolved around him, that I might have a life of my own. The impositions were bad enough living in the same city. What would they be like living in the same house?

His side of the river, I had to admit, had its allure, namely Wu Chon in Somerville's Union Square, where we could get our fill of Korean food—bibimbap, kalbi, and jaeyuk bokkeum—and the Porter Square Exchange, which housed the Japanese market Koto-bukiya and a handful of small Japanese restaurants that were practically stalls, yet offered cheap and tasty comfort foods.

Our favorite was Cafe Mami, where we usually sat at the counter, and it was there that Joshua dispensed his latest harangue about my dating habits.

"All these years, it's like you haven't learned a thing," he said. "You haven't changed at all."

"I could say the same about you. You've never had much luck with the ladies."

"By choice, man. It's by choice."

During college, Joshua hadn't had a single real girlfriend, and the same held true when he was in Iowa and the Bay Area, a fling here and there, never lasting longer than three weeks, at the end of which the women invariably left him. He was lazy, not interested in expending the least amount of effort required to sustain a relationship. He couldn't be bothered with courtship, with sharing, with being complimentary or attentive or supportive or sensitive. He couldn't care less about flowers or romantic gestures or fun excursions. He didn't want to go out on dates or hold dinner parties. He didn't want to talk to the women on the phone (why would he, when he had me?). He didn't really want to spend any *time* with them. He needed to protect his time, for writing and mulling, for reading and pondering. He needed space and sovereignty, not be tied down with commitments and compromises. He needed women only to slake the periodic biological urge. In other words, the last thing he wanted was a girlfriend or a wife, though he could do with a mistress or a married lover, but, barring that, he would settle for a prostitute, which he still employed on occasion.

He had solicited one not too long ago from the escort pages of the *Boston Phoenix.* "You know, you should watch out," I said. "They're cracking down on johns these days."

"It's so stupid and hypocritical. Everyone pays for sex in one form or another, marriage being the most common and extortionate. It's all about money. All these laws are designed to oppress women so they can't take control of the industry and get their fair share. It's so parochial and anti-feminist, not to mention inconvenient for people like me."

"Somehow I've never thought of you as a feminist."

"I am, at heart. I'm an equal-opportunity asshole. But you," Joshua said, "you'd never hire a hooker, would you? Because you believe the concept of love is real and attainable and not merely a myth perpetrated by religious demagogues and prohibitionists and crypto-fascist conglomerates."

"Yes."

"Okay, then, if you have to go down this path of *felo-de-se*, at least do one thing."

"What?"

"Look around you."

From our perch in Cafe Mami, I looked at all the young, attractive Asian women in the Porter Square Exchange, milling through the passageway to eat at the sushi bar or the ramen place, to buy bubble tea from Tapicha or pastries from Japonaise or cosmetics from the Shiseido kiosk.

"Why can't you just go out with a nice Asian girl?" Joshua asked me.

I had tried. My parents had set me up on a few blind dates, daughters of friends or friends of friends from their Garden Grove church, Korean girls purportedly seeking a nice Korean boy from a good Korean family. By and large, they turned out to be typical KAPs—Korean American Princesses. Stuck up, superficial, very high-maintenance. They had salon hairdos, wore heavy makeup, and dressed to the nines in designer clothes, especially prizing Gucci and Louis Vuitton handbags. They expected me to take them to dinner at Biba or Blue Ginger, Mistral or Clio, Maison Robert or No. 9 Park, then go clubbing at Aria, followed by a nightcap at Sonsie, and pay for everything. They were disappointed I didn't wear a suit—Prada, Armani, Joseph Abboud, or at least Zegna. They were bewildered I didn't own a car—a Benz or a Beemer, or at least a Lexus. They were flummoxed most of all by my career.

"I'm working for *Palaver* magazine and teaching adjunct at Walden right now."

"Is there much money in that?"

"No, but I'm trying to become a writer."

"What kind of writer?"

"Fiction. Short stories. Novels."

"Is there much money in that?"

"No. Not in the type of books I'm interested in writing."

"But—I don't get it—what would be the point, then?"

Joshua chewed on his tonkatsu curry, and I munched on my yaki donburi, thinly sliced beef with onions and bean sprouts served over rice.

"Those girls were civilians," he said. "What can you expect from civilians? Of any color? They can't understand. They see an unre-mittingly sad film, and they think it's depressing, whereas we're fucking enthralled, because the catharsis for us is in witnessing great art, seeing the undiluted truth, in the shared recognition that life is pain. You need to go out with an artist. An Asian artist."

"You find me a nice Asian artist," I said, "and I will."

Later that summer, Joshua told me to come over to his house, he had a little surprise for me. He opened the front door and intro-duced me to his new roommate—Jessica Tsai.

I broke the lease to my basement apartment in the Back Bay and moved into the house on Walker Street.

9

That first month, with just the three of us in the house, was idyllic. There were three bedrooms on the second floor, the master and two smaller ones that had once been home offices for the Meers. Joshua couldn't bear to sleep in his parents' old room, although he said one of us was welcome to it. Jessica and I didn't feel it'd be proper, either, and moved futons into the two smaller rooms, while Joshua encamped in the converted attic upstairs, an expansive, sunny haven with dormers and skylights and its own bathroom.

Jessica was hired as a waitress at Upstairs at the Pudding. She also got a daytime gig proofreading at the law firm Gaston & Snow downtown. She would look for a third job—her student loans were quadruple what I owed—but none of this employment would start for a few weeks, so she had much of August at her leisure, time to relax and work on her art.

Serendipity visited me, too. *Palaver*'s managing editor, a feminist poet who had never gotten along with Paviromo, quit without notice, and he asked me to take over her slot. The salary was shit, and still I wouldn't have benefits, but it was a full-time job, allowing me to take a leave from teaching freshman comp at Walden College.

For once, we could all take a breather. We went to the Kendall Square Cinema and Brattle Theatre to watch indie and foreign films, to Jillian's to play pool, to Jae's for pad thai and the Forest Café for mole poblano, to Redbones for ribs and the Burren for Guinness, to Hollywood Express to rent DVDs, to the Harvard Book Store and Wordsworth to browse books, to Tower Records, Newbury Comics, and Looney Tunes to scope out CDs.

Joshua's musical tastes now leaned toward Fugazi, Outkast, Massive Attack, Beck, and Marilyn Manson, but he was obsessed at the moment with Jeff Buckley's *Sketches for My Sweetheart the Drunk*, a double-disc set of unfinished songs. He played it incessantly. Whenever the opening chords for "The Sky Is a Landfill" wafted down from the attic, Jessica would groan, "God, why does he have to keep playing that thing over and over? It's driving me fucking insane."

It was a strange album, at times soulful, bluesy, psychedelic, and incoherent, filled with weird, discordant riffs, Buckley's falsetto spooky and haunting, all the more so knowing he had died after recording the demos. Joshua was convinced that Buckley had committed suicide.

"It was an accident," I told him.

"He goes for a dip wearing jeans and Doc Martens?"

The story was that Buckley, frustrated with the production of his second album in New York, had fled to Memphis and cloistered himself in a cabin with just a mattress, a four-track, and his guitars. He had quit drinking and smoking and was working nonstop. He had just completed writing all the songs for *My Sweetheart the Drunk* when, enigmatically, he took an evening swim in the Wolf River Harbor, fully clothed. He was last seen floating away on his back, singing Zeppelin's "Whole Lotta Love" at the top of his lungs. The official cause of death was listed as an accidental drowning, the theory being that he had been pulled into the Mississippi by an undertow created by a passing tugboat. Joshua didn't buy it.

"He'd finished the album. That's what he'd set out to accomplish, and he was done. He didn't have any more reason to live. Writing the songs, not releasing them, was his raison d'être."

When we were at Mac, Joshua had once taken us to the Washington Avenue Bridge, from which John Berryman had jumped. Jessica had asked why he'd done it, and Joshua had said, "Life, friends, is boring. We must not say so." I had thought Joshua was making a general declaration about existence, but it was a line from Berryman's book *Dream Songs.* "Who knows why he did it," he told us. "Most people inclined to kill themselves don't out of cowardice. That's why William Carlos Williams said the perfect man of action is the suicide."

That summer on Walker Street, Joshua's other obsession was with Haruki Murakami. *The Wind-up Bird Chronicle* had just come out in paperback. Previously he hadn't been much of a fan of Murakami's—too lightweight and gimmicky, too many pop culture references and cyberpunk sleights of hand—but this novel was a monumental breakthrough, he believed, right up there with *Blood Meridian* and *The Remains of the Day.* (Joshua had photos of McCarthy and Ishiguro on his bulletin board, along with Kafka, Jim Morrison, and Thích Quảng Đức, the Buddhist monk who had been famously photographed in the moment of self-immolation on the streets of Saigon, reportedly not moving a muscle or making a sound as he charred and shriveled.)

Joshua had heard Murakami was living in Cambridge, somewhere between Central and Inman Squares, while filling a titular post as a writer-in-residence at Tufts, and Joshua spent several days crisscrossing the neighborhood, trying to find the pumpkin-colored house that Murakami was reportedly renting. He read interviews in which Murakami said he rose at five a.m. and wrote for six hours and then went running, read for a bit, listened to some jazz, and was in bed by ten p.m. He kept to this routine without variation, Murakami said, because the repetition induced a deeper state of mind, a form of mesmerism.

So Joshua, formerly a sedentary, inveterate night owl, decided to change his schedule and start running himself, and he enlisted me to train him. I had continued running after Mac, doing the loop nearly every day on the Esplanade between the Museum of Science and the Mass Ave bridge when I'd lived on Marlborough Street.

We bought shoes for Joshua at Marathon Sports. He had in mind two things: first, to emulate Murakami's work ethic, helping him wrap up a draft of his novel, and second, to possibly spot Murakami along the Charles River, his preferred route, and befriend him, perhaps become running buddies with him, do the Boston Marathon together.

I thought I'd start Joshua off with an easy jog down JFK Street to the Eliot Bridge, but Joshua—a chain-smoker since high school—was sweating and hyperventilating after a mere quarter mile.

"You're going to have to quit smoking," I told him.

"Yeah, yeah," he said, bent over, hands on his knees.

"And eat better." At the moment the only meal he was making for himself was a fried egg and bologna sandwich on Wonder bread, slathered with mayonnaise and splotched with soy sauce. He considered himself a gourmand, yet could subsist on the worst junk imaginable.

"Yeah, yeah," he said.

Maybe his dietary habits never improved much, but in time he did become a diligent runner. It was always he who would drag me out on cold or rainy weekends. He would never miss a day. It was one of the few things that gave him peace, he would tell me.

He never ended up meeting Murakami. We would soon learn that he had left Cambridge three years earlier, in 1995, compelled to return to Japan after the earthquake in Kobe and the sarin-gas attack in Tokyo. Yet before we knew that, Joshua would look ahead expectantly as he puffed along the Charles, and whenever he saw a middle-aged Asian man approaching us, Joshua would say, "Is that him?" It became a private joke between us. In the years to follow, anytime we saw an Asian man with a broad forehead, sunken cheeks, and short bangs, one of us would say, "Is that him?"

Jessica had stopped running quite a while before then, her joints beginning to bother her. She had become an Ashtanga Vinyasa devotee, and she was going to Baron Baptiste's Power Yoga studio in Porter Square. I accompanied her for the first time one night in mid-August.

The class was for all levels, and it was first-come, first-served, cash only, ten dollars a head. A line of people waited on the sidewalk for the door to open. What struck me immediately upon entering the studio was the heat—sweltering and oppressive, the thermostat intentionally set at ninety degrees, hotter than it was outside. "Baron calls it healing heat," Jessica told me as we filed in.

The place was bare-bones: no dressing rooms, showers, or lockers. Everyone—mostly young women, mixed with a few post-hippie graybeards—began stripping off their T-shirts and shorts and piling them against the walls and in the corners. I was astonished by how beautiful their bodies were, Jessica's included.

I had seen her over the years—she'd sometimes take the train or bus up from Rhode Island or New York to visit us when Joshua was in town—but she had not ventured out of Provincetown at all during her fellowship. In the intervening year, she had cut off her hair, not much longer than mine now, and it was spiky and highlighted with burgundy streaks. She had acquired an eyebrow ring and a

tongue stud, and she favored clothes in the cross-genres of Goth/
punk/grunge. Zippered corset tops, cargo pants, skater shoes, a
Mao cap with a red star. She had also gotten tattooed—not with
3AC, but with a large green feather, a peacock quill, that plumed
up the inside of her right forearm, and also, to my regret, a tramp
stamp of barbed-wire twists that defaced her lower back.

But her body—good Lord, how she had transformed her body.
In her sports bra and skintight spandex shorts, she was lithe, sin-
ewy, and buffed. So were most of the other women, and as they
packed into the room and began warming up in front of me with
sun salutations and downward dogs, I was afforded close-up views
of curved, supple ramps of ass and distinctly delineated furrows
of ungulate. I thought it impossible I'd be able to make it through
the ninety-minute class without embarrassing myself with an
erection.

I needn't have been concerned. This was not yoga as I had imagined it. There were no smoldering sticks of incense or Tibetan
tingsha cymbals to guide us into oneness, no Sanskrit chants or
quiet moments of sitting meditation to harmonize our pranas. This
was an unadulterated, ball-busting workout. This was boot camp,
absolute hell on earth.

The instructor, Kenta, was Japanese American, dressed in a long-
sleeved T-shirt, loose pants, and a bandanna. He was not an impos-
ing man—short, and even, it seemed, a little pudgy. He walked
with a strut and spoke with a nasal voice that betrayed a faint metro
lisp. But he led the class through a series of torturous stretches and
lunges and contortions. Cobra pose, warrior pose, I couldn't keep
up with the poses, couldn't flex or twist the way everyone else did.
Soon I was out of breath, in pain, and sweating. Really sweating. I
had never sweated so much in my life. With the heat turned up and
the doors and windows sealed, with all the straining bodies so close

together, the temperature must have been over a hundred. It was a sauna, a convection oven.

"Superglue your nips to your kneecaps," Kenta ordered the class.

Sweat dripped onto the floor and was puddling—not just from me, from my mat neighbors, too.

"Don't let fear interfere," Kenta said. "You might feel like you're struggling, but just transport yourself into the eye of the storm. Now sweep up and inhale."

Sweat from my neighbors hit the backs of my legs, the wall mirror, the ceiling.

"You feel that decompression?" Kenta said. "It's all about letting go. Now rotate."

Sweat from my neighbors flew through the air and splattered my face.

"Awesome," Kenta said. "This is warm molasses. Love your body. Don't push. Just flow."

I had to pause repeatedly to rest. I'd drop down into child pose, kneeling pathetically, and then rise and try to follow along, grunting and squealing. I lost my balance several times and fell over, almost instigating a dominoic catastrophe.

"I thought you were in shape from running," Jessica said when the class ended.

"Some of those poses were inhumane."

I stumbled through the door, into the relief of the cool night air. "Your wrists don't hurt?" I asked. I hadn't noticed her modifying her poses or using any of the foam blocks or apparatuses.

"No. Yoga seems to help, actually."

"I don't know if I can walk home. Let's take a cab."

"It's less than a mile. Come on."

We stopped at the White Hen on Mass Ave so I could buy a jug of Gatorade. "Is Kenta gay?" I asked.

"No. Why do you ask?"

"He seems gay."

"He's married and has two kids. He used to be a professional kickboxer. Before this, he was a trainer for the Celtics. Have you become homophobic?"

"Of course not."

"Homophobia's always a sign of latent homosexuality."

"I'm not homophobic, and I'm not gay. I was just asking," I said. "Slow down. My legs are killing me."

"I love the feeling after class," Jessica said. "It feels like I've just had incredible, hot, sweaty, slippery sex."

Sex. Sex with Jessica—hot, sweaty, slippery, or any other variety. I had been imagining it quite frequently in the two weeks we'd become housemates, in even closer proximity now than we had been on the fourth floor of Dupre. "Do you ever talk to Loki?" I asked.

"Loki? Not in years."

From Skidmore, Loki Somerset had gone to Yale for a combined PhD in film studies and East Asian languages and literatures. RISD was only two hours up 95 from New Haven, so they had seen a lot of each other and had even begun talking about marriage. But then Loki spent a summer in Beijing and fell in love with a Chinese woman ("I guess I wasn't authentic enough for him," Jessica told me). Last she'd heard, he had gone back to China for a postdoc at the Beijing Film Academy.

"Have you been seeing anyone?" I asked as we crossed Linnaean Street.

"No, not really, nothing serious."

This was her patented answer, invariably circumspect about the particulars. I didn't really know anything about her romantic life in the last four years, whereas, if prompted, I was unfailingly forth-coming with her.

"Is it that you're not looking for anything serious?"

"I don't know," she said. "I've been going through a lot of shit, and people are always trying to analyze me, saying it's because of Loki or what happened with my parents, or bottom-line I'm a cold heartless bitch, or that I'll only go out with people who are so fucked up or unsuitable or unavailable, it guarantees it won't work out, which must be secretly what I want, but you know what? Fuck all that. I just want to be alone right now. What's so wrong with wanting to be alone?"

"Because being alone frightens people."

"Does it frighten you?"

"A little," I admitted.

"That could be your downfall as a writer," she said.

"Why do you say that?"

"To produce art, great art, you've got to be willing to alienate people and suffer the consequences."

I wanted to see what she had been working on in Provincetown, and the next day she led me into the basement of the house, where she had stacked her canvases against the foundation wall and cov-ered them with tarps.

She had changed mediums again. At Mac, she had expanded on her elaborate ink drawings, then had started adding water-color to them, then had gone back to representational painting, mostly hyperrealistic portraits. She entered RISD with painting as her discipline, only to become interested in doing small-scale sculpture—not a true departure, rather a redefinition of the pen-and-inks, with the same kind of intricacy and exactitude. Joshua and I drove down to Providence for her thesis exhibition, and what had fascinated us were her table sculptures. She had made them out of architectural model materials: styrene sheets, basswoods, open-cell foam, and chipboard. One sculpture, called *Wushu*, was shaped like the Pentagon, an ordinary replica, it appeared, except the concentric polygons were made up of miniature pairs of Nike shoes. Another, called *Yawn*, was a one-hundred-Taiwan-dollar bill, only, if you looked closer, you could see that the bill consisted of infinitesimal logos for McDonald's, Coca-Cola, Kentucky Fried Chicken, and the like. All of this was rendered with the utmost specificity, down to the swoosh and laces on the shoes, and Jessica had done it all by hand, using craft knives and fine saws, files, sandpaper, and glue.

But she had started paying a price for such precision. Her hands began to hurt. Her fingers tingled and numbed, her wrists locked up on her, she couldn't grip a knife or a brush with any vigor, and she couldn't sleep at night, she was in such torment. She had developed carpal tunnel syndrome. She had hoped it might be temporary, but it persisted, so she began trying every conceivable remedy. She slept in wrist braces and propped her arms on pillows. She took anti-inflammatories. She stretched and massaged her forearms and wrapped them in gauze. She applied ice packs and rolled Baoding balls. She dipped her hands into baths of hot paraffin wax. She saw an acupuncturist and a chiropractor. Finally she paid out-of-pocket for cortisone injections.

"I don't know how you can function at all, much less do yoga and art," I said in the basement.

"They don't hurt all the time," she told me. "I notice it most when I'm drawing or carving, or when I'm trying to sleep. I might need to get the surgery, but I'm afraid it'll make things worse— relieve the pain at the expense of agility. I can't afford it, anyway, without health insurance."

"I'll lend you the money if you want."

"You don't have any money."

"You could borrow it from Joshua."

"Maybe," she said, "but that's something I'd be loath to do. I'd rather not owe anything to anyone, especially Joshua."

"Why especially him?"

Joshua was magnanimous with his money, overly generous, really, always offering to pay for dinner or drinks when we went out. True, we'd already had some issues at the house. He pilfered our food and toilet paper and detergent without asking and didn't replace them. He left dishes and crumbs everywhere. He relied on us to mop and sweep, take out the trash, scrub the toilets. When we complained, he would smile and say, "Listen, you know I'm not going to change."

"He uses people," Jessica told me. "Don't you know that by now?" She pulled the tarps off the paintings and leaned them against the wall one by one.

This was something completely different. Gone was her fetish for minute detail. The paintings were abstract, a series of heavily textured acrylics. The paint was thickly and haphazardly applied in dozens of layers, and the colors were almost all dark—blacks, blues, browns, some purples, with a few wispy swirls of white, yellow, and green, a dab of red. They all portrayed a stick figure in what appeared to be a forest, the figure brushed in ghostly smears, as if it were disappearing, evaporating. The paintings were luminous, with a three-dimensionality that was technically cunning, yet, looking at them, I felt uncomfortable—very disturbed, actually.

"These are . . . ," I started to say, but couldn't finish.

"Weird," she said. "I know."

"They're stunning. They're like nothing you've ever done. They're—I don't know how to describe it—unruly."

"I like that. 'Unruly.' That's what I was trying to do, let everything go."

The stick figures were based on ancient pictographs for the Chinese calligraphy character *nǚ*—woman. In its earliest forms, the character was drawn as if a woman were bent or kneeling, her arms lowered and crossed, in a show of meekness and subservience. The titles for the paintings were words that combined *nǚ* as a radical to form other characters: *jiān* (traitor), *yāo* (witch), *nú* (slave), *biǎo* (whore).

"What's the series itself called?" I asked.

"*The Suicide Project.*"

"I'm a little worried about you. Is this a reflection of your present mood?"

She laughed. "I'm fine."

"Are you going to keep working in this vein? I think you should. I think you've found your medium."

"I'm not sure. I might try doing some installations."

"What kind of installations?"

"Mixed media. Maybe found objects. I have to come up with a proposal soon. I'm applying to the Cambridge Arts Council for an exhibition."

She had been in discussions, too, about being included in group shows at the Creiger-Dane Gallery in Boston and the DNA Gallery in Provincetown. I had to confess, I was jealous of her—jealous of the palpability and immediacy of her talent.

Between paintings and sculptures, Jessica churned out watercolors, collages, crosshatched charcoals, ink washes, linear perspectives with mechanical pencils and rulers. She was always doing *something*, a myriad of exercises. I loved her impromptu drawings the most. She would grab a napkin or a paper towel or the back of an envelope and a felt-tip or a stub of graphite, whatever was within reach, and dash off a quick sketch—little still lifes, figures, portraits. She drew one of me once as I was chopping an onion, and somehow she captured the essence of my movements with a casual scattering of lines, a touch of shading. It took her all of four minutes to complete. These drawings and studies, they were effortless for Jessica, a pleasure (something I never felt when trying to write), but they were mere doodles to her. She might pin them up on the walls of her bedroom for a while, but eventually she would toss them. I would sometimes pick them out of the trash to preserve (I still have a portfolio of the discards in my garage). "Can you believe she's throwing these away?" I'd ask Joshua, and we'd look at the drawings and marvel at Jessica's dexterity, the splendor of her skills. Of the three of us, Joshua and I believed Jessica had the best chance of making it. Anyone could see right away that she had an immense gift. It wasn't nearly as obvious or tangible for writers.

In college, Joshua and I had each made a vow to publish our first books before we hit thirty. We were twenty-eight now. It was still a distinct possibility for him, tapping away up there in the attic. For me, the chances were dubious. I wasn't writing at the moment, just occasionally tinkering with revisions of old stories. The fact was, I hadn't written anything new since grad school. I blamed adjunct teaching and *Palaver* for waylaying me, but they were poor excuses. There were no excuses, Joshua always said. If you want to write, you write. You find the time. You make the time.

I spent most of my time with Jessica. We cleaned up the backyard, which was small but quite pretty, with a Japanese maple, dogwood, and black tupelo. Jessica and I pruned the trees and shrubs, mowed and edged the grass, and weeded, tilled, and composted areas along the deck and fence, where we planted perennials and bulbs.

We shopped for groceries together, took walks, went to museums. For hours, we would sit in Café Pamplona or the Algiers or the Someday, Jessica with a sketchpad, me with a book. At each opportunity, I'd hover close to her, casually touch her arm or back, sit so our bodies adjoined. And, despite the torment, I kept accompanying her to Baptiste Power Yoga.

One night, after we returned home from another brutal session, I walked out of my room with a towel around my waist, thinking Jessica had already finished with the shower. But when I opened the door to the bathroom (the lock didn't quite function), she was still in there, spiking her hair with pomade, and she was naked. Her skin was slick with water, and her body was everything I had always imagined it would be—lissome, toned, beautiful. There was one thing, though, that I had never imagined. She had no pubic hair—shaved or waxed off.

"I'm sorry," I said.

"I don't think you really are," she said, glancing down at my towel, which was tented. "We need to talk." She took me into her bedroom and shut the door.

For one thrilling second, I thought she might seduce me. But then, as she put on her bathrobe, Jessica said, "I can't keep having you stalking and puppying after me all the time. It's draining. It's exhausting, actually." The opening chords to Jeff Buckley's "Yard of Blonde Girls" drifted down from the attic. "Christ, not again."

She sat down on her futon and motioned for me to follow suit. Clumsily holding my towel together, I squatted down on the foot of the futon, several feet away from her. I was embarrassed and glum, my hard-on beginning to dissipate. I knew a lecture was in the offing, one that would irrevocably puncture all the daydreams and hopes I had harbored for years.

"I thought we were over this," she said. "I thought we'd moved past this. It can't go on, Eric. If we're going to be living here together, it has to stop."

"I know," I said.

She tore a frayed thread from the hem of her bathrobe. It was the same white silk bathrobe she had worn in Dupre, accented with flowers and branches, now faded, threadbare, and tattered. How many times had I stared at the folds and outlines and knolls of that robe, and fantasized about what was underneath? How many times had I dreamt of running my hand over her bare skin, down the runnel between her spine muscles and over the small of her back, reaching that delectable cleft and progressing over her ass?

"Sometimes," Jessica said, "I think the only reason you want to be with me is because you can't fuck Joshua."

"What?"

"Your connection to him is much more real, honest, than to me."

"That's ridiculous," I told her, perplexed. "I don't love Joshua."

"You idealize me," she said. "You don't even know me. If you really knew me, you wouldn't like me very much."

"I've known you for ten years, Jessica." I looked at the small mole on the side of her neck, and I thought of when she'd told me that, as a child, she used to rub the mole over and over, trying to expunge it.

"We've been friends," she said, "but we've become different people. Or at least I have. Really what's kept your glorification of me alive is the idea of conquest, but you don't actually want to achieve it. You're in it for the longing and the yearning. The culmination of it, having a relationship with me, wouldn't really interest you. So let's just get this over with, once and for all."

"Okay," I said, expecting she would now make me promise to cease and desist.

"Let's just fuck," she said.

"What?"

"Let's just do it once and get it over with."

"Are you insane?" I said. "Just like that?"

"Why not? Do you need more foreplay? More courting and romancing?" She slid her fingers down the lapels of her robe, unveiling the inner halves of her breasts, her stomach, the mound above her pubic bone. "From what I've seen, men don't need a lot of foreplay. We'll just have sex this one time and satisfy your curiosity, and then maybe we'll be able to move on. It won't mean anything."

This was a cruel trick, I thought. She was taunting me. "This is crazy."

"I'll admit, there have been times I've been curious myself. This will be good for us. We'll feel stupid afterwards, and it'll be awkward for a while, but then we'll be fine. I don't suppose it'd do any good to say we shouldn't tell Joshua."

"Stop," I said.

"Stop?"

"Can you cover yourself up? I can't talk to you this way."

She tied her robe together. "You're going to deny me now," she said, "after all those years of hangdogging? You're going to pass up free pussy? There are no strings here, Charlie."

"But don't you see?" I said. "I want there to be strings. I want this to mean something. Jessica, I've been in love with you from the moment I saw you."

"Okay, this was a terrible idea," she said. "Idiotic."

"You've been curious at times. Haven't you ever felt more than that for me?"

"I've always seen you as a friend."

"You just said we're not even that, really."

She scooted to the edge of the futon and put her feet on the floor and stared at them. She needed to cut her toenails. "I'm sorry, Eric," she said. "I don't feel anything for you. Not in the way you want."

"Why can't we try and see? Maybe it could work out between us."

"I really don't think it could."

I went to my room. The next day, we felt stupid, and it was awkward, and it didn't seem at all like things would ever be fine between us. Even Joshua noticed it. At the kitchen counter, he watched us avoiding each other, then asked me, "What's up with you two?"

"Nothing."

"Did you finally crack the walnut, pogo her pachinko?"

"No. We had an argument."

"About what?"

"You."

"What about me?"

"She said you're a user," I told him. "She said you'll take advantage of anyone or anything if the opportunity presents itself. She said you don't give a fuck about anyone except yourself."

"Huh," Joshua said. "That's hurtful. Probably all true, but hurtful nonetheless. She really said all that?"

"Yes," I told him, and then regretted it.

I was full of regrets. I should have taken Jessica up on her provocative if misguided offer, because, regardless of what she'd said, if she had been attracted to me enough in that one spontaneous moment to fuck me, her feelings were malleable, and had the potential to become larger and more substantive, given time and familiarity. This is not to say I thought my powers of lovemaking would have made her swoon, but I believed that if we had gone ahead, it would have been more than a flyby. I think eventually I would have won her over. Why had I turned her down? What kind of a limp-dick wusswank was I? I wanted to say it had all been a mistake. I wanted to tell Jessica that I had changed my mind.

Cautiously, I worked to get back in her good graces, trying to act as relaxed and nonchalant as I could around her, trying to make her trust me again. As she was coming down the stairs and I was going up a few days later, I said, "Listen, we're all right, aren't we?"

"Sure," she said. "I am if you are."

"Let's forget about it, then, okay?"

"Okay."

My plan was rather pedestrian. I was hoping to go out with Jessica one night, get her a little tipsy, and, once home, trundle up to the second floor with her, and into her bedroom. My chance came at the end of the week, when Jessica invited Joshua and me to tag along with her to an opening in the South End, a special group exhibition featuring Asian American artists called *Transmigrations*. "I think you guys should come," she said. "It's an important show."

Joshua, normally so opposed to going across the river, offered to drive us in his parents' old car, a blue Peugeot 306. The show was at Mills Gallery in the Boston Center for the Arts, and by the time we found a spot to park on the street, it was in full swing, filled with more Asian Americans than I had ever seen in one room in Boston. And these were no ordinary Asians. They were young, hip, good-looking, fashionable.

"Can you believe this?" I said to Joshua.

"Where the hell have all these people been hiding?"

The art was a mishmash. There was a pair of videos projected onto a wall, side by side, the one on the right showing white people on a city sidewalk sampling a slice of honeydew melon, the one of the left showing, in synchronicity, the same white people eating a piece of bitter melon—an Asian staple. On the right, the faces expressed pleasure. On the left, they winced, they scrunched, they gagged, they spit the melon out onto a napkin.

There were steel boxes stacked on the floor that resembled the balconies of an apartment building, with miniature pieces of laundry hanging from lines. There were two wigs on Styrofoam stands of faceless heads with elongated necks. One wig was blond, the hair gathered in a tight bun, secured by lacquered chopsticks. The other wig was Oriental black, the hair in the same tight bun, but secured this time by a sterling silver fork and knife set from Tiffany's.

There was a series of large-format color portraits of Asian women in various nail salons, all from the vantage point of the photographer getting a pedicure from them (I saw Jessica lingering in front of the photos, no doubt thinking about the years her mother had had to work as a manicurist in Flushing). There was another set of portraits, this one of human skulls, evoking the Khmer Rouge's killing fields. The skulls were embedded in a white wall of the gallery itself. The artist had cut out pieces of the drywall with a keyhole saw, distressed the edges, then reinserted them with glue so they protruded out toward the viewer. It seemed the wall was bulging and cracking with rows and rows of hollow socketed bone, made even eerier by the holes for the eyes, noses, and mouths exposing the dark recesses behind the wall, punctuated in places by splintered studs of wood.

In the middle of the gallery was a performance piece. Two men, dressed as peasant farmers with coolie hats and their pants rolled up, stood in a shallow twenty-by-fifteen-foot pool of mud and water, planting rice seedlings. They worked methodically, staying bent over for the duration of the opening. Every so often, a woman in silk pajamas and sandals, carrying a bamboo yoke over her shoulder with two baskets, came out and replenished the men's supply of seedlings. All three were silent, solemn. A sign said the audience was welcome to participate—a tub of clean water, a stack of neatly folded towels, and a stool awaited the intrepid—but no one dared.

I wasn't quite sure what to make of the performance piece, and none of the art, excluding the skulls, had the visceral brilliance of

Jessica's paintings, but for me the show still radiated an invigorating buzz—just the idea of it, the esprit de corps.

Jessica knew some people there—a couple of classmates from RISD and a Chinese American woman named Esther Xing who had been a fellow with her at the Fine Arts Work Center. "Esther's a fiction writer," Jessica said as she introduced us, then left to corral someone else across the gallery.

"I think I read a story of yours in *Bamboo Ridge*," Esther told Joshua.

"Yeah?"

"I thought it was groovy," she said.

He chuckled, bemused by the turn of phrase, but was pleased. "That was an excerpt from my novel, *Upon the Shore*."

"Have you finished it?"

"Almost. What are you working on?"

"A collection."

"Eric is, too."

"Oh, yeah? How's it coming?"

"Good," I said. "Pretty good."

"Have you had stories from it published anywhere?"

"No."

"You were in that venerable Minnesotan journal, *Chanter*," Joshua said.

I couldn't decide whether he was trying to be facetious or helpful. "I don't send my stuff out much," I told her. "What about you?"

"I had a thingie in *Salamander* and a few other small places."

Instinctively, I did not like Esther Xing. I wasn't certain why. She hadn't uttered a single unpleasantry, yet she came off as snooty and disagreeable. It might have been that I had yet to see her smile or do anything other than glower. Moreover, I found her ugly. She was short, and, though not overweight, her body was shapeless and disproportioned, her arms and legs too stubby for her torso, her head seemingly enormous. She had a choppy pageboy and no makeup, her features bland and flat. She wore a quirky outfit that was not at all becoming—a black halter dress over another dress, a gray sweater jumper, and white leggings and black platform boots.

After the show, we had been planning to have dinner together, but Joshua started chatting up Tina Nguyen, the Vietnamese American artist who had done the skulls, and Jimmy Fung, the Australian/Hong Kong transplant who had assembled the wigs, and Joshua told me, "Hey, I'm thinking of going with this crew to the Franklin Café. Want to join?"

"You go on ahead," I said. "Jessica and I want to go to the DeLux."

The DeLux was a tiny neighborhood restaurant on the corner of Chandler and Clarendon, with maybe just ten tables and a small bar, but it had a kitschy, retro-cool vibe—dimly lit and smoky, the music running from Louis Armstrong and Sinatra to Astrud Gilberto and Petula Clark. The food was exceptional yet cheap, no entrée over ten dollars. While everything else in the South End had become chic-gentrified, the DeLux had remained a hole in the wall—my favorite hangout when I'd lived in the Back Bay. After hearing me talk it up, Jessica had been eager to try the place. And now, with Joshua gone, it would almost be as if we were on a date.

She invited Esther Xing.

"Does she have to come?" I asked.

"You don't like her?"

"I don't, actually."

"You just need to get to know her," Jessica said. "She comes off as dippy at first, but she's actually whip-sharp—like, Joshua-sharp. You should ask to see one of her stories. She's really good. I think you'd be surprised."

The DeLux was jammed. We squeezed to the end of the narrow

room, left our name with the lone waitress for a table, and then waited near the little Christmas tree that twinkled on top of the bar (a year-round decoration).

"This is cool!" Jessica yelled to Esther. They gazed around at the Elvis shrine and the collage of posters, postcards, and record album covers stapled to the pine-paneled walls. The crowd was boisterous, a mix of local artists, yuppies, and bike messengers. Brenda Lee was blasting from the stereo. "I love this place!" Jessica said to Esther.

I bought a round of Schlitz tallboys, as well as shots of Bushmills Black label, for the three of us. I was aggravated. I should have been the one receiving credit for introducing Jessica to the DeLux, not Esther, who heretofore had never set foot in the bar.

We were seated at a table, a two-top with an extra chair, and the waitress eventually returned to collect our orders: the salmon potato cakes and a bowl of chili for me, the grilled cheese with arugula pesto and sweet date spread for Jessica.

Esther was torn between the quesadillas with black beans and the vegetable pie made with puff pastry. "They both sound so yummy. I just can't decide," she said. "This is too much responsibility." Defeated, she leaned her head on Jessica's shoulder.

"How about the quesadillas?" Jessica said.

"Perfect," the waitress said, turning to walk away.

"Wait!" Esther said. "I think—oh, maybe the vegetable pie might be better?"

As we drank and chitchatted, Esther divulged that, after spending the summer in Italy, she had just arrived in Cambridge for a Bunting fellowship—a very prestigious yearlong appointment at Radcliffe College that came with a hefty stipend, an office at the Bunting Institute, and a cut-rate apartment on Brattle Street.

"I thought you needed to publish a book to get a Bunting," I said.

"You do, usually," she said, "although you need just three stories in magazines to apply."

"Did you know someone?" I asked, and Jessica knocked her knee against mine under the table.

The girls talked about the show, concurring that Tina Nguyen's wall cuts of the skulls and Annie Yoshikawa's pedicure photographs had been the best of the lot. But Esther had qualms about the fundamental premise with which the exhibition had been organized.

"What's *Transmigrations* supposed to mean, anyway?" she asked, abruptly shifting into highbrow mode. "Okay, it's a play on trans-oceanic and immigration, I get it. But that's precisely what I object to. None of those artists are immigrants, yet in order to have a show with Asian Americans, there always has to be a rubric, a theme about crossing borders or bridging the diaspora or whatnot, even if it has nothing to do with the works or the artists themselves. It might as well have been called *We're All Oriental Fuckers*."

It sounded exactly like something Joshua would posit. I agreed with the overall sentiment, but didn't want to say that I did. "I happen to have liked the show," I told her. "It felt good, seeing so many Asian American artists in one place."

"The camaraderie's great, I agree, but it was such a hodgepodge of stuff, a free-for-all. Like Annie Yoshikawa, I'd love for her to be included someday in a show with Rineke Dijkstra and Sharon Lockhart—okay, maybe that's a stretch, she's got a long way to go before she reaches that level, but you know what I mean—included not because she's Japanese American, but because she's an interesting photographer, period."

I didn't know who Rineke Dijkstra and Sharon Lockhart were.

"What do you think of all of this?" she asked Jessica. "You're not saying anything."

"I don't have an opinion, because a part of me agrees with both of you."

I had lost the thread myself. It was one of those pointless arguments you enter without any strong formulations, but then, by dint of the opening parry, find yourself heatedly defending a position in which you don't really believe, yet from which you can no longer withdraw. "Where'd you go to school?" I asked. "Did you get an MFA somewhere?"

"Yeah, Cornell," Esther said. "You went to Walden College, right? How was it? I've heard some bad things."

"Like what?"

"I've heard it called a trust-fund MFA. They'll let anyone in if you have the money."

This was basically true, but still, it was an appallingly rude thing to say.

"Eric just got promoted to managing editor of *Palaver*," Jessica said.

"Ah, *Palaver*," Esther said. "Evan Paviromo's written me a few notes about my stories. What's his deal? He seems kind of full of himself."

"He's a terrific editor. He was great as a teacher, too," I lied.

"But *Palaver* is, like, so old school, you know. It's kind of become stale and moribund, don't you think?"

Would this woman stop at nothing? Never mind that her assessment had some validity.

"Although I *will* say," Esther then told me, "if I had to be absolutely honest, that I'd kill to be in it," and finally she smiled, exposing a mouthful of bucked teeth. "Do you have much to do with the editorial process?"

At last I could claim a measure of superiority. Esther Xing was as susceptible as any young writer to sycophancy. "Some," I said, lying for the second time in succession. She waited. I knew she was hoping I'd ask to read one of her stories. I let her wait. I went to the men's room to take a leak.

When I returned to the table, our food had arrived, each dinner plate different, like the flatware that did not match. Esther tasted her risotto (she had nixed the vegetable pie after the order had gone to the kitchen), and her face wilted.

"What's wrong now?" Jessica asked.

"Miss? Miss?" Esther said to the waitress. "I don't want to come off as a pest, I know you hate me already, but could you ask the kitchen to reheat this a little?"

"I don't know this person," I told the waitress.

We managed to get through the rest of the meal without incident, although the girls talked interminably about people they had known at the Fine Arts Work Center, shutting me out. As Esther left for the women's bathroom, Jessica picked up Esther's pack of American Spirits.

"You don't smoke," I said.

"I do once in a while now."

"Since when?"

"There wasn't much to do in Ptown. Yoga saved me from complete dissolution."

"Your friend's a piece of work," I said.

"Sometimes she doesn't think before she speaks—a lot like someone else we know. I wish you two would get along. We've become really close."

I didn't gather how close until dessert. Jessica and Esther ordered a chocolate-chip pound cake to share, and, forking bites, they burbled and purred about its scrumptiousness. At one point, Jessica had a smidge of whipped cream on the corner of her mouth, and Esther delicately scooped the cream up with her index finger and deposited it into her own mouth. Smiling moronically, they stared at each other—finger still hooked between Esther's lips—and held the pose for a second too long, in which all was revealed. I didn't know how I had missed it, Esther always hovering close to Jessica, touching her arm and back, sitting so their bodies adjoined. They were lovers— former, current, soon to be, or all three.

Jessica didn't come home that night. After the DeLux, she and Esther ditched me to go dancing at Club Café, a gay bar.

In the morning, Joshua and I sat at the kitchen counter, eating cereal. "No shit?" he said.

"Did you know?" I asked him.

"I had no idea."

Right then, Jessica opened the back door and walked through the kitchen, bedraggled, as if she had not slept a wink. "Hey," she mumbled, and headed upstairs.

Joshua and I were caught midspoon, suspended in the wake of her chimera.

"I guess we'll need to think of something else for you," Joshua said, and slurped up the rest of the milk in his bowl.

10

I t started casually—dinners at Cafe Sushi and Mary Chung's and Koreana, then beers at the Cellar, the Plough & Stars, and the People's Republik—and at first there was just Jimmy Fung, the wig artist.

Jimmy was ten years older than us, in his late thirties, handsome, ponytailed, and voluble, a rather flashy guy, inclined to wear clingy shirts and black leather pants. He'd been a hairstylist in Sydney and Hong Kong and had moved to the States just before the 1997 handover. He spoke with an Aussie accent, yet had three passports, including an American one. "I'm a multinational juggernaut unto myself." Recently he had taken over a decrepit antiques store on Arrow Street in Harvard Square and had made it into an antiques store/hair salon/art gallery called Pink Whistle. "You want Asian chicks?" he said to Joshua and me. "I'll get you Asian chicks."

He got Tina Nguyen, the wall cutter, to come, then Danielle Awano, a Japanese Brazilian dancer and capoeira teacher, and Marietta Liu, a Chinese Italian harmonium player. ("What's with all these mixed-blooded Asians?" Joshua asked. "It's like the UN had an orgy.")

As the group grew, incorporating a filmmaker, playwright,

actress, and other artists and writers—alas, some of them male—
we decided it would make more sense to congregate at someone's
house, and eventually it became a regular happening, Sunday night
potlucks on Walker Street.

All through the fall, the rice cooker was always going in the
kitchen for our buffets of Sichuan peppercorn shrimp, futomaki,
dim sum, japchae, and bulgogi, washed down with sake and OB
beer. Jessica, who worked Sundays at Upstairs at the Pudding,
would come home after her shift finished at ten and be befuddled
to find the crowd ever larger and more raucous.

But we weren't merely partying, we weren't playing poker or
charades or singing karaoke. We were talking, hatching plans.
We talked about organizing our own exhibitions and performances and showcases and reading series. We talked about starting a newsletter, a literary journal, maybe a publishing press.
We talked about volunteering in Asian communities, offering
workshops and fellowships and a youth arts program, becoming
a 501(c)3 tax-exempt organization. Already we had staked out the
domain "3ac.org."

We talked about the representations of Asians in the media,
particularly in movies and on TV shows. We lamented the China
dolls, the Chinese waiters, the Japanese tourists and kung fu mas-
ters and Uncle Tongs. We bemoaned the computer nerds, the dirty
refugees, the gang members, the greengrocers, and the sweatshop
and laundry workers. We deplored the geishas and bargirls and
lotus blossoms and Suzie Wongs and dragon ladies.

"Orientalist masturbatory fantasy figures," Joshua said.

"I hate that shit so much," Annie Yoshikawa, the photographer, said.

"The expectation that we're either servile or hypersexual,"
Trudy Lun, a theater costume designer, said.

"Mama-sans or dirty little yum-yum girls," Tina Nguyen said.

"It's the Madonna/whore complex for bamboo fetishists," Marietta Liu said.

"I'm so sick of white guys hitting on me all the time," Danielle Awano said. "I'm, like, are you for *real*, asshole? You think someone like you could ever have a chance in hell with someone like me, just because I'm Asian? You think I have no *standards*?"

We complained about *Miss Saigon* and *The Killing Fields*, *Seven Years in Tibet* and *Breakfast at Tiffany's*, about yellowfacing, about always having white actors in the lead and relegating Asians to the backdrop, even when it was an Asian story.

"You know the worst?" the composer Andy Kim asked. "*Sixteen Candles*."

"The Donger!" the glassblower Jay Chi-Ming Lai said, and all the men in the group groaned, recalling the character of Long Duk Dong ("The Donger") in the teen movie, the foreign-exchange student who had embodied every possible malignant stereotype about Asian males.

"How many of you suddenly got nicknamed the Donger after the movie came out?" the guitarist Phil Sudo asked, and they all raised their hands.

"People would run up to me—I mean, literally people I didn't know, people on the street—and shout their favorite Donger lines at me," the painter Leon Lee said.

"'Donger need food!'" Andy said.

"'What's happenin', hot stuff?'" Leon said.

"'Oh, no more yanky my wanky,'" Jay said.

Some of the women laughed, which the men did not appreciate. "It's not funny," Andy said.

"It sort of is," Tina said.

I had seen *Sixteen Candles* in ninth grade, and at the time I'd thought everything about it, including the Donger, had been hilarious, unaware that I should have been offended. I knew better now. Joshua, I could tell from his silence, had never seen *Sixteen Candles*. He never went to comedies.

"That goddamn movie," Phil said, "pretty much guaranteed I'd never get laid in high school."

And then, as if released by the true import of the matter, it all poured out—the various indignities and assaults everyone had had to endure, the misassumptions and slurs, the stupid, annoying questions: "What's a good place to eat in Chinatown?" "Do you know kung fu?" "How can you guys tell Asians apart?" "No, where are you really from?" One by one, we disclosed altercations. Joshua related what had happened to him on the pier in Southie, and I described the chalkboard incident at Mac.

"And let's not forget Vincent Chin," Joshua said.

In 1982, Vincent Chin, a twenty-seven-year-old Chinese American, had been beaten to death by two laid-off autoworkers in Detroit. Chin was attending his bachelor party at a strip club called the Fancy Pants Lounge—he was to be married in five days—and the autoworkers shouted insults at Chin, calling him a Jap and saying, "It's because of you little motherfuckers we're out of work." There was a fight, they were all thrown out of the bar. Outside, the autoworkers cornered Chin and bludgeoned him, teeing off on his head with a baseball bat. They received only two years' probation, and did not spend a single day in jail. Before slipping into a fatal coma, Chin had mumbled, "It's not fair."

We pledged to change things with the 3AC.

"Fuck oath we will, mates!" Jimmy Fung said.

We would instigate a grassroots movement, Yellow Power redux, through our art. We would support one another as Asian American artists, writers, and intellectuals, as brothers and sisters. We'd celebrate our heritage in our work and foster unity, and we'd help shape our generation's literary and artistic attitudes.

"We'll be the vanguard," Trudy said.

"We'll provide healing," Tina said, "a restorative for all the Asian American artists before us who were ignored and marginalized."

We would deform and reform the stereotypes. We'd decrypt and decorrupt and decalcify all the old codes and symbols.

"A mass social praxis," Joshua said. "We'll create counternarratives to the status quo and disorient the entire concept of what it means to be Asian American."

We toasted our resolve with shots of soju and baijiu. "To the 3AC!"

"We'll be the Asian version of Bloomsbury," Joshua said. "It'll be our own Harlem Renaissance. We'll be legendary."

All this talk, developing these plans, was exhilarating, enlivening. I felt a remarkable accord with this group, indeed as if we were brethren and sistren, a family. With them I did not have to explain or justify myself or worry about how I was being perceived. I could just be. No one questioned my origins. No one recoiled at the sight or thought or smell of my otherness. No one needed lessons on how to use chopsticks. There was something to be said, I had to concede, for sticking to your own kind.

■　■　■

Outside, the leaves turned, the foliage revising in hues of heavenly orange, citron, russet, and scarlet. Inside, the cast of members of the collective changed as well, sometimes growing larger, sometimes succumbing to attrition.

There were, predictably, hookups, which led, predictably, to breakups. Posthaste, Jimmy Fung laid claim to Marietta Liu, the most exotic and sensual beauty in the 3AC, and then dumped her with awkward alacrity. Annie Yoshikawa started seeing Phil Sudo.

Andy Kim asked out a poet new to the gatherings, Caroline Yip, who after their first date never returned to the collective. Joshua had a fling with Tina Nguyen. It lasted his usual three weeks, near the end of which Tina said to me, "What the fuck is wrong with your friend? He's not interested in ever doing anything with me or even talking on the phone. The sex is pure routine. He just lies there. He doesn't care about satisfying me at all. This is just a boys' club, isn't it? Tell the truth, you guys put this whole thing together just to get laid."

Jessica, when her schedule permitted, began to infiltrate the potlucks and gab sessions, though she hardly ever spoke. Her main contributions were oyster omelets and T-shirts, which she made, upon Joshua's request, on a borrowed silkscreen machine at the Brickbottom Artists Building, one of the shirts reading 3AC in Futura Bold, another reading 6.19.82, the date of Vincent Chin's fateful encounter.

Inevitably, she invited Esther Xing to the house one Sunday. I watched Esther load up her plastic plate with every offering from the buffet and then take just one small bite of each item—squashing up her face, rodentlike, as she nibbled—leaving the bulk untouched. At least she didn't pipe up much that first night, except to deliver a few antediluvian exclamations: "That's far out." "That's trippy."

But the next week, to my dismay, after learning that there were several other fiction writers in the 3AC, she made a suggestion. "We should form a writers' group," she chirped. "What night is everyone free? What about Tuesdays? We could call ourselves the Tuesday Nighters." She looked to Joshua.

"You know, I'm pretty workshopped out at this point," Joshua said. "But you guys can meet here if you want."

"What about you, Eric?" she asked.

Everyone turned to me and waited. "I don't know," I said. "I might be workshopped out as well."

"Come on," Esther said, "it'd be a gas."

"Let me think about it."

In the kitchen, as Jessica and I were cleaning up, she said to me, "You know, a writers' group might be good for you."

"How so?" I didn't want to have any more to do with Esther Xing than absolutely necessary. I should have been thankful, I supposed, that Jessica had enough propriety not to let Esther spend the night at the house—not yet, anyway.

"It might jump-start something new for you," Jessica said.

I resented this not-so-oblique criticism that I wasn't writing. "I don't see you producing anything new yourself other than sketches." I tossed out the heap of uneaten food from Esther's plate.

"A studio hasn't opened up yet." She was on the wait list to share a space at Vernon Street Studios.

"Why don't you just work in the basement?" I asked.

"I can't work in the basement. It's depressing down there."

"I'll help you clean it up."

"It's not that. It's the light. I need light, although with the hours I'm logging these days, I don't know if it'd make a difference. When would I have the time?"

She was now working a total of sixty-six hours a week. In addition to Upstairs at the Pudding and Gaston & Snow, she had picked up a part-time job proofreading for the *New England Journal of Medicine*.

Everyone in the 3AC had day jobs: wedding photographer, waitstaff, house painter, seamstress, carpenter, temp, freelancer, the ubiquitous adjunct teacher. Yet some had more gainful avenues of income. One woman was an immigration attorney, and more than a few were working for Internet start-ups as programmers, content developers, illustrators, graphic designers, and software test analysts. They were always discussing IPOs and when they would become vested.

Joshua frowned upon these temptations. "You need to be willing to live on the street to be an artist," he'd say. "Getting sucked into a career is an invitation to bail. It makes it too easy to give up. It makes it almost inevitable that you will."

There was certainly no danger of *Palaver* ever becoming a career for me. The magazine had just been turned down for an NEA grant (panel conclusion: the journal didn't publish enough women and writers of color), and our funding from the Massachusetts Cultural Council had just been halved. We couldn't afford to hire anyone to help me in the Watertown office. I was working solo in the shithole, save for a couple of itinerant interns, and it was likely that, unless a new grant came through, my hours would soon have to be cut drastically—possibly eliminated altogether.

My immediate preoccupation, though, was taking delivery of the new issue and preparing to send it off by presorted third-class bulk mail.

I would have to unload and wheel in about forty boxes—each weighing fifty pounds—from the delivery truck, and stack them in the office. I would then have to stamp a thousand Jiffy No. 1 mailing bags with two impressions: *Palaver*'s return address on the top left, the bulk-mailing permit indicia on the top right. Stuff each envelope with a copy of the issue and close the flap with three staples. Stick on the subscriber address labels and sort the envelopes into bundles according to zip code. Wrap two rubber bands around each bundle by length and girth, then cram them into No. 3 canvas sacks. Tag each sack for delivery to the proper district hub. Rent a cargo van from U-Haul and load, transport, and unload the fifty or so sacks at the post office in Harvard Square—a total of twelve hundred pounds.

I was in the middle of bundling and sorting envelopes when Joshua made his maiden visit to the office.

"Jesus, this place is a dump," he said. "I had no fucking idea."

The storefront office was sandwiched between a T-shirt shop and a pizza parlor on Waverley Avenue. One long room, the place was furnished with castoffs and street finds and stuffed with boxes of unsold issues and masses of junk, a museum of antiquated publishing paraphernalia: broken typewriters, light boxes, T-squares, strips of old Linotype, paste-ups of covers and galleys.

"Not a good time," I told Joshua. He had gone to the RMV in Watertown to renew his license and had asked to stop by on the way back. Reluctantly I had given him directions, but had said he couldn't stay long.

"What are you doing?" he asked.

I summarized the undertaking at hand.

"Why do *you* have to do this?" Joshua said. "Can't you get interns or something?"

"It's faster if I do it myself."

"Look at yourself, dude."

My T-shirt was wet with sweat, my jeans filthy. My forearms were scratched from lugging boxes, my hands black from the ink-pad, and my fingertips bled from wayward staple prongs.

"You are being fucking *exploited*, man," Joshua said. "You're being treated like a *slave*. And you know why?"

I heaved another stack of envelopes to the sorting table. "Why?"

"Because you're Asian," he said. "Paviromo assumes, since you're Asian, that you're meticulous and good with numbers and conscientious—read: *docile*—like all Asians are, so he'll make you do all the shit work, the clerical and computer crap, but damn if he'll ever let you touch anything that involves any aesthetic sensibilities or, God forbid, any real editing."

What he was saying was accurate. The only thing Paviromo allowed me to do editorially was screen the fiction manuscripts in the slush pile. Occasionally I'd uncover a terrific story, but Paviromo never once accepted any of the submissions I passed on to him. "Can we have this conversation later?" I said to Joshua. "I'm a little busy here, if that's not obvious enough."

But Joshua wouldn't leave. He poked around the office, playing with the Pantone flip book, punching keys on the old broken Olivetti typewriter ("You know Cormac McCarthy has used the same Lettera 32 since 1963?"), cutting some scraps of Lino with an X-Acto knife.

"If you're bored," I said, "you can take off. I'll be okay by myself."

But then he discovered the stacks. *Palaver* didn't publish book reviews, but the journal did run a list of "Books Received" in the back of every issue, in the tiniest print, a curious feature (the lists were arbitrary in what they included, not at all comprehensive) whose sole purpose was to ensure that we were sent free books and advance reader editions by publishers.

"This is a fucking gold mine," Joshua said. "I can't believe you've been holding these out on me."

He began pawing through the stacks, which were heaped precariously against the wall. We didn't have enough shelves for the books and the many literary journals with which we exchanged subscriptions, so I had crisscrossed some bungee cords to keep them from falling over. He tugged out the new William Trevor, the new Gass and Sebald and Beattie. "Can I have this?" he kept asking.

He smuggled the books into the backseat of his Peugeot and then, for a late lunch, bought a meatball grinder (jumbo, with extra provolone and mayonnaise) at the pizza parlor next door, eating it in the office while I continued to label and sort and rubber-band. "Don't you have to go home and work on your novel?" I asked.

When at last he was about to leave, we heard the screen door creak open, and unexpectedly, Paviromo, wearing his trademark blue suit and dapper bow tie, blustered in. Usually he never came to the office except to drop off the mail every few days.

"Oh, what's this?" he said. "An interloper in our midst, breaching the sanctum sanctorum?"

They introduced themselves. "Yes, yes," Paviromo said. "I read your story in the *North American Review*. Fabulous, I thought. I'm good friends with Robley, you know." Over the years, whenever one of Joshua's stories came out in a journal, I always pointed it out to Paviromo, but never imagined he would actually read one of them. "Robley kept boasting about it. It was nominated for a Pushcart and got on some other short lists, correct?"

"Nominated, but not ultimately selected," Joshua said.

"Mandarins and halfwits, the committees that make these decisions."

Joshua, easily charmed by this sort of flattery, grinned broadly.

They gossiped about this year's prize annuals, opining which stories were best and which shouldn't have been included, Paviromo confounded and outraged that *Palaver* had not parlayed more selections. One writer in particular intrigued them. Her story, which had been her first publication, had snared the literary triple crown, the trifecta, picked for all three prize anthologies: *The Best American Short Stories*, *Pushcart Prize*, and *The O. Henry Awards*. The woman had a compelling background, raised on a hippie farm in rural Pennsylvania, studying at Columbia and the Sorbonne, writing screenplays with her Argentine film director boyfriend, teaching English and coaching girls' soccer in a village in Punjab,

Pakistan. She also happened to be young, twenty-eight, the same age as Joshua and me, and drop-dead gorgeous. *New York* magazine ran a two-page photo spread on her, glammed up like a movie star. Agents and editors were clamoring after her. All for publishing one little short story, which was, Paviromo and Joshua admitted, dazzlingly good.

"She'll be a phenom," Paviromo said. "It's all before her."

"In the palm of her hand," Joshua said.

"Let's salute the girl with a drink." From a file cabinet drawer, Paviromo pulled out a bottle of Macallan's single malt that I had not known was there. "Eric? Care for a nip?"

"I still have some work to do."

"You sure?"

"Maybe later."

"This young man," he said to Joshua, "is entirely too industrious."

"I couldn't agree more."

Paviromo rinsed out two coffee cups, poured the Macallan's, and gave one to Joshua. "To youth," he said.

"To fortuity."

After a second round, Paviromo began regaling Joshua with a story about once getting drunk on Macallan's with Robert De Niro in the White Horse Tavern in the West Village, and how, as a favor to the director John Frankenheimer, his longtime mate, he had been a silent partner and (by choice) uncredited executive producer on De Niro's latest film, *Ronin*, and how some of the film's characters were composites of Paviromo—the screenwriter, David Mamet, was an old friend, and Paviromo had disclosed details to him of his escapades as an arms dealer and his covert operations with the Special Forces—and how once, long ago, he had dropped acid with Mamet and Lawrence Ferlinghetti, and in the middle of the night Ferlinghetti had gotten the brilliant idea that they should

go fishing, and somewhere they had found three fishing poles and a
Spanish longaniza for bait and drove out to a pond and stayed there
all night, sitting on the edge of the water and casting and reeling,
yet mysteriously not getting a nibble, constantly snagging and losing their hooks, and then had woken up in the morning to discover
that all night they had not been fishing at the edge of a pond, but at
the edge of a cabbage field.

Joshua and Paviromo nearly cried, laughing. The cabbage fishing acid story sounded familiar to me. I had heard it before—not
from Paviromo, but as an oft-told yarn from Beatnik lore.

When they had recovered sufficiently, Paviromo said, "So, I
have a question for you, young sir."

"Yeah?" Joshua said, wiping the corner of his eye.

"Why, pray tell, did you send your story to Robley's esteemed
but vastly inferior publication, and not to *Palaver*?"

Joshua set down his coffee cup and leaned forward. "Do you
really want the truth?"

I cringed, because I knew the truth, having heard it many times
from Joshua whenever I suggested shepherding one of his stories
to Paviromo.

"It sounds like I might not like this," Paviromo said, "but go on."

"Because," Joshua said, "although *Palaver* got its fair share of
awards in the past, I find most of the work you publish these days
dull. You rely almost exclusively on the safe choices, the old guard,
the same writers over and over again, most of whom are white.
Overwhelmingly white. You don't take enough risks—with new
writers, with writers of color, with anything that's unfamiliar."

Paviromo was taken aback. "But we're known for our discoveries. We're known for launching careers."

"Early on, but not lately. Maybe it's time to be proactive, try something different. Bold. Why not do an entire issue of discoveries?"

Paviromo nodded. "You know, that's rather brilliant." They hashed out ideas for a special Fiction Discoveries issue—all writers who had yet to publish a book. Writers under thirty. A good percentage of women and writers of color. "We'd get a lot of attention, I would wager," Paviromo said.

"It'd be big news," Joshua said, and it occurred to me then that, all along, he might have been loitering in the office with this proposition in mind.

"There could be peripheral benefits as well," Paviromo said. "A boon with grants, perhaps even a pop in our circulation."

"You'd be back in the game."

"I love it," Paviromo said. He refilled their coffee cups. "So will we see you submit a story for me to consider for this special issue?"

Joshua took a drink of the Macallan's and savored the taste. "We'll have to see if I have anything available," he said.

11

I can no longer recall who introduced Mirielle Miyazato to the 3AC. All sorts of people were coming and going then, and Joshua grumbled that the group was getting too large, too slipshod, that maybe we should have a nominating committee and screen and interview potential members—an idea that the rest of the 3AC rebuffed as elitist.

Seeing Mirielle across the living room, I was struck first by how elegantly she was dressed. A fitted black blouse, gray twill pencil skirt. She was tall and thin. She wore no makeup—she didn't have to. Her hair was straight and soft and parted in the middle, falling to her shoulders, where it rested in a layer of subdued curls.

"You like that?" Joshua said to me.

I didn't really have a chance to speak to her, though, until a few weeks later, at Leon Lee and Cindy Wong's wedding in early November. The couple had been together since college, both of them painters with similar approaches, Leon mimicking the techniques of eighteenth-century Korean genre painters to make contemporary portraits on scrolls, Cindy adopting Chinese watercolor and brush schemes to produce modern still lifes on rice paper.

The wedding was in Fort Point Channel, and Leon and Cindy

had invited everyone in the 3AC to attend. We packed into the art-ists' loft space, which had been cleverly divided by hanging surplus parachutes from pipes—one area for the ceremony, another for the banquet, and a third for dancing.

Friends, all Berklee grads, had been cobbled together to form a band, with Phil Sudo on lead guitar. Mirielle was standing near the dance floor beside the bar, wearing a black dress that had a zippered mock turtleneck with boots that snugged her calves—a simple out-fit, yet vaguely haute couture.

"What are you drinking?" I asked. "Want a refill?"

"Oh, it's just Diet Coke," she said. "I need the caffeine."

"Out late last night?"

"I was breaking up with my boyfriend," she told me.

I perked up.

"Don't look so happy," she said.

I laughed. "It was rancorous, I take it?"

"He had to know it was coming. We haven't touched each other since September."

The band launched into a bluesy Latin song, which no one quite knew how to dance to, until Jimmy Fung led Danielle Awano out to the floor. He held her very close, his right thigh thrust force-fully between her legs. They took three steps and then paused for a beat, and on the pause they took turns lifting their knees or doing a little kick or flip with their feet, à la the tango. All along, their hips were swaying, gyrating, grinding pelvis to pelvis. The dance was unmistakably sexy, but there was also something unbearably melancholy about it. They glided and turned and twirled, and once in a while Jimmy dipped her into a back bend or raised her hands up and then slowly down, clasping her arms by the wrists behind her head, captive. He winked at the 3AC men, raised his eyebrows to Joshua.

"It's called the bachata," Mirielle told me. The dance had its origins in the shantytowns of the Dominican Republic, where the music was considered the blues of the DR. The bachata was banned from being shown on Dominican TV.

"How do you know this?" I asked.

"Jimmy offered to teach it to me—when he was trying to pick me up."

The band switched to hip-hop, and everyone spilled onto the floor, even Joshua, who held a little girl, someone's kid, up by the arms, her feet balanced on top of his. Delighted, the two of them were. I'd never seen Joshua play with a child before; he'd never expressed the least bit of interest in kids.

"Do you want to dance?" I asked Mirielle.

"I only dance to old standards."

"Like?"

"Jazz ballads. Johnny Hartman, Little Jimmy Scott."

She was from Washington, D.C., Cleveland Park. Her parents, who were divorced, both worked in international trade, specializing in the Far East, her father a lobbyist, her mother an economic policy analyst.

Mirielle had gone to Walden College and had just graduated this past spring with a BS in political science—sidetracked in her studies somewhere along the line, apparently, since she was already twenty-six. She had taken a few creative writing and literature courses as electives, including one with Paviromo, and she wanted to be a poet.

I thought back to my class assignments at Walden. "I could have been your teacher for Intro," I said.

Like Jessica, she was currently working as a waitress in Harvard Square, at Casablanca. In three days she would be moving from the Brookline apartment she had shared with her boyfriend to a place in Somerville, Winter Hill. She was crashing temporarily on a friend's couch in Beacon Hill.

"Let me walk you home," I said as the wedding wound down.

As I was getting my coat, Jessica, who'd seen me with Mirielle, told me, "She's pretty. She's your type."

"What's my type?"

"Skinny. Wounded."

We walked through downtown and across the Common to Pinckney Street, a nice night, not too cold out. In the vestibule, I asked, "Can I come up?"

"My friend goes to bed early."

I kissed her. I was a bit drunk. I didn't expect her to respond with much enthusiasm, but she did, and we made out rapaciously in the vestibule. I took off my gloves, opened our coats, pressed against her.

"Can I come up?" I asked again.

"No," Mirielle said. "You're just taking advantage of me because you know I haven't had sex in two months."

The next night, I went to Casablanca. There were two sections in the restaurant, a bar/café and a more formal dining area. Mirielle worked in the latter, but she had to get her drink orders from the bar, where I sat, drinking beers, throughout her entire shift.

"Still here?" Mirielle kept saying.

After she cashed out, I asked, "Want to stay here for a drink?"

"No, let's go somewhere else."

Each place I suggested, she vetoed. "You know," I said, "we could just go to the house, hang out there, talk."

"Can you behave this time? Last night was a mistake. We can't do that again. You got me when I was weak."

The house was empty, Jessica at Esther's, Joshua who knew where. "Do you want a glass of wine?" I asked Mirielle. "I have a good bottle of Sangiovese."

"Water's fine."

I fetched a beer for myself and took her upstairs for a tour, and, in my room, I lit candles and put on *All the Way* by Jimmy Scott, a CD I had bought that afternoon. We slow-danced, began kissing.

"You're a pretty good kisser," she said. "Where'd you learn to kiss like this?"

We ended up on the floor, where I gradually disrobed her— everything except her panties.

"There's something very premeditated, almost professional about this seduction," she said. "The candles, the music, the slow-dancing. Have you ever been a gigolo? Did you ask Jimmy for tips?"

"Jimmy's a gigolo?"

"I wouldn't put it past him."

"Let's move to the bed. We'll be more comfortable."

We crawled onto my futon. "Oof," she said. "You call this more comfortable? This mattress is a lumpy abomination. No one's going to do you in this bed, honey."

"I think you should spend the night, Mirielle. It's too late to go back to Beacon Hill."

Reluctantly, she agreed. "I can't believe I'm doing this," she said. "You haven't even taken me out to dinner yet."

As much as I tried, I couldn't convince her to have sex with me that night. "I think my libido's taken a vacation," she said.

"To where?"

"To Tahiti." She giggled. "It's gone to Tahiti. Wouldn't it be wonderful to go somewhere tropical right now?"

In the morning, I made her coffee and an omelette. She was anxious. She needed to finish packing, the movers coming early tomorrow.

"I could take the day off and help you," I said.

Her hair was in a tussle. She was wearing one of my flannel shirts, the tails down to her thighs, and a pair of my thick woolen socks. She looked adorable. "I can tell already," she said, "your kindness is going to give me nightmares."

The apartment was near Coolidge Corner, a spacious one-bedroom. Her boyfriend had cleared out most of the furniture from the living room, but there were books and tchotchkes and lamps on the floor to pack, and neither the kitchen nor the bed-room nor the bathroom had been addressed at all. Mirielle had done nothing thus far. "You haven't even gotten boxes?" I said.

I made several trips to Coolidge Corner, collecting boxes from the liquor store and Brookline Booksmith, foraging recycle bins for old newspapers, buying markers and rolls of tape from CVS. We worked all day, breaking only for take-out burritos from Anna's Taqueria. At one point, while Mirielle was in the kitchen and I was clearing out the hallway closet, I came across a shoe box of photographs of Miri-elle and her boyfriend. Crane's Beach, Mad River Glen, Ghirardelli Square, the Golden Gate Bridge. She had told me the relationship had lasted a little over a year. They had rushed into it, moved in together after a few weeks—too impulsive. He was handsome. White.

We finished everything by evening. "I don't know what I would have done without you," Mirielle said.

We took a cab back to Cambridge and showered, then I treated her to dinner at Chez Henri, the Franco-Cuban bistro a few blocks away on Shepard Street. "Let's celebrate with mojitos," I said. "They're famous for them here. It's a nice tropical drink."

"I'm not really in the mood for a mojito," she said.

"How about the pinot noir?"

She shrugged, noncommittal.

When the waitress brought the bottle and tipped it toward Miri-elle's wineglass, she put her hand over it and asked, "Can I get a Diet Coke instead?"

We ravished our meals, both starving. As we waited for our desserts, I said, "Are you sure you don't want any of this?" In my nervousness, I had almost finished the entire bottle of pinot noir.

"I don't really drink," Mirielle said. "I quit drinking when I was twenty-one."

She had been out of control as a teenager, she told me. Booze, coke. She had, at one time or another, flunked or dropped out of Sidwell, National Cathedral, and Maret, then Bowdoin College, Oberlin, and Walden—the latter because she had been institutionalized for three weeks. "I tried to kill myself with a razor," she said matter-of-factly. After the nuthouse, as she called it, she went to a halfway house in Northern Virginia, and, once released, moved back to Boston. She lived in a rooming house in the Fenway and worked as a receptionist for a year, then reenrolled in Walden College, waiting tables to support herself. She attended AA meetings at least three times a week.

I recalled when we'd walked into her apartment earlier that morning. She had run over to the stacks of books on the floor, embarrassed, turning the covers over and the spines away. I had glimpsed a few titles. They had been mostly self-help books. *Reclaim Your Life. The Narcissist Within You. Be Happy to Be You.*

"I'm flabbergasted with myself," I said. "I've gotten a little soused every time I've seen you."

"I was beginning to take note of that," Mirielle said.

"Did you suspect I had a drinking problem?"

"I thought maybe you might," she said, "but—I don't know, you don't seem tortured enough, to be frank. Sobriety's not much fun, either, you know. Now that I've been sober five years, I get depressed a lot more."

I glanced down at her wrists. I could see a faint scar on one of them—a tiny keloid shaped like a comma, trailed by a thin whisper of discoloration.

I was surprised by her disclosures, but they didn't scare me. If anything, they made me respect Mirielle even more. I had never known anyone with a history of substance abuse of such magnitude, nor anyone who had tried to commit suicide and been institutionalized. Suddenly my problems—my entire life—felt, in comparison, benign. She seemed so strong and self-possessed now. I admired the fortitude it must have taken for her to piece her life back together, and the fact that she was comfortable enough with me to make these admissions drew us, in that moment, immeasurably closer, I thought.

We walked back to the house and decided to turn in early. It'd been a long day. In my bedroom, I undressed her—completely this time.

"What's going to happen now, Eric?" Mirielle said, smiling impishly.

We made love.

"Don't look so proud of yourself," she said afterward. "It's just sex."

"No, it's not just that," I said. "I have a confession to make."

"What?"

"You're the first Asian woman I've ever slept with."

"Really? That's surprising. Why haven't you before?"

"Maybe I was a Twinkie, I don't know. But sometimes it seems Asian women aren't, in general, very interested in Asian men. Sometimes it seems they prefer going out with white men. Is that true?"

"I don't know about that."

"Is it because they've bought into all those clichés about Asian guys?"

"Well, I'd never say this to the 3AC, but some of those clichés have a basis in reality. A lot of Asian men *are* kind of nerdy and wimpy and boring. They can be very traditional."

"You've dated a lot of Asians?"

"Not many," Mirielle said, then allowed, "Okay, I've gone on a few *dates* with Asians, but I never fucked any. You're my first. You popped my Asian-boy cherry."

"I'm honored."

"I am, too," she said. "Although I'm Japanese, you're Korean. If I had any ethnic pride, I wouldn't be consorting with you at all. God, this futon. I swear, I'm not coming over here again until you get a new bed, an actual bed. Having a mattress on the floor is bad feng shui. And sheets. You need better sheets."

They were cheap knockoffs from Filene's Basement—so cheap, they hadn't advertised a thread count on the package, just that they were one hundred percent cotton. "Any other complaints?" I asked.

"No, I'm pretty impressed with you," she said. "You can make perfect omelettes, and you're a hell of a kisser."

"There's something else I can do pretty well," I told her, and slipped down the futon.

Later, she said, "Do you have this effect on all women? Make them crumble?"

"I think your libido's back from Tahiti."

"You may be right," she said.

The next day, I went to Big John's Mattress Factory in Lechmere and ordered a new mattress, box spring, and frame for delivery.

■   ■   ■

Joshua, never one to be outdone by me, had started his own romance the night of Leon and Cindy's wedding. He had gone home with Lily Bai, another new 3AC member who was a ceramic artist.

"I tell you," he said in his attic room, "this chick, she's a little pistol. She gives unbelievable head. She could suck the chrome off a trailer hitch."

"Isn't that a line from an old movie?" I asked, but laughed nevertheless.

He had been spending the past few days at the Ritz-Carlton. Lily was from Ann Arbor, her father a geneticist who'd developed several patents that had made him a fortune.

"Room service!" Joshua said. Lily lived in a two-bedroom condo attached to the Ritz, and the hotel's services were fully available to the condo residents. "I've been fucking this hot little kumquat and eating room service the entire time! You can't ask for much more in life." He was going back; he'd just come home for some clothes.

"You're able to write there?" I asked.

"Sure. She's at her studio most of the day." Joshua had long ago abandoned his Murakami regimen, and ever since the 3AC had formed, he had become more susceptible to distractions, far less disciplined.

I told him about Mirielle, about her going to AA.

"Fuck, man," he said, "that pious, sanctimonious twelve-step shit bores me to tears. It's just an excuse for self-absorption. Oh, poor me, poor me. Whatever you do, don't fall in love with this girl. I know you. You're a complete sap when it comes to women. Will you promise me you won't fall in love with her?"

I broke my promise to Joshua almost immediately. For the next two weeks, I helped Mirielle unpack and set up in her new apartment in Winter Hill. She was sharing it with two PhD students at Tufts who were a couple, and her room was small, without much closet space. We went to hardware and furniture stores. I installed shelves for her, and miniblinds. I hung up photos. I assembled bookshelves and storage carts. I bought her a garment rack on wheels.

Still, we spent nearly every night back in Harvard Square. She liked my new bed. I'd pick her up after one of her AA meetings or from Casablanca, and I'd walk her back to the house. "Are you living with that Chinese guy now?" a fellow waitress asked Mirielle.

I made breakfast for her every morning—omelettes, poached eggs, French toast, pancakes. I gave her massages. We went to movies and poetry readings at the Blacksmith House and the Lamont Library. We ate in the Porter Square Exchange, where she ordered food in Japanese. We stopped by Toscanini's each night for ice cream, a weakness of hers. We ran on the Esplanade together. That path at sunset, coming down Memorial Drive toward town—the water on the Charles blustery and whitecapped, the gold dome of the State House gleaming above Beacon Hill, the skyscrapers in the Financial District orange-lit—was glorious. With Mirielle running beside me, my chest would squeeze, and I'd love the city.

The 3AC kept meeting on Sundays. The glassblower Jay Chi-Ming Lai had just returned from giving a lecture at a university in butt-fuck rural Missouri. He hadn't wanted to go, but they had persisted, saying they had found more money for him from the minority scholars initiative. He had pictured this group of minority scholarship kids marooned in the Midwest, and thought they'd appreciate having an artist of color visit. At the lecture, there was not a single nonwhite student in attendance. It turned out *he* was the minority scholar. Insult to injury, for dinner the hosts drove him deeper into the country to a restaurant called Jasmine Cuisine, where the menu was not Thai or Chinese or Japanese, just generically Asian. The food was terrible.

"Why do they always assume if you're Asian, you'll want Asian food?" Jay said. "I'd really been looking forward to some *barbecue*."

The entire staff at Jasmine Cuisine had been white. One of the waitresses had a tattoo of Chinese letters on her arm, which she proudly displayed to Jay. She thought it read, "Life won't wait." Jay didn't have the heart to tell her it actually spelled out, "General Tso's Chicken."

"No shit?" Trudy Lun said. "I've heard of that happening, but I always thought it was an urban legend."

"The thing is," Phil Sudo said, "whenever I go out with a bunch of Asian friends, even in Boston, we get stares. You know, getting asked if we're a tour group or an MIT reunion. So I'm more comfortable going to Asian restaurants, even though I'm sick to death of eating Asian all the time."

Joshua, as much as he appreciated these soul sessions, pushed us to come up with an issue we could adopt, a protest or a cause. "We need to actually *do* something as an organization," he said. "We need to get our name out there as a force to be reckoned with. We need to agitate."

"Foment," Jimmy Fung said.

One night, Joshua proposed picketing some of the old Brahmin men's clubs in Boston, like the Algonquin and the Somerset. It was only in 1988 that the private clubs had begun, grudgingly, to admit women, but an Asian American financier, Woodrow Song, had carped recently that the clubs were still discriminating against people of color, his applications for admission repeatedly denied.

"I don't know," Annie Yoshikawa said. "This financier, I'm not sure *I* would have admitted the guy. I heard he—"

"Can I say something?" Lily Bai interjected.

Unlike Mirielle, who never uttered a peep at the 3AC potlucks, Lily had a habit of interjecting. She was just twenty-one years old, yet did not let her youth stop her from voicing her many opinions, which seemed, at least for the moment, to charm Joshua.

"We'll see how long that lasts," Jessica said to me in the kitchen.

"You know," I said, "I was thinking, this is a first, all three of us in relationships at the same time."

"Does that mean Esther's grown on you?" she asked.

"I wouldn't go that far."

"You seem happy," Jessica told me, looking at Mirielle in the living room.

"I am."

A couple of evenings later, Joshua invited Mirielle and me to join him and Lily at Diamond Jim's Lounge, the piano bar in the Lenox Hotel. We went because they were supposed to play old jazz standards there, yet, unbeknownst to any of us, it was open mike night. Amateur singers, one after another, trundled up to the piano and belted out terrible renditions of "The Look of Love," "As Time Goes By," and "My Funny Valentine." The whole scene was corny and boring and tacky. What's more, Lily kept swaying and singing along to the songs, even though she was lyrically challenged with most of them.

"Stop being a brat," Joshua told her. "You're acting like a little kid."

"You're always belittling me over my age," Lily said. "I'm a member of Mensa! I graduated college at twenty!"

"Maturity's not about IQs. It's a function of experience," Joshua said. "You might think you know all you need to know right now, but you haven't lived *through* anything yet. Once you do, you might not be so annoying."

"You might have more experience than me, Joshua, just a tiny, tiny bit," she said, "but *I'm* more brilliant."

They dragged us back to her condo at the Ritz, which had a view of the Public Garden. Joshua brought out a bottle of Macallan's scotch.

"What's the matter?" he said when I declined a glass. "You a teetotaler all of a sudden?"

I had stopped drinking around Mirielle. Sometimes I would still imbibe before I picked her up from Casablanca, and when I kissed her, she would say, even though I had brushed my teeth and gargled with mouthwash, "You taste like beer. Have you been drinking beer?"

Lily wanted to play strip poker. "Oh, don't be poops!" she said after we demurred.

Joshua took photographs of us.

"Come on, that's enough," I said. "That flash is blinding. Why are you always taking photos?" He had become a shutterbug of late, always snapping group portraits of the 3AC.

"Take one of me and Lily," he said, and as I did, Lily stuck out her tongue and lifted her sweater, showing us her boobs.

Mirielle eyed me, and I said, "It's late. We've got to go."

"It's still early!" Lily said.

"Yeah, stay," Joshua said. "We could order room service. It's available twenty-four hours, man."

"The T's going to stop running soon."

"Wait," Joshua said. "What are you guys doing for Hanukkah? Or Christmas, I mean. Do you want to come to the BVIs with us?"

Mirielle and I walked to the Charles/MGH station. "What was that all about?" I asked. "Were they trying to get us into a foursome?"

"You tell me. They're your friends," she said.

"I barely know Lily."

"You ever notice how much Joshua drinks?" she asked.

Yet, as we were waiting for the Red Line to Harvard Square, Mirielle surprised me by saying, "The BVIs would be nice, wouldn't it? A tropical vacation. It's not Tahiti, but it might be fun."

Lily's parents owned a house on Great Camanoe, a private residential island across the bay from Tortola, the most populous of the British Virgin Islands. We'd have the place to ourselves. Her parents would be in St. Moritz.

"You serious?" I asked. I usually went to California for Christmas, and in fact had bought my ticket months ago, snapping up a sale fare.

"No, it's stupid," Mirielle said. "I don't have the money for a trip like that. Who am I kidding?" She had terrible credit history and virtually nothing in her checking account, and had been using her father's gold card to buy things for her new apartment. "It's just that I hate going home for the holidays," she told me. "I'm dreading Thanksgiving."

She flew down to D.C. on Wednesday night. Joshua, Jessica, and I stayed in town and baked a turkey for ourselves, and on Sunday, although most everyone was away, Joshua still hosted a 3AC gathering. I skipped it to pick Mirielle up at the airport, borrowing the Peugeot.

Her flight was delayed on the tarmac at National Airport for over an hour and a half, and by the time she got off the plane at Logan, she was flustered, on the verge of tears.

"What's wrong?" I asked.

"Everything," she said. She had first stayed at her mother's house in Wesley Heights, and her mom had suggested Mirielle might try to get into modeling, she'd arrange for a photographer she knew in New York to take shots of her for a zed card. But her father, who lived in a co-op in Kalorama, ridiculed the idea, telling Mirielle she wasn't pretty enough, she had bad skin, she was too short, her shoulders were too narrow, she had fat calves.

"I can't believe he said all that," I told Mirielle. "You're beautiful. Your skin is perfect."

"He said, being Japanese, there wouldn't be much demand for me in the industry, anyway."

Then her father, who had promised to spend the entire weekend with her, took off on a business trip on Saturday afternoon, leaving her alone in the apartment with his friend, a lobbyist whose wife had just kicked him out, and the lobbyist friend was drinking and doing lines of coke in front of Mirielle, entreating her to join him. "He was trying to seduce me!" she said. "My father probably told him to give it a whirl, what the fuck did he care. My mom, she said I was imagining things. I loathe going to D.C., shuffling between them. I can't go back there for Christmas, I'll have a nervous breakdown. Is there any way we can go to the BVIs?"

"Wouldn't it bother you, being with Joshua and Lily? The way they drink?"

"I'd be all right," she said. "Could you do it?"

"I don't know."

"Please?"

I called my mother the next night and told her I wouldn't be coming to Mission Viejo for Christmas after all. "But you always come," she said. "I don't understand."

"I'm sorry," I said. "It's just this once. I'll come next year for sure. Maybe Mirielle will fly out with me. What do you think of that?"

"Mirielle," she said, trying the name on for size. "How do you spell that?"

I spent the next hour on the phone with American Airlines, trying to roll over my ticket to Tortola, then walked down Brattle Street to Casablanca. Inside, Mirielle was talking to the restaurant manager and a cop. Her purse had been stolen from the employee room.

"What else can go wrong?" she said to me.

Everything had been in her bag—her wallet, driver's license, cash, her BankBoston card and checkbook.

From my bedroom at the house, she called her father, telling him he would have to cancel his gold card, and they argued. "I wasn't rude to your guest," she said into the telephone, then: "No, I didn't tell Mom he tried to *rape* me!"

She hung up. "He's not going to send me another credit card. How am I going to pay for my plane ticket, then? Shit, my passport was in my bag!" She began crying. "I'm such a fuckup," she said. "I don't know what I'm doing with my life. I finally graduate, and then what, I'm still a waitress? This poetry thing, who am I kidding. I miss David. I don't know why I broke up with him anymore. So I could move into an ugly little apartment with strangers?"

I wrapped my arms around her while she wept.

"I feel so lost," she said. "I feel so alone."

She told me that her parents had divorced when she was five years old, and not long afterward her mother had remarried. Her stepfather repeatedly molested Mirielle as a child, but neither her father nor her mother would believe her. "She's the most gullible person in the world," Mirielle said. Her stepfather was a con artist. He stole tens of thousands of dollars from Mirielle's mother, and disappeared before he could be charged for any of his crimes.

"I've never been happy since I quit drinking," Mirielle said. "Look at me: I have no self-esteem, I'm lousy with interpersonal relationships, I don't have a connection with anyone. I'm completely alone."

"You have me," I told her.

"I've been miserable sober," she said. "I was so much happier when I was drinking. I can't imagine not having another drink again for the rest of my life. I quit when I was so young. I was an unbelievable slut then. You'd choke if you knew the things I did, but I'm a lot more mature now. I think I could handle it. Listen, let's get a bottle and get wasted."

"No, this is what we're going to do," I told her.

We'd replace her passport—we had time, three weeks. I'd lend her the money for her plane ticket to Tortola. She'd resume therapy with her old shrink. She would talk to her AA friends and find a new sponsor (her previous one, Alice, had died of breast cancer seven months before). I would quit drinking entirely and go to meetings with her. The most important thing was for her to focus on remaining sober.

"You'd do all that for me?" she asked.

"I'd do anything for you, Mirielle."

■   ■   ■

"Jesus, this girl is more fucked up than I am," Joshua said later in the week. "You know what it all boils down to? Forget the addictions and the underlying abuse, forget the recovery rhetoric and the pop psychology. It all boils down to one thing for her. It's because Daddy doesn't love his little girl."

"Give her more credit than that," I told him. "She's had more to deal with, she's far tougher than you and I will ever be." I didn't want to admit that her breakdown—especially the revelation that she'd been molested—had unsettled me.

We were in the living room, and Joshua was going through his mail. "You really quit drinking for her?" he asked. "Why deny yourself one of the few pleasures in life?"

"Actually, it's been good, not drinking," I said. "It was harder for me to stop than I thought. I had cravings the first few days for a beer. But then that passed, and I started sleeping better. I feel this new kind of energy and clarity now."

"Yeah? Maybe I'll try it myself."

"You?" I said.

"Why not?"

"Self-restraint has never been your forte."

"I could stop anything cold turkey if I wanted. My discipline is nonpareil."

"Is that why you've been screwing around with Lily instead of sitting in front of your computer?"

Joshua set down his letter opener and exhaled laboriously. "I don't know what happened. I was in such a great flow with the novel—I thought for sure I'd finish a draft by the end of the year—and then all of a sudden everything just fizzled. I'm sort of panicked, to tell you the truth. What if it never comes back?"

"Why don't you show it to me?" I asked.

"Not ready for external perusal yet."

"How many pages do you have?"

"Hundreds. But it's a mess."

"Just keep at it," I told him.

"Easy for you to say. If I'm not able to write, the world is intolerable to me. Utterly without purpose. Lily's tiresome, but at least she's serving as a form of provisional entertainment. I'll be ditching her soon enough, no question, but I'm going to wait until after the BVIs."

"That's the only reason you've gone beyond your usual three weeks?"

"That, and the room service, and the fact that she drains old blind Bob with the efficacy of an industrial Hoover every night," Joshua said. "I think the BVIs, the change of scenery, would do me good. And it'd be research. My characters live on an island, some of them are fishermen, but I don't really know anything about living on an island, about boats or the sea. I think I could justify writing the whole trip off on my taxes."

"I'd love to see how that flies with an auditor."

"What are the AA meetings like?" Joshua asked.

I had only been to two thus far—one at Trinity Church, another at the Boston Center for Adult Education. Mirielle liked to rotate locations. "They're less somber, funnier, than I expected. Still, some of the stories are brutal."

"Can I tag along sometime?"

"Why would you want to?"

"I'm curious," Joshua said. "Maybe I'll get something out of it for my novel, hearing these people talk."

I was skeptical. I didn't want to bring Joshua to a meeting, afraid he might deride the proceedings, which was the last thing Mirielle needed. For several days, things had been very tenuous for her, Mirielle thrown by the smallest hiccups, such as not being able to find her birth certificate, which she needed to replace her passport. Her parents were unobliging. "How do they not know where my birth certificate is?" Mirielle had said. "They didn't think it was worth *keeping*?" I made phone calls for her, found out the Vital Records Division in D.C. would mail a copy of her birth certificate to her if she sent verification of her identity with a driver's license, which of course had been stolen. I drove Mirielle to the RMV in Watertown and waited in line with her for two hours. She stayed sober.

She thought it might be fruitful for Joshua to go to a meeting. "This might be his way of acknowledging he has a problem," she said.

So on Saturday, Joshua accompanied us to the Church of the Advent on Brimmer Street. The meeting was being held in the basement of the Beacon Hill church, attended mostly by gay men, who, Mirielle assured us, would keep the mood light, in spite of any horrors they might relate. This was an open meeting: families and friends of AA members could come as guests, and we wouldn't be expected to speak or state that we were alcoholics, Tim, the chairperson that night, told us when we entered the basement.

The room was crowded, around fifty people or so. With cups of coffee and cookies, we sat down on the beige metal folding chairs, and Tim began the meeting by asking, "Would all of you who care to please join me in opening with a moment of silence for those who are still sick and suffering?" Then he led us into the Serenity Prayer: "God, grant me the serenity to accept the things I cannot change, courage to change the things I can, and wisdom to know the difference."

We said amen, and then there were introductions, and then Tim announced the topic for discussion that night—Self-Acceptance—and several members went to the podium to speak, sharing their drunkalogues, the stories familiar yet affecting. An ex–Navy SEAL used to sneak into bathhouses and public restrooms, blind drunk, and have anonymous sex with men and then beat them up, all the while in the closet in the military. A doctor started drinking and taking Benzedrine in med school, which progressed to injecting Demerol and Pentothal and losing his medical license, his wife, his kids, and his house. A man whose partner had died of AIDS found himself going to bars and picking up men and having unprotected sex with them and becoming HIV-positive himself.

The meeting was wrapping up. They handed out baskets for the Seventh Tradition, asking for contributions, and Tim was about to close with the Lord's Prayer when Joshua, who had been silent and respectful all evening, raised his hand without warning. "Could I come up and speak?" he asked.

Tim squinted at him, disconcerted. "Well, this is a little unorthodox, but I suppose it'd be all right."

Joshua rose out of his chair, and I grabbed his arm. "Don't do this," I said.

"Don't worry, this will be great," he said, and walked to the head of the room.

"What's he up to?" Mirielle whispered.

"Nothing good, I'm sure," I told her.

At the podium, he said, "My name is Joshua."

"Hi, Joshua," everyone said.

"I've been listening very carefully to the testimonials this evening—they've been truly inspiring and courageous. But I have to admit discomfort standing here, in the basement of a Christian church. I'm Jewish, you see. Call me cynical, but I have difficulty putting much stock in Christianity, when the entirety of the religion was built upon believing an unmarried fifteen-year-old girl's explanation for how she got pregnant."

The audience crowed.

"I was born on Cheju Island, off the southwestern tip of the Korean Peninsula. I was abandoned when I was four days old and sent to an orphanage on the mainland, in the port city of Pusan. I know nothing about my parents. It could be that my mother was an unmarried fifteen-year-old girl who couldn't manufacture a clever explanation for how she got pregnant. When I was five, one of the teachers at the orphanage molested me. I told the administrators, but no one would believe me. They took me into the courtyard, where they'd assembled all the kids, and made me proclaim that I had been lying and then shaved off all the hair from my head.

"I ran away the next year. I stowed away on a cargo container ship and ended up in Hawaii, where I begged on the streets and worked the sugar plantation fields. An old Chinese hooker got me drunk one night and absolved me of my virginity when I was seven. Thereafter, sex and alcohol were forever enjoined for me. After a few years, I got into a bit of trouble with the law and had to decamp. I hitched a ride on a tanker to San Francisco and picked Brussels sprouts and artichokes in a small town called Rosarita Bay."

"Goddamn him," I muttered. "Goddamn him."

"A family of Mexican migrant workers took me in, sort of as their mascot, and I followed them down the San Joaquin Valley and through Arizona to Brownsville, Texas. Oddly, in the Lone Star State, I found myself discriminated against more than the wetbacks."

He recounted the Southie pier story, only he changed his age to ten and the setting to Port Isabel, on the edge of Laguna Madre. In the church basement, when he got to the climax about the duct tape, there were gasps and soughs of sympathy.

"I became a syrup head. I'd steal prescription cough medicine and mix it with Sprite and drink it by the gallon. Texas tea, it was called. I was also a compulsive masturbator. I'd create these ornate fantasies with which to beat off, using a variety of props: gym socks, milk bottles, and, once, a big piece of liver that was sitting in the refrigerator. I got addicted to porn. I literally wanted to fuck anything that walked."

"Um, the profanity?" Tim cautioned from the front row.

"Sorry. I'd have sex with anything ambulatory, including—I regret to say—three times with the family dog, a rat terrier named Pepe. I started snorting coke and smack, and I became a street hustler—men, women, whatever. I'd do anything for money. I had this beautiful blond girlfriend in junior high school, Leigh Anne Wiatt."

"Just first names, please," Tim said.

"Leigh Anne, Leigh Anne—a tasty little majorette with a bad-girl streak. I took her across the border and got her doped up and sold her to some cholos for a donkey show. She couldn't pee straight for a year."

Now there were guttural protests, not laughter. Some men looked at each other, bewildered, angry. Beside me, Mirielle was furious. Joshua had gone too far. He was enjoying himself too much. People were beginning to catch on that he was playing an elaborate hoax on them, constructing a grand tour of misfortune and debauchery. He was ad-libbing, slapping his narrative together by tapping into a few raunchy movies and dysfunctional memoirs of the day, as well as *Portnoy's Complaint*, sparing no one (Mirielle, me, my parents, Kathryn Newey), and, worst of all, lampooning the earnest speeches that had been shared earlier that night. He was making a mockery of the entire program. Once the rest of the crowd figured it out, there'd be mayhem. They would lynch him. And I would let them. It was unpardonable, what he was doing.

"The Mexican family eventually kicked me out. I made my way to Detroit to join the hip-hop scene there, and I got jumped by two laid-off autoworkers with baseball bats. I was in a coma for three weeks. I still get seizures, can't hear out of my left ear. By the time I got out of the hospital, I was hooked on painkillers: roxis, percs, Captain Codys, vikes, Miss Emmas, I'd take whatever I could get my hands on, and do whatever I had to in order to get zombed. I kited checks. I robbed johns. I jacked cars. I scammed a bunch of Hmongs with a pyramid scheme.

"I got sent to juvie, where for a while I was a regular dick cushion. What saved me was a counselor, a girl from Massachusetts just out of college. Her name was Didi. She said while I was incarcerated, I might as well make use of my time and get an education. She figured out I was dyslexic and tutored me. I started keeping a journal and writing letters—long, intimate letters—to imaginary relatives. I'd actually mail them, picking out addresses at random from an atlas: Uncle Dae-hyung in Kittery, Maine, Grandma Soobong in Weeki Wachee, Florida.

"Didi and I fell in love. She was a sweet, modest girl who'd never done anything wrong, born and raised in Lowell, where her family owned a bakery store renowned for its sourdough bread. I moved with her to Lawrence, got my GED and a job at the New Balance factory, and went straight. For the first time in my life, I was happy. But her family, this large Irish clan, wouldn't accept me—they said they never would, not this degenerate ex-junkie gook—and eventually Didi couldn't take the pressure anymore and left me.

"I started drinking and pharming again. I felt so alone. I wanted to die so many times. Just shut everything down. Why—" Joshua's voice cracked, and he closed his eyes. "Why did everyone I ever care about leave me?"

He clutched the edges of the podium, stared down at the microphone, and didn't speak again for more than a minute. The crowd, which had become increasingly agitated and hostile, quieted. They all knew by now that his entire monologue had been a fabrication, but they could sense, as I did, a subtle change—that inadvertently Joshua had stumbled upon a cavity of undisguised emotion.

"I don't know who I am," he said finally. "I don't know my real name, my real birthday. Other people, they have photos of themselves as babies, family albums. I have nothing. There's no record of my existence. I'm nobody. I'm nothing. I'm worthless."

He stopped again. "I don't know what to do. What will I do? No matter what I do, I can't get anyone to love me. I've had my chances, but I always fuck it up. It never fails. Why do I keep doing that? It mystifies me. My parents, though, they knew. They could tell when I was born, they could tell I was a lost cause. They saw the truth right away. The truth is, I'm unlovable. That's why they abandoned me."

He began to cry. He stayed up there, helpless, and a number of people in the audience, including Mirielle, cried with him.

"I'm sorry. I'm awfully sorry," he managed to say, and walked back to his seat. The audience applauded. People patted Joshua on the back as he sidestepped to the chair next to me. Tim asked us to stand and hold hands, and we bowed our heads and recited the

Lord's Prayer. "Our Father, who art in heaven, hallowed be Thy name." I squeezed Joshua's hand as he continued to whimper.

When the prayer was finished, everyone shouted the standard coda to AA meetings—"Keep coming back! It works!"—and clapped.

Mirielle hugged Joshua. Others did, too, and shook his hand benevolently. "You'll always have a home with us," they said. "You'll always have a family here."

Outside, while we waited for Mirielle, Joshua lit a cigarette and shivered in the cold. "Man, that was fucking nerve-wracking, making that story up on the spot like that," he said. "I was, like, Okay, push it, push it, keep going, let's create a Dickensian epic here, then I'd feel I was losing them and I'd have to tell myself, Come on, think of something, you weenie, reel them back in. I couldn't figure out a way to explain how I got to be Jewish."

"Joshua—"

"Story time for the wretched and woebegone. Not bad, huh?"

"I want to tell you," I said, "I was really . . . moved by that."

" 'Moved'?" He cackled. "Come on, you didn't buy a word of that shit, did you?"

"The last part . . ."

"The last part was no different than the rest. I needed an arc—an ending of contrition, of implied redemption—to round the fucker out. The whole thing was a crock."

"Okay," I said.

"Don't okay me like you know something," he told me. "Believe me, there wasn't a shred of sincerity to anything I said up there."

12

Everything changed the following week. Paviromo accepted an excerpt from Joshua's novel-in-progress for the special Fiction Discoveries issue of *Palaver*, which he was now planning to publish in June. Then he shocked me by finally, after three years of toying intimations and broken pledges, taking my story "The Unrequited" for the issue as well. I didn't know what to make of the offer at first. I was, in fact, initially torn about it.

"Did you have something to do with this?" I asked Joshua.

"I might have impressed upon him the obvious grandeur of your story, which he's been a blinkered arse and bloody ninny to overlook all this time."

"I can't have a story in a magazine where I'm the managing editor," I said. "Everyone will say the only reason I got in was nepotism. No one would count it as a real publication."

"Look, you and I both know the story stands up, that it's had to undergo quadruple the scrutiny of anything that's ever come over the transom at *Palaver*. Am I right?"

"It didn't pass the scrutiny of all those other journals I sent it to."

"Mandarins and halfwits, those editors."

"Maybe I should withdraw it," I said.

"Are you fucking kidding me? So what if a few curmudgeons chirp about it? Fuck 'em! You deserve this, man. More than anyone else, you deserve this. I'll never forgive you if you withdraw it. It'd be such a fucking loony act of career self-sabotage to pull it right when you're on the cusp. I'm telling you, once people actually read the goddamn story, there'll be no question that you belong."

I deliberated for a few days, and even though I still had reservations, I signed the publication contract (which I had had to draw up myself), and let Joshua take Jessica and me out for a congratulatory dinner at Rialto in the Charles Hotel—a threefold celebration, since Jessica had received some good news herself. Her application to the Cambridge Arts Council for an exhibition had been approved.

"This is going to be our year, man," Joshua said. "1999 will be when everything comes together for us."

I believed everything just might. I began dreaming. Dreaming that our stories would be selected for prize anthologies, and agents and editors would come clamoring. That we'd get book contracts and fulfill our vow to each publish a book before we turned thirty. That Jessica's exhibition would be a smash and lead to her signing with a dealer in Boston and another in New York. That *Vanity Fair* would ask to do a two-page photo spread of the 3AC, but only of the three of us, Joshua, Jessica, and me, because we were the founders, the core, the real *fin de siècle* noisemakers who were heralding the arrival of Asian American artists in the new millennium, the ones who had everything before them, a future that promised to be bright and glamorous and extraordinary.

I began writing again—not just revising old stuff but embarking on something brand-new, a novella to round out the collection, about a third-generation Korean American from Mission Viejo who moves to Boston to work for a management consulting firm and encounters the bamboo ceiling. I even yielded to Jessica and several 3AC members' supplications to form a writers' group after the holidays.

For the next week and a half, I wrote every minute I wasn't at *Palaver* or with Mirielle. She was getting stronger—and more affectionate toward me—with each day. "I feel good around you," she said.

By the time we boarded the plane to Tortola, my spirits were at their highest since college, and Mirielle was giddy as well, excited about the trip. "How long till we're there?" she kept asking me during the flight. "Can I wear your watch?" I handed her my black digital chronometer. A flight attendant, serving drinks, said to Mirielle, "And what would your husband like?," and throughout the rest of the journey, Mirielle referred to me as her "*husband*," and I referred to her as my "*wife*," and with each reference, we chortled.

Joshua met us at the airport on Beef Island. He had been in the BVIs a week already, and he was tanned and relaxed. He wore a white captain's hat with a black bill, cocked on his head at a jaunty angle. "Just call me Commander!" he said.

He led us down a dock at the end of the runway to a seventeen-foot Boston Whaler. "You sure you know how to drive this thing?" I asked.

"You'll be impressed by what I've learned here," he said, and bragged that he'd been taking sailing and diving lessons.

Joshua maneuvered the workboat slowly out of the bay, and once we were in open water, he pushed down on the throttle, and we roared out to sea. Mirielle and I unwound, enjoying the sun, the wind, the panorama of boats and islands and ocean.

"I'm so glad we're here," she said to me, and I put my arm around her.

It was a ten-minute ride to Great Camanoe. "Pull those fenders out," Joshua said as we entered a marina, and then he adroitly piloted the boat alongside a concrete pier. He secured the Whaler to cleats and posts, showing off various knots: bowline, sheet bend, clove hitch, daisy chain. For a second I pictured Joshua being tied to the railing on the Southie pier, but the *mise-en-scène* didn't seem to hold any residual trauma for him.

We walked to an old Land Rover parked at the end of the dock. It was rusty and battered, and there was no top to it, no roof or windows, just a windshield. The steering wheel was on the right side, and the interior had been stripped bare, foam poking out of the seats. "What is this?" I asked. "A relic from World War II?"

"Could be," Joshua said. "But it climbs like a motherfucker."

Great Camanoe was a volcanic doublet joined by an isthmus. The island was small, two and a half miles long and one mile at its widest, and only the southern half was inhabited, with fewer than thirty houses, the northern half a national park. There were no commercial businesses on the island, which accounted, perhaps, for the poor condition of the roads.

We quickly reached the end of the two-track of gravel that had begun at the pier, and thereafter it was just ruts and dirt that humped in steep ascents and descents. The Land Rover had a complicated gearbox with a long black shifter, a red lever, and a yellow knob, and Joshua kept having to stop and manipulate the gears—no built-in shifting on the fly—occasionally grinding them. "Come on, you son of a bitch," he said. Soon the dirt road narrowed even further and pitched precipitously up the hill, hanging sheerly off escarpments, twisting and hairpinning. Finally, near the top, at four hundred feet, was the house, in front of which was Lily, passed out on a chaise longue, topless.

"Hey, you big cow," Joshua said, kicking the chair, "wake up."

She opened her eyes and smiled. "Is it cocktail hour already?"

The property was cut into the side of the hill on two terraces and was made up of four small buildings—boxy little cottages—all of them built with white stucco, red galvanized roofs, and terracotta tile floors. There was one cottage for the kitchen and another for the living room, connected by a breezeway that served as an open-air dining area; a cottage for the master bedroom suite; and up a stone walkway from a stone courtyard lined with boulders, a cottage for the guest suite, which had, Mirielle and I discovered, a bathroom that was agape on one end to the rock face of the hill, into which a shower had been carved.

"How cool!" Mirielle said.

The views from the property were magnificent—the lush green slope of trees and the white beach below, the horizon of blue ocean beyond. All around the cottages were flowers: orchids, bougainvillea, huge vines of petrea with mauve-blue flowers, hibiscus, oleander. And the trees: palms, white cedars, loblollies, whistling pines, figs, organ pipe and prickly pear cacti, frangipanis with feral branch sculptures. I could hear songbirds, the plants and trees rustling and swaying with the trade winds. I could smell wild sage and jasmine and thyme.

"I love this place," I told Mirielle.

On the veranda in front of the dining area, Joshua was making drinks. "Gin rickey?" he asked me.

"No, thanks," I said.

"Oh, come on. You're still not drinking? We're on vacation, man." He squeezed half a lime into a tall glass of ice, added gin, threw in the lime, and topped it off with club soda. "You sure?"

Despite the wind, it was hot, and I was sweating. We had left Harvard Square at six-thirty a.m., and it had taken us nine hours to travel to this spot. For the first time in three weeks, I really wanted a drink. I looked to Mirielle, who shrugged. "Go ahead," she said.

"Gin rickeys were Fitzgerald's drink," Joshua told me.

"You know what I could really use?" I said. "A swim."

We changed into bathing suits and walked down the hill on the dirt road, then hiked through the trees on a trail littered with rocks and roots. After a few minutes, the path opened to the curved beach of Cam Bay, surrounded by canopies of sea grape trees and patches of bay lavender. We all ran into the water.

Mirielle hugged her arms and legs around me, and we floated with the swells. "Heaven," I said, and she kissed me.

Joshua was splashing Lily. "Stop it!" she screamed.

He had left his captain's hat on the beach, and now that his hair was wet, I realized he was going bald at the temples.

We returned to the house, and, perspiring from the climb, Mirielle and I took an outdoor shower together. We soaped each other up, and I became erect. "Turn around," I said.

"That's so impersonal."

Facing her while we stood in the shower, I tried to arrange our bodies into a feasible position.

"This is impossible," she said. "I'd never get all that soap out of my vagina, anyway."

I barbecued chicken for our dinner, throughout which Joshua and Lily, drunk on gin rickeys, jousted with each other.

Mirielle and I went to bed early. "It's more rustic than I thought it'd be," she said. "I was kind of expecting a villa on the water"—she kicked off the sheet—"and A/C in bedroom, at least."

"I'm okay with the ceiling fan and the breeze. Are you hot?"

"They don't have a Christmas tree or any decorations at all, not even some stockings."

"Well, Joshua's Jewish."

"He always says that, but he never goes to temple. Lily's Episco-palian. It doesn't feel Christmasy without decorations."

"We'll get some in town tomorrow." I kissed and stroked her.

"Aren't you tired?" Mirielle said. "I'm wiped."

"You don't want to?" I said. I could hear Joshua and Lily gab-bling on the veranda, the tinkling of ice cubes.

"Can you be quick?" Mirielle asked.

I complied.

She curled up against me. "It was a good day," she said before falling asleep.

■   ■   ■

She woke up with big red welts on her face—five of them. "Are these zits?" she asked. "How could they appear out of nowhere?"

They were mosquito bites. I had a few on my arm as well.

"Here, my father showed me this once," Lily said. She mixed baking soda and water in a bowl and told Mirielle to apply the paste with a finger to her face.

Mirielle used a mirror in the living room, and when she rejoined us at the dining table, we looked at her white-spotted face and burst out laughing.

"Don't laugh at me!" she said. "They really hurt."

She didn't want to go into town with us. "I look like a total freak," she said.

"No one will notice."

"You're not helping."

"Don't you want to shop for souvenirs?"

She washed off the spots of white paste and covered the welts with thick concealer, and we made the trek to Tortola, riding the Land Rover to the marina, then the Whaler to Trellis Bay, then a taxi across the bridge to Road Town, the capital city.

It was crowded—high season, a cruise ship in port. The streets and buildings were festooned with Christmas decorations: wreaths, tinsel, garlands, poinsettias. There was a large Christmas tree in the main plaza, and a band was playing reggae versions of "White Christmas" and "Jingle Bells." Everyone wore Santa hats, along with their Hawaiian shirts, shorts, and flip-flops. It was eight-five degrees, blindingly sunny.

Joshua took photos of us in front of the tree, then we strolled through some shops. Mirielle and I bought T-shirts, and surreptitiously I purchased a pair of silver earrings for her. She found decorations for the house, especially captivated by ornaments made from seashells—a nautilus striped like a candy cane, turritellas glued together and hand-painted as Santa Clauses.

We went to a restaurant on the water for lunch, but had to wait an hour for a table. The lines were just as long at the grocery store, where we carted up a week's worth of food and supplies, and then, outside the store with all our sacks, we couldn't flag a taxi.

"Everyone's staring at me," Mirielle said.

"No, they're not."

"They're thinking, So sad, she could be a pretty girl if she didn't have such horrible acne."

It was getting hotter, the wind stilling. "There's a tropical wave forming in the northeast. A trough's blocking the trades," Joshua said.

The ocean was rougher as well, the Whaler rolling and yawing as we motored back to Great Camanoe, making Mirielle feel seasick.

Onshore in the Land Rover, I asked her, "Did you put suntan lotion on? Your face is a little pink."

"No. I didn't want to smear the makeup. Am I sunburned?"

When we arrived at the house, she trudged up to the guest cottage without a word, not helping us unload the sacks.

"Is she PMS-ing or something?" Joshua asked.

After we put away the food, Joshua and Lily suggested another swim in Cam Bay. I went up to our cottage, where Mirielle was lying on the bed, and asked if she wanted to come along.

"You go," she said. "I don't feel well."

On the spur of the moment, Joshua and Lily opted for a snorkel in Lee Bay, on the other side of the isthmus. Joshua knew the names of most of the fish: reef squid, a big tarpon, a beautiful blue-green queen angelfish with yellow rims. At one point, a huge stingray swam underneath me. "Did you see that?" I exclaimed to Joshua.

Mirielle was hanging Christmas lights from the eaves of the breezeway when we returned. "You went snorkeling without me?" she asked when she saw our masks and fins.

For dinner, I grilled steaks, and Joshua and Lily switched to Myers's rum with pineapple juice, garnished with slices of fresh pineapple and maraschino cherries. As Mirielle and I washed the dishes, she said, "Why are we doing all the cooking and cleaning? We're the guests. Those two haven't lifted a finger since we got here. They're just getting shitfaced every night."

"That's the deal I made."

"What deal?"

"With Joshua. For letting us stay here."

"It's not even his house. They invited us. It's not like we begged to come. They didn't even offer to pitch in for the decorations." She had bought stockings and tinsel in addition to the lights and seashell ornaments. "No one even thanked me for putting them up."

"They're beautiful," I said. "Thank you, Mirielle."

The wind dissipated further, and the heat and humidity surged, as did the insects. Our alfresco bathroom, which had seemed so charming, was now a mosquito den. Even after dousing ourselves with bug spray, we were swarmed brushing our teeth. We saw teeth marks on our bar of soap in the shower—a rodent of some sort.

"This is like camping in a jungle," Mirielle said. Her face was spotted with white paste again and red from the sun. "God, it's so hot."

In the bedroom, she checked the screens on the windows. "There must be a hole in one of these things. Those mosquitoes got in here somehow. Wait, do you hear that?" There was a faint mechanical humming noise outside. "They have an air conditioner in their bedroom!"

She got into bed and eventually calmed. I hovered over her, kissing her. "You're dripping on me," she said. I wiped the sweat from my forehead on the pillow, but then she said, "Oh, God, what is that?"

"What?"

"I'm burning. I'm burning inside. What's happening to me?" Moaning, she covered her crotch with her hands and drew her knees to her chest. "It's the fucking bug spray," she said. "It's on your fingers."

I went to the bathroom, washed my hands, and got back in bed.

"Get that erection away from me," she said.

We tried to sleep, but floundered in the heat. "This is an awfully long date," Mirielle told me. "I'm not used to being around someone so much. Even when I lived with David, we never spent twenty-four hours together like this."

"You never went on a trip with him?"

"He was always working," she said, then told me, "I saw him last week."

"You did?"

"We had to exchange some stuff," she said. "He wanted to get back together."

"What'd you tell him?"

"What could I say?" She billowed the sheet and shifted on the bed, trying to get comfortable. "I wonder what the hell I'm doing sometimes, going from one man to another, this long string of boyfriends—not even boyfriends a lot of times, just guys who want to fuck me. Sometimes I feel like I'm nothing but a sex object."

"You're not that to me."

"No?"

"I'm in love with you, Mirielle."

I waited for her to say something in response. In the dark, I watched as she lay on her back, breathing. Finally, she turned onto her side, toward the far wall. "Good night," she said.

■　■　■

She slept in the next morning, and by the time she came down the stairs—her hair matted, her face pinked, the welts recessed but still visible—the three of us had already finished breakfast. "Do you want me to fix you an omelette?" I asked.

"I'll just have coffee," she said. She saw the carafe perched upside down in the dish rack. "You finished the pot?"

"I'll make you some more."

"*I* can make it," she said irritably.

After lunch, Joshua and Lily wanted to go snorkeling in Lee Bay again, this time with the Whaler so they could explore the outer tip of the reef. I decided to give Mirielle some room. "I think I'm going to do some work on my novella," I told her, "but you can go if you want."

"I *know* I can go if I want," she said.

I spent the afternoon alone at the house. I tried to write for a few hours, but whatever momentum I'd had before coming to Great Camanoe had disappeared. I cracked open Joshua's copy of Nabokov's *Pale Fire*, yet found myself reading the same paragraph over and over. I didn't know what was going on with Mirielle. I'd never seen her like this, so testy and brusque toward me.

When they returned, she seemed in a better mood. The three of them talked animatedly about seeing a school of squirrelfish, a green sea turtle, elkhorn coral, a nurse shark, and a barracuda. Yet when I said to Mirielle, "I'm glad you got to go snorkeling," she looked at me with barely concealed contempt. As dinnertime neared and she was going up to change, I stood to follow her, and she told me, "Can't you leave me alone for a few minutes?"

We took the Whaler to a waterfront restaurant in Trellis Bay to sample the local cuisine, sharing orders of conch fritters, chicken roti, lobster, spicy goat, and johnny cakes.

Joshua and Lily were drinking painkillers, a rum cocktail that was a BVI specialty. After three or four of them, Joshua heard the bar next door playing a recording of the Wailers' "Duppy Conqueror" and began bemoaning the commercialization of Bob Marley, how the white colonial culture had exploited his music and image and debased his message beyond recognition ("Don't people listen to the lyrics at all?"), so Marley was now simply a symbol of island party life and sybaritism, his songs a sorry, spurious anthem to the glories of ganja for white-bread narrow arrows who'd never touched a doobie in their lives. This got him on the topic of hip-hop sampling—he remembered the Beastie Boys had poached a part of "Duppy Conqueror" for "Funky Boss"—and the concept of *détournement* ("which, of course, was the primary impetus behind Jessica's table sculptures, remember?") and other situationist pranks intended to subvert the capitalist system, although these approaches ironically inherited the same problems of reflecting or refracting a culture ("Can there be such a thing as genuine *weltanschauung* or any kind of normative postulate when everything's been so bastardized and imperialized?"), which led to a digression about Duchamp's readymades, the anxiety of influence, T. S. Eliot, and the objective correlative.

"What about—" Lily started to say.

"It's not just with poetry," Joshua said. "It's the perpetual conflict with all text, language being both the material object on the page and the signifier for meanings that reside beyond it. How can you reconcile those contradictions and find a way to acknowledge them yet still allow a specificity of discourse? I don't know if it's possible now to create a definitive statement about any subject that's mimetic to actual experience when every word bears a semantic, ideological charge."

"Can I say something?" Lily asked.

"I want to agree with Valéry, who famously contended that order and disorder are equal threats in a poem. Great writing should function as a bearer of alterity, but language continually fails to contextualize the inequities of the cultural moment. You're always reduced to privileging one thing over another."

"You're ignoring me," Lily said.

"I'm sorry. You have something pertinent you wish to add?"

"I was going to say something about metaphors, but now I've forgotten what exactly because you were babbling so long."

"Ah, you see, this is where you're misapprehending the basic rules of etiquette, Lily. Conversation is not dialogue, it's monologues. No one ever really listens in conversations. It's civility that makes you wait and pretend you give a fuck what the other person is saying. You've got to learn to ignore that shit and just butt in."

"Everything you were saying was pompous bullshit, anyway," Lily said. "Not that it matters to you, you love the sound of your own voice so much. It's like when the 3AC meets: my theory this, my project that. Sometimes it feels like you guys don't think what I'm doing is as important as what you're doing."

"You design cute little plates and bowls," Joshua said. "You display them at trade shows for distribution to home accessories stores. You hardly ever go to the studio, you have your helpers do all the actual work. You've never made a profit, but it doesn't matter, because you can always rely on your father's seemingly inexhaustible moola. You wonder why we might not regard what you're doing as important. The fact is, it's not."

Lily threw the rest of her painkiller in his face.

"Okay," he said, "maybe that was a little too blunt." He rose from his chair and stumbled to the beach, taking off his shirt along the way, and dove into the water. Tittering, Lily joined him there, stripping down to her underwear.

Mirielle watched them frolicking in the bay. "Joshua's a total prick," she said. "Why are you friends with him?"

"Well, you've only seen his good side," I told her.

"I thought after that meeting, he might actually change. That's how stupid I am. But he's a classic narcissist. He gets gratification by tearing apart everyone around him, because it feeds into his self-hatred. He likes to inflict pain so he won't have to focus on his own. He'll destroy you in the end. Don't let him. Don't be a second banana to him."

"So to speak."

"What?"

"Banana?"

"I don't get it," she said.

"What's going on, Mirielle?" I asked. "There's this weird wall between us all of a sudden."

"You're condescending to me," she said. "You get it from Joshua, obviously, the way he treats women. He's a misogynist. Did you notice how he went on and on about poetry and never asked me, the only poet at the table, for my opinion? You've been doing it all vacation. Like this morning, telling me I could go snorkeling. You're always telling me what I can and cannot do, making decisions for me."

"That's not true," I said.

"Yes, it is."

"Is it because I told you I'm in love with you?"

"You need to readjust your expectations for this trip," Mirielle told me. "You want a romantic trip, but it's just a vacation we happen to be on together."

■   ■   ■

We exchanged Christmas presents in the morning. I gave Mirielle the silver earrings from the shop in Road Town, a black BCBG dress from Jasmine Sola in Harvard Square, and a necklace from the Cambridge Artists Cooperative Gallery. Mirielle gave me a novel, *Blindness* by José Saramago, the Portuguese author who'd won the Nobel Prize a few months ago. A book, the most unimaginative gift you could give to a writer, plucked from a rack of prize-winners. She couldn't have put less thought into buying a present for me.

It was cloudy and sprinkling intermittently. We repaired to various corners of the house, reading and napping. It cleared up later, and Mirielle came down the stairs in her bathing suit, on her way to Lee Bay, plainly not interested in company.

That night, she said to me, "We only have two days left."

I didn't reply.

"Are you okay?" she asked.

"Just readjusting my thinking," I said. "Evidently I'm just this guy to you."

She rolled her eyes and turned off the light.

I couldn't sleep, and in the middle of the night I walked down from the guest cottage to the veranda, where I found Joshua on one of the chaises longues, smoking a cigarette.

"Insomnia?" I asked, sitting down beside him.

"Stomach's a little queasy. Nice night for stargazing, though." We peered up at the stars pinholing the black sky. "Breathtaking, isn't it? 'My little campaigners, my scar daisies.'"

"Roethke."

"Sexton," Joshua corrected me.

"Mirielle's favorite poet."

"Figures," he said. "Manic-depressive, suicidal, anorexic—the perfect role model."

"I'm totally baffled by her," I said. "Things were going so well."

"Don't be so nice to her," Joshua told me. "Women, especially little girls like her, like men who are jerks. They don't know what to do with themselves if they're treated well. They can only function when they're in despair. That book she gave you, Saramago—there's a Portuguese word, *saudade*. It's like nostalgia, but not quite. More like yearning, a vague acedia, a desire for something that can never be obtained or might not even exist. We all have that, don't we? All of us who are artists, who are outsiders. It's what your man Fitzgerald was alluding to when he said in the real dark night of the soul it's always three o'clock in the morning. We get down, but it's manageable, and it's essential to our creativity, that occasional glimpse into the dark night. But for someone like Mirielle, it's pitch-black every hour of the day. You're not going to be able to save her, you know. If you keep trying, she'll break your heart."

He was right, of course, but I didn't want to believe him just then.

The wind freshened, luffing leaves and branches. "The trades are back," Joshua said, then asked, "What kind of tree is that?," gesturing toward a large hardwood with peeling red bark. "Do you know?"

"Turpentine, a.k.a. gumbo limbo," I said. I pointed out other species around the house: tamarind, flamboyant, aloe.

"One of my great failings is that I don't know the names of trees and flowers," Joshua said. "How'd you learn?"

"You've never noticed all the work Jessica and I have done in the backyard, have you?" I said. "My mom's a gardener. She used to take me to arboretums and botanical gardens when I was a kid."

"She did you a real favor. That was a gift," Joshua said. "You should appreciate her more. You take your family for granted, you know."

"Did I ever tell you what she did with the oranges for my sack lunches?"

In a year, I would go home to Mission Viejo for Christmas, as promised. It'd be the last time I would see my mother. She would die a few months afterward, and Joshua, in the throes of his own grief and guilt, would fly out to California for the funeral. In the church, he would read aloud the eulogy I had written—I wouldn't be able to do it myself. He would follow us to the wake, then would sit with me in the house as I clicked through the old slideshow of my parents' honeymoon, telling me, "She was a beautiful woman," and would console me as I wept. I'd never forget that he did that for me.

■   ■   ■

We walked down to Cam Bay for a swim. "You seem unhappy," Mirielle said as we treaded water. "You seem like you're sulking."

"It's just a long date, right?" I said. I didn't know why I was being truculent instead of seeking rapprochement. I couldn't help it. My pride was wounded, and I didn't want to be accommodating.

"I guess I can't give you what you want," she said.

"I guess not."

She swam farther out into the bay, then floated back to me. "It's stupid," she said, "not having sex when you want to have sex. Just like with David. It's not unreasonable, what you're asking."

For the first time in days, there was clemency in her voice. Her hair was slicked back from the water, and she looked at me with a forbearance that suggested a submerged well of regret. Or pity. But then I did exactly the wrong thing.

"Let's go to where it's shallower," I said.

"Why?"

"Put your legs around me."

"I didn't mean I want to have sex with you right *now*," she said.

We gathered our towels, and as we were leaving the beach, I glanced back and saw pink jellyfish, dozens of them, washed up on the sand. It was a miracle we hadn't been stung.

Our bar of soap was gone from the shower, purloined by the rodent. The insects—centipedes, ants, termites, spiders—as well as the geckos, were proliferating. "I can't wait to get the fuck out of here," I said in our room. Stalking a mosquito, I rolled up a magazine and smacked the wall.

Mirielle was packing clothes into her suitcase. We were leaving early the next day. Holding one of her souvenir T-shirts, emblazoned with the slogan VIRGIN ISLANDER, she sat down on the bed. "I've always made a lousy girlfriend," she said. "I'm always a bitch.

I know I'm a drag to be around. There's no reason you can't have a drink. I want a gin rickey, too, you know."

I put the magazine down. "Maybe we should get you to a meeting tonight. There have to be some on Tortola."

"Don't tell me to go to a meeting. I'm not a child."

"All right, then. Don't go."

"I'm not what you're looking for," she said. "I just can't deal with getting into another heavy-duty, exclusive relationship so soon after David. I don't want to feel obligated or possessed, I don't want to settle down into a routine again as a couple. I think maybe we should date other people."

"What?"

"It might be healthy, not seeing each other so much." She folded the T-shirt and tucked it into her suitcase.

"Have you met someone else?"

"No."

"Did you sleep with David when you saw him?"

"Not that it's any of your business, but no."

"Did someone ask you out?"

"Could you give the questions a rest for one fucking minute and let me pack?" she said. "God, I hate clingy men."

I left the guest cottage. Joshua and Lily were making gin and tonics on the veranda. "Fix me one of those," I told Joshua.

I wasn't in the mood to cook dinner. We went back to Trellis Bay, and this time ate at De Loosey Goosey, the outdoor beach bar, which was decorated with the usual thatched roof, tiki torches, nautical flags, and picnic tables. It was quizo night there, and after some cajoling from the bar's owner, we played the pub trivia game. Joshua named our team the Broom in the System of Cyclones.

"Which punk rocker was born in 1947 and originally named James Newell Osterberg, Jr.?" the owner asked.

"Too easy," Joshua said, writing down *Iggy Pop*.

"How many keys are there on a standard piano?"

Lily scribbled *eighty-eight*.

"What condiment is served with sushi?"

A man at the bar—part of a French sailing crew—groaned. "They have unfair advantage," he said, apparently referring to our team's all-Asianness.

"What the fuck?" I said, jotting down *pickled ginger*.

We came in fourth, lagging on the sports questions. Yellow Polka Dot Bimini was first. Mary Poppins Was a Drug Dealer was second. The French sailor's team, Bill Clinton Is President of the Wrong Country, was third. When the standings were announced, the Frenchman faced our table, palms upturned, smiled, then put his hands together and bowed Orientally to us.

"Did you see that?" I said.

"See what?" Joshua asked.

"That guy at the bar."

"What about him?"

"He's fucking mocking us."

"I didn't see."

"What the fuck's his problem?" I said, glaring at the Frenchman.

"I wish you guys could stay until New Year's," Joshua told me. He and Lily still had another four days to go on Great Camanoe.

"A shame," I said drunkenly, and turned to Mirielle. "I've had such a grand time. Fabulous company."

We'd started with painkillers, and now were ordering rounds of bushwackers, another potent BVI specialty.

"Enjoying those?" Mirielle said.

"Absolutely," I said. "I don't know why I've been denying myself, when I've been deprived of everything else."

I knew I'd never see her again after we landed in Boston. For all intents and purposes, she had just broken up with me, and I felt murderous, thinking of everything I had done for Mirielle, all the time and money I'd spent. For what? I had been nothing but caring and solicitous and doting—indeed, worshipful. I had loved her.

I headed to the bathroom. The French sailor was roosting on a stool beside the door, leaning against the wall and calling out the nationalities of the men who entered, along with culinary associations about their endowments. "German bratwurst. Russian kupaty." When he saw me, he shouted, "Ah, Chinese wonton!" and his chums guffawed. I kicked the stool out from underneath him, and as he was trying to get to his feet, I punched at his face, connecting with an ear. I was grabbed, a free-for-all, and Joshua flew into the throng to my aid. We started a near-riot.

"You are such an asshole," Mirielle said to me as we climbed into the Whaler.

On the plane the next day, she wouldn't talk to me. Every time I said something, she pretended not to hear. "What?" she'd ask, peeved.

She didn't like our assigned seats, which faced a bulkhead. I didn't care for the alternatives she chose, next to the lavatories. We switched to another pair of seats, but she thought they were too close to the movie screen. We moved back to the ones beside the toilets.

"You can sit somewhere else, you know," she said.

"You'd like that, wouldn't you?"

I was hungover. After takeoff, I asked for a Heineken, and as the flight attendant handed me the can, she stared at me curiously. My cheek was bruised, my nose scratched, my bottom lip cracked and scabbing. "Does your wife want anything?"

"I'm not his wife," Mirielle told her.

Halfway through the flight, I asked Mirielle for the time. She unbuckled the strap of my black chronometer watch, which she had been wearing all week, and handed it back to me.

13

On the first Sunday of January, the 3AC resumed its pot-lucks (I had to explain the scrapes on my face to every-one, and Joshua said, "You should have seen him lay out the fuckwad. It was beautiful"), and two evenings later, the Tues-day Nighters convened for the first time. With Joshua declining to participate, I was the de facto leader of the writers' group, and I set down the ground rules.

I wouldn't endure any of the pussyfooting that Peter Anderegg had mandated at Mac. I wanted people to be forthright, speak to the authors directly, address them by name and "you," and have the authors respond to the critiques at will—peremptorily and conten-tiously, if warranted. But there were only five of us in the group: Grace Kwok, the immigration attorney; Rick Wakamatsu, who sold windsurfing gear at Can-Am, near the Galleria; Ali Ong, a sous chef at the Green Street Grill; me; and, unavoidably, Esther Xing.

It was too small and unschooled of a group for candor or asper-ity. Grace, Rick, and Ali did not have MFAs. They had never taken a fiction workshop other than a couple of weekend classes at the Grub Street writing center in Boston. They were complete neo-phytes, and they were good-humored and ebullient about it. They wrote terrible, cloddish stories, and they loved everything that was presented. They wanted the writers' group to be supportive and fun, not confrontational—an exercise in boosterism for dabblers and tenderfoots. They were too busy to read the manuscripts ahead of time, preferring to listen to them *in toto* the night of the meetings, and they didn't care for the formality of penning commentary or marginalia. It was all impromptu, the pronouncements slapdash and facile. They had nary a criticism for the opening to my novella. The sessions in the living room were bush league, amateur hour. The writers' group was a waste of my time, without utility or challenge. Until the third Tuesday night, when Esther Xing read her story to us.

"Say What You Will" was about two women, Leona Hood and Caroline Bates, who lived in the former quarry town of Severn Springs, Vermont, in 1954. Leona ran a spa-turned-inn-turned-boardinghouse with her husband. Caroline was the assistant town clerk and a spotter for the civilian Ground Observer Corps, assigned to scan the skies and alert the Air Force to any irregular or unscheduled aircraft. Leona and Caroline were lovers, had been for many years, but in 1950s small-town Vermont, they both knew that such a relationship could never be made public. The story was a subtle portrait of their everyday routines, without sentimentality or opera, culminating in a single touch, or nearly a touch, Leona furtively brushing her fingertips across the sleeve of Caroline's blouse as they said good night after a town meeting.

"I'm totally blown away," Ali said.

"You know, I feel honored to have read this," Rick said.

"It's really, really beautiful," Grace said.

It was. It pained me to acknowledge, but it was. The story was haunting, the prose crisp: "She caught a wink of light in the sky, at once bright and flimsy. There was no contrail, nor any sound, none of the typical buzz or hum. She didn't think it was a spy plane or a drone, yet it had form, movement, and she had a sense that it had come from a place unfathomably far away. She found something comforting in its unexpected appearance and in the fact that she could neither explain nor identify it."

Esther Xing was a better writer than I was, perhaps rivaling Joshua in the quality of her work. There was a patient assurance in the story, an honesty of emotion, that I had never come close to producing. Sitting there, listening to Ali, Rick, and Grace fawn over her, I knew, no matter how hard I tried, I would never be as good as Esther, and the knowledge galled me. There was, however, a conspicuous omission in the story, one that was instantly recognizable to me, toward which I could channel my envy.

"I guess I'll have to be the lone dissenter here," I said.

"Oh, no!" Esther said, clamping her hands to her fat cheeks in mock horror. She smiled kookily with her crooked teeth, then pouted. "You didn't like it?"

"The story's craft aside, I have a question for you—something more fundamental and profound."

"Okay."

"Why are all the characters white?"

"What?"

"Why are you writing about white people in Vermont in 1954?"

"My mom had a friend who grew up in Severn Springs. She told me about these women, and I thought it was so sad they were never able to come out, but it really, you know, touched me that they kept being lovers, till the day they died."

"Why didn't you make at least one character Asian?"

She laughed. "There were no Asians in Severn Springs in 1954."

"You couldn't have fudged it?"

"I did a lot of research on the town and period. I really wanted to get the historical details right."

"Let me ask you something," I said. "Are you ashamed of being Chinese?"

"What?" She giggled. "What are you talking about?"

"I just find it very curious you'd choose to write a story like this instead of something about Asians."

"Why should I restrict myself to writing about Asians?" Esther asked, becoming more sober. "Why can't I write about anything I want?"

"Isn't it obvious?"

"No."

"Because not doing so is denying who you are. Because it's a form of whitewashing. Because it's betraying your own race."

I had to say, it was satisfying being in this position of power, assuming Joshua's usual role for once.

"That's ludicrous," Esther said, then asked the others, "Don't you think so?"

But Grace, Ali, and Rick, clearly uncomfortable with the emergent direction of the conversation, said nothing.

"Expression should be expression," she said. "I'm interested in other things besides race, other themes. Aren't you? Are you planning to write the same identity/racism story the rest of your life?"

"Until things change, I just might have to."

"Come on," she said. "Art's not about being didactic. There's nothing more boring or tedious than that. Art should simply be about what makes us human. Its only obligation, if anything, is to try to break the frozen sea within us."

I knew the quote. "Kafka."

"Look," Esther said, "if we limit ourselves to the subject of race, it's equivalent to self-segregation, to ghettoizing ourselves. Like, don't you remember when you were back in college, and you'd go in the union and see all the Asians at one table, all the blacks at another table, all the Hispanics at yet another? I thought that was such a shame, these groups huddled in self-exile."

"Whites don't do that all the time, sit with other whites?"

"The whole victimization motif of minority narratives—they drive me crazy," she said. "They just end up indulging in the same old tired clichés of romantic racialism that have been around since Gunga Din—characters speaking pidgin English or in that bizarre, singsong, Confucian/koan/proverb-laden Orientalese that's supposed to pass for lyricism. I mean, if I see one more book by an Asian American with *moon, silk, blossom,* or *tea* in the title, I'm going to have to hang myself. At least give me some Asian American characters I can recognize, not just the virtuous or the persecuted, but some freaky, flawed motherfuckers like me. But really, why do we have to follow that path at all? We should be trying to de-label the identities of artists as Asian or African or whatever. We should insist on being regarded as artists, period."

"And ignore the Asian American experience altogether?"

"What *is* 'the Asian American experience'?" Esther asked. "There's no single way all Asians think and behave and feel. This panethnic identity as Asian Americans is an unmitigated fraud. Besides, everything's not all about race, you know. It's more often about class. That's much more interesting and insidious."

"You don't believe in anything we're doing, then?" I said. "We're marginalizing ourselves, and the 3AC should disband?"

"No, I like that we have a common bond, artificial as it is," Esther said. "I just don't want to be told that being Asian is all that I'm about, it's all I can explore in my fiction. *That's* racist, when you get down to it."

I looked at the others in the living room. Ali and Rick were nodding, seemingly in concord with Esther's last statement, and I knew I would not win this argument, especially since, as in the DeLux the first time I met her, a part of me was beginning to side with Esther. "Okay, then, let's talk about what else is missing in the story," I said.

"Okay," she said, "let's."

"There's not much," I told her, "except, oh, I don't know, maybe wit, and tension, and originality. Maybe one or two other things."

She smirked at me. "You're kind of a sexist pig, aren't you?"

"Now you're talking, sister."

■   ■   ■

"You *are* a sexist pig," Jessica told me the next morning in the kitchen. "Esther's story was good. More than good. Superb. Admit it."

"I can't. Not unless you want me to lie." I opened the cupboard. "Did you eat all the cereal?" I asked Joshua, who winced apologetically.

"You're being pissy and argumentative out of spite," Jessica said. "When did you become such a dick? You used to be a nice guy."

"It was a perfectly reasonable discussion. She has issues being Asian."

"I thought you were more mature than this. I thought you were above such pettiness."

"She should be kicked out of the 3AC," Joshua said. He had come back to Cambridge after New Year's Day and, as promised, had promptly broken up with Lily, but the BVIs had not, as he'd wished, rekindled his creative juices. He had been moping around the house all month, rarely changing out of his *manga* pajamas.

"Have you read her story?" Jessica asked him.

"No. Why should I?"

"It's brilliant," Jessica said. "If anyone deserves to be in the Fiction Discoveries issue, she does."

"That was her whole motivation behind the writers' group, wasn't it?" I said. "It was just an underhanded way to get me to read her work, hoping I'd push it onto Paviromo for the issue. She was looking for a shortcut. It was so transparent to me."

"She suggested the group before the issue was even *conceived*."

"You know what I mean," I told her. "She's a user."

Jessica looked at Joshua, then at me, grasping that a confidence had been broken.

"Let's banish her," Joshua said.

In truth, it didn't matter all that much to me—my quarrel with Esther. At that moment, the only thing I really cared about was Mirielle, and how I might win her back.

I didn't hear from her for almost a week after Great Camanoe, during which, despite my anger and disappointment, I missed her terribly. Finally I gave in and called, asking to see her. She granted me lunch. We met at the Harvest Restaurant in the Square, where I learned that, in the short time since our return, she had decisively moved on with her life. She had quit her job waitressing at Casablanca, found another one as a medical secretary at Mount Auburn Hospital, and would be applying to MFA programs in poetry for the fall.

"Wow," I said, feeling defeated by the developments.

"I know!" she said.

"Where are you thinking of applying to?"

All the schools she mentioned were outside Massachusetts. "Maybe you should apply to Walden as a backup," I told her.

"I've had enough of Walden," she said. "I want a clean slate."

We went to Wordsworth so she could buy some GRE prep

books. Her grades at Walden College had been spotty, and she would need to do well on the test.

"I could help you study," I told her.

"I don't know if that's a good idea," she said. "Would you have a problem seeing me platonically?"

"It'd be painful," I admitted.

"This always happens. Can't you be my friend?"

I told her that I would try. "Are you going to date other people?" I asked. "Have you?"

"No. It's important for me to be alone right now."

"I won't be a nuisance to you, then," I said. "I'm not going to call you. When you want to see me or talk, you should call."

She ended up calling me every day, sometimes three or four times a day. Almost immediately, her newfound confidence collapsed. After her first day of work at Mount Auburn Hospital, she was barely able to mumble hello on the phone before bursting into tears. I went over to her apartment. She was slumped in her nightgown, her face swollen from crying. "It's so demeaning being a secretary again," she said.

Then, during a thunderstorm, she came home to find water pouring from the windowsills, the ceiling leaking in rills, ruining her bed and sheets and her clothes on the garment rack. "Can I sleep over at your place?" she asked.

We saw each other just as much as before the BVIs. We went to movies and poetry readings. We dropped by Toscanini's for ice cream. We drilled through GRE practice tests. I quit drinking again and accompanied her to the occasional meeting. I made her coffee and French toast and omelettes. And we kept spending nights together in my bed, though chastely.

The denial of sex now, however, instead of pushing me further away, oddly intensified my feelings for her. I waited for Mirielle to swing around. At times, it seemed she was coming back to me, but then she would abruptly retreat.

"You never call me," she said. "I always call you."

I reminded her about our arrangement, about not being a pest.

"That's silly," she said. "We talk every day, anyway. What are you doing Saturday?"

"Seeing you," I said.

One morning, she told me she was going to the Square to hang out, maybe see a movie. "You want company?" I asked.

"No," she said. "I think we're spending too much time together."

"Why'd you call me, then?"

"I don't know," she said. "You sound strange."

Later that day, she appeared at the house, depressed by the movie, throughout which the characters had drunk copious amounts of wine. She had gone to a meeting afterward at the First Parish Unitarian Church but had left early, restless.

I had been about to head out. A jazz combo, Phil Sudo and Annie Yoshikawa's friends, was playing at the Lizard Lounge, and I was supposed to meet them there. Yet Mirielle didn't want to go. She had not attended any of the 3AC potlucks since December, and she felt it would be awkward seeing Phil and Annie again with me.

"It'd be like we're double-dating," she said. "As if we're a couple."

"God forbid anyone would think we're a couple."

"We're not a couple."

"We're more of a couple than most people who have sex."

"We have a weird relationship," she conceded.

Another night, she was limp with exhaustion—she had been on her feet all day.

"Come here," I said. "I'll give you a foot massage."

"No. You're too nice to me."

"I know I am. Should I be meaner to you? Less nice?" I asked.

She shook her head in alarm. "That'd be disastrous."

Several nights later, we lay in bed. We had gone to see a film at the Kendall and then had eaten pizza at Emma's. "You're so quiet," she said.

"It gets to me sometimes. You know how I feel about you," I told her. "Do you think there's a chance things could ever become romantic between us again?"

"I don't know if I'm capable of feeling romantic with anyone right now."

I mulled this over in silence, dispirited.

"You hate me, don't you?" she said.

"No, I don't."

"I can tell by your face. You hate me."

"No, just the opposite, Mirielle."

The next week, Planned Parenthood contacted her. Her Pap smear had come back abnormal, and they wanted to schedule her for a biopsy. "Nothing I do makes a difference," she said. "Another job or another apartment or another city won't change anything— I'll still despise myself. This grad school thing is a pipe dream. And now I might have cancer."

I escorted her to Planned Parenthood, and then, on the morning she was to get the results, I waited for her to call me. She didn't. I left two messages for her at her office at Mount Auburn, but she didn't return them. Late in the afternoon, frantic she might have received terrible news from the pathologist, I finally reached her.

"Oh, it was nothing," she said. "I'm fine."

"Why didn't you call me?"

"It's just that I've been on the phone practically all day," she said. She was typing, then I overheard her talking to someone and laughing.

"Who was that?" I asked.

"No one. The new temp."

"We can talk later," I said.

"No, I can talk," she said, and continued to type.

"Well," I said.

"What?"

"If you're busy, we can catch up later."

"Okay," she said, and hung up.

The following night, when she slept over, I explained how worried I'd been about her the day before. "I always go into a tailspin when you do things like that," I said.

"Like what?"

"When you don't call me back."

"I don't *always* have to call you back," she said.

Throughout January and into February, we worked on her applications to MFA programs. I convinced Paviromo to write her a strong letter of recommendation, despite the B-minus she had received in his British poetry class, and I also persuaded a local poet I knew, Liam Rector, to add his own endorsement of Mirielle, even though they had never met. We revised and revised her personal statement, deliberating over whether she should delve into her former addictions. Eventually, we decided she should, since her writing sample was filled with recovery poems.

She read a new one to me about the sponsor, Alice, who had died. I tried to be encouraging.

"You don't like it," she said.

"No, I do."

"I can tell you don't."

"I think it's really powerful."

She was dejected, but then said, "Well, I think I should be proud of myself for at least sitting down and completing a first draft."

Joshua was more frank about the poem's merits, or lack thereof.

While we were watching the Celtics on TV, I showed him a copy of the poem. I still didn't trust my ability to judge poetry. Maybe I'm wrong, I thought.

"This is unadulterated crap," he told me. "Pure excreta. She actually said she's proud of herself? You see, she comes from the school of the emotionally crippled wherein they pat themselves on the back for accomplishing what people do as a matter of course. We come from the school where only national recognition will satisfy ambition, and that's the way it should be. What's this chick's appeal to you? I know she's pretty, but why are you so in love with her? Because you can't have her?"

"It's not that."

"What is it, then? You spend the night together, and what, nothing? No hand jobs, even? You don't touch each other at all?"

"I give her massages sometimes."

"You give her massages. Jesus, she's walking all over you. You're embarrassing yourself. What she wants is someone to support her and be a slave to her, and you happen to be available. Let's face it, she feels nothing for you. Either she puts out, or you get the fuck out. You're making a complete fool of yourself."

■   ■   ■

I lit candles. We slow-danced to Johnny Hartman. I gave her a massage. She was wearing her nightgown, lying on her stomach, and I straddled her ass while I kneaded her back.

"This is all very familiar," she said.

When I finished the massage, I lay down beside her. "Let's make love," I said.

"Are you crazy?"

"It's been almost two months."

"We're friends."

"Will you give me a kiss? Just one kiss?"

She pecked me on the cheek. "What's gotten into you tonight?" she asked.

"What's gotten into me? Look what we're doing. How am I supposed to feel?"

She got up and pulled on her jeans underneath her nightgown. "You know what you should do?" she said. "You should go out to a bar, have a few drinks, get loose, and pick up someone who'll fuck your brains out."

"I don't want to fuck anyone else. Why won't you make love with me?"

"To be honest," she said, "I don't know if I'll ever be able to have sex with you again."

"How come?"

"The closer I get to someone, the less I feel like having sex with him—whereas I could probably let some stranger fuck me twelve ways to Sunday."

"That doesn't make any sense, Mirielle. Why do you feel that way?"

"Because I can only have sex when it's degrading," she said.

■　■　■

"That was a mistake," Jessica told me. "You're not being sensitive to her at all. You should have gotten it by now. Pushing sex, even playfully, is going to upset her after her history."

"You're right."

"Honor her privacy. Don't make demands on her. Don't try to change her or pressure her. If you're there for her, she'll come around eventually."

"Joshua thinks I've been humiliating myself."

"He's just jealous. He'd love to see you guys break up so he can have you all to himself again. Can't you be patient?"

I apologized to Mirielle the next time we saw each other, which seemed to mollify her, but something was different. All of a sudden she was mysteriously busy on weekends, and there were fewer nights when she was able to sleep over, worn out or feeling sick or wanting to nest in her own room. More and more, her roommates would have to tell me that Mirielle wasn't home when I called. I'd leave messages for her with them, and still I wouldn't hear back from her. Sometimes she'd claim not to have received the notes, and I thought she was lying, just like when she would insist that she had called me back and had left a message on our answering machine, until Joshua confessed to me one night, "Oh, yeah, I forgot. I must have accidentally erased it," whereupon I installed a code and disabled the erase function on the machine.

She would say that she was on the run, could she call me back, then wouldn't. She would make plans to get together with me, then renege.

"You've been canceling on me a lot," I'd say.

"It's been a rough week," she'd say.

I knew full well what was going on, but I wanted it not to be true. She had gotten back together with David, or she had met someone new altogether. Someone older, with money, in AA. Someone who could relate to her in ways that I never could. A father figure.

I thought about her every moment of the day—wondering what she was doing, imagining her going on dates with anonymous men, having impersonal, degrading sex with them. I was in torment, yet I had such pity for her, for her horrible childhood, for being so sad. I wanted to continue seeing her somehow. I wanted to tell her that

I loved her, that I cared about her, that no matter what, we'd find a way to remain friends. I called to tell her all of this. She wasn't home. She didn't return my message.

In the morning, when she picked up the phone at her office, she was laughing, in the midst of a conversation with a coworker. She never laughed like that with me anymore. "Can I call you back?" she asked me.

"Will you promise to call tonight?"

"I don't know when I'll be home," she said.

"It doesn't matter. I'll be up late."

"Okay," she said.

She never called.

Three nights later, we met for dinner at Pho Pasteur. She was uneasy, nervous. At last, she said, "I have something to tell you. Something big."

"I know already," I said.

"You do?"

"You're seeing someone else."

She nodded. "I've been afraid to tell you."

"Who is he? Where'd you meet him?"

"At the office. He was a temp there."

"How long has it been going on?"

"A couple of weeks," she said. "I couldn't figure out how to tell you. I didn't want to lose you as a friend."

"So you tortured me instead."

"I should have told you. It's stupid I didn't."

"The worst part," I said, "is that you deceived me. You lied to me that you were busy or tired when really you were going off to see him. You only called me when you needed me for something."

"I'm sorry."

"Are you?"

"I'm disgusted with myself," Mirielle said. "I thought of killing myself last night."

"Don't do that," I said. "Don't make this into another excuse to feel sorry for yourself."

She took a folded check out of her purse. It was for the money I had lent her to buy her plane ticket to Tortola.

The waiter brought us the bill, and Mirielle and I split it down the middle—the first time I had ever let her pay for her share of a meal.

"Do you think we could stay friends?" she asked. "I'd like to."

"Is he white?"

"What?"

"Your new boyfriend."

She nodded.

"I knew it," I said. "A yellow cab."

"What?"

"All the crap about not wanting to jump into another relationship, how difficult it is for you to get close to people—it was all bullshit. It wasn't that at all. It's just that you didn't want to be in a relationship with *me*."

"Can't you be my friend?"

"I'm right, aren't I?"

She wouldn't look at me, stared down at the caddy of sriracha and hoisin sauce on the table.

"I never thought you were capable of something like this," I said. "I thought I knew you, but I guess I don't. You're a stranger to me," I told her. "You're a bad person, Mirielle."

Joshua was home, sitting in the dining room, eating sandwiches of pan-fried hot dogs, cheese, sauerkraut, and barbecue sauce on raisin bread, paired with a bottle of dolcetto.

"What the hell was I thinking the entire time?" I asked him. "What did I expect? I was a fucking fool. I was pathetic. How could I have been so blind, so fucking weak?"

"It's okay," he said.

"I'm sick of being such a fucking pussy. I'm *pathetic*."

"It'll be all right."

"How come you never fall in love, huh, Joshua? What are you? Totally heartless? Do you ever feel anything? Is there nothing inside?"

He stood up from the dining table. "Let it out, Eric. You want to hit me? Go ahead, hit me."

I sagged and began to mewl, and Joshua embraced me. "You're going to be okay," he said. "This will pass. Everything passes eventually."

"The fucking thing is," I said, "all I can think about right now is Mirielle, what she must be going through. I'm worried she might jump off a bridge. She must be so depressed tonight."

■   ■   ■

I waited months to deposit Mirielle's check. When I did, it was returned, the account closed, and the bank charged me a fee for the voided transaction.

14

Suddenly *Palaver* was flush with money. In the fall, Paviromo had had me spend weeks on an application for a new program sponsored by the Lila Wallace–*Reader's Digest* Fund (coming full circle with Mac's major donor), and in February, we were miraculously bestowed a grant for $100,000, almost double our entire annual operating budget. I got a bump in salary. We bought new computers, and I was able to appoint a part-time office manager to assist me, Sandra Tran, a graphic designer in the 3AC who had previously worked at *Granta*. (Despite her qualifications, Paviromo was initially wary of hiring her, no doubt thinking that having one Asian in the office was good for the diversity checklist, but having two might be an Asian invasion.)

The two-year program was for audience development, or, in plainer terms, marketing, and involved fifteen magazines. It was an experiment of sorts. The Lila Wallace foundation wanted to see if literary journals, given the resources and the know-how, could actually find readers. They hired a group of professional magazine consultants to educate us at a series of seminars. Yet at the first panel session in San Francisco, it became clear that the consultants might need some educating themselves.

"Why do you print in this format and not in standard trim size?" one of them, Lester Dillenbeck, asked. He picked up a trade paperback journal from the stack on the table and thumbed through it. "There's just so much *text*."

The program allowed two people from each magazine to attend the seminars, and Paviromo accompanied me to the first one, but only the first, too exasperated with these "philistines" and "charlatans" and "apparatchiks" to return. "Do you recall James Carville's famous slogan during the '92 campaign, 'It's the economy, stupid'?" he said to the consultants. "Well, in our field of endeavor, quaint and stuffy and bizarre as it may seem to you, it's what we print that is paramount, indeed sacrosanct"—and here he paused and stared directly at Dillenbeck—"stupid."

Paviromo liked the money we were receiving and the possibility that *Palaver* might gain a wider audience, but he didn't really want to change anything or do any work himself, and he couldn't have cared less about the nuts and bolts of the program. He left all the details to me.

I threw myself into the project. I began to learn the lingua franca of marketing, which was strangely fetishized, creeping into the realm of BDSM, with terms like *bind-ins* and *blow-ins*, *branding* and *penetration*. I was assigned two consultants, Dillenbeck and another fellow named Ryan Hickel, and they came up with a plan. They decided that the Fiction Discoveries issue was an ideal marketing opportunity. They wanted me to embark on a subscription acquisition campaign—more commonly known as direct mail—and coincide the drop date with the issue's publication in June.

My period of leisure was over. My novella would have to wait. I taught myself how to do projections and budgets on spreadsheets, segment lists on a relational database, and put together RFPs and consolidate bids. I was busier than I had ever been in my life, in the shithole until late every night, working on weekends as well, but, still hurting over Mirielle, I was grateful for the distraction, and I was even, to my surprise and embarrassment, sort of enjoying myself. I was learning things, getting things done. The work was tangible. You set goals, deadlines, and there was an end result. I realized I had an aptitude for number-crunching and strategic planning, and, for the first time, I felt like a grown-up.

At Filene's Basement, I bought a blue blazer, khaki trousers, wingtips, and a couple of button-downs and ties, in addition to a rollerboard. I took the US Airways shuttle to D.C. for the next seminar, spending three nights at the Marriott, not far from the Capitol, where the Senate was wrapping up Clinton's impeachment hearing. When I got back to Cambridge, Joshua took a gander at me in my outfit, wheeling my rollerboard behind me, and said, "Dude, what is *happening* to you? What are you turning *into*?"

Since I was working much of the time, Joshua had been hanging out with Jimmy Fung, whose business at Pink Whistle had flourished for a while, largely due to the 3AC's extended network. The thing about Jimmy was that he knew Asian hair, which was different from Caucasian hair—thicker, heavier, coarser, harder to cut, more prone to cowlicks. Moreover, like Asian faces, the backs of Asian heads were broader and flatter, and needed extra volume. When Asian hair was cropped ineptly, every mistake was magnified. After childhoods of mothers giving us bobs and bowl haircuts with square bangs (the China doll, the Caesar, the Cleopatra, the Stooge), after being butchered at salons with white hairdressers, it was a relief for Asians to find someone like Jimmy, who used texturizing scissors and razors to chop off some of the bulk before styling, then could layer and shape and soften the hair so it was feathery and light, so it fit the face and skull, so it had some brio and élan. "You have to conceive it like art," he would say. "It's like doing sculpture."

Jimmy was, actually, very good at what he did. Clients came in, asking him to replicate the styles of Asian pop and movie stars, and he could readily turn them into Faye Wong (*Chungking Express*), Norika Fujiwara (*CanCam* model), or Chow Yun-Fat (the coolest actor in the world). I myself got my hair cut by Jimmy at Pink Whistle, partial to the Yun-Fat.

For several months, the place was hopping. Jimmy renovated Pink Whistle, making the interior slick and flashy, with several TVs continuously playing music videos, Cantopop blaring all day long. He hired another stylist, a colorist, and a manicurist. But then things took a downturn. Clients failed to return, and new ones weren't materializing. He had to fire all his help and now worked alone again. The problem was, Jimmy Fung—ever the hustler—was also a lecher. He kept hitting on his female clients, as well as his staff.

"He's an inveterate sleazebag, isn't he?" I said to Joshua.

Joshua, who had been acting as Jimmy's *pro tempore* advisor, said, "He's not so bad."

Only guys continued going to Pink Whistle, lured in by the increasingly salacious videos, but men's haircuts weren't nearly as profitable as perms, body waves, color treatments, and highlights. Jimmy was in trouble. He had overextended himself with the renovations, for which, Joshua told me, he had borrowed money from a less than savory source. Jimmy was trying to think of what else he could do to bring in more income.

I went into Pink Whistle for a trim one day, and noticed a change. There was a girl in the salon—a very young Asian girl, possibly only sixteen or so. She was wearing a spaghetti-strap tank top and tight capri pants, and she was feather-dusting the bottles on the shelves.

"Is Jimmy here?" I asked. "I have an appointment for a haircut."

She was pretty, although her appeal might have been that she was so young, and therefore illicit. Normally I would have censured this kind of pedophiliac impulse, the mere thought of it, but she was staring at me in an openly provocative way, eyes unwavering. They were dead eyes, though—disdainful, sullen.

"Jimmy come back fifteen minute," the girl said, her voice nasal and grating. "You want shampoo?"

"I'll just come back later."

"I give you shampoo!" she shouted shrilly.

I sat down in the chair. She wrapped a vinyl cape around my neck, attaching the Velcro much too tightly, yet I was too cowed to complain. I leaned my head back into the basin, nestling my neck into the curved cradle, and she sprayed water (much too hot, but again I kept quiet) onto my hair, then lathered it up, leaning over me, her arms squeezing her breasts—not large, but perfectly contoured—together so they distended and contracted inches from my face. She was rough, raking her fingers against my scalp, yanking on my hair. I doubted she had had any professional training as a shampooist at all.

"You want massage?" she asked me as she rinsed. "I give you massage."

I thought she meant a scalp treatment, one that would undoubtedly require paying for an expensive oil or conditioner. "No, thanks, that's all right," I said.

"I give you massage!"

"No! Thank you, but no."

"Why no massage? You gay? You like boy?"

Then I began to comprehend what was going on. Sitting in the stylist chair while I waited for Jimmy, I looked up at the mirror and saw a new sign Scotch-taped to the top corner: *Pink Whistle special massages now available. Many varieties. Fifteen minutes, half hour, full hour.*

By the time Jimmy returned, my hair was already dry. The girl had sat in the room with me for a while, slapping aside pages in a magazine, occasionally glaring at me, then had disappeared into Pink Whistle's antiques store/art gallery section.

"Hey, man, sorry about that," Jimmy said, spritzing water onto my hair. "I was sitting in the Dolphin, getting lunch, and I was having a coffee, thinking, Man, the day's going so slowly. Then I realized my watch had stopped. Believe that? It's a fucking Rolex. Okay, it's a knockoff Rolex, but a good one. It's lasted me years."

"You got it in Hong Kong?"

"What? No. New York, mate. Canal Street."

He clipped away at my hair, tousling strands and switching between the scissors, shears, and razor. "The girl washed your hair?" he asked. "Yeah, course she did. Don't expect you did it yourself." He had on a vintage paisley shirt, unbuttoned nearly to his navel, dzi beads dangling from his neck. He was the only one among our group who had gotten a 3AC tattoo, on his upper left arm, just like Joshua's. "What'd you think of her?"

"She's Chinese?" I asked.

"Thai."

That figured. "I don't know, seems competent enough."

He snipped and whittled. "You're not going out with anyone right now, are you?" he asked near the end of the haircut. "You and Mirielle broke up, right?"

"Almost a month ago."

"You haven't hooked up with anyone else?"

"No," I said. Then I added, ridiculously, maybe out of machismo, "Been too busy."

"Understandable, understandable. What do you do again? A science magazine, is it?"

"Literary journal."

"Right, right. As I was saying, a lot of guys I know are in the same position, too jammed to even breathe these days. Can't stop to take a goddamn break and relax for one minute, am I right?"

"I guess so."

He flipped a can of mousse up into the air and deftly caught it nozzle-down, oozed out a dollop onto his comb, and threaded it through my hair. "So I bet a soothing massage would be just the ticket, right? I'm trying to build word of mouth, you know, so how about I give you a massage on the house?"

"I don't really need a massage."

"No? You sure? You seem *tense*, mate. Think about it. On the house. I converted the old office in back for privacy. I'm telling you, the girl's got some talent, mate."

■ ■ ■

In his attic room, Joshua plunked on a *geomungo*, a six-stringed zither usually reserved for Korean folk songs, that he had been teaching himself how to play. He was trying to accompany Hendrix's "Little Wing" with the instrument—not very successfully.

"It was your idea, wasn't it?" I said to him.

"What? What'd I do now?"

"The 'massages' at Pink Whistle."

"I don't want to take all the credit, but I might've mentioned to Jimmy that they could be a boon to his business." He was wearing a tie-dyed T-shirt and a traditional Korean *gat*, a black, wide-brimmed, cylindrical hat made of horsehair. "What, you didn't like the girl?"

"You guys think this is a lark, a game," I said, "but it could land Jimmy in jail. You, too, if you're getting a cut of the action."

Joshua put Hendrix on pause. "What the hell are you talking about?"

I looked at the piles of books on the floor, the strewn clothes and CDs, the pig piñata dangling from the ceiling and the collection of swine postcards on the bulletin board. "You and your fucking prostitutes."

"You think she's a prostitute?"

"Obviously she is."

"Is it because she's Thai or because she's a masseuse that makes you assume that?" he asked. "Because they're equally dim-witted, loathsome stereotypes."

"Come on, you're actually going to deny it?"

"She's a licensed massage therapist. She's a health professional. Just because she's a masseuse and/or from Thailand does not make her a sex worker."

"Is she in the country legally?"

"She must be if she got licensed."

"How old is she?" I said. "She can't be more than sixteen."

"Nineteen. She's nineteen."

"That's been verified?"

"What are you asking me for? I don't have a stake in this. But yeah, Jimmy says he checked it out."

"Like he's such a trustworthy source."

"What is your problem?" Joshua said. "I'm telling you, it's on the up and up. Don't worry about it. What's it got to do with you, anyway?"

As it happened, it would have a lot to do with me, for when I got back from another seminar in New York several weeks later, I walked into the second-floor bathroom of the Walker Street house and barged in not on Jessica, but on the young Thai girl. She wasn't naked, at least, but she was in a somewhat compromising position, sitting on the toilet with her skirt and underwear bunched at her ankles. "*Pai hai pon!*" she screamed at me, hunching over.

"Oh," Joshua said. "She got kicked out of the place she was living in, and Jimmy asked if she could sack out on the couch here for a while."

"How long is a while?"

"I don't know, a few days, I guess."

"Why can't she just stay with Jimmy?" I asked, although I assumed that he'd been sleeping with the girl all along and it'd gotten messy somehow.

"Jimmy's got a new girlfriend," Joshua told me.

"Who? Not anyone from the collective." After Marietta Liu and Danielle Awano, after his shenanigans at Pink Whistle with his staff and clients, Jimmy was persona non grata with the 3AC women.

"Naw, some random chick he met at the Toad," Joshua said. "Hey, where you *been*, man? You're never around anymore. You've disappeared on me. First it was Mirielle, now these *business* trips."

"You didn't think to run this by me first?"

"What?"

"The girl staying here."

Joshua cocked his head to the side. "I know we operate like this is a co-op, but it's not really a co-op, is it?"

"You're fucking her, aren't you?" I said.

"No way. I have some scruples. I don't partake in jailbait."

"I thought you said she's nineteen."

"She is!" Joshua said. "What is this? The only times I see you, you just rag on me."

I was short-tempered with nearly everyone those days, overworked and stressed out and more than a little depressed. Yet Joshua in particular nettled me. All of his antics and tirades and lectures and riffs had become tiresome. Everything I used to admire about him now seemed fatuous. He did nothing all day but attend to his whims. He needed to grow up.

"You swear this is aboveboard?" I asked.

"Yeah," he said. "You see, the thing is, I don't think the girl likes me very much. In fact, I don't think she likes *men* very much. She likes Jessica, though. She seems infatuated with her, actually. Keeps following her around like a newborn pup."

"What's she have to say about this?"

"Jessica? She's fine with it. She doesn't care. She doesn't seem to care about anything anymore. Have you talked to her lately?"

Jessica was home less than I was. She had tacked on a fourth job, teaching a beginning painting class at Martinique College of Art as a last-minute replacement for the spring semester, hired on the recommendation of a former RISD professor. Two mornings a week, she would borrow Joshua's Peugeot and drive up to Beverly to teach, then would rush back to town for her other jobs. The schedule was taking its toll. She was often sick, and she looked terrible—thin and wan.

"Is there any way you could back out of the class now?" I asked her. "The pay's not really worth the commute, is it?"

"That's not the point," Jessica said. "I'm trying to ingratiate myself so maybe I'll be able to teach there full-time someday or get a tenure-track job somewhere else. I can't string along these part-time gigs forever. They're killing me. I need to build up my CV."

"How's the installation coming along?"

"You had to ask, didn't you?"

She had yet to start work on her one-woman show sponsored by the Cambridge Arts Council. The exhibit was scheduled to be shown on the second floor of the City Hall Annex, beginning on May 7, for three weeks. It was almost the end of March.

Nothing had gone right for her this winter. The Creiger-Dane and DNA galleries, after teasing Jessica repeatedly with promises to include her in group shows, passed in the end. She was turned

down for every grant and fellowship she applied to. She was delin-
quent on her student loans. The IRS had nailed her for not paying
self-employment tax on an independent contractor job three years
ago in New York, and she now owed five hundred in back taxes and
interest, plus an additional fifteen hundred in penalties. Her carpal
tunnel was flaring up, and she was back to wearing wrist braces
while she slept. She'd had a panic attack one day in Bread & Circus, and a shopper had called 911; a phalanx of emergency vehicles
had converged on the grocery store, exacerbating the attack even
further, and Jessica had to be hospitalized overnight. And, most
devastating to her, more than I could have ever imagined, she had
been undone, waylaid into dark submission, weeping in her room
for days, when Esther had left her.

Jessica had had an inkling something was amiss when all of a sudden Esther was not home when she was supposed to be and didn't
return her messages right away, when she was mysteriously busy on
weekends, when they spent fewer and fewer nights together, Esther
saying she was tired or coming down with something. Eventually
Jessica forced her to come clean. "It's another woman, isn't it?" she
asked. "Not exactly," Esther said, then revealed that she had fallen
in love with a Strategic Studies Fellow at Harvard's Olin Institute
named Jon Stiegel.

The Tuesday Nighters never met again, and in short order—
and not without coincidence, in my view—the 3AC began to lose
its fervor and energy. The main problem, actually, arose with the
preliminary plans for our website, or, more specifically, the notion
that we needed a manifesto, a formal mission statement, to post
on it.

First, we affirmed that the 3AC was a not-for-profit organization devoted to the creation, celebration, and dissemination of art
by Asian Americans. Simple enough. But then Andy Kim said we

should specify art by *young* Asian Americans, since we wanted to accentuate the hip, the new, not the traditional, and Phil Sudo said that would be ageist, and Annie Yoshikawa said *young* made it sound like the 3AC was an after-school program for kids, so we changed it to *modern*, but that word had narrow critical associations, so we settled on *contemporary*.

We wanted to emphasize the importance of these Sunday night gatherings on Walker Street, so we added that the 3AC was also devoted to creating a foundation to gather and exchange ideas and experiences, but *creating* was repetitious because we already had *creation*, so we changed it to *building*, and *foundation* was stodgy and made it appear that we were a philanthropic organization, so we changed it to *network*, and then, because *network* was too geeky and wonkish and corporate, we changed it to *community*, and we added that we exchanged resources and information as well. But then Trudy Lun thought this might come off as too insular and cliquey, since we were trying to reach out and disseminate, so we attached a clause that we promoted the intersections between art and audience.

Yet we wanted, too, to declare our commitment to social change, so we modified that to intersections between art, audience, *and activism*, and asserted that we were dedicated to subverting stereotypes, then decided we should also say we were confronting prejudice and discrimination and oppression against Asian Americans through our art, but scratched the last phrase, since it was something we were trying to do in all facets of our lives, not just through our art, and then we agreed we should also remove *Asian Americans* there, because weren't we opposed to the oppression of any group? But then Grace Kwok wondered if this might jeopardize our future 501(c)3 application, since the IRS had restrictions on giving tax-exempt status to organizations that were involved in political campaigns or lobbying, and we thought of deleting the entire sentence, but Joshua said fuck it, this is who we are and what we're trying to accomplish.

Cindy Wong said she wanted *synergy, empowerment,* and *coalition* somewhere in the statement, and Phil threw in *diasporic,* all of which we liked, but we couldn't find a place for them. We went back to *exchanging ideas, experiences, resources, and information* because Jay Chi-Ming Lai said the connotation there was still primarily about networking, even though we'd expunged *network,* and that wasn't all we espoused, so we put in that the 3AC was devoted—was there another word? I asked. We'd already used *devoted* twice, along with *committed* and *dedicated*—maybe *faithful,* no, *believed in,* no, *entrusted with,* definitely not—we'd fix it later—devoted to nurturing artistic expression. But what about the collaborative nature of the 3AC? Danielle Awano asked, so we inserted *collaborative,* but then Jessica objected, since it might seem our art projects were produced jointly as a group, so we changed it to *individual and collaborative,* and then Jimmy said we needed to highlight how many different types of artists comprised the 3AC, so we slid in *multidisciplinary.*

We had yet to clarify who our target audience was, Sandra Tran reminded us, who our constituents were, and we wrote down that we sought to engage with other Asian Americans, then had to stipulate on a local, statewide, national, and international level, then reconsidered, since what we really wanted to do was engage with people of all racial, socioeconomic, generational, and ethnic strata, don't forget genders and sexualities and political affiliations, too, so, unable to come up with a solution, we deleted the entire sentence this time, and replaced it with another that said that we sought to build—no, already used it, I said—*foster* solidarity with other communities of color, or should that be *all* communities of color, but why just *of color,* it should extend to everyone, be more encompassing, so we ended the line, as a compromise, with all communities of color *and beyond*.

The acronym 3AC troubled Leon Lee. It was familiar shorthand to us, the phrase we all used, and it was catchy, in-the-know, hip, but wasn't a fundamental principle of organizational marketing to have the name plainly advertise its purpose? We spelled out *Asian American* (hyphen? categorically no hyphen?) *Artists* (apostrophe or no apostrophe? singular or plural possessive?) *Collective, known as the* (cap or lowercase article?) *3AC* (space after the number? periods after the letters?).

The real contretemps began when Joshua returned to the original statement, *art by contemporary Asian Americans.*

"Listen, we should specify that it's art by and *about* contemporary Asian Americans," he said.

I could feel the room curdle.

Although Esther Xing was no longer part of the collective, everyone had heard about my dispute with her, thanks to Rick Wakamatsu and Ali Ong, who now seemed to reveal themselves as converts to Xingism.

"I've been thinking about this a lot," Rick said, "especially pertaining to the goals for my own fiction. At a certain point, if we keep rehashing the same themes, always writing about being Asian, it's going to get stale."

"So what?" Joshua asked. "Faulkner said every writer has just one story to tell. It's all in the telling."

"It's just that all this race stuff is starting to come off as, well, *whining*," Rick said. "Know what I mean?"

"Maybe it's time to move on," Ali said. "That's exactly what I've been thinking of doing with my next story."

"How many stories have you published, Ali?" Joshua asked.

Startled, she said, "None."

"You, Rick?"

He shrugged, embarrassed.

"Uh-huh," Joshua said. "I'm glad we can rely on your combined authority and experience to make such pronouncements."

"Hey," Jessica said, "that's a little harsh."

Joshua launched into a peroration about being true to one's race, about not playing into the hands of the WSCP, the White Supremacist Capitalist Patriarchy. We'd heard it all before. As much as I agreed with him—more than ever, in fact—I meditated on how monotonous Joshua had become, with a limited reservoir of ideas, some of which he borrowed without attribution, e.g., bell hooks's WSCP. Nonetheless, it was hard for the group not to be swayed by him. He was the incontestable founder of the 3AC. After all, it was his house, therefore his rules.

There was a general though tepid consensus that we could stick in *and about* after *by*, but then we had to pull *contemporary*, since sometimes we might want to address historical Asia or Asian America. This started a tiff about whether we were being too provincial. If we were going to reference Asia, Jay said, we should include Asian Asians, not just Asian Americans, so we changed it to say *art by and about Asians and Asian Americans.*

Then another squabble emerged. What did we mean by *Asian Americans?* Annie asked. We should be specific and say *Asian Pacific Americans,* Cindy said. But instead of APA, shouldn't it be APIA, *Asian Pacific Islander Americans?* Leon wondered. What about splitting the difference, Andy suggested, and using AAPI, *Asian Americans and Pacific Islanders?* But it would confuse the geographic origins further, I said, and by the same token—sorry, a slip of the tongue—what would we then call Asians who were foreigners—no, that had become a pejorative term—okay, nationals? Would we have to enunciate *art by and about Asian Pacific*

Islanders and Asian Pacific Islander Americans? That would be very clunky. What about the biracial among us, or those who were multiracial? Danielle asked. Would we have to adopt a one-drop rule?

Then Trudy mentioned South Asians. Shouldn't we include them, too? This led to a skirmish about what *Asian* meant. There was no question that Southeast Asians qualified, even though many were Muslim, so weren't Pakistanis and Indians and Bangladeshis eligible?

"Russia is technically in the continent of Asia," Joshua said. "Why not include Russians, too? Hey, man, let's include everybody! Let *anyone* in! We can be one big happy multifucking family!"

Five Sunday nights in a row, and we never were able to finish the mission statement, which was revised, elided, diluted, dumbed, appended, particularized, and parentheticalized into incoherence. Slaughtered by committee. After that, fewer people showed up for the meetings. Rick Wakamatsu and Ali Ong dropped out altogether.

We would never fulfill any of our grand ambitions to sponsor exhibitions, showcases, or publications. Although the 3AC would persist as an ersatz organization for seven more years, with the Sunday potlucks rotating to various members' apartments, and although many of us would remain close friends, the 3AC's activities would recede into just holding parties, playing poker and charades, singing karaoke, and watching Wong Kar-wai films.

Maybe everything that happened with the 3AC was Joshua's fault, or even mine, but I would always resent Esther Xing's intrusion, however brief, into our cozy little collective. She introduced the first kernels of division into the 3AC, and I would forever wish I could blame her for its eventual demise.

In early April, Jessica finalized the concept for her installation, which she would be calling *Dis/Orienting Proportions*, and she said she would need my help for the project. As she detailed what she required of me, I was certain she was joking.

"Funny," I said. "Anything to eat in the house?" I had just returned from a two-day road trip to Vermont, meeting with the list broker for our direct-mail campaign in Rutland and the CSRs at our printer/lettershop in Essex.

"It's not a joke," Jessica said. "If you do this for me, I'll buy you dinner at the B-Side."

"It'd take a lot more than that. Are you really serious?"

"Yes."

"You've gone completely off the deep end, haven't you?"

"Maybe," she said. "I think it's going to be great, though. I got the idea after seeing *W.R.: Mysteries of the Organism* at the Film Archive the other day. Will you do it?"

"Absolutely not."

"You have to. Who else am I going to ask? Jimmy Fung?" she asked.

"I'm sure he'd be willing."

"Too willing."

"Exactly. No one but someone like Jimmy would do it."

"Joshua did," she said.

My imagination reeled with lurid scenarios. "When?" I asked, subsumed with jealousy.

"Last night," Jessica said. "I just need one more. It's not a big deal. It's kind of clinical, the whole procedure."

"I don't think anyone would ever compare it to a simple doctor's visit. Not by a long shot. It's kind of sick, to be frank. It's fucking weird and totally depraved, actually. Can't you see that?"

She couldn't, and after I made us a quick dinner of linguine with shredded zucchini, onions, garlic, chopped walnuts, and parmesan, during which Jessica badgered me continuously, I consented, mainly because I wanted to know precisely what she had done with Joshua.

"Where is Joshua, anyway?" I asked.

"He went to a rave in Northampton. He took the girl with him."

"Like on a date? That fucking asshole. I knew it wouldn't stay innocent for long. She was only supposed to be here a couple of days."

"They went with Jimmy. They won't be back until morning."

"Convenient," I said.

"She keeps stealing my clothes."

"Joshua thinks she's infatuated with you."

"Or it could be that we're the same size and she likes my taste and she's a thief." After we finished washing the dishes, Jessica said, "There's something I need you to do first."

"What?"

"Shave."

"Shave?" Instinctually I rubbed the stubble on my chin.

"Your pubic hair."

This was a mistake—a terrible mistake. "All of it?"

"All of it. Your balls, too."

"How can I shave my balls? Don't I need to get them waxed or something?" I asked, although waxing seemed a more painful alternative.

"I'll shave them for you, if you want."

"Have you gotten into S&M? Is that it? You're getting off now by cutting people?"

I opted to do it myself, although Jessica insisted on standing outside the bathroom door, shouting instructions. First I sat on the toilet and trimmed my pubic hair with scissors ("Crop it as close as you can!"). Then I took a hot shower ("Really steam up the room! You want to soften up the skin and relax the follicles"). Then I had to exfoliate with a cleanser and a washcloth ("That'll get rid of dead skin cells"). Next, I dabbed on some shaving oil, keeping my skin damp ("It'll make the razor glide better and prevent razor burn"), and used a brush to apply a special cream called Brave Soldier Brave Shave, which had been originally formulated for bicyclists, swimmers, and bodybuilders, but which was now favored for extracurricular body shaving ("Work the brush in circles!").

Jessica had given me a new pivoting razor, and, staring at the three sharp blades, I hesitated, questioning the rationality of this entire project, especially my participation in it. I stood in the tub and began with the easiest area, above and around the shaft ("Pull the skin taut and go in the direction of growth! Keep rinsing the blades! You don't want to clog them up"). The scariest part was my testicles ("Just go slowly! Use this!" she said, and slid a small hand mirror underneath the door, the lock on which I had thankfully fixed three weeks ago). I had never noticed how wrinkly and ugly the skin of my scrotum was. I had never, actually, really looked at my scrotum.

It took forever, but finally I finished, somehow managing not to nick or cut myself ("Now rinse and pat it dry and put that moisturizer on!"). I climbed onto the edge of the tub and examined my newly bared genitalia in the mirror above the sink. It was, I had to say, a very clean look, even a good look—everything pristine, and seemingly larger.

I came out of the bathroom with a towel around my waist. Jessica stood waiting for me in her ratty white silk robe. "Why are you in that?" I asked.

"You might need some inspiration," she said.

"This is getting too kinky for me," I told her. "You said it'd be almost clinical. Can't I just do it myself?"

"It's very complicated stuff."

"You could shout instructions to me like just now."

"Just come in my room. It'll be over in ten minutes."

There was plastic sheeting spread over the floor. Jessica had fashioned a work table with a piece of plywood and two sawhorses, and on it was a small combo TV/VCR, a bunch of disposable containers and stirrers, scissors, a kitchen timer, duct tape, measuring cups, and a glass bowl with water in it. On her bed were some porn magazines (*Barely Legal, Stuffed, Asian Climax*) and porn videos (*Doin' the Ritz, New Wave Hookers 5, Fresh Meat 4*). Scattered underneath the table were various boxes that were labeled Casting Willy, Create-a-Mate, Clone-a-Willy, Clone-a-Pussy.

"You're going to use one of those kits?" I asked.

"No, I experimented with them, but I figured out a better way to do it," Jessica said. "Okay, let me see."

Reluctantly, I undid my towel, and she cranked a gooseneck lamp into position for an up-close-and-personal appraisal, getting on her knees to stare at my genitals. "Not bad, not bad," she said. She lifted my cock to look at the underside, and I became half aroused. "But you missed a few spots." She grabbed a razor and pulled on the stray pubes for a dry shave—no oil or cream.

"Hey, careful!" I said.

"Don't worry," she said, shifting and twisting my penis and testes this way and that for a thorough inspection. "You know, you have a very nice penis."

"Thanks," I said. What else could I say?

She plugged in an immersion coil—one of those cheap contraptions to heat up a cup of coffee—and stuck it into the water in the glass bowl. She held up the magazines and videos. "Any preference?"

"No."

She popped *New Wave Hookers 5* into the VCR. "You want a

magazine, too? This is a two-part operation. I have to do a fitting first, so I need you to get fully erect for just a minute, then you can relax for a while. Feel free to beat off. Don't mind me."

"This is impossible," I said. "I can't get a hard-on at will."

"No? You had no problem the night you walked in on me in the bathroom." She sighed and took off her robe, under which she was nude, and waited for further developments. "Okay, that seemed to do the trick."

In spite of her recent weight loss, her body verging on gaunt, no longer hard-yogaed, Jessica remained incontrovertibly attractive to me.

She shot close-ups of my penis with a macro lens and a flash from every angle.

"You're going to give me all the prints and negatives when you're done, right?" I asked.

"I'm not shooting your face. Who's going to be able to tell it's your penis? I hate to disillusion you, but all penises look pretty much alike."

"Is that a yes or a no on the prints and negs?"

"Yes."

"No one will ever know?" I asked. "You'll never tell anyone?"

"I already promised." She took what appeared to be a clear plastic report cover and rolled it into a tube. "Is this fully erect for you, or do you still have a ways more to go?"

"This is essentially it," I said, betraying some deflation of ego.

"That wasn't a value judgment. I was just asking. You're pretty big."

She manipulated the tube, enfolding my erection and balls. "How big?" I asked.

"Oh, come on."

"Bigger than Joshua?"

"I'm not falling for this."

"Bigger than Loki?"

"This is exactly what my installation's going to be about, these kinds of insecurities." She cinched the width of the cylinder with duct tape, marked it up with a Sharpie, and removed the tube.

Over the table, she cut the tube with scissors, snipping curves on the bottom end and a triangle on the top end. She then capped the upper opening with a section of rubber and tape and checked the fit on me. The tube slotted over the shaft of my penis and had a flap that went under my scrotum and between my legs. She made a couple of more cuts on the tube, measured the temperature of the water in the bowl with an oven thermometer, unplugged the immersion coil, and turned around.

"We're flagging a little," she said, looking at my wilting erection. "Once I mix this stuff, we have to go really quickly, and I'm going to need you to be absolutely still and maintain a full erection for at least four minutes." She inserted another video, *Fresh Meat 4*, into the VCR and laid the *Asian Climax* magazine open on the table. "Do you think you can do that?"

"I'm not sure."

She walked over and began fondling me.

I put my hands on the small of Jessica's back and drew her to me and tried to kiss her.

"No," she said. "This isn't sexual."

"How's it not sexual? Everything about this is sexual."

"I can't have sex with you. I can't go into those emotions." She squatted down and took me in her mouth.

"Jesus," I said. "Jessica."

She worked her head back and forth, her tongue stud rubbing the underside of my penis.

"Maybe Bill Clinton wouldn't define this as having sexual relations, but I do." I should have been elated—fulfilling multiple fantasies I'd entertained for years—but it didn't seem right, or really even erotic. It felt, as Jessica had posited, clinical.

She said nothing, concentrating on the task at hand.

"Did you do this with Joshua?"

"No," she said, taking a breath.

Once I was rigid, she applied a rubber cock ring around the base of my penis, behind my testicles, cutting off the circulation and making me harder.

"Is that too tight?" she asked.

"Where'd you get this? How the hell do you know about these things?"

She snapped on a pair of vinyl gloves and mixed alginate powder with the water, which was precisely at ninety-eight degrees, in a disposable tub. The alginate, she told me, was usually used by dentists to make impressions of teeth.

"Did you give Joshua a hand job?"

"No," she said, stirring robustly. "He didn't need any encouragement."

"Were you naked with him?"

"No," she said.

"Have you ever fucked Joshua?"

"For God's sake, *no*, all right? I've never jacked him off or kissed him or done anything with him," she said. "What is this thing you have with Joshua?"

She had me hold the tube around my penis with both hands while she poured the pink alginate into the triangular hole she had clipped. The mixture was soft, wet, warm. It oozed down the tube, enveloping my cock, and pooled around my balls, then seeped between my legs and down my thighs and dripped onto the plastic sheeting on the floor in clots.

"Can you move around a little?" Jessica asked. "Just a little. Like you're doing a shimmy. But keep the tube in place. I want to get rid of any air pockets. Otherwise we'll have to do this again."

She pulled out a woman's vibrator from a drawer and turned it on, and I felt a wave of momentary panic, thinking she had nefarious intentions for it, like lodging it into my anus to create an internal shimmy, or purely to attach an evil, twisted subtext to the whole endeavor in the name of art. But she simply held it against the tube in various spots, letting it clatter, plastic to plastic, to rid the alginate of microscopic bubbles. She set the kitchen timer for three minutes. "You're not losing your erection, are you?" she asked. "Is there something you want me to do?"

I wanted to touch her. I wanted to kiss her. I wanted to make love to her. "I'm okay," I said.

When the timer dinged, there was an unexpected problem. I couldn't get out of the tube. Jessica snipped off the rubber cock ring, put her robe back on, turned off the TV, and tucked the magazines away, yet I stayed priapic. "Can't you get it to go down? Just shrink out of it."

"It's not a voluntary thing," I said. "I can't mentally switch it on and off."

"Such a mysterious organ."

The alginate had gotten cold and firm, and I stood there, holding the tube, my legs cramping, Jessica waiting for me anxiously. At last, after a few minutes, I was limp enough to extricate myself.

"Gently, gently," Jessica said. She tipped the tube up and looked inside at the mold of my penis and balls.

"I'm not doing this again," I told her, wiping myself with the towel and the bucket of water she had set aside for me.

"I don't think you'll have to. It looks pretty good," she said. "Here. Rub this on if you start getting itchy the next few days."

I covered my groin with the towel with my left hand, and with my right I accepted the small tube of cortisone cream.

"You see, that wasn't so bad, was it?" she said.

■　■　■

Her name was Noklek Praphasirirat. Once she had moved from the couch in the living room to the master bedroom, which had its own bathroom, she was hardly visible. Sometimes I would forget she was staying in the house. She didn't interact with us at all, never talked to us or ate with us. I never saw her in the kitchen. I didn't know what she did for meals. She didn't keep food in the refrigerator. It didn't seem she used the washing machine or the dryer in the basement, either. She never made a sound. Perhaps she did everything in the dead of night, when we were all asleep.

The only conversation of substance I had with her was in mid-April, when I came home from work just before twilight and, through the sliding glass door, saw her on the back deck. She had gotten her hair chopped off. It was now spiky and streaked, just like Jessica's. She was also, it appeared, wearing a pair of Jessica's cargo pants.

She had assembled a shrine on the deck—three small Buddhas, one brass, one stone, one faux-marble, surrounded by candles, incense, two vases of flowers, and framed photos of a Buddha and of a man, woman, and girl. She was kneeling in front of the shrine in a posture of prayer.

"I'm sorry," I said. "I didn't mean to disturb you."

"You sit?" she said. "You pray with me?"

I knelt down beside her. It seemed disrespectful not to.

"This my father, mother, sister," she said. "This Gautama."

Noklek lit the candle on the right side of the Buddhas, then the candle on the left, followed by three incense sticks. She sat stiffly upright, her palms pressed together, then bowed down, forehead on the redwood boards, and I followed suit. She chanted, *"Annicā vata sankhārā, uppāda vaya dhammino. Uuppajjitvā nirujjhanti tesam vūpasamo sukho,"* and bowed three more times.

She pulled out a folded piece of paper from her pants pocket. "Your mother, father alive?" she asked.

"Yes."

"You have brother, sister?"

"One older sister."

"You love sister?"

"I suppose so," I said, "even though she represents every bourgeois SoCal value that I despise. Southern California—that's where I'm from originally."

"My home, very far. Chiang Mai. You know Chiang Mai?"

"In Thailand, right?"

"Yes. Thailand."

"Do you miss it?"

"Miss, no miss, no different. I no go home. This my home now. My sister dead. My father, mother dead. Everybody dead. This paper, my sister, father, mother name, my family name, ancestor name."

I wondered how and when everyone had died. In her photograph, her sister was in a school uniform and looked no more than ten years old. The photographs of her parents seemed to have been taken a long time ago, when they were still in their late twenties. No one was smiling. They were rather grim black-and-white portraits, formal head shots, as if for passports. Yet I didn't ask about the particulars, for without warning Noklek flicked a lighter and lit the corner of the paper with the names of her family and ancestors, holding it over a plate until it was completely enflamed. I was unsettled, assuming there was bitterness in her memories of them, not understanding until later, after I had researched Theravada

Buddhist rituals, that this was a tribute to the dead, a passing of merit to their spirits.

She chanted some more, then lifted a bowl of water with flower petals floating on it. Jasmine. I breathed in the sweet scent. Where she had gotten the jasmine, I did not know. I gazed around the backyard. None of the perennials or bulbs that Jessica and I had planted late last summer had bloomed just yet.

Noklek gently sprinkled a bit of the water over the Buddhas and the photo frames, catching the runoff in another glass bowl—the same one, I recognized, in which Jessica had stuck the immersion coil for the alginate mixture. With the collected water, she doused the ashes of the paper. Then she startled me by tipping some water onto my shoulder, down my back.

"Hey!" I said. I was wearing a new button-down, and the water was cold. It was barely fifty degrees outside.

"Luck!" she said. "Songkran! New year!"

This was, I remembered then, a rite of the Songkran festival in Thailand, a three-day new year's celebration in April. The tradition of pouring cleansing water had degenerated into a national water fight, caravans of celebrants driving down streets with water guns and cannons, drenching bystanders, who would retaliate with buckets and hoses. I had seen videos on the news.

"You water me?" Noklek asked.

I dribbled water onto her shoulder, and she momentarily shuddered from the chill.

She mixed a white powder, maybe chalk, in a small bowl with some water, then dipped her fingers in the white paste and daubed her face—a consecration, vertical lines on her forehead, swirls on her cheeks. She handed me the bowl. "You paint?"

I rubbed the chalk onto my face, mimicking her design pattern.

"*Sawatdee pee mai*," she said, pressing her palms together and bowing to me. "Happy New Year."

"*Sawatdee pee mai*," I said, bowing.

"*Suk-san wan songkran*," she said.

"*Suk-san wan songkran*," I said, bowing again.

When I rose, she squirted my face with a tiny water pistol. "Hee hee hee hee," she hiccupped in childlike squeaks. It was the first time I'd heard her laugh.

"Now you're going to get it," I said, and I jumped up and grabbed the larger of the bowls and whirled around and threw the water at the same time she tossed the contents of a bucket into my face. I had been errant in my aim and missed Noklek completely. I, on the other hand, was soaked. We ran on and off the deck, into the backyard, fighting over the garden hose, filling bowls and buckets and trash cans from the utility shed, screaming and laughing, the chalk smearing and streaking down our faces, until dusk fell and we were exhausted and deluged and shivering, yet blithe.

We never really spoke again. I think of that evening, of Noklek, our abbreviated conversation and gestures of communion, every now and then. I think of the jasmine petals she had spread in the bowls of water. I think of her youth, how alive and joyful she was in those few minutes we had shared—for once, carefree. I think of the Thai Buddhist beliefs of renewal and rebirth, of the Songkran custom of washing away misfortune and receiving the blessing of protection, the making and passing on of merit. I think of the practice of commemorating the dead by writing down their names, and then incinerating them. I think of devoting myself to more acts of kindness and goodness, as you are supposed to do during Songkran, and of dedicating those acts, in part, to Noklek Praphasirirat, wherever she may be now.

15

On Sunday, May 2, five days before her exhibition would be open to the public, Jessica gave the remaining members of the 3AC a preview of *Dis/Orienting Proportions*. We walked up the stairs to the second-floor foyer of the City Hall Annex on Inman Street, and there, in the exhibition space known as Gallery 57, past a knot of freestanding partitions that had been temporarily assembled to conceal the installation until its unveiling, stood three life-sized mannequins. They were of Bruce Lee, Charlie Chan, and Suzie Wong.

Bruce Lee was dressed in the yellow tracksuit with black stripes that he had sported in *The Game of Death*. He was positioned in a three-quarters fighting stance, one arm up, ready to parry, the other forward and down to block. Jessica had silkscreened a black-and-white photograph of Lee's face onto a sheet of rubber and stretched it over the mannequin's head, which was crowned by a high-end wig. All the mannequins had very realistic wigs, styled by Jimmy Fung. The clothes had been just as skillfully sewn by Trudy Lun, the theater costume designer/seamstress.

Charlie Chan—made portly with foam padding—was in a tweed

three-piece suit and bow tie, with slicked-back hair and a Fu Man-
chu mustache. He was bowing slightly, his palms pressed together.

Suzie Wong had her hip cocked to one side, fist resting on it. She
was in a form-fitting cheongsam, the silk the lightest blue with a
hint of lavender, accessorized with a matching hair band and open-
toed pumps—the outfit Nancy Kwan had worn in *The World of
Suzie Wong* when she modeled for William Holden's painting.

What made the mannequins distinctive, though, was that Bruce
Lee and Charlie Chan had their zippers open, baring erect penises
and scrotums. Suzie Wong's cheongsam also had an open zipper, but the zipper and the vulva that it exposed (a clone of Jessica's vulva) were *horizontal*, an allusion to the old myth that Asian
women had sideways vaginas. Framed by the lashes of the zipper's
jagged teeth, the labia resembled a slitted eye. There was a one-
yuan coin stuck between the folds.

The dental alginate molds Jessica had made of Joshua's and
my genitals had been the first of a four-part process. For the
second, she had poured plaster of Paris into the molds, then dismantled the alginate to reveal the casts of the plaster erections,
which she filed and sandpapered and filled with spackling paste
to fix voids and defects. After that, she applied a coat of acrylic
polymer to smooth out the surface even further, then painted on
a thin layer of latex rubber molding compound on the plaster,
waiting twenty-four hours for it to dry before painting another
layer, repeating until she had accumulated ten coats. She then
dislodged the latex molds from the plaster penises, sprayed the
insides with a release agent, filled them with two-component
RTV silicone, and suspended the molds inside two-liter soda
bottles with the tops cut off (the water in the bottles equalized
the pressure, since the weight of the silicone had a tendency to

bulge). After another twenty-four hours, she peeled the rubber off to uncover the replicas.

They were, in fact, exact replicas. Contrary to Jessica's assertion, all penises did not look alike. I identified mine right away. It was on Bruce Lee, and I could see every vein, ridge, and anatomical detail, every little bump and crease and crinkle. It was, as far as I could tell, a perfect facsimile, although I looked much thicker and longer than I had imagined—far bigger, I was pleased to see, than old Charlie Chan (Joshua).

But there was one anomaly in sacrifice of verisimilitude—the color. Jessica had made all the genitalia bright fluorescent yellow, and what's more, they glowed in the dark. Spotlights overhead were programmed to alternate what was illuminated and what was not, a face, an arm, a leg, sometimes making an erection or labia dramatically luminescent.

Among the group, there was a lot of twittering and giggling, but I was, relatively speaking, assuaged. When Jessica had described her plans for the installation and enlisted my help, I had feared it'd be a stunt, a one-off for which she would be ridiculed and humiliated, yet there was (almost) a tenable integrity to the mannequins, and the political implications were provocative, the stretched silkscreened rubber of the faces making the Asian icons seem as if they were yowling in horror and agony, eyes monstrously slanted.

Characteristic of all of Jessica's work, there were hidden elements, pieces within pieces. She had carved a cavity in each head, prying their mouths open, and inside each maw was a menagerie. In Bruce Lee's mouth were miniatures of dogs—dozens of them in every variety, running, leaping, lying, snarling, shitting. In Charlie Chan's mouth were rats. In Suzie Wong's mouth were snakes. And the miniatures were fluorescent yellow, glow-in-the-dark as well, creating a spooky, contrapuntal incandescence whenever the spotlights changed, as if the skulls were lit from within, while the genitals appeared disembodied, floating apart. Moreover, since the mannequins were mounted on platforms, you had to get on your tiptoes and lean close to peek into the mouths, and the figures were purposely positioned so you couldn't avoid brushing or bumping up against the genitalia, contributing to the exhibition's gestalt of discomfiture—indeed, of disorientation.

After the preview, we migrated to the house on Walker Street for the usual potluck. The group included Jimmy, Trudy, Grace, Leon, Jay, Cindy, Phil, and Annie—the smallest turnout we'd ever had. We congregated in the kitchen, unwrapping and heating up various dishes: yakisoba, salt-and-pepper squid, cucumber suno-mono, bean sprouts, chicken karaage, gyoza.

"I have to admit," I told Jessica, "I had my doubts, but the exhibit works. You pulled it off. It's pretty fabulous."

"Hear, hear," Joshua said.

"You really think so?" Jessica said, flush with relief. "I knew I was taking a risk, doing something so different, with huge poten-tial for disaster, but I kept following my instincts."

"The stretched faces, the mouths, the lighting—it's all really ingenious," I said.

"I didn't have time to finish the installation part. I was going to have these Judd-like boxes and some table sculptures."

"You didn't need them," Joshua said. "The mannequins have enough depth on their own."

I went outside to the deck to barbecue kalbi on our grill, and Joshua soon joined me there, bringing a bottle of Tsingtao out for me. "So what'd you really think?" he asked.

This was the lesson I'd learned about being friends with artists: at first, you were honest in your critiques, just like you had been in grad school. But when you were honest, you'd find it would cause

days, weeks of tension and bruised feelings, a rift that would sometimes never fully mend. You learned what artists really wanted from
their friends. It wasn't honesty, it wasn't constructive criticism, it
wasn't the truth. They'd get the truth soon enough, from dealers, editors, directors, agents, grant-makers, foundations, critics,
and the public. What artists really wanted from their friends was
simply support, and encouragement, and, if it wasn't too much of
an imposition, unconditional adoration. About works in progress,
they wanted you to tell them: It's perfect. You don't need to change
a thing. It's good to go. About works that had already been released
to the world, fait accompli, they wanted you to tell them: It's brilliant. You're brilliant. I love it. I love you. What was the point of
saying anything else? Yet, this did not prevent us from disparaging
our friends' work behind their backs.

"It's not as silly as I thought it'd be," I said to Joshua, "but it's still
kind of silly. What about you? What'd you think?"

"Ditto."

"I wish she'd kept going with her latest paintings. Have you seen
the series in the basement?"

"No."

"They're my favorite of anything she's ever produced," I said.
"I guess it doesn't matter. No one's ever going to see this show,
anyway." Gallery 57 was small-fry, almost a nonentity, in Boston's
art world.

"It's pretty wild, though," Joshua said, "seeing your breakfast
burrito up there, isn't it?"

I rearranged the kalbi on the grill. "When Jessica was making
the mold of you, what was she wearing?" I asked.

"What do you mean?" he said. "I don't know. Jeans, a T-shirt.
Why?"

"Did she do anything to you?"

"Like what?"

"You didn't have trouble staying stiff?"

"My piccolo never needs prodding. Yours did?"

"She never, like, handled you? Even when she was checking out your shaving job?"

"She used chopsticks to turn over my dick, which I have to say was a little antiseptic, not to mention ironic and insulting and not very erotic," he said. "She didn't use the chopsticks on you? What the fuck happened between you guys?"

"Nothing happened," I said, and flipped the kalbi. For the moment, no one knew that the penises on the mannequins were casts of Joshua and me, everyone believing they were scrupulously carved sculptures based on dildos.

In the dusk, I looked at the crocuses and daffodils that had bloomed. Glancing up at the pink flowers of the dogwood, I saw the lights on the second floor, in the master bedroom, turning on. Joshua noticed them, too.

"You know, you could invite her down," I told him. "She doesn't have to stay in her room all the time. We have a lot of food—more than enough."

"She doesn't want to," he said. "I've asked her before, but she's shy."

"When there aren't so many people around, then. She must get bored up there all by herself."

The other week, after coming home from work, I had slipped into Noklek's room. On the second-floor landing, I had thought I smelled something burning. I knocked on her door, waited, then entered the master bedroom. She had a hot plate on the bureau. I put my hand over the coil element, and it was still warm. She must have just cooked something. Beside the bureau was a small refrigerator, and in the bathtub there was a dish rack, a freshly washed pot and bowl drying in it. A braided nylon rope stretched

across the bathroom, laundry clipped to it. She had few possessions overall—the Buddhas, the framed photographs. On the
neatly made bed was the pig piñata that used to hang in Joshua's
attic, which he had named Claudette, in homage to Claude, the
pig piñata that Pynchon had owned when he lived in Manhattan
Beach, where he wrote *Gravity's Rainbow*. Otherwise, there was
not much personal in the bedroom, just a stack of celebrity gossip
magazines.

"I've been thinking—" Joshua said. He picked up a slab of kalbi
from the grill with my tongs and bit into it. "Ow, that's hot—of
marrying Noklek."

"What?"

"So she can get a green card. Jimmy told me she's worried about
getting booted out of the country. Her visa's expired. I've been talking to Grace about it," he said—Grace, the immigration attorney.

"Joshua," I said, "that is utterly fucking nuts. Did she offer you
money? Or something else."

"I offered."

"In exchange for what?"

"Nothing," Joshua said. "My intentions are entirely honorable.
I haven't laid a finger on her. I just feel sorry for the kid. I mean,
yeah, there are things to be concerned about, like being financially
responsible for her for ten years, like her maybe trying to take me
for a ride down the road with a divorce and busting my balls over a
settlement. But I'd have her sign a prenup."

"You realize what the penalty is if you get caught?"

"Up to five years in prison and two hundred fifty thou."

I had not actually known the penalty. It was more severe than
I had assumed. "The INS is always trying to crack down on these
sorts of scams," I said. "You can't fuck around with shit like this."

"That's why we wouldn't do it right away. We'd wait at least six

months. We'd be careful. Even though she's illegal now, if everything went through, she'd be entitled to residency."

"She says she wants to do this?"

"We've talked about it. She hasn't said yes for sure yet, and neither have I. I'm gathering facts. Grace told us we need to build
evidence of a relationship history—you know, ticket stubs to events
and vacation photos and birthday cards, shit like that. I'm thinking
we could go to the Virgin Islands together—to St. John this time."

"What are you looking to get out of this? You'd be risking a hell
of a lot just to get laid regularly."

"I like having her around," Joshua said. He pinched the kalbi by
the ribs and, with his teeth, tore meat off and gnawed on it. "You
know a couple of weeks ago she cleaned the entire house top to bottom? She even mowed the lawn."

"That was for Songkran," I told him.

"Songkran?"

"New Year's in Thailand. It's a ritual, to clean your house. You
don't know anything about her, do you? She's not as tough as you
think. You know her entire family is dead?"

"Jimmy told me."

"Tell me the circumstances," I said, as if I were testing him.

"Ferry accident," he said. "Her parents and little sister were on
holiday, and Noklek got left behind with a neighbor because she
was sick. The ferryboat captain tried to cut across the path of a
chemical tanker, and the ferry got cleaved in half. Eighty-seven
people died."

I thought of the black-and-white head shots, the paper burning
and curling in layers of ash.

"She's an orphan, just like me," Joshua said. "She's all alone in the
world. You'll laugh at this, but maybe, I mean, who knows, maybe
we'll even fall in love and it'll become a real marriage."

"Don't do this," I said. "Don't fuck with her. She's a teenager. She's practically a child. You know you don't want a real marriage. You want a maid, a concubine. That's the only reason you're considering this."

"No, you're wrong," Joshua said. "You know I consider us a family—you, me, Jessica. I would love it if we could live here together forever. Love it. But I know someday you guys will meet someone, maybe even get together with each other finally, and you'll want to move out and have a place of your own. You'll be tired of having old Joshua around all the time. Then where will I be? I mean, I know I'm no prize. I know I'm a pain in the ass. I'm demanding and strident, I'm lazy and messy and difficult. Who would have me? No woman in her right mind, that's for sure. I don't want to get married, not for real. I don't want to have kids. All I want to do is write."

"You might change your mind someday," I said. "You might fall in love and want a family. There's always the possibility of that happening."

"No."

"I saw you dancing with that little girl at Leon and Cindy's wedding. You were enrapt."

"I never told you. I had a vasectomy."

"You did?"

"Years ago," Joshua said.

"There's always adoption," I said, and saw him flinch in distaste. "Or you might meet a woman with kids."

"I'm not going to change," Joshua said. "People don't change. If there's one thing I've learned by now, it's that. I'll never fall in love, because I could never trust that I wouldn't be abandoned. The only problem, the only noisome little contradictory wrinkle, is I don't want to be alone. The truth is, the idea of dying alone terrifies me. Remember those journal excerpts by your hero, Cheever, about ending up cold, alone, dishonored, and forgotten? An old man approaching death without a companion? As much as I try to thwart it, I know that's my fate. That's why I'd never arrange for a memorial service. I'd be afraid no one would show up."

"You won't die alone, Joshua. I'll always be around. So will Jessica."

"You say that now, but you can't guarantee it. You guys have been the only true friends I've ever had, but sometimes I've felt I had to buy your friendship."

"What are you talking about?"

"If I didn't have this house, would you—or anyone else here, what's left of the 3AC—be hanging out with me at all?"

"That's an absurd thing to ask."

"Is it? I don't know," Joshua said. He finished the rest of the kalbi and chucked the bones over the crocuses into the shrubs. "Sometimes I'm just barely hanging on, you know. Just barely hanging on. And I'm beginning to feel there's only so much more I can do to keep us together."

■　■　■

The second floor of the City Hall Annex housed several municipal offices that encircled Gallery 57, including the Animal Commission, which issued dog licenses. On Monday, one of the clerks who worked at the commission, Maryanne Costa, called Councilman Vivaldo Barboza, a fellow Portuguese American parishioner at St. Anthony's Church, and complained about the sculptures to him. The mannequins were still sequestered behind the temporary partitions and draped by sheets, but Mrs. Costa, curious about the exhibition, had availed herself of a sneak peek, and had been appalled.

Vivaldo Barboza had been on the City Council for four years.

Campaigning on an unimaginative platform of quality-of-life (noise abatement) and traffic (on-street parking) issues, he had been, to everyone's surprise, elected to two terms, and was now the chair of the Public Safety Committee. He went to examine the sculptures in Gallery 57 himself and, equally horrified and disgusted, took matters into his own hands.

He bore down on the erections with his full weight and broke them off the Bruce Lee and Charlie Chan mannequins. He tried to pry the vulva off Suzie Wong as well, but couldn't gain purchase on it enough to tear it off, so he simply yanked closed the horizontal zipper, the one-yuan coin plinking away to recesses unknown, never to be found again. He hid the erections underneath his suit coat and marched around the corner to City Hall, straight into the city manager's office.

In Cambridge, the nine members of the City Council were elected at-large through a proportional electoral process, and the members themselves appointed a mayor and vice mayor from the council, but the city manager, John Toomey, was the true chief executive of the city, with the power to enforce laws and ordinances and hire and fire employees.

Barboza dumped the erections on Toomey's desk and demanded that the exhibition be dismantled at once. Toomey—amused rather than outraged, which infuriated Barboza—told him that it was neither the city manager's responsibility nor purview to decide what was or wasn't art, and Barboza would have to take his grievances elsewhere.

It was two p.m. From January until June, the City Council met on the first Monday of each month at five-thirty, and Barboza entered a last-minute emergency item to that evening's agenda. At the meeting, he summoned the director of Gallery 57 and the members of the Cambridge Arts Council (only two of three could appear on such short notice), and asked them to account for themselves. How could they have sponsored such an offensive and obscene exhibition? How could they justify showing such rubbish in a public space? What in the world had they been thinking? Never mind what they owed their constituents; they had left the city vulnerable to a sexual harassment suit by its workers, and by God he wouldn't blame them one bit if they filed one.

"This is not art," he said. "This is pornography."

The council recessed the meeting so all the members could read Jessica's artist statement—about addressing issues of cultural appropriation, ethnicity, identity, sexuality, and stereotypes in media representations of Asian Americans—and go to Gallery 57 to view the exhibition, replete with the lights. Two councilmen held the erections in place on the mannequins, and there were some oohs and ahs when they discovered that the pieces glowed in the dark and there were hidden caches of miniature sculptures in the heads. They resumed the meeting in City Hall, and Barboza called for the Gallery 57 director and Arts Council members' immediate resignations. They refused, so Barboza submitted two proposals: the first to hold a public hearing to investigate the Arts Council's selection process, the second to include, on all future arts juries, a councilperson and a representative of the clergy. The first proposal was accepted. The second—only the motion about a councilperson, the stipulation about the clergy roundly dismissed—was tabled, pending review. Barboza then asked for an injunction to cancel all current and future exhibitions in Gallery 57 until the hearing was held and resolved to everyone's satisfaction. The injunction divided the City Council, but ultimately was shot down. The show could go on, with a few caveats.

"There need to be certain adjustments," the Gallery 57 director, Gustaaf Dekker, told us that night in our living room.

"What adjustments?" Jessica asked.

"In order for the exhibit to proceed," Dekker told her, "they want the temporary partitions to be permanent, so people who are going to get their dog licenses won't see it unless they intend to, and they want signs posted." He pulled out a sheet of paper and read: " 'The works in this exhibition address provocative issues of sexuality and identity. To be specific, this exhibition contains explicit displays and symbols depicting genitalia, and these objects may be offensive to some viewers. Please use discretion in entering the exhibit space and viewing the artwork. Because of the sensitive nature of the exhibit, it is not recommended for viewing by minors.' "

"That's ridiculous," Jessica said.

"That's blatant censorship," Joshua said.

"There's a last little bit, a disclaimer of sorts," Dekker said. " 'The City Council is not responsible for the contents of this exhibition and in no way endorses it.' "

"What kind of chickenshit nonsense is that?" Joshua asked.

"I'm not going to do it," Jessica said. "I won't accept it. It's complete bullshit. Why am I the one who has to compromise? This asshole decides he's the guardian of morality for the city, and he vandalizes my exhibit, yet he's allowed to get away with it without any punishment? If anyone walked into a gallery or museum and defaced the art, they'd get arrested. Why hasn't this guy been arrested?"

"I'm behind you one hundred percent," Dekker said. "All the members of the Arts Council are, too. We'll stand by you, whatever you want to do. It's tragic and reprehensible, that's what it is, this whole thing. Tragic."

He bowed his head, as if to solemnize the depths of the tragedy. Tall, with a trim, muscular frame, Dekker had thinning curly blond hair, and there was a bald spot beginning to form on top of his head. He was Dutch, born in Curaçao and raised in Maastricht, and he had come to the States because he had fathered two children with an American expatriate. He lived with her and the kids, but remained unmarried. Jessica had told Joshua and me that when Dekker was helping her move the mannequins from the Vernon Street Studios to Gallery 57, he had hit on her.

"But I wonder if this is not so onerous of a compromise," Dekker said. "At least the mannequins would not have to be covered or altered in any way, and the exhibit could carry on as scheduled. That is, if you are able to repair and reinstall the sculptures by Friday. Do you think you can do that?"

"I don't know," Jessica said.

We all stared at the two erections on the coffee table, which rested on the base of the scrotums and were sitting upright, glowing feebly. They had been attached to the mannequins with epoxy, and parts of the shafts and testicles were cracked and tattered. The labial folds on Suzie Wong in Gallery 57 were also chipped, marred.

"There's a lot of damage," Jessica said. "What it would mean is patching and doctoring them, and the whole point had been going for strict authenticity. But I don't really have any other option at this point, do I? It'd take me at least twelve days to do them over. They're not sculptures, you know. They're replicas. They're from molds of live models."

Dekker glanced at her, then at Joshua and me. As he caught on, his face bloomed vermilion, and he twitched his head in aversion. "Well, why don't you see what you can do."

"That information does not leave this room," I said.

He looked at me dully. "Of course," he told me.

■   ■   ▥

It started on Tuesday with a small article in the *Harvard Crimson*, recapping the previous day's City Council meeting, headlined "Phallic Art Exhibit Gives Rise to Councilman's Protest." On

Wednesday and Thursday, more newspaper articles appeared, the puns too inviting to resist: "Artwork Neutered by Politician," "Dildo Sculpture Manhandled," "Cambridge Mannequins Castrated."

And in the articles, Vivaldo Barboza was talking. "The potholes are so bad in Cambridge, people can't drive down the street without getting their wheels knocked out of alignment, yet the Arts Council decides to spend taxpayer money on this?" he said. "What's this exhibit have anything to do with art? There's a boundary between what's art and what's junk, and this is undeniably junk. It's trash. There's no redeeming social or artistic value to it at all. As an elected official, I had a civic responsibility to take action and protect my constituents from this kind of smut."

Reporters called the house, but Jessica declined to give comment. She was too busy. She carefully restored the genitalia and managed to reattach the penises to the mannequins just in time for the exhibition to open on schedule on Friday at noon, with a line of people winding down the stairs—the biggest crowd to ever appear for a show at Gallery 57. Certainly a good number were lookie-loos, merely curious or seeking titillation, but many were serious arts patrons, far more than would have come to this particular venue without the attendant publicity, and they seemed appreciative. There were no snickers, no cries of outrage, no scowls of denunciation. And there was a rumor that among the crowd was a critic for the *Boston Globe*.

"Maybe," Jessica said, ecstatic over the attention, "in a strange way this was the best thing that could have happened."

"How about doing an interview, then?" Joshua asked. "This is exactly what the 3AC needs. There's this chick who's been calling. She's Chinese American—fourth generation from New York."

Meredith Yee worked for the *Boston Record*, a new alternative weekly that was trying to compete with the *Phoenix*. She came out to the Walker Street house on Saturday, and we fixed her a lunch of sesame noodles and salad. We told her about becoming friends at Mac as freshmen, then reuniting last year and forming the 3AC, about the shared purpose of the collective, to support one another as Asian American artists, gather and exchange ideas and experiences, subvert and provide a counternarrative to stereotypes—all the catchphrases that had survived the vetting of the mission statement.

"That's what's behind the exhibit," Jessica said. "It's not about sex or eroticism. It's about identity, sexual identity, and how Asian Americans are affected by external tropes. Asian women are objectified, and Asian men are encumbered with these emasculating anxieties, like about penis size, which isn't an accident, since the phallus is a symbol of male power."

"Basically," Joshua said, "Asian American men have been relegated as the eunuchs of the world."

"So I wanted to provoke debate about all of this," Jessica said. "What the councilman did was a violation of my constitutional rights, my civil rights. This is yet another hegemonic attempt to suppress the voice of Asian Americans."

Meredith seemed receptive to everything discussed. She told us she had grappled with many of these issues herself, and was interested in attending a 3AC gathering sometime. But she was oddly, persistently nosy about our personal lives, saying, "I'm sure there's been some pairing-off in the group, yes? That's natural in any group dynamic. Have the three of you ever been involved? In any combination?"

We shook our heads no.

"Really?" she said. "In all these years? Never been tempted?"

Jessica refrained from delving into her sexual orientation.

Later, Meredith asked for a tour of the house, and as we led her around upstairs, she seemed to be absorbed with the sleeping arrangements. "So who's got this room?" she asked, pointing to the master bedroom.

"Noklek," Joshua said.

"Who's Noklek?"

"She works with Jimmy at Pink Whistle," he told her.

"She's just crashing here temporarily," I said.

A photographer arrived, and after he set up his lights and reflectors, Meredith arranged us on the couch, shifting us into different arrays, asking us to pose with our arms and hands here and there, to gaze forward, to the side, at one another and away. It all felt a bit silly, yet, succumbing to vanity, the three of us kept checking our hair and wondering if we should change clothes. "Is this going to be in color or black-and-white?" I asked.

At the potluck the next day, some 3AC members were less than thrilled hearing about the interview.

"Why didn't you call the rest of us?" Annie asked. "If the article's going to be on the 3AC, all of us should have been interviewed."

"No one should've been excluded," Phil said.

"It wasn't intentional," Jessica said. "It was all last-minute."

"She interviewed me," Jimmy said.

"She did?" I asked.

"I made the wigs, remember? She came over to the shop after she finished with you three."

"Did she contact you about the costumes?" I asked Trudy. She told me no.

"A little starchy, that Meredith," Jimmy said, "but kind of a babe, don't you think?"

"Listen, we did the interview to promote the 3AC as an organization," Joshua said. "It wasn't about us, it wasn't an ego thing."

"Did you mention all of us by name and discipline?" Jay asked.

"Yeah, we did. Didn't we?" Joshua asked me.

"Yeah," I dissembled.

"At the very least," Cindy said, "I wish we could've been part of the photo shoot, you know? That's what I'm most disappointed about."

Yet on Tuesday, when the *Boston Record* came out, the group quelled any objections they might have had, because it became apparent that Meredith Yee had been planning to sandbag us all along.

Her article was entitled "Slits and Eunuchs: A Most Unusual Collective." She accurately described the aims of the 3AC and quoted us without error, but often out of context, and her tone was mocking throughout. She sketched us as a bunch of pretentious twentysomething layabouts with ample time for "almond-gazing," as "wannabe Asian Panthers" whining about racial injustice while lolling, rather comfortably, in a tony Harvard Square house, where the bedroom assignments appeared to be "very fluid." She profiled Jimmy individually in a sidebar, with a photo of him—shirt open, leather-panted legs spread wide—sitting in front of Pink Whistle, "in which 'massages' are offered by a Thai teenager who happens to be the kneader-in-residence on Walker Street."

Our own photograph had Joshua and me on opposite sides of the couch, squared around so we morosely faced Jessica, who was between us in her zippered corset top and eyebrow ring as she leered forward, sticking out her tongue with its silver stud. An Asian sandwich in which Jessica was the dominatrix meat. Meredith described her as "a shock artist whose most recent exhibit has her focusing her hooded eye on two Asiatic erections, standing head to head, the casts for which were made, expediently or perhaps extra-collectively, from the in-the-flesh molds of her two houseboys' aroused penises. Whether they measure up or not is in the hands of the beholder."

"That cunt," Jessica said.

"It had to be Dekker who told her," I said.

"The article could have at least been well written," Joshua said. "Her prose is abominable."

On the same day, the *Boston Globe* published a review of the exhibit, penned by the chief art critic, Kate Roper. Not a full review, but the last item in an omnibus. It read in its entirety: "Jessica Tsai's new show in Gallery 57, *Dis/Orienting Proportions*, has been stirring up a tempest in Cambridge, namely because her triumvirate of mannequins—modeled after famous Asian movie stars—flaunt rather aggressive anatomical appendages. The artist's intentions, as explicated in her statement, are earnestly political and identity-based, yet betray a bit of jejune thinking about the work's impact. Instead of contending with codes of power, race, and typecasting, the exhibit exposes conspicuous shortcomings, failing to attain the density of expression, or at least wit, that is required for any art medium to succeed."

"It's not that bad," I told Jessica.

"My career's over," she said.

The following morning, Barboza went on a Boston talk radio show and yukked it up with the hosts. "The human body's a wonderful thing, no doubt about it, nothing wrong with it at all," he said, "but displaying their *own* genitalia like that is just perverted, not to mention self-indulgent and—what did you call it?—yeah, self-aggrandizing. I don't know what this so-called artist and her friends do in that house in Harvard Square, and I don't really want to know. Maybe it's a commune or a cult, maybe it's a club for Asian swingers and they have orgies in there, who knows. That's their prerogative, I guess. But that doesn't give this woman any right to foist her sordid lifestyle unto the public, shoving these obscene little egg rolls and bonsai bushes in our faces."

"That does it," Joshua said. "He's a racist! It was a fucking hate crime! And now he's insulting our manhood!"

"There's nothing ambiguous about this," Jessica told me.

For the first time, the controversy no longer felt abstract to me. It was personal. "We have to get this fucker," I said.

I went to see Grace Kwok at her office, which was on the third floor of 929 Mass Ave, a concrete high-rise across from the Plough & Stars. She shared a suite with half a dozen other attorneys, all sole practitioners who split the expenses for the receptionist, conference room, copier, and kitchenette.

Grace didn't think we had enough evidence to file a civil rights case—certainly not a hate crime complaint. "It'd be difficult to prove he broke off the penises because of an inherent bias against Asians," she said.

"What about a First Amendment case?" I asked.

"Maybe. I don't know. It's not my area of expertise. I'm just an immigration attorney." She freelanced for several high-tech and biotech companies, obtaining H-1B visas for foreign engineers and scientists, as well as F-1 student visas.

"This green-card marriage between Noklek and Joshua," I said, "you really think they could get away with it?"

"It's not inconceivable. It's been known to happen," Grace said. "But not if she's involved in something illegal. The INS tends to frown upon applicants engaged in criminal activity. What the reporter was insinuating about the massages, is it true?"

"She gives massages. I don't know what else she provides. She's a sweet girl. I doubt she'd let herself be talked into doing anything more than wearing sexy outfits."

"Well, it's not my business, I suppose," Grace said.

"You're not going to represent them?"

"Joshua asked for my professional opinion. I met with him and Noklek and gave it to him, and I billed him for it. That's it, as far as I'm concerned."

"Look, Barboza can't get away with this," I said. "We have to make him accountable somehow. His comments—instead of condemning him, people think it's funny. Do you know someone who might be able to help us?"

"Not really."

"Any ideas at all?"

"Sorry."

"You don't seem too upset about this," I said.

"It's all kind of embarrassing, don't you think? The sculptures?" Grace asked. "And then all of the proselytizing—politicizing everything. Does it have anything to do with art?"

"You've fallen into Esther Xing's camp."

"I don't know. Why do there have to be camps at all?" Grace told me. "What I do know is that Joshua is a snob, and sometimes you and Jessica aren't much better. I don't blame Rick and Ali for not coming back. I doubt I'll be coming back myself. You're all very ambitious, but it seems you'll exploit pretty much anything or anyone, including the 3AC, to get ahead. It's a shame, because I thought we had something great there, something worthwhile, before the three of you ruined it."

16

Joshua solicited the ACLU, the NAACP, the Anti-Defamation League, the Southern Poverty Law Center, and various Asian American advocacy groups. All of them initially seemed interested in the case, but then, without explanation, dropped out. Finally he found an organization that was eager to become involved: the Cambridge Coalition for Freedom of Expression. Its core mission was to assist artists and organizations facing attacks on their artistic freedom. I had never heard of them.

The CCFE representative who came to our house, Stan Margolies, was around fifty, heavyset, with salt-and-pepper hair tied in a ponytail. He wore a hunter-green corduroy sports jacket and sneakers, and he had the right leg of his jeans rolled up, exposing a hairy calf and a vivid red sock. He had ridden his bike over, and he smelled rank. He was, supposedly, both a lawyer and a painter. "I've been in this house before," he told Joshua. "Your parents were my professors, years ago. They were terrific teachers and people. I loved them."

In the dining room over a cup of chai, Margolies said, "There's no doubt this is a First Amendment issue. The city of Cambridge is under no obligation to support the arts, but having chosen to do so, they can't retroactively impose content or viewing restrictions on exhibits. They are, in fact, prohibited from so doing by the Constitution. The First Amendment also precludes public officials from acting as freelance art vigilantes. Having said that, however, I'm not confident we could pull off a First Amendment case against Barboza and the City Council."

"Why not?" Jessica asked.

"It might take years to litigate, and it'd entail an enormous amount of resources and money, and still we might not win, especially in the current climate."

"But this is *Cambridge*," Joshua said. "I can't believe this is happening in fucking Cambridge."

"There are powerful constituencies at work, well-funded ones on the extreme right, and they're driven by a general hysterical fear of the unknown, which of course is, at its root, about intolerance."

"Barboza's got to be a closet queen," Jessica said. We turned to her, faltering over the non sequitur. "So there's nothing we can do?" she asked.

"There's one tactic I can suggest," Margolies said. "File a criminal complaint of malicious destruction." He cited Chapter 266, Section 127, of the Massachusetts General Laws, which set the penalty for wanton destruction of personal property at a maximum of ten years in prison or a fine based on the value of the property. "It's unlikely he'd get any jail time, but it'd be an expeditious way for us to make our point."

"What are the chances he'd be convicted?" Joshua asked.

"Fifty-fifty," Margolies admitted.

"How long would it take to litigate?" I asked.

"We could submit the complaint as early as Monday, the arraignment would be in a week or two, the trial five or six months after that."

"What about the costs?" Jessica asked.

"We're willing to do this pro bono," Margolies said. "There is a monetary threshold, however, for filing the charge as a felony. We need to be able to claim that Barboza caused damage in excess of $250. Is that something we can claim?"

I could see Jessica mentally tallying the expenditures for the repair material, which could not have been much.

"You should also factor in the reduction in the mannequins' market value, since they're no longer in their original condition," Margolies said. "That loss would be irrevocable, I imagine."

Jessica had arbitrarily priced the mannequins at $3,000 apiece, never believing anyone would buy them. "In that case," she said, "yes, definitely more than $250 in damage."

"All right, then, we can do this," Margolies said. "But I have to warn you, if we go forward, you'll have to be prepared for the resultant shitstorm. It won't be just Barboza. The Christian Coalition and other factions will probably marshal their forces to support him under all sorts of guises. I wouldn't be surprised if there were protests and dirty tricks to try to discredit you and the 3AC."

"Are you shitting me?" Joshua asked.

"No, I'm deadly serious."

"That's beautiful, man," Joshua said. "This will be war."

Margolies gave us the weekend to think it over.

As Sunday evening approached, one 3AC member after another phoned to say he or she could not make the potluck that week. All good reasons—a deadline, a relative or a friend visiting, a gig out of town, tickets to a show. Jimmy was the only one available. When he heard no one else was coming, he said he'd give this one a miss. Grace didn't bother to call at all.

I made pajeon—scallion pancakes—from the batter I had already prepared, and Joshua, Jessica, and I ate them with rice and kimchi in the kitchen.

"I checked these guys out," I told them. "The CCFE. They're a bunch of kooks. They want to ban prayer in the schools and eliminate the word God from all government entities, including money."

"So they're atheists. More power to them," Jessica said.

"Yeah? You know they also support NAMBLA?" The North American Man/Boy Love Association. "They've gone to court for convicted sex offenders. They're trying to get the sale and distribution of child pornography legalized."

"That's nothing new," Joshua said. "The ACLU's been doing that for years. When you're trying to protect civil liberties in absolute terms, you end up having to defend the indefensible."

"I think we should let everyone have a say in this," I said. "It affects the rest of the 3AC. We should tell them what's going on and put it up for a group vote."

"Screw that," Joshua said. "Do you see anyone else here? Fucking cowards. The first sign of trouble, they bail."

"They all had legitimate excuses this weekend."

"Every single one of them? By coincidence?"

"Let's wait until next Sunday," I said. "They'll all be back then."

"That's bullshit, and you know it. They deserted us. It's just us now. We're the only group that matters. What's your problem? This is just like at Mac. Why are you so afraid?"

This was not just like Macalester. I had always regretted my initial reluctance to act then, chagrined by my passivity, and I had been committed to proceeding now. I wanted apologies. I wanted retractions. I wanted denunciations. Yet that was before Margolies had promised a circus. I did not want that kind of strife or notoriety. Not over this.

"This just doesn't feel right," I said. "It might escalate and get out of hand, and that's exactly what Margolies wants. That's why they're pursuing this. They're not looking out for us at all. They want to use us."

"I'm being publicly humiliated, and now you are, too," Jessica said. "You're going to let that pass? This is about our dignity."

"Once Barboza made the egg roll comment, he crossed the line," Joshua said. "He made it racial. There's no way we can back down now. The crazies and detractors will come out, but so will supporters and admirers. This will make us famous. It'll help our careers, I'm not too disingenuous to say. And the timing couldn't be better for you and me, bro, with the Fiction Discoveries issue coming out next month."

"That shouldn't be our motivation," I said.

"No? Let's not be naive. We can't sit around waiting for things to happen. We've got to make them happen. Nothing's going to fall in our laps. That only happens to beautiful white people. I'm telling you, that photo of us in the *Record*, someday it'll be reprinted in magazines and biographies as a watershed moment for the three of us."

I knew I wouldn't get anywhere with Joshua, but I tried to sway Jessica privately when we were in the basement later, doing laundry.

"This is a mistake," I said.

"I've become a joke," she said, putting her clothes in the washer after I had moved my load to the dryer. "I've got to salvage my reputation."

"You can do that with another exhibition."

"No one's going to give me another show now—not if I let this go. Joshua's right. Even if the shit comes down, at least my name as an artist will get out there."

"Are you sure it's worth it?" I asked. "Are you sure that's how you want to make your mark?"

"Are you implying the show's not worth defending?" she asked. "That it's something I should be ashamed of?"

"I wish you had exhibited your paintings," I said, looking at the stacks of canvases against the wall. "I think these are wonderful. I really think that's the direction you should've followed."

"Don't obfuscate. Answer my question. Say what you really mean."

"Why do you think all those other organizations wouldn't take the case? Purely out of legal considerations?"

"Answer me."

"Maybe," I told her, "the *Globe* review had some validity. Maybe there could have been more substance, fewer gimmicks."

"You've got a lot of fucking nerve," Jessica said. "I can't believe this, coming from you. You've written one good story in your life, and you took what could have been Esther's slot in the Discoveries issue, no compunction whatsoever, even though you're on the staff. For what?"

"That's not fair," I said. "I did have compunctions. A lot of them. I wanted to pull my story. Joshua convinced me not to."

"And he's the god of propriety," Jessica said. "I hate the bitch right now, but Esther's the real deal. You know that. She works hard, she deserves to be recognized. Whereas you're always complaining you don't have time to write. Let me ask you: When will you? Will you ever do anything instead of just talking about it? Maybe you should just quit, Eric. Give up trying. The world doesn't need another dilettante, and that's all you've ever been."

■   ■   ■

Barboza filed a counter-complaint against Jessica, Chapter 272, Section 29, for public dissemination of obscene and pornographic materials, which was punishable by a maximum of five years or a fine of $10,000. Both the malicious destruction and obscenity complaints would be heard in ten days by the clerk magistrate of the Third District Court of Middlesex County, who would determine if criminal charges should go forward against either party.

"This is scandalous," Barboza told the *Globe*. "I can't believe she and her misfit cronies want to waste taxpayer money on this. But if they want a fight, I'll give them one."

This time, in addition to newspaper reporters, local TV crews showed up at the house, and Margolies and Joshua were all too happy to grant interviews.

"Freedom is about tolerating what you might despise," Margolies said. "If you can't do that, you're un-American."

"It's clear with the councilman's recent remarks," Joshua said, "that he's a bigot. We're demanding his resignation. We will not condone this kind of racist conduct. Asian Americans will not be anyone's patsies."

Some City Council members began to backpedal from their initial decision not to cancel the show. "It's possible that the exhibit constitutes a form of artistic recklessness," the vice mayor said. One of the Arts Council members alleged that she did not know the exhibit would contain sexually explicit material when they had approved the project—a barefaced lie, since Jessica's application had described exactly what she planned to do, her only alteration using casts of real genitalia instead of sex toys.

With increased ardor, the story was rehashed on talk radio stations, and the head columnist for the *Boston Herald*, Joe Quinney, addressed the subject with particular zeal. "Over in the People's Republic of Cambridge," he wrote, "where the diversity-university PC police run amok and City Hall is banned from displaying Christmas trees, it's apparently permissible to display your private parts in public, as long as you call it 'art.'" ("P-p-please. Is it possible to alliterate any more than that?" Joshua said.) "This is yet another example of the sordidness polluting our society, where this cheap, imitation Mapplethorpe with penis envy is being allowed to parade her perversions in a public place." ("Yes, it's possible!" Joshua cackled.)

Paviromo, in one of his rare visits to the *Palaver* office, asked me, very amused, "What in the world is going on in that house of yours? I didn't think you had it in you, my boy."

There followed, as Margolies predicted, protests and rallies. Demonstrators gathered in front of the City Hall Annex with signs that read THE FIRST AMENDMENT DOES NOT PROTECT FILTH, STOP PORNOGRAPHY NOW, GOD HATES SINNERS.

Anonymous hate mail was sent to the house, and anonymous hate phone messages were left on the machine: "You gooks are pervs" and "Fucking chink whore, go back to China."

We unlisted the number and stopped answering the telephone. "Still think this was such a great idea?" I said to Joshua.

"Give me the damn code so I can erase this shit."

"No. We might need the tape later for evidence."

The story was picked up by the wires, the AP writing "City Councilor Charged in Stolen Porn Case," and presumably the article was reprinted in the *Saratogian*, the local paper in Saratoga Springs, for one evening I came home to find that Jessica's father had called the house. They had had no communication in seven years, although, surreptitiously, her mother and younger sisters had been in occasional touch with Jessica.

Her father had left a two-sentence message on the answering machine. "You shame me," he said. "You are not my daughter."

I knocked on her door. "Jessica?" She was lying on her bed in the dark, turned toward the wall.

"You heard it," she said.

"I heard it," I said, squatting down on the futon.

She sat up and leaned her back against the wall to face me. "I should have listened to you," she said. "I never thought it'd get so crazy."

I don't think any of us really had. At Mac, with Kathryn Newey, everything had gone so peaceably, so easily for us, we had been lulled into believing that we would be sheltered from true adversity. "It'll die down soon," I said. "It can't get any worse, right?"

In the last two days, she had been told by Martinique College of Art that her contract as a teacher would not be renewed, and she had been fired from Gaston & Snow.

"I'm finished as an artist," Jessica said.

"You'd be surprised how quickly people forget things. In a year, maybe even less, I bet no one will remember any of this."

"I went to Mount Auburn Hospital this morning," she told me.

"You did?" Reflexively I thought about Mirielle, wondered if she was still a medical secretary there, if she had heard from any MFA programs, if she was still seeing the temp. "Was it another panic attack?" I asked.

Jessica picked up her wrist braces. "My hands have been killing me. I couldn't stand it anymore, so last week I went in to find out about the surgery, and they did a bunch of tests. I got the results today. After all these years, now they tell me I might not have carpal tunnel at all. They think I might have rheumatoid arthritis."

I didn't know anything about the condition. "Is it treatable?"

"It's chronic and progressive." She flexed her hand, opening and closing her fingers, the tattoo of the green peacock quill on her forearm pulsing. "They don't know, it might be a different kind of arthritis altogether. I'm supposed to see a rheumatologist next month. But I went over to Longwood"—where she proofread part-time for the *New England Journal of Medicine*—"and did some research. It all fits, all the symptoms. My bones could start fusing. My fingers could twist up and become permanently deformed. It might get so I can't grip a paintbrush or craft knife anymore."

The image of Jessica crippled, no longer being able to do what she loved most, was heartbreaking. "Try not to dwell on it right now," I said. "Wait till you hear from the rheumatologist."

"It doesn't matter," Jessica said. "I don't think I was ever cracked up to be an artist in the first place."

"How can you say that?"

"The mannequins," she said, "they were just a device. The *Globe* critic saw right through me. You did, too. All the stuff with the 3AC, everything we've been spouting off about since Mac, they've been a crutch. It's been a way of adding agency to my work when there hasn't been any. I'm just a technician with nothing to say, really. Maybe I should have just gone to med school."

"You couldn't be more wrong, Jessica."

"Am I? What's it mean, then? What's the point? Why can't I do something of substance, like you said, something real, something from here"—she jabbed her fist against her gut—"and not from here?"—she knocked her fist against the side of her head. "From *here*"—she hit her stomach again, harder—"not from *here*"—she punched her head. "From *here*—"

I grabbed her wrists. "Stop it, Jessica."

She was crying now. "All the hoopla, even before it all turned to shit, I ask myself, Did I really want this? Any of it? Because the truth is, if I could take it all back, I would."

"It's not too late," I said.

"It's too late."

"We could drop the complaint."

"Even if we did, Barboza would never let it go. It's an election year. He wants a trial. This is the most fun he's ever had."

"Maybe he'll listen to reason."

"I wish it could all go away," Jessica said. "I wish it could all just end."

■   ■   ■

I knew from news reports that Vivaldo Barboza was forty-seven, and that he still lived with his mother. They had emigrated from the Azores when he was nine. His father had already been in the U.S. for two years, working at a glassworks factory near Lechmere, and once reunited, the three of them had settled in the Portuguese community of East Cambridge.

Vivaldo had arrived knowing no English, but eventually managed to earn a bachelor of science degree in business administration from Suffolk University. Nevertheless, other than getting licensed as a justice of the peace, he never pursued a career outside of the family business. From the time he was seventeen, he and his mother—a widow since the late sixties, when Vivaldo's father had died of a heart attack—had been running a small corner market near Inman Square.

I took Joshua's Peugeot and drove down Broadway. I didn't know the name of the Barbozas' store, and I couldn't remember whether it was on Columbia or Windsor Street. I crisscrossed the vicinity known as Area 4, which was largely an African American neighborhood. I stopped at several bodegas and markets, but the merchants were Brazilian, Indian, Syrian. I searched closer to Cambridge Street, and finally spotted Azores Variety on Columbia.

"Hello," a woman said when I walked in. Friendly, energetic. She was in her early seventies, perhaps—almost certainly Barboza's mother. The family resemblance was uncanny. A thick body, a wide face with a prominent brow and heavy-lidded eyes, downturned at the corners like the mouth, only Vivaldo's wavy hair was dark while hers was white, and she was quite short, the counter she stood behind too high for her.

I browsed the aisles, temporizing. The place was dimly lit, rather dismal. I had been expecting Portuguese staples like salted cod, fava beans, and linguica, but there was none of that here, just sundries that could be found in any store, odds and ends, everything dusty, overpriced, the stamps on many of the products past expiration. There wasn't much of a stock, either, one or two of each item on the sparse shelves, like the one bar of soap or the one package of thumbtacks or the one can of shaving cream. I pulled a gallon of milk from the cooler and set it on the counter.

"Anything else?" the woman asked.

I picked out some gum from the rack of candy bars.

"Bag?"

"Yes, please." There was a sign on the cash register, written with a Sharpie, that said CASH ONLY. NO CHECK. NO CREDIT CARD.

She slowly counted out my change. She was wearing very thick glasses.

"Is Vivaldo home?" I asked. I had read in the paper that their apartment was above the store.

She brightened. "You friends with Vivaldo?"

"Is he home?"

She pressed a doorbell buzzer screwed to the wall, and I could hear it ringing above us, then the thump of footsteps coming down the stairs a few seconds later.

I was facing the back of the store, assuming he would enter from there, but the stairwell apparently led out to the street. He came in through the front door. "Yes, Mãe?" he said.

"A friend has come to visit you!" his mother told him, as if it were a very rare occurrence.

Hesitantly, he shook my hand, confused. "I'm sorry, could you tell me where we know each other from? I can't place you."

"I'm Eric Cho," I said. When my name didn't register, I added, "Jessica Tsai's friend. The 3AC."

He recoiled. "Let's go outside." We stepped out onto the sidewalk. "What do you want?" he asked.

"I was hoping we could talk," I said. "Maybe calm things down a bit. Everything's gotten a little out of control, don't you think?"

"You guys started it. I didn't do a thing."

"I think we've all said a few things—without really meaning to—to stoke the fire."

"I'm not going to apologize," Barboza said. "I'm standing by my principles. I'm just doing what I believe and what's in the best interests of my constituents."

"Don't you think it'd be mutually beneficial," I asked, "if we could take a step back and, you know, discuss this rationally?"

"I am being rational," he said. "I ask again: What do you want?"

"We'll drop our complaint if you'll drop yours."

He smirked. "Pressure gotten too much for you and your friends?" he said.

"I admit, we didn't anticipate this level of hysteria," I said, willing to bend a little.

"Well, you asked for it," Barboza said. "I'm not going to drop the complaint."

"The show will be over in a week. You've already made your point."

"Not going to happen."

"We listened to bad advice, okay?" I said. "We shouldn't have brought the courts into it. We see that now. So wouldn't it be better for the taxpayers if we both pulled back?"

"If I dropped it, it'd look like I caved in to you."

"What about this, then?" I said, encouraged by the small opening. "Let's agree to both withdraw the complaints at the end of the month, when the exhibit's over. That way, it won't look like anyone compromised. In the meantime, how about we impose a gag order on ourselves and not talk to the media anymore?"

Barboza was wearing a short-sleeved white dress shirt. He tugged on the knot of his tie—it was a clip-on—and removed it. He rolled the tie into a compact spool, stuffed it into his front pocket, and loosened the top button of his shirt. "You see this street?" he said. "Look how brightly lit it is, every streetlight working, the reflectors in the road in front of the crosswalks. Before I took office, this was a pedestrian hazard. Two kids got hit in one summer. One of them died. You think I'm uncultured and stupid. What makes you think you're so much better than everyone else, just because you're an artist? What do you contribute to society? At least I've made the streets safer, at least I've gotten foot patrols increased and put bike paths in and reduced the rodent population. Maybe these are small things to you, things that don't matter, but they're not to the people who live here. I've worked hard to make their lives a little better. What have you done?"

The street was, in fact, impressively well lit. I could see the crease marks on his neck from his shirt collar, a mole in the notch of his jugular. "We're trying to improve the lives of Asian Americans," I said.

"I'm an immigrant just like you. You think I wasn't made fun of, being Portuguese? You think I didn't get teased as a kid?"

Briefly, I wondered if Barboza ever experienced *saudade*. What did he yearn for? I knew he had never been married, did not have children. I doubted very much he had a girlfriend. A part of me wanted to feel sorry for him.

"Why'd you say that thing on TV?" he asked. "Why'd you have to bring race into it?"

He thought I was Joshua. "We didn't. You did. Remember? 'Little egg rolls'? 'Bonsai bush'?"

"One of the hosts on the talk show, Louie, he fed me that line. I regret it. But I ask you, should it have been such a big deal? Now people think I'm a bigot. Yeah, it was colorful language, but that's talk radio. You get caught up in the hyped-up energy of the show. There wasn't any harm intended. It was just creative license."

The milk was getting heavy, the handles of the plastic bag cutting into my fingers. "What's that mean, 'creative license'?"

"They're just words," he told me. "What's it matter? Race has nothing to do with this. It's about decency. It's about whether government agencies should be sanctioning perversion. So to say what you did, using the race card, that was a cheap shot. I would have reacted the same way if the artist was white."

"Don't you see?" I said. "It makes all the difference that the artist isn't white. The context is what separates her exhibit from pornography."

"Just because you're Asian American, you get a free pass?"

"You don't understand the cultural references."

"Explain them to me, then."

"The whole exhibit is about caricatures, the stereotypes that Asian Americans are saddled with."

"Uh-huh," Barboza said.

"It's a satirical treatise on—"

"Listen," he said, "you guys always say how you don't want to be treated any different."

"We don't."

"But anything happens, you automatically say it's racist."

"A lot of times, it is. You think your comment was innocent, but these things are never innocent, it's never just a joke, they're never just words. If you really think about it, you'll realize what you said was racist."

"Oh, yeah?" Barboza said. "Tell me, who made you Martin Luther Kim?"

A car drove by, going much too fast, the windows tinted black, hip-hop thumping from inside, the bass concussive enough so we could feel it out on the sidewalk. "Hey, hey, slow down!" Barboza yelled. He stared after the car until it had sped out of sight. "Fucking . . . ," he began to mutter, then caught himself. He turned to me with a sheen of embarrassment.

"I know what you were about to say," I told him.

"You don't know shit."

"By the way, I'm not an immigrant, and it wasn't me on TV. That was my friend Joshua. I realize we all look alike to you."

"We're done here," Barboza said.

"Forget the offer," I said. "We're not going to back down. We're not going to drop the complaint."

"Neither am I."

"Go give your mother a break, Vivaldo. You shouldn't make her work so much."

"Fuck you."

"Here, dump this. It's expired—a public safety hazard," I said, and left the milk on the sidewalk.

■　■　■

We received another anonymous letter, this one written in crayon on a page torn from a spiral notebook. "Its because of sodamight motherfuckers like you this country is going to Hell. Enoughs enough. Im coming after you. Prepare to meet the reeper and be delivered to pain. Prepare to die you crepes."

The misspellings, punctuation errors, and childlike handwriting aside, we were chilled by the threat, more so because it did not include any racial epithets. Rather, the envelope contained hundreds of tiny pieces of sheet metal, methodically snipped into razor-sharp triangles.

"I don't know why," Joshua said, "but it's the green crayon that puts it over the top. It makes it feel truly deranged."

"Keep the front door locked," I told him. "You're always forgetting."

Glumly, Jessica nudged pieces of sheet metal across the dining table with her finger. "You said it couldn't get any worse."

I gave the envelope to the police, along with the rest of the hate mail and the microcassette of hate messages from the answering machine, but they didn't seem overly concerned. Instead, they chose to investigate the 3AC.

I was dealing with a crisis at work. Our list broker had screwed up, and I realized we would be woefully short of addresses for our direct-mail campaign. Then I stumbled upon another snafu. The lettershop had neglected to apply for an additional mailing office in Vermont, and the process usually took thirty days. I phoned the General Mail Facility in Boston to plead for an exception, but was told that they had just canceled our bulk-mailing permit, claiming we had not used it in over fifteen months.

In the midst of all of this, Joshua called me. "Dude," he said, "Jimmy and Noklek are in jail."

The police had set up a sting operation on Pink Whistle, sending two undercover detectives to the salon the day before, both requesting massages. The first cop told Jimmy that he was in a hurry. "You want the fifteen-minute, then, for fifty," Jimmy told him. According to the police report, the cop gave Jimmy a twenty and three tens (marked bills) and was led into the back office, which was furnished with a massage table, towels, assorted body oils, a low-lit lamp with a red shade, and mirrors framed by tassels and black lace. Noklek entered the room, wearing a tube top and hot pants, and she offered him a menu of "Extras": Topless, Nude, Doctor, Foot Fetish, Domination, Russian Ending, and Pop the Cork, priced between $25 and $150. The detective chose Topless, and Noklek, after taking a twenty and a five from him (also marked), removed her tube top, massaged his chest and stomach, fondled his testicles, and gave him a hand job until the timer rang. Three hours later, a second detective stepped into Pink Whistle for the same services, whereupon they arrested Jimmy and Noklek. They had been held overnight and were being arraigned this morning.

Joshua picked me up at the office and drove us to the courthouse. "Why'd they have to spend the night in jail?" I asked. "Couldn't they get bail?"

"I don't know. Jimmy called me less than an hour ago."

"Why didn't they let him call earlier?"

"I don't *know*, okay? I've been scrambling around, trying to find Margolies and Grace. I'm still fucking half asleep. I was up all night writing. I finally got on a roll, man."

In court, Jimmy was charged with keeping a house of ill fame, Chapter 272, Section 24, and deriving support from prostitution, Chapter 272, Section 7. The penalty for the first charge was no more than two years, but for the second charge it was no *less* than two years in state prison, with no chance of early release, probation, or a reduced sentence. Noklek was charged with engaging in sexual conduct for a fee, Chapter 272, Section 53A, punishable by up to one year or a fine of $500. I discovered that Chapter 272 of the Massachusetts General Laws—the same classification under which the counter-complaint against Jessica, dissemination of obscene materials, had been filed—was entitled "Crimes Against Chastity, Morality, Decency, and Good Order."

Both Jimmy and Noklek pled not guilty, and Margolies and Grace, representing them in court, arranged for their release, Jimmy on $500 cash bail, Noklek on personal recognizance, pending a hearing in one month. After the arraignment, however, Grace told us that the INS had been alerted to Noklek's immigration status, and she might be deported before her case ever reached trial, green-card marriage or not.

"That's fascist crap," Joshua said. "Cambridge is a sanctuary city. The police aren't supposed to cooperate with the INS."

"She gave them a fake name. She had a fake ID," Grace said. "That's what set everything in motion. The line gets fuzzy if they learn someone's illegal while in custody. Even then, they normally wouldn't bother doing anything, especially for a minor offense. But this isn't normal. Not with so much about you guys in the press. You know, you could have given the rest of us a little warning you were going to file the complaint against Barboza. Or maybe even have let us weigh in on it. But what did I really expect from you three prima donnas?"

Joshua and I waited for Noklek and Jimmy to be released from holding. "This is total bullshit," Joshua said. "Since when is it acceptable for cops to get their pugs yanked, not once but twice, on the city's dime for an investigation? This is all retaliatory, you know. It's because we're Asian."

"Jesus fucking Christ," I said. "You did this, Joshua. This is all your fault. The massages were your idea. You knew how this would turn out. It was entirely predictable. The whole green-card scam, did you and Jimmy cook it up to get Noklek to prostitute herself?"

"No, man. That was sincere."

I thought of all the trouble he had caused over the years, all the preening and disquisitions and rebukes, all the bad decisions that he had suckered me into, all those moments of anxiety and queasy discomfort I had had to endure as he harassed and manipulated and bullied me into servitude. How much better, I wondered, would my life have been if I'd never met Joshua?

"I don't believe you," I said. "Nothing you do is sincere. It was just a whim. You were never serious about it. You get these impulses and you go on these crusades, but you never stop to think how people will be affected. You keep fucking up everyone's lives, Joshua. You realize that? I think you do, but you keep doing it anyway. Why is that? Is it entertaining to you? Amusing? Are you getting writing material out of it? Let me tell you something. The world doesn't owe you anything because you're Asian, because you were abandoned. I can't do this anymore. I can't take this shit. I'm done. I'm done with you."

Noklek came out first, hugging her arms around her chest. She was still wearing her tube top and hot pants and a pair of strappy shoes with ludicrously high stilettos. I touched her on the shoulder, and she yelled, "*Yaa ma jap chan!*" and ran away from us, clacking down the hall.

"I need a drink," Jimmy said when he emerged. "Is it too early for a drink?"

I took the T from Kendall to Harvard Square and then rode the bus to the *Palaver* office. I spent the rest of the day calling the General Mail Facility about our permit and searching for documentation in our files to prove that we had, in fact, sent out three mailings in the past year. After hours of faxing and being put on hold, I was able to get the permit reinstated.

Drained, I went home early, splurging on a cab. I walked into the kitchen, and through the sliding glass door I saw Jessica in her white silk robe, kneeling on the deck outside.

But it wasn't Jessica. It was Noklek in Jessica's robe, and she was soaking wet, from water, I assumed, reenacting the Songkran festival rituals. She had the shrine before her, the three small Buddhas, the flowers, candles, incense, and framed photographs of her mother, father, and sister. Rice grains were scattered on the redwood boards of the deck, and white string was wrapped around her ankles. Somehow she had tied her wrists together with the string, too, and between her palms she held two flowers, two lit candles, and a twenty-dollar bill.

I stood at the glass door, looking down at her, and, sensing my presence, she slowly turned to me. Instead of white chalk, it looked as if candle wax was smeared over her lips and eyelids. She stared at me, emotionless, for a moment, then faced the shrine again, the photos of her family.

I noticed the red plastic can beside her, the depressions of an X on its side, and I realized then that it was the spare canister for the lawn mower. She had drenched herself in gasoline, not water. That was when she closed her eyes, tipped the candles against the left breast of the robe, and set herself aflame.

17

At what point is it acceptable to give up? The years go by, and there might be some validations, a few encouraging signs, a small triumph here and there, but more often than not, failure follows upon failure. You get into your thirties, and every day you wonder if it's worth it to keep going. How long can you continue being a starving artist? Will it ever happen for you? Very possibly, it will not. Then where will you be? Sometime or another, you have to decide.

The oblique questions and snipes from civilians and your family become a babel in your head, insisting that you grow up, be practical, find a real job, give up on this fruitless dream, because, really, it's become kind of pathetic. You tried, but it came to naught. It might have been due to a lack of providence, yet more likely, although no one will ever say so outright, it was probably due to a lack of talent. Even among ourselves, there are doubts and judgments. We still go to one another's shows and exhibitions and readings and performances, rare as they may be now, and afterward we dole out all the appropriate accolades, but secretly we wonder if, perhaps, our friends never quite lived up to their promise—if we believed they had promise to begin with—and if, perhaps, it's time for them to give up.

We love our friends. We hate them, too. It's easy to feign support and sympathy for them when they're failing. It's much harder to affect elation when they start to succeed. It's a terrible feeling—a sterling reminder of your underachievement and inertia. This is when the schadenfreude begins, the invidious whispers that maybe your friend's success is undeserved, when you revel in the publication of an unkind review or the unexpected exclusion of your friend's work from that year's major awards. You detest this about yourself. You've become exactly the type of person you've always despised. It eats away at you. You promise to reform, to be more generous, to focus on your own work with renewed vigor and diligence. Yet it seems that there's never enough time, or that when you finally do find the time and embark on a new project, you falter right away, feeling dispirited and desperate, knowing that it's all wrong, that it'd be pointless to continue because the whole thing is misconceived, and even if it isn't, you know you could never pull it off, anyway.

The thought of giving up gains appeal. People might not change, but situations do. You've acquired different priorities, and inevitably some things must be left behind. Your parents always told you that life is about money, and you refused to believe them, but as you've gotten older, you've begun to reconsider. You wouldn't mind a few bourgeois creature comforts, a new car, vacations, actually owning property instead of living in rented shitholes, and you start to admit that there is something to having money.

Would it be so shameful to give up? Of course you'd never admit to giving up. You'd say you're continuing to toil, you're making great progress, you're almost finished. One by one, your friends begin dropping out. If they haven't compromised themselves already, in their hearts they want to, because being true to one's art, keeping the dream alive, is utterly exhausting.

What stops you is fear—fear that you'll always see yourself as someone who couldn't hack it, fear that you'll become even more bitter than you already are, that you'll always wonder what could have, should have, and would have happened if you'd kept at it a bit longer. Mainly, you're afraid of abandoning the sole thing that makes you distinctive, your identity as a bohemian artist, that allows to you be blasé and condescending about your mindless service job or your soul-sapping position as an admin assistant in an office where everyone talks in acronyms.

I hung on for about five more years, until I was thirty-four, although I never finished my novella, never got a story published, never assembled enough material for a book manuscript. I withdrew my story, "The Unrequited," from *Palaver*'s Fiction Discoveries issue at the last minute, when the issue was already in final galleys. I told Paviromo that I wanted to earn my first publication, not weasel my way into print through favoritism, and that he should publish Esther Xing's story in its stead. I will confess that, at the time, I was pretty certain I could get "The Unrequited" taken elsewhere, but I was never able to. A pity, since it really was, as Jessica said, the only good story, the only honest story, I ever wrote. It was about my parents' courtship, the months that my father went to the post office in Monterey Park to woo my mother, mailing blank letters to phantom recipients.

I stayed at *Palaver* for another year and a half to finish out the Lila Wallace program, then worked a series of freelance and temp jobs, doing everything from copyediting business articles to writing newsletters for a trade association of bus operators. Finally, in 2004, I accepted a full-time job in downtown Boston at Gilroy Prunier, a boutique marketing firm that catered to invest-ment banks and financial services companies. My primary area of responsibility was direct marketing, i.e., direct mail. I wrote and edited the copy that went on letters, envelopes, slip-sheets, forms, brochures, and postcards.

Joshua told me I was squandering my talent. I was betraying our vow to be artists. I was no longer a believer. I had sold out.

In truth, I felt relieved.

We all moved out of the Walker Street house after Noklek immolated herself. How could we stay there, with the scorched wood on the deck, the soot whispers on the clapboards, the singed patches of grass? And the smell—the smell that could not have pos-sibly lingered, yet that we imagined did.

When skin burns, the blood vessels below begin to dilate and weep. The skin bubbles and blisters. It chars and blackens. As flames eat through the flesh, raw tissue starts to appear. Fat is exposed, and it sizzles. There's an awful odor. It's like charcoal at first, not unpleasant, then quickly becomes putrid and vinegary, almost metallic, like copper liquefying. The hair is the worst—sul-furous—but then, mixed in there, there's a queerly sweet scent, the searing of fat and tissue blossoming into a thick, greasy perfume.

Unlike the monk Thích Quảng Đức, who had remained silent and still while he burned, Noklek began screaming at once. She tried to stand, but her ankles and wrists were tied by the string, and she tumbled, knocking over the shrine and crashing against the side of the house and keeling back onto the deck. I grabbed her and rolled her on the grass in the backyard, using my own body to smother the flames, then, as she shrieked and writhed, I sprayed her with the garden hose until she passed out, steam rising from her flesh and what was left of the white silk robe.

I was burned on my hands, forearms, and chest, the dim scars of which I carry to this day, but of course they're nothing compared to what Noklek had to endure. She spent over a year in Bigelow 13, the burn unit at Mass General, and in a rehabilitation center. She suffered second- and third-degree burns on sixty-five percent of her body and required agonized procedures of debridement and grafting. More than once it was questionable whether she would survive, in danger of sepsis, renal failure, and infection. I had saved her life, but what kind of life did I leave her? I sometimes wondered, in the brutal light of her pain and disfigurement, if it would have been more merciful to have let her die.

I never told anyone about my conversation with Barboza, which undoubtedly had provoked the police investigation into Pink Whistle. For once, instead of waffling in indecision, I had done something, just as Joshua had always exhorted me to do, and it had been the wrong thing. The guilt I feel over this will never abate, it cannot be absolved.

I couldn't bring myself to visit Noklek in the hospital very much, as opposed to Joshua, who went to see her every day. He put the house on the market, rented an apartment in Beacon Hill, and paid for the entire cost of Noklek's hospitalization. He still wanted to marry her (the assistant district attorney had dropped the prostitution charge, and the INS chose not to pursue her), but she said no, and as soon as she could, she left the U.S. for Thailand, where Joshua sent her international money orders for two years, until the envelopes started to get returned, forwarding address unknown.

The Walker Street house was sold at the height of the real estate boom. Joshua, however, did not invest the proceeds very wisely, putting a lot of it in tech stocks, which took a dive during the dotcom bust. He became an itinerant, going from one artists' colony to another for extended residencies or accepting short-term visiting writer gigs at colleges, only reappearing in Boston for sojourns of one to six months. I missed him. Regardless of what I'd told him that horrible day, I was never really done with Joshua. We would remain friends, though it would be a changed friendship, less urgent, less pervasive, with an unspoken falseness that would stiffen with time, neither one of us able to overcome a niggling discomfort with each other.

He got the attention he wanted from the Fiction Discoveries issue—calls from several literary agents. He signed up with the most prominent one, and the agent sent out his novel for auction when he finished it, but puzzlingly there were no takers. In the end, just before his thirtieth birthday, they were able to sell the book to a small press, a prestigious house as far as noncommercial publishers went, but nonetheless it was a disappointment to him.

Upon the Shore was about the inhabitants of Cheju Island during the rebellion that began there in 1948 and resulted in the massacre of tens of thousands of people by the (U.S.-backed) Korean government. Almost universally, the novel engendered stellar reviews, even getting a half-page rave in the *New York Times Book Review*, yet not much else happened. No bestseller lists, no book prizes, no esteemed fellowships. Joshua complained that it was because he had been marginalized, dismissed, as an ethnic writer. There might have been some truth in this. One midwestern newspaper presumed he was a South Korean writer, that his book had been translated from Korean into English.

His second novel, *The Base*, was set in the 1970s and portrayed the Itaewon merchants, bargirls, and civilian workers who serviced the American soldiers on Yongsan Eighth Army base. His third novel, *And I Will Be Here*, was about a drug-addicted Korean American female poet in a wheelchair who was stalking her Cambridge neighbor. The critical reception was less glowing, often dwelling on how unlikable or unsympathetic his characters were (the first line of *And I Will Be Here* was: "Just so you know, I am a hateful person"), and neither book sold well. They weren't crossing over. With all the screeds on racism, readers felt they were being preached to. He wasn't connecting, even, with Asian Americans. The younger generation, he was baffled to discover, wasn't interested in the subject of race.

To me, each book was more profound and lyrical than the last. All three were beautifully bleak, quietly heartrending. They deserved better. (For years, whenever I went into a bookstore, I would locate the spines of his latest novel, rearrange the shelf, and turn the copies of his book ninety degrees so the cover would face out. I still do that now, though more and more, I cannot find any of his books in stores.)

Obsessively Joshua checked the sales rankings for his novels online. He tortured himself by reading book industry blogs and *Publishers Weekly*, fulminating whenever he learned about a large advance that was being given to a pretty young white writer. He railed and brooded whenever a contemporary received a rhapsodic review or prize, especially when it pertained to one writer—"our nemesis," he called her—Esther Xing, who was offered, after her story appeared in the Discoveries issue, a two-book deal from Knopf for a story collection and a novel. The latter, which had all white main characters, became a Pulitzer Prize finalist, a first for an East Asian American writer.

The person from the 3AC who had the most success was Tina Nguyen, with her wall cuts. Annie Yoshikawa was also able to make a living from her large-format photographs, although she never reached the stature of Dijkstra or Lockhart. Leon Lee and Cindy Wong did fairly well, exhibiting their paintings regularly and teaching in an art school—a joint appointment they shared as a married couple until they divorced. Phil Sudo started an improvisational jazz band, Avant Garbage, then wrote a book called *Zen Guitar* and traveled around the country, giving motivational speeches about incorporating Zen philosophy into music, art, everyday life, and business. He died of stomach cancer at the age of thirty-five.

Jimmy Fung served his mandatory two-year sentence in state prison, MCI-Norfolk, then disappeared. I lost track of a lot of people. Jessica withdrew the malicious destruction complaint against Barboza, and, in kind, he dropped the obscenity complaint against her. She moved to San Francisco and then to L.A., and we kept in frequent touch for a while, but talk less now.

After our breakup, I never spoke to Mirielle Miyazato again, but occasionally I checked up on her on the Internet. She didn't go to an MFA program in poetry. She became a research assistant at a think tank in D.C., then ended up in Miami, where she sold commercial real estate. A few years ago, she married the founder of a sustainable building company. High-res images of their wedding were online, posted by the photographer to market his services. Mirielle looked beautiful, ecstatic. More than once, I clicked through the album. In one photo, she was holding what might have been a wineglass, but I couldn't be sure what was in it—possibly just water. Her husband was about her age, good-looking, stylish with his short dreads, Afro-Cuban American. Recently they had a baby, I read on her website. I've always regretted telling her that she was a bad person.

The last time I saw Joshua was in July 2008, two months before he killed himself, when I drove out to his rented cottage in Sudbury to say goodbye to him. I was leaving Cambridge for good—a relocation, a wholesale life change, that had come about swiftly.

"Unbelievable," he said as I got out of my car. "You never got rid of your mayonnaise streak, did you?"

Two years earlier, I had gone to the Boston Athenaeum, the private library catty-corner from the State House. The Athenaeum was trying to recruit a younger membership, and they were hosting a mixer that day. These receptions, besides the draw of exceptional wine and hors d'oeuvres, had acquired a reputation as a meat market.

I was already a member. I often spent my lunch hour at the library, and that evening I had gone there after work to get a novel I wanted to reread, not knowing a mixer was being held. After checking the catalog, I wended through the crowd, past the busts of Petrarch and Dante, into the reading room with its leather chairs, vaulted ceiling, and arched windows. A woman was leaning against the very bookshelf I needed to access, listening to a fellow trying to chat her up.

She had an old-fashioned air about her, blond hair parted in the middle and tied into a thick ponytail that ran down her back, a vintage indigo dress with subtle white piping rather than the ubiquitous power suit. She wore little makeup, and had a narrow face.

I waited, not wanting to interrupt their conversation, but finally said, "Excuse me, could I reach behind you for a second?"

She looked at me blankly, then said, "You trying to find a book?"

"It's supposed to be on that shelf. If I could—"

"I don't think you understand the parameters here."

"Sorry?"

"I saw a sign posted at the entrance. You didn't see the sign?"

"Which sign?"

"The one that said no reading allowed. It was very explicit."

She grinned slyly, and I knew then who she was. I hadn't seen her in fourteen years. "I guess I was misinformed," I said. "This isn't a library?"

"Apparently not," she said. "Which book?" She stepped aside, and I pulled out William Maxwell's *So Long, See You Tomorrow* from the shelf. "Oh, I've read that," she told me.

"You have?"

"Sure, several times. My father went to elementary school with the author."

"No kidding."

"He said Billy was a smart kid, but kind of antisocial. The sort of kid who goes to cocktail parties and sits in a corner with a book."

"I didn't know elementary kids went to cocktail parties back then."

"Astonishing, isn't it?" she said. "A different era. They started them young."

Her prospective suitor excused himself and retreated into the crowd.

"Do you think it was something I said?" she asked me.

"How have you been, Didi?"

I moved in with her less than a year later. "Why'd we break up at Mac again?" she asked. "I can't remember."

In many ways, it was as if she were an entirely different person. I remembered what Joshua had told me once, long ago—that Didi had no soul—but she was nothing like she'd been in college.

After Macalester, Didi had gone to Manhattan, working as a computer programmer for an insurance corporation before landing at Cantor Fitzgerald, on the 103rd floor of the World Trade Center. In 2000, she was transferred to Cantor's Milan office, and the following year, all her friends and colleagues in New York died on 9/11. She quit Cantor, found a job at an Italian brokerage firm in Rome, met Alessandro Pacelli, the creative director of an ad agency, and almost immediately got pregnant by him. They had three children in quick succession, Matteo, Wyatt, and Finnea. Didi became a stay-at-home mom and was content, she thought, until she discovered that Alessandro had been sleeping with two different women, one of whom was their housekeeper. She fled to Chestnut Hill with the kids, and their divorce proceedings, involving U.S. and Italian courts, were a contentious mess, Alessandro calling Didi all manner of Italian variants for bitch, his favorite being *stronza*, fucking bitch, saying she had never loved him, had trapped him by deliberately getting pregnant when she knew he'd never wanted children, which was supremely ironic, since ten months after they separated he had a son with one of the women he'd been fucking (not the housekeeper).

Didi got what she wanted, sole custody of the kids, bought a house in Huron Village, and then looked for a job, a formidable challenge since she had been out of the workforce for almost five years. At last, she was hired as a software engineer at Fidelity Investments, specializing in Web applications for their online brokerage program.

She was with the technology group, not on the investment side, so she wasn't being yoked and pummeled by the upheavals in the market like the fund managers and portfolios analysts. Nonetheless, there had been two rounds of layoffs at Fidelity in the space of a year, and she was nervous. So was I. Everyone in the financial sector—and in businesses like Gilroy Prunier that depended on it—was on tenterhooks in the spring of 2008. Then Fidelity announced that it was consolidating some of its operations, and Didi was presented with a transfer to the Research Triangle in North Carolina. We talked about it. I applied for a job in Fidelity's marketing communications department down there, and was offered a position as a senior copywriter. I proposed to Didi. (We would join the circle of sixty percent of Mac grads who purportedly marry one another.) We were moving to Chapel Hill next week.

"I don't get it," Joshua said in his driveway. "Isn't her father loaded?"

"We want to support ourselves."

"But his money will always be there, won't it? It'll corrupt you eventually," he said. "You'll get emasculated by it."

I chose not to remind Joshua that he'd had money himself, that he had never really had to work a day in his life.

I liked Didi's parents, actually. Mr. O'Brien sometimes told me stories about his father, who had been the first in the family to immigrate to Boston from Ireland, and who, upon arrival, had been confronted with NINA signs: HELP WANTED—NO IRISH NEED APPLY. Mr. O'Brien thought the Irish and Koreans had more in common than any other ethnic groups: they shared a history of subjugation and divided homelands, they had violent tempers yet liked to carouse and sing, and they both drank like fish.

Joshua led me into the cottage and gave me a tour, which took all of two minutes, the place was so small. The living/dining room was one space, with a Pullman kitchen. It was sweltering inside from the July heat and humidity, and Joshua had two fans blowing at full speed, billowing the yellowed sheets he'd tacked to the windows. The furniture included with the rent—what little there was of it—was old. A round pedestal café table and two ladder-back chairs with rush seats, the pine painted white; a Windsor rocker; a little sofa with plaid cushions. I laughed seeing the stacks of books bungee-corded against the wall—my bygone trick at *Palaver*'s office.

"I thought you kept some of the furniture from the house," I said, remembering the beautiful bentwood tables, rugs, and Eames chair. "Don't you have stuff in storage?"

"I sold it all."

The bathroom was tiny, just a narrow shower stall, commode, and corner sink. In the bedroom was an oak four-poster, but the mattress was twin-sized, making it appear to be a child's. The cottage felt even more dismal with its low ceilings, and everything needed a thorough scrubbing, the smell of mildew pungent.

"I see you're the same old neat freak," I said.

"Yeah, well, I can't really be bothered with cleaning. Besides, I never invite anyone in here."

"You haven't met anyone lately?"

He shook his head. "I had a little flirtation at Yaddo last month, but it didn't go anywhere. I don't know, women don't seem to like me anymore. It's better this way, living like a monk. I'm writing up a storm. Haven't you heard? Celibacy induces a form of mesmerism."

I stared at the fluffs of dust on the floor, wavering with the fans' currents. "You ought to hire a housecleaner, anyway. Purely for sanitary reasons."

"You want something to eat?" Joshua asked. "I could make us some ramen."

While he boiled water and cut up some bologna, he asked, "You've been reading about these credit default swaps? It's a total racket, a Ponzi scheme sanctioned by regulators and the government that allowed these companies to get unconscionably rich. It's not an industry I'd be proud of, you know."

"Fidelity's not Bear Stearns," I told him. "It's a different type of financial institution."

"You'll never write a book now for sure," he said. "This was your fatal flaw—you always had a backup plan. You were never willing to risk everything."

I couldn't argue with this assessment.

"Jesus," he said, "fucking Sourdough. And North Carolina. Prime-time redneckville." He tore up some cabbage leaves. "You want an egg in your ramen?"

He had quit smoking a year ago and had put on a good fifteen pounds since I'd last seen him in the fall. He was wearing Nikes, madras shorts, and a T-shirt that read FOOD SHARK, MARFA that was too tight on him. Running religiously did not offset his awful diet.

His hair had thinned further and was going a little gray, and he now kept it at a buzz cut with clippers. We were the same age, thirty-eight, but he looked much older.

I walked over to his desk and glanced at the piles of papers, files, Moleskines, manila envelopes, and index cards surrounding his laptop. Several articles and books on 9/11 and Asian immigrants in Manhattan rested on top of the laser printer that was on the floor.

"How's the novel coming along?" I asked.

"Really, really well," he said. "I think I'll be done with a draft by the end of the year. It's going to be a doorstopper."

I noticed a framed photograph on the wood-paneled wall above his desk. It was of the three of us—Joshua, Jessica, and me—at Mac, when we were eighteen, during the first snowstorm our freshman year, standing beside a snowman we had built. Didi had taken the photo. I had a copy of the same snapshot hanging in our hallway.

"Hey," Joshua said, "why don't you turn the game on? I want to check the score."

He carried bowls of ramen to the kitchen table. "It's not the same anymore," he said. He had been euphoric when the Red Sox had won the World Series in 2004, ending eighty-six years of futility, but when they won again in 2007, it had transformed them from a perennial underdog to just another big-market franchise with a bloated payroll. "The whole Bosox-Yankees agon, the way they'd find a way to lose in the most excruciating fashion, that's what I really lived for, when I think of it. There was something exquisite and poetic about those fucking catastrophes."

After we ate, we took a walk down Waterborne Road. "Why are you on that side?" I asked.

"To watch out for cars. It's safer to face the traffic."

"I don't think so," I said, but joined him on the left side of the road.

He was tired. He had just returned on the red-eye from Crescent City, California, a coastal town of four thousand (not counting the three thousand residents of Pelican Bay State Prison) close to the Oregon border. The library there had chosen *Upon the Shore* for its one-book program, in which the entire town was supposed to read and discuss his novel. Only about two hundred people did, or at least picked up a copy, and fewer than a hundred showed up for Joshua's reading, but the audience was attentive and appreciative, staying past the appointed hour to ask questions and have him sign their books. A young man lingered in line. "It must be so great to be a published author," he said, "to get all this adulation." Joshua smiled at him. What could he tell the young man? That he had published three books, but they had not made him rich or famous, or feel loved or admired? That he knew he was a journeyman destined to go out of print and be forgotten? That he had, in essence, achieved everything he had set out to do, and then had found out it was not the life he had wanted?

"I couldn't tell him what always happens," he said to me. "I couldn't tell him that no matter how well an event goes, without fail I'll wake up at two, three in the morning obsessing over a comment or a question someone asked, wondering if it was a veiled dig, or about an answer I gave, or about some old lady frowning at me in the front row, and I'll think to myself, God, I am such an asshole. I hate myself."

For the past few nights, I had been having trouble sleeping myself. Finnea, Didi's three (almost four)-year-old daughter, had for weeks been fascinated with scary stories, and she had pleaded for me to make one up for her. "It has to be long, something I've never heard before," she had said, "and it has to be really, really scary!" I had watched the horror channel on cable for inspiration, then, as I tucked her into bed, I told Finnea a story about a haunted house, a demon house with an underground river in which a monster was trapped. Finnea had squeezed her eyes shut and covered her ears. "Too scary? Should I stop?" I had asked her. "Keep talking," she had said. Afterward, it had been I, not Finnea, who had been frightened into waking in the middle of the night.

I thought of relating this to Joshua, describing to him, too, the simple joy of playing Frisbee with Matteo and Wyatt in the dying light of a summer's day, but I knew he would not be interested, that indeed he would scoff at my sentimentality. It'd be further evidence to him of what my life had come to, how I had sunk into pitiable domesticity.

By the side of the road, he stopped to stretch.

"What is it? Your back?" I asked.

"Yeah, I've been having spasms," he said. "I'm taking Vicodin for it. You know what my doctor suggested? Yoga. Could you ever see me doing yoga?"

Before leaving the cottage, I had used the bathroom, and I had been startled by the number of prescription bottles inside Joshua's medicine cabinet—in addition to the Vicodin: Xanax, Effexor, Diazepam, Ambien, Valium.

"You know," he said, flexing his stomach forward, "when I was at Yaddo, I walked by an optometrist's shop in Saratoga Springs. I saw this old Asian couple inside, running the store. I think they were Jessica's parents. Do you know the name of their shop? I almost went in."

"I'm not sure what it's called."

"Have you heard from her lately?"

"Not for a while." The last time I had spoken to Jessica was when I'd flown out to California to see my father and sister. Rebecca and her husband, Howard, a Korean American high school teacher, now had two children, and my father was living with them in

Pomona. During the beginning of the housing crisis, Rebecca had quit working for the mortgage industry, and was now volunteering for a nonprofit group that assisted homeowners facing foreclosure.

Jessica was in Silver Lake. Her rheumatoid arthritis had gotten worse over the years, and she had had to undergo several surgeries, getting plates and pins and polyethylene implants inserted into her wrists and ankles. When we met for coffee at a café on Hyperion, she showed me her gnarled fingers. "This is the worst part about RA," she told me, "how ugly my hands have become." Her feet caused her the most pain, but she was mobile, and her fingers were flexible enough to work. She operated a lucrative private business, making custom dildos and novelty porn clothes for celebrities. Her partner—both professionally and romantically—was Trudy Lun, who had been in L.A. working as a costume designer for the movie industry. Trudy was seven months' pregnant, inseminated with sperm donated by a (white) friend, and she and Jessica had bought a house together.

"So you're happy?" I had asked Jessica. I didn't broach what I really wanted to know. Whether—and how—she had reconciled that she was no longer making art. She wore a simple sundress with a cardigan draped over her shoulders. The tongue stud was gone, as were the eyebrow rings. She wasn't dyeing her hair anymore. She looked for all the world like a housewife.

"I guess so," she told me. "But you know, as Kierkegaard once said, happiness is sometimes the greatest hiding place for despair." One of Joshua's favorite quotations.

As we went down Waterborne, Joshua pointed out the high-bush blueberries and clethras, which he said would become very fragrant later in the summer; the royal and cinnamon ferns; the purple loosestrifes, which were vivid and pretty but terrible invasives. In late spring at night, frogs would come out onto the warm pavement, thousands of them, which would make a casual drive down the road, just to go out for an errand or takeout, a terrorizing experience—a massacre.

We heard a bell ringing in the distance—a church bell, it sounded like. "Hey, remember Weyerhaeuser?" Joshua asked, and revealed to me then that he had been a virgin—not just on-campus—when we were freshmen.

"You fucker," I said. "I can't believe you lied to me about that."

"That's between us. Have to safeguard the mythography, you know."

I've thought since then, of course, of what else Joshua might have lied to me about—being called a chink at the Sonic Youth concert, perhaps, the chalkboards, the extent to which he knew what was going on at Pink Whistle, maybe even what had happened on the pier in Southie.

We walked farther, and as we rounded a corner, we saw a jogger, a middle-aged Japanese man, coming down the crest of the next hill toward us. "Is that him?" Joshua asked, squinting, and we chuckled.

"You know what I've been thinking?" he said. "Tell me if this is crazy. I've been thinking about Lily Bai. Remember her? The BVIs? In retrospect, I think I should've tried harder to make that work. I've been thinking of calling her."

"Lily Bai?"

"You're right. It's a dumb idea."

We returned to the cottage, and after Joshua gave me a book he thought I should read (*Stoner* by John Williams), as well as a CD (*End of Love* by Clem Snide), we said our goodbyes beside my car.

"It was a good run, wasn't it?" he said.

I was confused, thinking he meant the jogger, or maybe our walk on Waterborne.

"Us," he said. "You, me, and Jessica. The real 3AC."

"You're talking like an old man."

He rubbed his hand over his scalp. "I feel old. You know, next month will be twenty years since we first met. Isn't that something? How the hell did we get here?"

I hugged him, and he squeezed me tightly. It was sad to behold, Joshua so tired and beaten down, living alone in that depressing little cottage. "Come visit us in North Carolina," I said.

He laughed. "I can pretty much guarantee that will never happen." He bent down gingerly and pulled some weeds out from the gravel driveway, then brushed his hands together. "You've been a great friend to me, Eric. My best friend," he said. "But you stopped needing me a long time ago."

"We'll be back for Thanksgiving," I said. "I'll see you then?"

"I'll see you then," Joshua said.

"And the wedding," I said. "Don't forget the wedding."

Didi and I were planning to get married next Memorial Day in Marion, at the O'Briens' summer home on Buzzards Bay. I was going to invite nearly everyone from the 3AC, for old times' sake, and, despite everything, I had asked Joshua to be my best man, although he had dithered about it when I phoned him in the spring, saying he couldn't predict his whereabouts so far in advance, since he would be applying to several artists' colonies for a residency.

"You'll be there for sure?" I asked, holding open my car door.

"I wouldn't miss it," Joshua told me.

We want to think that there's an inviolable continuity among old friends, a bond that cannot be fissured despite years of lassitude and neglect. We want to believe that there's truth and solace in our memories, that there's meaning and purpose to the things that have happened to us. I'm not sure that's really the case. Youth is about promise. As you approach your forties, it's about how you've come up short of those dreams, and your life becomes what you do with that recognition. Inevitably, you begin to identify your old friends with what you're trying to discard; you associate them with wreckage.

Joshua was a liar, a narcissist, a naysayer, a bully, and a misogynist; a whiner, misanthrope, and cynic. He was a user. Sometimes I wonder why we tolerated him at all, and for so long. Didi thinks he was a cancer to me, a malignancy to everyone within his crumbling, nihilistic orbit, and I was lucky, as his enabler, not to have been pulled down with him. If not for Joshua, Didi is convinced, we would not have broken up in the first place at Mac. What drove him to kill himself, she says, was realizing that he would never have what I now possess—a life beyond the pursuit of art—because being an artist, a writer, means isolating yourself in a room for hours, days on end, going into the darkest parts of yourself, and really, what sane person would want to do that?

I think she's wrong, of course. I still respect that sort of sacrifice, for the sake of art. I disagreed with many of Joshua's choices. Fundamentally I believed in solving how people are more alike than different; he believed in the antithesis. But he stayed constant to his principles to the very end, and he was as loyal a friend as anyone could ever ask for. I can never discount the fact that, for better or worse, he made me into the person I am today.

I can't justify what he did, resulting, however inadvertently, in the deaths of the man and the little girl (her name was Emma Dunford, and she was almost exactly Finnea's age). I can't explain to Didi or anyone else why he did it. How can you explain that it's just that he was sad, that he'd been sad all his life, and he knew he'd always be sad?

I keep returning to the last conversation I had with him in Sudbury. He was down, but no more than usual in recent years, given more to brooding and self-denigration than braggadocio. Was there something I had missed—a sign? Something meaningful in the way he had said goodbye? Did he know then that it'd be the last time we would see each other?

I ask myself what I could have done differently. If I could have prevented it. If I could have saved him. In hindsight, I think everything—his entire life—had been coalescing toward that moment on the road. He had trapped himself. He had had no other option. He had wanted too much. You see, the problem was, he had been the idealist, not me.

All this I am projecting, of course. I'll never know for sure. We can't fully understand what plagues each other's hearts, much less our own at times. Ultimately even our best friends are unknowable to us.

And it could be, I will allow, that I am trying to acquit myself of responsibility. Jessica implied as much when I called to tell her about the accident. I was inveighing against Joshua, his selfishness, his reckless, last-second deviation into the car's path instead of gassing himself in his cottage—why couldn't he have waited?—and she said, "Oh, Eric. You've always been so hard on him."

"Shouldn't that be flipped around?"

"No," Jessica said. "You keep using the word pathetic."

"Never to him."

"Don't you think he knew?" she asked. "He was always trying, so desperately, to live up to your expectations. It was agonizing for him. Can't you see that?"

I couldn't, and I still can't—not really. As the years went by, I saw less and less of Joshua, especially after Didi reentered my life. Yet, all that time, maybe even long before then, while I thought Joshua was passing judgment on the choices I was making, had he felt the opposite, forever afraid I might disavow him? Did he believe I was deserting him after years of weathering my scorn—blaming him for things in which I had been, through my actions and inactions, just as culpable?

It's been three years now. I sit in my kitchen and watch the kids outside, climbing the old mockernut hickory tree in the backyard. Didi's nearby, cheering them on, vigilant. There's a pot of kalbi jjim—braised short ribs, my mother's recipe, Matteo's favorite— simmering on the stove.

I look at the refrigerator door, festooned with the kids' drawings and paintings, photos of them with goofy captions. Hanging from the patio trellis, canopied by wisteria, is a bird's nest that Wyatt made this morning, ingeniously constructed—in minutes—with paper towels, disposable Styrofoam trays, yarn, and buttons. Even now, I know he will be an engineer. Or an artist.

It's warm today, the sliding glass door open to the wavy heat of summer and the sounds of their laughter. It's never quiet in this house, someone always around, which I don't mind—which I've come to prefer, actually. I gaze at Wyatt's bird's nest rotating in the breeze, starting to wheel a little tumultuously, and I picture Joshua spinning through the air, the car rolling and tumbling, and I finally arrive at what Joshua might have been contemplating on Water-borne, why he had stepped into the car's path, what he had been hoping would happen: the driver skidding to a stop after hitting him, opening the car door, and running back to where Joshua lay on the road, kneeling down beside him and saying it would be all right, an ambulance was on its way, and maybe squeezing his hand a little, a complete stranger, yet the only person Joshua could turn to, the only person he thought available, who could provide him with, in his last few seconds, a small measure of intimacy, ensuring he wouldn't die alone.

Not long after the accident, I received an envelope. It was addressed to me in Huron Village in Joshua's familiar chicken-scratch scrawl. He had misspelled the street name and put down the wrong zip code, transposing the first and second numbers, so the envelope first went to Calverton, Virginia, then was rerouted to Cambridge, then had to be forwarded to me in North Carolina. The original postmark was the Saturday of his death. I let the envelope sit on my desk all afternoon, overcome by what I might find inside. At last, I opened it. All it contained was a utility bill and a check.

I could imagine an accounts receivable clerk at NStar opening the envelope that Joshua must have mailed on the same morning, the clerk unfolding the letter that was within, looking curiously at it for a second, not exactly surprised, since this sort of thing happened practically every day, before tossing it into the recycle bin—whatever it was that Joshua had meant to tell me.

AUTHOR'S NOTE

This novel would not have been possible without a residency provided by the Lannan Foundation. Thanks to Jo Chapman, Martha Jessup, Douglas Humble, Ray Freese, and, of course, Patrick Lannan, and to all the townspeople of Marfa, Texas, in particular Tim Johnson and Caitlin Murray.

For their editorial insights and support, I would like to thank my editor, Alane Salierno Mason; my agent, Maria Massie; and my friends Jennifer Egan and Fred Leebron.

I'm also indebted to Hans Evers, Katherine Bell, Kathy Herold, Ben Lerner, Paul Yoon, Richard Haesler, Maryanne O'Hara, Ruth Ernst, Om Paramapoonya, Elliott Holt, Meghan O'Rourke, Alan Vana, David Opdyke, Leland Cheung, Don Smith, Katie Mitchell, and the Corporation of Yaddo for their assistance.

Thanks, too, to Denise Scarfi, Dave Cole, Don Rifkin, and Alice Rha at W. W. Norton.